THE BLOOD LANCE

Also by Craig Smith:

Silent She Sleeps
(published in the United States as: *The Whisper of Leaves*)
The Painted Messiah

The Blood Lance

Craig Smith

MYRMIDON

Myrmidon Books Ltd
Rotterdam House
116 Quayside
Newcastle upon Tyne
NE1 3DY
www.myrmidonbooks.com

Published by Myrmidon 2008

A catalogue record for this book is available from the British Library.

ISBN: 978-1-905802-22-7 Hardback
ISBN: 978-1-905802-23-4 Export Trade Paperback

Set in 11.5/14.75 pt Sabon by Falcon Oast Graphic Arts Limited,
East Hoathly, East Sussex

Printed and bound in the UK by
CPI Mackays, Chatham ME5 8TD

1 3 5 7 9 10 8 6 4 2

For Martha, the love of my life, and for my good friend
and wise counsellor, Burdette Palmberg,
keeper of the Blood Lance.

Prologue

Kufstein, Austria
March 16, 1939.

The dead man wore the uniform, coat and high black riding boots of an SS officer. Missing were the officer's cap, his sidearm, his identity papers, and the SS *Totenkopf* ring every officer wore. The first military personnel on the scene understood at once the gravity of the situation and rang Berchtesgaden for assistance. The Wilder Kaiser, after all, fell within the outer defences of the Eagle's Nest.

Less than an hour later, Colonel Dieter Bachman arrived in Kufstein with two platoons escorting him. A tall, thick, balding man, Colonel Bachman watched with a dispassionate gaze as his men began to search the village. The Austrians were frightened of course, but they came out of their houses without offering any resistance. Satisfied with the progress, Bachman took a squad of men to the base of the mountain. The day was cold, just as the night before had been. Snow fell in flurries mixed with sleet. The sky was grey, the ground frozen and white. Bachman met the two Austrian SS guards standing at the base of a hill that was covered with saplings. They pointed him toward the body. Ordering these men back to the village to help with the search, Bachman walked up the hill alone.

As he approached the corpse, he saw that the victim was on his back. The eyes were open and gazing up at the sky. The body and head were deep in the snow. The arms and legs appeared to have been relaxed at impact. Bachman shook his head in wonder and looked up at the snow-capped ledge from which the man had dropped. The snow stung his face as he tried to count the metres. Enough at any rate that he had fallen for several seconds, three or four at least. A long, harrowing moment before the end. And what had he thought about as his life came to a close? What image did he bring down the mountain with him? God only knew.

Bachman stepped closer to have a better look at the face and suddenly sobbed. The emotion hit him so suddenly he could not control it. He bent down on one knee, hoping to cover the sob, hoping to sound like a man struggling to kneel down. The effort was wasted. His men did not seem to have heard him. Or pretended as much. He took one of his gloves off and ran his fingers across the cold, waxy cheek of the handsome face. He felt the stubble of a day-old beard. He traced his fingers over the delicately turned lips. He touched the finely arched brow. The serene expression confounded him. How was it possible?

He looked up at the mountain again. It had been night, of course. In the dark he might not have seen the mountain flashing past him. He might have been looking into the sky without any point of reference, but he surely would have heard the wild scream of the wind. He would have felt the acceleration pulling at him. Four seconds to live. It was enough to terrify any man, but here was the plain truth looking at him. Yes, Bachman thought, he had gone to his death like a Cathar walking blissfully into the Grand Inquisitor's fire . . .

Chapter One

North Face of the Eiger, Switzerland
March 24, 1997.

Those who knew it best called it the Ogre. Its solitary neighbours they named the Monk and the Virgin. For almost a hundred years after climbing became a sport, it killed anyone who dared its gnarly north face. In the process its shelves and slots and crevices and steep monolithic pitches had earned a litany of fanciful names. On the outskirts of the rock there were the Red Chimney and Swallows Nest. Higher up Death Bivouac marked the site where two German climbers, having got farther than anyone before them, froze to death in 1935. There was the Traverse of the Gods – a vertiginous piece of rock that had to be crossed before coming to the White Spider – the last and most treacherous ice field, so named for the numerous crevices spinning out from its centre – and finally the Exit Cracks, thin almost vertical channels of stone leading to the summit.

The first successful ascent of the Eiger's north face occurred in 1938. Two teams, one German and one Austrian, had started a day apart from each other but consolidated in order to come up through the Exit Cracks tied to a single rope. The next climb came nine years later with better equipment and the traces of the first climb still in place. Like the first team, these left their ropes and anchors in their wake and walked out across the western shoulder. Later teams did the same, simplifying the more difficult pitches with strategically placed anchors and the occasional rope.

After that, Eiger's dark face became a proving ground. National teams attempted the summit, then solo climbers. The first single day ascent occurred in 1950. A woman summitted the north face in 1964. A year before that, a team of Swiss guides accomplished a harrowing descent by cable from the summit in an attempt to rescue two Italian climbers. They saved one and lost three of their own in the effort. There was a most direct route, called the John Harlin route after the climber who died trying to make it, a successful ski descent on Eiger's western flank, a youngest climber, and then even a seemingly impossible eight-and-a-half-hour climb in 1981 – shattering all records.

But even after it had been domesticated with ropes and anchors, detailed narratives of its various challenges and helicopter rescues, the Ogre could still sometimes awaken from its slumber and come roaring out of the alpine south with howls like that of a wounded beast. Its winds were capable of ripping climbers from their tenuous hold on life and rock. The ice was notoriously unstable, the stone pitted and fragile. Fog made a habit of following the sweet clear *foehn* like night follows day. It swept across the face so thick and close one climbed by touch alone. Then there were avalanches of rocks and ice and snow, the unrelenting cold of shadows never warmed by the sun's rays and the bone-tired weariness that comes of crawling across vertical walls. Nine had died before the first successful climb. More than forty had perished in the decades since.

By the time Kate Wheeler made her first attempt in 1992 all the records, it seemed, had been set. The Eiger was a rock in the Bernese Alps with a storied history; dangerous, yes, but well travelled and almost comfortable as mountains went. Kate was seventeen – not even the youngest to climb the Eiger. She had been involved in the sport seriously for three years. She had already summitted a great many of the glories of Europe, including the legendary Matterhorn.

On the first day, Kate and her father climbed for ten hours and were making jokes about the first father-daughter team –

the list of firsts having grown so long as to be the stuff of humour. They planned to summit late the following evening because things had gone so well, but a snowstorm that night came in fast and white and cold and pushed them back. They made camp and tried to wait it out, but when their supplies ran low they finally retreated.

Kate tried it again the next summer, partnering this time with a young German climber she had met that spring. After forcing their way across the lower ice fields over the course of two days, they made love at Death Bivouac. They intended to climb out on the third day, and awoke to perfect weather. They started the day confidently by ascending the ramp and completing the Traverse of the Gods. Then an ice screw broke free at the Spider and sent Kate's partner tumbling across almost a hundred metres of ice and rock. He was lucky that the worst of it was a pair of broken legs.

On her third attempt Kate partnered with Lord Robert Kenyon and a Swiss guide who had been up the mountain more than a dozen times. It had been Robert's idea to make it a honeymoon climb. 'We'll take it,' he had told Kate with the quiet confidence of a man who never failed, 'or it will kill us both. One way or the other.'

An individual without Kate's passion might have hesitated at such an awful promise, but Kate loved it. Robert Kenyon's life was not about compromise and patience. He seized the moment with audacity and savoured his victories as though they were his God-given right.

They followed the classic route of the 1938 ascent and planned a three day climb. On the evening of the second day, Alfredo, their guide, found a bit of winter snow lingering in a large crevice and dug a snow cave, whilst Kate and Robert commandeered a narrow shelf hanging like a nightmare over an abyss.

After two days of scrambling across pitches and hammering their axes into rotting slabs of ice, Kate was exhausted, but with the prospect of only a three or four hour ascent the following morning and good weather promised, she realised she had never been happier. Below them night had already settled on the village of Grindelwald, but from where they sat they could still see the faint glow of the setting sun reflected on the distant snow-capped peaks to the west. Having secured themselves with ropes, they let their legs hang off the ledge as they ate a cold meal and drank hot black tea.

Their meal finished, they fell into a comfortable silence, like an old married couple, though in fact they had said their vows only four days earlier. Finally, longing to bring Robert into her thoughts again, Kate whispered with a sigh, 'Our last night.'

Kate was a fair skinned beauty of twenty-one years, slender and tall and preternaturally strong. With Nordic blue eyes and pale honey blonde hair she might have been a model or an actress but, as she was the first to admit, she wasn't suited to taking directions or pretending at romance. Robert was thirty-seven, ruggedly handsome, wealthy, athletic and even-tempered. They had met only six months earlier at a party Kate's some-time boyfriend Luca Bartoli had given in a resort town south of Genoa. Robert, as it happened, was an old friend of Luca's. Kate and Robert had spent that first night together talking – just talking – and by dawn they both knew nothing was ever going to be the same. Kate supposed they ought to have gone a bit more slowly, that was how one was supposed to do things, but they both lived like they climbed. Nothing stopped them, least of all common sense.

Robert laughed pleasantly at Kate's mournful sigh and took her hand with an affection that was so much sweeter than desire. 'You sound like you wish we had a couple more nights up here.'

'I wouldn't mind another night or two,' Kate answered, letting her eyes sweep across the dark world below them, 'as long as we could keep climbing.'

Robert groaned good-naturedly. 'My God, what have I married?'

Kate laughed, 'You can't say you weren't warned!'

'I *was* warned!' Robert agreed.

Kate smiled ruefully. 'Between an ex-boyfriend and a possessive father you pretty much got the worst of it right off!'

'And all true as it turns out. You know if I hadn't been madly in love I probably would have listened to them!'

There had been no one willing to tell Kate stories about her fiancé. Certainly there were no dire warnings about his obsessions, the kind her father and Luca had given Robert about her. In fact it was weeks before she knew Robert was the seventh Earl of Falsbury and the owner of a country manor in the rolling hills of Devon. At Falsbury Hall she had been surprised to see photographs of Robert in a British military uniform receiving an award. He had admitted under close questioning – a virtual interrogation, actually – that, yes, he had been decorated 'for valour and distinguished service and the like a few times.' A hero? 'More like making a habit of standing in the wrong place at exactly the worst time. . .'

Kate was too young to be practical, too accomplished to be overly ambitious for a courtesy title, but it wasn't a bad thing, she discovered, being called Lady Kenyon and seeing men her father's age looking at her husband with a sense of awe. Not that it really mattered. She had married for the best of reasons. She had fallen in love. And why not? Robert Kenyon had the storybook dark features and mysterious air of a Heathcliff, the sweetness, natural pride and uncompromising virtue of a Mr Darcy. He knew the Prime Minister and had served at the side of several of the Royals during his time in the army. He had travelled the world, was fluent in five languages and had a working familiarity with several more. But what she liked best about her husband was that he backed down from absolutely nothing.

Kate's only hesitation, and it had been a slight one, came because of the differences in their ages. At thirty-seven he was a full sixteen years her senior. Of course she had always dated older men, at least from her sixteenth birthday onward. Her occasional flings with a younger man, inevitably a climber, never failed to end with a row and hard feelings.

With older men she had rarely endured the churlish resentment that comes of besting a young man in a physical contest. Older men simply had more confidence and seemed to enjoy her remarkable skills as a climber. So it was inevitable that the man she finally married was solidly placed in his world and comfortable inside his own skin. Eight, ten, sixteen years? What difference?

'I hope they aren't planning to bivouac with us.'

Kate's gaze left the snowy peaks in the distance and fixed on two figures coming up the rock. They were not easy to see in the gathering dusk, but she could tell they were moving with the steady rhythm of climbers who have worked together for years. They certainly came up faster than she and Robert and Alfredo had done. Of course that was the nature of two on a rope. All the same, they were very good.

Reflecting on Robert's remark about their bivouac Kate looked down at the ledge where they sat. The two climbers might ask to share it, she thought, but it wasn't going to get them very much. The sleeping area was a couple of feet wide and hardly sufficient in length to accommodate two individuals. Above them an overhang protected them from falling rocks. Below a vertical descent of several hundred feet ended in a glacier.

'I doubt they intend to take the Traverse of the Gods in the dark,' she answered. As the fact of the sudden intrusion dawned on her, Kate felt a bit of unfriendly irritation. She didn't want company in these high altitudes. She wanted her husband's complete and undivided attention. She had not even wanted Alfredo, had in fact argued against the use of a guide, but Robert had been insistent. If something happened, he had said, a third climber could make the difference.

Robert continued to watch their approach. 'I don't know,' he said finally, 'it might be interesting.' He was talking about a night-climb across a rock that only the top climbers in the world would dare in the sunlight.

'*Interesting* is what you call the Traverse of the Gods on a sunny afternoon,' Kate answered. 'At night it's just plain crazy.'

'There's a full moon coming up in a couple of hours,' he told her. 'If the sky stays clear a couple of strong climbers could summit by two or three o'clock in the morning.'

Kate considered the prospect and felt a throb of excitement hit her. The idea hadn't occurred to her previously, but now that it had, a moonlight climb sounded like just the finish she was looking for.

She heard Alfredo offering the obligatory Swiss greeting, *Gruezi-mitenand*, to the climbers as they scrambled up the pitch. They answered Alfredo's greeting in High German, expressing a bit of surprise at finding someone bivouacking so close to the ramp. With simply no extra space to share, it was an awkward situation but climbers are famous for helping out and making do.

'You want to bivouac here?' Alfredo asked them in an ambiguous mix of High and Swiss German. Alfredo was Robert's age but with his leathery skin and flecks of grey in his beard he looked closer to fifty. He spoke a countrified version of the Bernese dialect – an unimaginably sluggish patter with its own peculiar mountain charm.

'Not unless we have to,' the larger of the two men answered. 'We're hoping to move on once the moon comes up.' He spoke with an Austrian accent. 'But you don't mind if we settle down here and wait a couple of hours, do you?'

Alfredo looked in the direction of Kate and Robert, 'Up to the man.' The Austrians looked out toward the ledge in surprise, apparently having not seen Kate and Robert.

Robert called from the ledge in good High German that it was fine with him. 'Take as long as you want! When did you start up?'

'We took off at four this morning,' the man answered. 'We are still hoping to make it in under twenty-four hours, but it is going to be close.'

'It took us two days to get this far!' Robert answered.

'Are you the two love birds on the honeymoon climb?' the second man asked.

'That's us!' Kate called.

'If you want to come on up the rock with us, you're more than welcome,' the first man said. 'There's supposed to be a heavy fog coming in early tomorrow – might be a little tricky getting out of here if you wait for sunrise.'

'The last I heard, we were supposed to get clear weather for a couple more days,' Kate answered.

'I expect the three of us would just slow you two down,' Robert added.

'Hey, I read all about you two! There's no way you'd slow *us* down!'

Now Robert seemed to consider the invitation. 'You really wouldn't mind if we joined you?'

'Are you kidding? If we summit with you two tied to our ropes we could end up on the cover of the *Alpine Journal*!'

Robert laughed cheerfully. 'I hadn't thought of that. I'll tell you what. Give us a minute to talk it over.'

'No hurry. Take a couple of hours, if you want,' the man answered.

'Alfredo! Why don't you brew up some coffee for them!'

'I think I've got a cup or two that's still warm, sir!'

'That's just the thing!' the first Austrian answered. 'That's very hospitable of you!'

Alfredo, who had run his rope through a permanent anchor to walk down to greet the men, now turned and began pulling himself back to his makeshift snow cave. The Austrians followed up the steep grade using only their crampons.

When the three men had gone up the rock and were out of sight, Kate said, 'Do you really want to do it?'

Robert laughed pleasantly at Kate's enthusiasm. 'I should have guessed you'd be up for it!'

'With a fog coming, it might be the smart thing to do.'

Robert gave the matter some thought. 'I actually feel pretty good, all things considered. How about you?'

'It's what? Four hours?'

'If we keep up with those two, it might be a good deal less.'

Kate heard something like a club striking rock and looked back toward the pitch in time to see a shadow sweeping across the rock. *A body*, she realised with a jolt.

The shadowy form slid at first, then began to tumble with the indifference of an inanimate object. It dropped over the edge and plummeted toward the glacier below. Kate and Robert leapt to their feet in alarm. Inevitably they collided – his shoulder knocking her off balance. Kate could feel herself leaning out and reached for Robert's hand. He didn't seem to understand she was in trouble. She cried his name, and then she was beyond his grasp.

The rope she had anchored to the rock caught with a snap that sent her crashing back against the mountain. Something brushed across her head and dropped away. Her sleeping bag? One of their rucksacks? She wasn't sure. She looked down, but all she could see was the ghostly ice far below.

She blinked and tried to understand what had happened. She was hanging a few feet below the ledge, twirling slowly from her anchoring rope. She was groggy from colliding with the rock wall and felt a deep sharp pain in her knee, but at least for the moment she was so juiced with adrenalin she would not have any trouble pulling herself back to the ledge.

She studied her situation with a practised eye. She was probably eight to ten feet below the ledge. Her anchor was another three feet higher. The only difficulty was getting some kind of purchase. Unfortunately her ice axes were on the ledge, along with her crampons, so she was going to have to climb the rope.

Then a thought struck her: why wasn't Robert leaning out over the ledge to make sure she was okay? Without daring to answer her own question, Kate felt a sense of doom and loss take hold of her. *No*, she thought, before she could even articulate the terror urging itself upon her. He had tied himself in at the same time she had. She had seen him do it. She looked around, thinking he might have come over right after her and be hanging a few feet below her position.

'Robert?' she said. Her voice was timid, frightened.

Could his anchor have pulled free? The thought sickened her, and she could not stop thinking about the object that had fallen beside her. Sleeping bag, rucksack. . . Robert.

'ROBERT!'

From the ledge above she saw the silhouette of a man's head. Relief rushed over her.

'Robert? I'm here. I'm okay!'

'Cut the rope,' a voice called from the distance.

'No!' she cried in sudden panic.

The silhouetted head pulled back as Kate kicked wildly trying to get to the rock. Her efforts nudged her closer to the wall, but she could still not touch it.

'PLEASE, NO!' she cried.

Her fingers brushed against the rock, but she failed to get any kind of grip. She drifted out, her legs turning away from the wall. She kicked to lengthen the arc of her swing and started back. She lifted her legs and leaned back in her harness, stretching a lone arm toward the rock.

She got close enough this time to grab it but her legs kept twirling and she missed her chance. She looked above her and felt the rope give a slight bump.

'NO!'

When the rope broke free Kate gave a screech of terror and saw the shadow of a protruding boulder come at her. She slammed into its sloping shoulder and rolled away, too stunned to grab anything. Her hips and legs tipped off the edge, but then her rope caught on something.

Fearing the slightest shift might send her plummeting Kate searched the boulder for a fingerhold. What she found was a slight ridge, but it took some of the pressure off the rope. For the moment she was safe, and looked up at the shelf from which she had fallen. The shadows made it difficult to judge distances. She thought she might have dropped another six feet. Twelve, maybe fifteen feet back to the ledge? She saw the same silhouetted head leaning out again. When the shadow disappeared, Kate pulled herself up, realising as she did that her second fall might have cracked a rib. She found the fissure that had caught hold of her rope and struggled to yank it free but it was wedged in too tightly. She knew she could untie it at the carabiner in her harness or even lose the harness if she had to, but she didn't want to leave either behind. A climber's instinct: having a length of rope and a way to tie in might mean the difference between death and salvation. She reached into the zippered pocket in her coat for her Swiss Army knife.

She lost about a metre after the cut, but kept the better part of three metres – enough to tie in to something. She rolled the rope neatly and tied it off, then stuffed it in her coat pocket. Next she examined the mixed character of ice and rock rising up over her position. She glanced out toward the horizon and saw the faint light of the setting sun still reflecting above the mountains. It was going to be dark soon. Climbing in the dark without any kind of lamp was suicidal, but she had no real choice. She couldn't tie herself in here and wait for the moon. In two hours, exposed as she was to the wind, she would be too cold to move.

She tried to shake off the sorrow and fear creeping over her. She knew from hard experience that if she gave in to it she was finished. She had to climb her way out of this, that was all there was to it. But which way? She looked directly overhead. That way would bring her to the two Austrians. She looked to the west and thought she might be able to traverse the sheer face under the ledge. It would bring her out below the Austrians, but she hadn't the equipment to descend the mountain. She took inventory. She was wearing a coat and boots. She had a Swiss Army knife, three metres of climbing rope, and a harness. It was not enough. The only way to survive was to get hold of the right equipment. She looked up. Fire, water, food, crampons, axes, rope, sleeping bag: all of it only fifteen feet away. Without those things there was no way off the mountain.

After a delicate traverse on a narrow ribbon of stone, Kate headed toward the ramp, intending to come out above the two men, but almost immediately her head brushed into an overhanging shelf. She crouched and tried to study the shadow. A boulder was blocking her only way up and forced her to move laterally again. She held her weight with her fingertips and toes. Below her the void waited patiently.

The wind kicked up a notch as she moved round the obstacle. Getting out farther she could feel the wind tearing at her coat. It had been above freezing all day, a bit warmer than ideal for the kind of mixed climbing the Eiger offered, but at night the temperatures usually dropped fast and kept dropping. Tonight was no different. She reached overhead now and found an icy crack. It was impossible to get a grip. She needed her axes! Suddenly standing on a half inch ridge of stone over a yawing abyss with nothing but her boots and bare hands to keep her from falling – not even an anchor to hold her – Kate realised that she was never going to get up to the ramp! What was she thinking? What did she intend to fight – God?

She began to tremble and felt her eyes burning. *Lady Katherine Kenyon died yesterday in a mountain climbing accident on the Eiger. . .*

A fine thing titles, she thought. Mourned by the better classes, envied by the rest!

'No,' she whispered, shaking her head and hooking her fingers over a ripple of stone and ice, 'I'm not dead yet!'

She pulled herself up. The rock's contour pushed her hips out. For a moment her feet lost their purchase. She was forced to take her entire weight into her fingertips. She felt the panic every climber knows when there is no protection. But she knew this move. She had practised it repeatedly. So what if there was no anchor! She was good enough in the sunlight to do this move without *needing* a rope! This was just a free climb through a bit of fog. You grabbed on and you kept going up.

That was the way of the mountain. How many times had she really needed the security of an anchored rope? 'You take the mountain in your hands and you do what you know how to do!' she whispered.

She reached higher and caught a knob of porous rock. It felt like a handle in her grip, and she pulled herself up easily. She found a fissure with the toe of her boot. She came over the bulge entirely now and lay across it catching her breath. 'Not . . . dead. . . yet.'

The next stretch was easier, lots of fingerholds and ledges, typical of much of the mountain. She moved slowly because of the darkness and untrustworthy nature of the rock, but she kept moving. There were no outcroppings in her path, no sheer slippery faces to stop her forward motion. Not so bad, she thought. Then she found a wasteland of pure ice stretching out above her. Kate had been climbing icy slabs like this for two days. This one was actually easy. With a couple of axes in her hands and crampons on her boots she could have ascended the thing in a few seconds. Swing, swing, hop. Swing, swing, hop. When you got a rhythm going there was nothing faster. Without equipment she knew that if she started to slide it was over.

'Stop,' she whispered. 'Stay here. Wait it out. You won't freeze.'

Lady Katherine Kenyon died yesterday in a mountain climbing accident on the Eiger. She is survived by her father. . .

Father. What would Roland Wheeler do with this in front of him? Would he lie to himself, settle down and go to sleep with a cold wind blowing a gentle death into his bones? The thought almost made Kate laugh. It was not in his nature! The man had a number of failings – amongst them a complete lack of morality when it came to other people's property – but the one thing he would not do was quit. No gentle goodnight for him! And he had never allowed Kate to do it either. Once, on their first real climb, she had panicked. She stood frozen on a ledge she would have killed to have at the moment, and her father had told her, 'You won't get off this rock with tears, Katie. You got here by climbing, and you'll get off by climbing!'

And she had said, 'I can't!'

'Well then you're not the girl I thought you were,' he told her and started on. Started on! Left her! Fourteen and shivering, and he left her behind and did not even give her a backward glance. The fury of it had burned away the panic – which was the point.

Kate touched the carabiner running through her harness, but it was not made for something like this. She searched her coat. Rope, knife. . . *piton*! She brought the knife and piton out. With her knife in one hand and the piton in the other she might be able to work them like a couple of ice picks.

Or die trying.

Kate punched the blade of her knife into the ice and felt it catch. Then the piton. She caught enough resistance to pull away from the rock. Once on the ice, she risked a glance below. She could see nothing but a sheer grey wall with a slope of some forty degrees. It ran out for a few metres and then became sky.

The hard way lay above her. She pulled her knife from the ice and struggled with trembling fingers to keep a grip on the piton. She drove the knife into the ice fast, and caught her weight with it. Now the piton, now the knife.

The fury of driving small steel objects into the ice was exhausting, but hanging drained the last of her strength. Better to keep moving. . .

They had cut her line! They had meant to throw her off the mountain! Had Robert watched them do it? Had he cried out without her hearing his shout? His silence bothered her because it meant what had fallen past her was a body. Not a sleeping bag. Not a rucksack. *His* body. She nearly gave out at the thought, but she couldn't be certain. It was possible he screamed as they cut her loose. She had hit hard, maybe lost a few seconds. It was possible he was alive. Maybe they meant to kidnap him. Take him out by the light of the moon and demand some obscene ransom. . .

She stopped to breathe, to lament, to find deep in her core the rage it took to get up this last stretch. It was simply no good if Robert was dead. She looked back, her fingers beginning to cramp from the tension, her strength failing her. She had to finish this quickly!

She had been unconscious. She had missed his cry of terror when they cut her free because she had slammed into the rock. His silence did not mean he had fallen. She had simply lost a bit of time. He was up there! Thinking *she* was dead! Praying for a miracle exactly as she was! She drove the piton into the ice and pulled herself up another few inches. The hand holding the piton was on fire with the pain of a cramp, but a boulder loomed above her now.

She searched in vain for some kind of purchase, then traversed slowly to her left, resisting the urge to look down again, and came finally to a patch of snow. The slope was steeper here, the snow unstable. She could see several promising rocks just above her now – the end of the hard part of her climb – but when she pulled herself across the snow it broke under her. She got her belly and toes into it and could feel a bit of traction, but it wasn't much, and it wasn't safe. She could be gone in a second, the entire wall of snow sliding away. She drove her fists deep into it and got anchored into the ice. She pulled herself up a few inches and tried again and then again.

A moment later she was scrambling over loose stones until she came at last to the long steep ramp. Kate pocketed her piton and tried calculating the distance left before she got down to the two Austrians. She thought from her position that they were about twenty metres below her, but she could see nothing. She looked at the sky. The stars had come out but they were still pale. The horizon had gone black. If she stayed in the shadows and if she was quiet, she thought she could be on them before they understood what was happening. She touched her thumb to the blade of her knife. It wasn't much of a weapon, but at least it was sharp.

Kate descended as if she were climbing down a ladder. She held the rock with her fingers and toes, her knife clutched under her right thumb. She could see grey patches of ice and then the faint outline of the indentation where Alfredo had dug into the snow to get out of the wind.

She was almost to the ledge when she heard the unmistakable sound of steel tearing into stone directly above her. She looked up in surprise, but it was too late. Her attacker came at her fast. Kate went down hard under the impact, but slashed out with her knife and anchored herself momentarily in the man's coat and at least some of his flesh.

She was conscious vaguely of the man's scream as his fist slammed down on her head. The knife pulled free under the assault, and Kate began sliding. Before her speed had built, she caught a ridge with one boot. She was maybe three metres under the man, but he was already coming again. To move as he was, he had to be on a rope.

He could have run it through some kind of natural anchor easily enough. That would let him come down on her quickly, but if that were the case, the rope would be tied into his harness on one end and he would be holding the other end. That would allow him to keep the tension in the line and feed it out as he came down the rock, but it also meant he was not completely secure. When he hit her the second time Kate was ready and threw her arms around his knees. He kicked at her but she wrestled him to his back, so that they were both dangling from his rope. Then she lunged over his chest and cut his wrist.

They began sliding across the pitch together, the man clinging to her with desperation. Kate slashed at his face and gave a hard bump with her knee as she rolled out of his arms.

His cry was different now, his voice filling with raw terror as his speed built. Kate felt her legs slip off the edge of the ramp and caught a jutting piece of stone with both hands. The rock cut into her fingers as her body went over, but she held on, her legs swinging wildly into the sky.

The second man came from the ledge, calling out to his partner excitedly, but there was no answer. Hanging by one hand, her knife gone, Kate looked up, but she could see nothing other than the sky and dark shadows of the rocks. She reached below the ledge with her free hand and found a ridge. She took it and slipped off the ramp entirely, now hanging against the side of a vertical wall with only four fingers.

Above her the second man's shadow cut away the stars as his crampons scratched the rock where her hand had been. If he saw her now she was dead.

Kate's hand began to tremble, but she waited, not daring to search for a better hold.

'Jörg!' the man called as he walked above her, the teeth of his crampons just inches from her fingers. He was moving slowly, careful to keep his balance.

When he was lost in the shadows, Kate risked bringing her second hand into play and began probing for a toehold. She breathed quietly, slowly, resisting the instinct to gulp air.

'Jörg!' he called.

Kate caught a vertical crack and tucked part of her boot sole into it and pushed up until her chest and hips had cleared the rim. She settled quietly on her hands and toes, her belly inches above the surface. Each step came gently but, as quickly as she could, Kate ascended the steep pitch. She stayed in the blackest shadows close to the boulders. She needed to get above the man. She needed the momentum of a long slide to equalize the difference in their size and weight.

The Austrian called his partner's name again, but his tone had changed. He was a man alone on a mountain and maybe, for the first time, just a little afraid. Kate visualised the contours of the ramp. She could not see him or hear him. She tried to gauge the distance between them but he had suddenly quit making any sounds. Was he still close to the edge? Was he coming up toward her so quietly she could not hear him? Or was he just standing somewhere, careful to keep his balance and listening to be sure he was really alone?

He might imagine they had both gone over, but he had to know it was possible she was still here. She began to move laterally and heard him turn as if alerted to a sound. She froze, waiting. A step and then nothing. How close? She had her hands and feet and face pressed against the pitch. Her back was to the assassin. She turned as slowly and quietly as possible, leg over leg, arm over chest. Now face up, she stared past the shadows of her belly and knees.

She pulled the length of rope she had saved from her pocket and loosened the knot with her teeth. The man still did not move. He must be sure she was above him – somewhere. He apparently did not intend giving away his position before he had to. If she had to guess, she thought they were ten or fifteen feet apart. Both of them blind, both suddenly, perfectly still, both completely aware that they were about to meet.

She left some slack in the rope as she took it in either fist. She thought he was off to her right, not directly under her, but she couldn't be sure. She couldn't risk starting to slide. If she missed him nothing would stop her. She needed to know his position, but to do that meant she must expose her own. 'Please,' she whispered, hardly recognising her own voice. 'Don't hurt me.'

The assassin seemed to have been waiting for this and started up the pitch quickly. The moment he did, Kate had his position. With a hop she began her slide. The force of her impact let her sweep through his arms and come in hard against his legs. Once he had lost his footing, Kate looped her rope around his knees, and then rolled out from under him. She kept the rope taut and let her momentum send him into a slide. He shouted wildly, but Kate kept pulling, her own momentum failing as his built. When she finally let go of the rope his voice rose to a shriek.

She heard his body hit the glacier three or maybe four seconds later. Then there was only the wind.

Kate rose up on her hands and feet, calling out as she did, 'Robert!' She crawled down the ramp until she got to the ledge where she and her husband had been seated. 'ROBERT!'

Silence answered. They hadn't killed him, she told herself. They had not come up the mountain for that! No! They had wanted to kidnap him! He was tied up, gagged. . . somewhere. He was *here*! He *had* to be here! 'ROBERT!'

Kate slipped out along the dark ledge, but she found only two rucksacks and a pair of sleeping bags. She found a torch in one of the rucksacks and had a look about. Robert's gear was gone. She turned back, leaving the ledge and crossing the ramp. She turned the light here and there. She climbed farther, calling her husband's name again. Again, there was no answer. Kate told herself Robert was somewhere else, but even as she whispered the lie to help her endure the next few seconds, she knew there was no other place. If he were still alive he had to be here. *And he was not here!*

She called his name once more, but her voice broke. Robert was gone. She dropped to her knees and covered her face.

When she had finished with her tears Kate retrieved one of the sleeping bags and secured herself in it so she could sleep for an hour.

She woke up with the moonrise and discovered that her body was racked with pain. It did not seem possible to move, but she knew she had better try. The moonlight brightened the area and Kate crossed back to the shelf without using her torch to search through the rucksacks for equipment. She found no crampons but there were ice axes and ropes, helmets with light, food, fire, water, and aspirin. She even found Alfredo's stove. She thought about climbing out, but she was more confident with the way down – she had taken it twice. If she got in trouble, she knew the places where she could settle and wait for rescue. She had the fire and food and clothing to survive a few days if she needed that much time.

She made her bivouac in a patch of snow when the moon had finally set. At dawn she continued her descent, her body quivering with each movement. She found two climbers late that afternoon. 'What happened?' one of them asked, whilst they waited for a helicopter rescue.

She shook her head, unwilling to say. The medics wanted to know as well, but Kate refused to talk. Too tired, too sore, too scared too relive it. They understood or at least thought they did.

It was instinct that silenced her. Someone had sent those men after Robert, she was sure of it, and whoever had done it was still out there. If she lied about what had happened, he might imagine he was safe. He would certainly decide she was too timid to find him. But she would. She would have his life or die trying!

When Kate had to speak and could no longer hide behind the fog of exhaustion, she was off the mountain and lying safely in hospital. She said she, her husband, and their guide had decided to join two men who were hoping to summit by the light of the full moon, five of them on two ropes. They had hardly started, she said, when the lead team lost an anchor and fell back into her party. The force of the collision had broken their anchor as well and all five climbers had slid back across the ramp, tangled in their ropes. She said that as she had started to roll she had managed to cut free, but the others had gone over.

There were problems with her story – gear switched and missing. Why had she been carrying one of *their* rucksacks? How had she lost her crampons? What had happened to *her* rucksack? She said she didn't know. She found the equipment after she had lost her own. That didn't make sense, they said, and pressured her for details, but Roland made some phone calls and the following day the interrogation stopped. No more questions. The newspaper got the story, and Kate's version of what had transpired got written in stone.

The Swiss made a helicopter search at first light the morning after Kate had finally had the strength to tell the authorities exactly where the fall had taken place. By then a spring snowstorm had come and covered the bodies and gear. Another search was made that summer, this too without success.

The Ogre, they said, had claimed another four victims.

Chapter Two

Zürich, Switzerland
Sunday February 24, 2008.

Attendance at the inaugural party of the Roland Wheeler Foundation came by invitation only. The luminaries gracing the list included politicians, CEOs, and the directors of Zürich's most prestigious foundations and museums. Naturally the city's philanthropists attended in force. They never missed a chance to have a look at the goods others were offering. Lest people imagine the occasion was only about power and money, Wheeler's daughter, Kate Brand, extended half the invitations to musicians, painters, leading architects, authors, and scholars. The list was finished off with rock hounds – friends of Kate and her new husband, Ethan. Old, young, rich, accomplished, crazy or beautiful: everyone brought something to the occasion. It was the crowd Roland himself would have put together, if he had only lived to see this day.

Perhaps the most curious guest on the list was Captain Marcus Steiner of the Zürich police. A veteran of some twenty-nine years, Marcus had made his way in the world somewhat quietly, one might even say covertly. In the past his participation in functions of this sort had always been limited to providing security, but on this occasion he was a genuine guest – and nearly as mystified by this as everyone else. Marcus of course had no trouble fitting in. Unlike most cops the world over, he actually enjoyed the company of the rich. He had found out early in his career that the rich paid handsomely for their favours once they trusted him and understood there wasn't much he wouldn't do if the price was right.

Of course Marcus knew there were people at the party who imagined Kate Brand had invited him out of sheer bravado. Rumours had circulated for years that Roland Wheeler had made his fortune by stealing paintings in other countries and then selling them to Swiss collectors. As Wheeler had grown older, or so the gossip went, he passed the torch to his only daughter. No one could prove it, of course, but then again, no one much cared to try. Roland Wheeler had bought his way into Zürich society with lavish gifts to the city and with the confidences he kept for the sake of his Swiss clients. Besides, theft happening beyond the borders of Switzerland was not really a Swiss problem.

Marcus didn't mind a few snide remarks at his expense. The occasion was too grand to miss, and it certainly didn't hurt a man's career to make acquaintance with the likes of this crowd. He didn't exactly hand out his business card, but he wasn't afraid to tell people where he worked. After all, someone might need his help some day. It only made sense to let them know where they could find him.

As he made his way from room to room, Marcus took inordinate pleasure at reading the names on the various canvases. So much so he hardly considered the paintings themselves. But who cared? Rothko, de Kooning, Pollock, Kandinsky, Picasso: they threw paint at the canvas and it was worth more than he could earn from the city in a decade!

It was staggering to imagine the value, and all the more so when one considered that Roland Wheeler had started life in the East End of London as a common burglar. Following a series of encounters with the police and a suspended sentence for possession of stolen goods, Wheeler had made his way to Germany. In Hamburg Wheeler's life had taken a turn for the better, including marriage to an English beauty, a job in an art gallery, and finally the birth of a baby girl. No one knew much else about Wheeler's early career but a few years later he had his own shop in Hamburg, another in Berlin and a third in

Zürich. The rough edges of London's East End had all been knocked clean. Roland Wheeler had become respectable. Following the death of his wife in the early 1990s, Wheeler had left Germany and moved to Zürich. The move had apparently worked out well for him. Over the next several years he became extremely wealthy.

'Close to a hundred million,' one guest estimated when Marcus asked the value of the collection Wheeler's daughter had donated to the city.

'Francs?' Marcus asked with something akin to awe.

The man, who was English, offered a stiff smile, 'Pound Sterling – on a good day, at least. I'd say Swiss Francs in a weak market.'

Marcus, who had acquired a Monet from Wheeler in October of 2006, asked about the market at present. Was it a good time to buy or sell?

The Englishman hedged. 'It depends entirely on what you are talking about, I suppose.' He glanced at the watch Marcus wore, his shoes, and the cut of the cloth of his smoking jacket. Marcus gave nothing away in the details of his costume. He might be a respectable civil servant or a man worth ten million francs. More than that amount, he knew, and everyone in the room would know about it. The Swiss were a very polite people, as a rule, but when it came to money they were terrible gossips.

'A Monet, for instance,' Marcus answered.

The eyebrow cocked dubiously. 'You own a Monet?' The Englishman's German was impressive: he had mastered a quite gentle sarcasm by sheer inflection. Of course the arched English eyebrow helped.

Almost blushing, Marcus answered, 'A small one.' He made a gesture of slipping a small canvas under his jacket, and the man laughed.

'Of course there's always a market for Monet. . . whatever the size.' The gentleman scanned the walls but to no avail. 'Roland had an exquisite Monet as I recall. I remember him showing it to me one time! Surprised he let it go. I know he was very fond of it!'

'I can understand that,' Marcus smiled. 'I am certainly fond of mine!'

Having learned something about the value of Wheeler's posthumous gift to Zürich, Marcus happened upon a Frau Goetz, the wife of the president of a small private bank in town where he did some of his business. 'An extraordinary gift on the part of Mr Wheeler, don't you think?' he asked after they were introduced by a mutual acquaintance – the mayor as it happened.

Roland being gone well over a year, the mayor offered a slight bit of laughter, 'He couldn't very well take it with him, could he?'

Marcus smiled at the joke and let one shoulder kick up good naturedly. 'I only meant his daughter might have got some pleasure out of it.'

'As I understand it,' Frau Goetz answered, 'Kate, not Roland, is the one responsible for the gift.'

'Really?' Marcus asked. He had not heard this rumour and immediately wondered about Kate's accounts – that she could afford such a gift.

A brittle woman, Frau Goetz sniffed with indifference. '*Really.* I guess *I* should know. My husband handled the estate.'

'That was. . . quite generous of her. I hope she hasn't left herself destitute.'

'As I understand the matter, she had some troubles in Zürich last year. I expect she felt obliged to make the gift to get back into the city's good graces.'

'Two hundred and fifty million Swiss Francs can buy a lot of good will,' the mayor chuckled.

'Besides,' Frau Goetz continued, 'Kate has her own money – and very proud of it, too, I might add.'

'I was under the impression she has a trust from her mother's estate,' Marcus remarked.

'She had one, but it came to her when she turned twenty-one and she invested it in a business venture with her first husband, Lord Kenyon. This was. . . oh, ten years ago. When the company bacame bankrupt following her husband's death the poor thing lost everything. Imagine it!' Frau Goetz continued with a shake of her head and a strange wobbling of skin under her chin, 'losing her husband on her honeymoon and her entire fortune a couple of months later!'

The mayor gave a casual shrug of his shoulders. 'If this collection is any indication, Roland surely had a few million lying about to soften the blow.'

'He did, but Kate wouldn't a take a *rappen*! Her trust was *hers*. She had lost it, and so she set about earning it back – with interest, according to my husband.

Marcus's eyes twinkled mischievously. 'Any idea just how she managed it?'

The lady gave him a coy look. 'Dealing in art in the same fashion as her father, as I understand it. You know, money is the least of what children inherit from their parents!'

Marcus tipped his head and offered an expression of mild curiosity for Kate Brand. 'More than a pretty face then?'

'Oh, my goodness yes. I believe she is the most extraordinary individual I've ever met! You know of course she is one of the best climbers in Switzerland?'

'I think I saw something on TV about that a few years ago.'

'I get vertigo on a stepladder!'

The object of Frau Goetz's admiration stood radiantly in what had once been Roland Wheeler's library. At the moment she was laughing at something the director of the James Joyce Foundation was telling her. It was curious, Marcus thought, how she won people over so effortlessly. Kate Wheeler, the wealthy heiress, Lady Kenyon, the young widow of an English lord, or just plain Kate Brand, the wife of an American rock climber: whatever scandal they whispered seemed to slip away the moment one looked at that radiant smile.

It hadn't taken a hundred million pounds to buy her way

back into Zürich's fickle embrace. Kate's smile alone was sufficient for that. The gift to Zürich in her father's name was exactly what it seemed: a daughter's love for her father.

Kate's husband, Ethan Brand, slipped away from the director of the opera and found the rock hounds in the garden at the side of the house: Reto, the madman, Renate, the dark-haired beauty, Karl, who could tell a story better than anyone, and Wolfe, the German who had nearly climbed Eiger with Kate before breaking both his legs at the Spider. They were drinking white wine and passing a joint. By the glassiness of their eyes Ethan was guessing the joint was probably not their first.

At the sight of him Karl cried out in *Swinglish*, 'Ethan! What's the *los*, man?'

'There's a cop inside,' he told them in English.

Reto laughed and said to send him out, maybe he wanted to get high, too. Renate wondered aloud if he had brought his handcuffs. Wolfe ignored the matter entirely and offered Ethan a toke. He knew Ethan didn't smoke. He did it just so he could sneer once Ethan refused.

It didn't seem that many years ago when Ethan would convince himself he needed a joint just to get through his high school classes. Of course after he was high he had always felt like he would explode if he went back inside and listened to his teachers, so, inevitably, he went looking for a house where no one was home. At first Ethan had broken into places to see if he could get away with it. He would usually smoke another joint or two, watch TV, and then just take a look about to see what the people had and how they lived. If he saw any cash, of course, he would take it, but in his first few break-ins he didn't touch anything else. It hadn't taken too many times before he was seeing the world differently. He got himself a watch, his mother a microwave. Eventually he brought home a TV, a stereo, jewellery, and CDs. After a while he got a partner because it seemed a lot safer to have a lookout, but his partner was a talker and the two of them ended up getting arrested.

The next eighteen months had changed Ethan's life. He got straight for one thing – scared straight as they liked to say in those days – and he had met a Jesuit priest who spotted something his high school teachers had missed: Ethan had a near-photographic memory.

When he was released Ethan spent nine months in a Catholic school completing two years of course work and learning the equivalent of four years of Latin from the priest. In his spare time, he learned to climb – also with the help of the priest. The following year he entered Notre Dame on an academic scholarship, intending to join the priesthood after graduation. He had liked the course work, especially the history of the Church, and he was top in his class in Latin, but the more he studied the faith, the more his own began to falter. Finally, he realised he could give up the notion of becoming a priest – and ultimately his faith in God – without sinking at once into moral ruin. At least that was the plan. As it happened moral ruin only wanted a bit of encouragement.

He got accepted to law school at George Washington University following graduation with honours from Notre Dame. Before he went off to D. C., Ethan wanted to spend a summer travelling in Europe, the last month of which devoted to rock climbing. A week into the climbing phase of the trip Ethan was at a rock with a couple of friends. They were laying out the ropes when Kate walked up. She offered Ethan a pretty smile and then started up the rock in a free climb. Ethan left his friends and the ropes behind and followed her to the top. It was his first ascent without any sort of security, but worth the risk, as it had got Kate's attention. A couple of nights before Ethan's flight back to the U. S., he and Kate were walking together when Kate jumped a wall and went into an estate. Ethan knew what she meant to do, but just the thought of Kate in his arms in a stranger's bed stirred him, and he jumped the wall as well.

He had followed Kate over walls for the next seven years, making a good living in the process. Roland had fenced the paintings they stole. An ex-boyfriend of Kate's in Italy, Luca Bartoli, took care of the rest of it. Sometimes they went into a house for a single painting, the buyer already waiting for his new property, sometimes they went in on speculation. Their luck had run out in the summer of 2006 with a job that had gone very bad very fast. In the aftermath they got out of the business and left the country. They weren't exactly fugitives, but they had made a mess of things and didn't care to stick around in case the police wanted to ask a lot of difficult questions.

'Where do you find these people?' Reto asked him.

Ethan turned and looked through a window. *These people*, he thought, were some of the most amazing individuals on the continent, but in Reto's world if you didn't climb you weren't worth. . . well, the air you breathed, amongst other things.

'Kate's dad used to say if you want money, the first thing you need to do is find out where it drinks.'

Reto laughed, 'They're not letting go of it, dude!' For Reto, money was just something to get him to the base of a rock with decent equipment. 'Me? I'd rather do a *whipper* than talk to these people.' A whipper was American climbing slang for taking a dive without a rope.

'A bleeding penguin convention, it is.' Renate muttered in faux English.

Ethan looked down at his own penguin outfit. 'Is it that bad?'

Renate laughed, 'It's bad, dude! It's like I don't know you anymore!'

'So where have you been?' Reto asked him. 'I mean like we haven't seen you for years!'

'We've been living in France most of the past year. Before that we were hanging out in New York for a few months. *Hanging out* was Ethan's description of his short stint at NYU after giving up the life of a thief. As it turned out, scholarship, like virtue, hadn't taken. Most of his professors, he had discovered, were singularly without curiosity about certain aspects of the medieval world. Mention the Holy Grail, the Lance of Longinus, the Holy Face of Edessa, or even the Shroud of Turin and they vibrated with a kind of overt anxiety that he had at first found incomprehensible. After a few weeks he figured it out. To an academic, Templar and Grail studies weren't part of serious scholarship. 'If you are looking for the Holy Grail,' his thesis director had told him quite bluntly, 'you're in the wrong place.'

Ethan dropped out that afternoon – a total of six weeks into the semester. Kate, who was struggling with too much city and not enough rock, threw herself at him, wounding him with kisses. They had settled in France a week later.

'Where in France?' Renate asked him.

'We had an apartment in a village a few miles outside of Carcassonne.' A walled, medieval city, Carcassonne was impossible to endure in tourist season, but a different world once the weather cooled and only the locals and the long term visitors settled in.

'The Pyrenees!' Reto exclaimed with delight.

Ethan nodded, smiling. 'It was great,' he said.

Wolfe laughed. 'Americans. . . everything is always *great*.'

'What did you like best?' Renate asked.

Ethan smiled. 'Sun. . . rocks. . . old castles. . . everything! It was. . .' He stopped himself from saying *great*. To be more precise about what he had liked required confidences he didn't especially care to extend to the likes of Wolfe and Reto. Besides there was no explaining happily-ever-after, especially to a jealous ex-boyfriend.

'So why leave it for this?' Wolfe asked him. *This* was cold, dreary Zürich – a good two hours to the base of anything worth climbing.

'Kate wanted to get Roland's foundation set up, and we both thought it might be nice to come back and see everyone.'

'Kate!' Reto said. The others, turning and seeing Kate coming toward them, called out to her as well. No one complained to *her* about the penguins inside. Not one stuffed shirt joke. They told her she looked beautiful, which she did.

'The house,' Karl told her in English, 'is unbelievable.'

'The *paintings* are unbelievable!' Renate cooed. '*Three* Picassos?'

'It was Roland's collection. Ethan and I just picked out the wine.'

They lifted their wine glasses in *salute*. Wolfe said in English, 'The wine is *great*, Kate.' His eyes cut mischievously to Ethan.

'How were the Pyrenees?' Renate asked.

'Pure,' Kate whispered. 'There are places that haven't changed in a thousand years. And caves! You wouldn't believe what we saw in the caves!'

'What did you climb?' Wolfe asked her.

Kate smiled serenely. 'Absolutely everything.'

'Leave the ropes at home?' Reto asked.

'What do you think?'

Kate was a free climber as much as possible. She liked to say it was the only way up a mountain. She trained with ropes sometimes, and some mountains required it, but when she wanted to summit most peaks, she took it as a free climber if it was possible and sometimes even if it wasn't. Ethan usually tagged along with dreadful notions of his mortality nagging at him, but he always made it – close call or not. With Kate it just was not possible to hang back or hesitate. And at the top, you had done it with your own hands and feet, and that was a feeling that took the teeth out of every fear.

'That attitude is going to get you killed someday, girl!' Renate told her.

'Not Kate,' Reto laughed. 'Ethan maybe, but not Kate!'

Kate looped her arm into Ethan's and said, 'I want you to meet someone. Do you have a minute?'

'Bartoli,' she whispered when they were alone.

Ethan stopped. 'Giancarlo or Luca?'

'The old man. Watch yourself, Ethan,' she added. 'Giancarlo can read minds.'

Giancarlo Bartoli was standing at the lake with his back to them as they walked toward him. When Kate called to him, he turned and tossed his cigarette aside. Bartoli was somewhere in his mid-seventies, tall and gaunt with a mop of white hair, deep lines creasing his red face, and pale, grey, merciless eyes that missed nothing. Like Ethan he wore a tuxedo. Against the wind he also wore a yellow cashmere coat.

Roland had considered Giancarlo one of his closest friends. Kate had told Ethan she had vivid memories from her childhood of visits from Giancarlo when her parents were living in Hamburg – long nights in which the two men drank and talked about art and politics and history. About everything, really. Roland would send her off to bed and then laugh at her when she would sneak back and find a seat on her father's lap again. As she listened to their talk – always in Italian – Kate had always imagined that the two men controlled all of the important things in the world.

Ethan could understand the friendship between the two men. Kate's father had been an affable man with a salesman's instincts for putting people at ease. He had also possessed a razor-sharp intellect – to keep things lively. As a young man he had been like Kate – audacious and always searching for new challenges. By the time Ethan knew him, Roland had settled into a world of his own making. He was getting grey, but not so much slowing down as savouring things.

For his part Giancarlo Bartoli was a good deal more than a shrewd businessman. Like Roland, his passions were varied and complex. He loved art, opera, and history above all else, but he was well versed in languages and law. At university he had toyed with a career in higher mathematics before settling on the more practical aspects of that discipline. As a young man he went often to the mountains – skiing nearly at the level of an Olympian and climbing with the same enthusiasm as Roland had in his prime. As an older man Bartoli had taken up sailing, circumnavigating the globe once on a twelve man team that he captained.

Shortly after Kate was born, Giancarlo Bartoli had stood with her parents to take his vow as her *padrino* – godfather – at the christening. Kate was not Bartoli's only godchild, of course, he probably had twenty or so, but she was his favourite, and he made no attempt to disguise his special affection. Every year at her birthday – at least until she was completely grown – he would send her some elegant gift that showed genuine care in its selection. With it came long, hand-written notes that gushed with grandiloquent laments at time's passing or gave stirring anthems to the beauty of youth that fades before it is ever truly discovered in a mirror. Ethan knew enough Italian to be impressed with Bartoli's poetic accomplishments. He also understood that to Kate he was family.

Giancarlo greeted Ethan warmly in very good English. Ethan answered him in Italian. Hearing an American speaking Italian pleased Bartoli no end. Had Ethan lived in Italy? No, Ethan told him, but when he had first met Kate she had told him she could never marry a man who could not speak Italian. 'I took my first lesson the next day.'

Bartoli laughed with pleasure at this, turning to Kate. 'I like this man, Katerina! 'I'm just sorry to have missed your wedding. . . but of course I was not invited. . .'

'It was a small wedding,' Kate answered. She was blushing. 'The two of us, a witness and a priest.'

'You only needed to call. You know that. I would have been there to make it five if I had to travel halfway around the globe!'

'It was my fault,' Ethan told him. 'Once I got her to say she would marry me, I didn't want to give her time to change her mind.'

Bartoli asked them about their year in France and wanted to know about the mountains they had climbed. Talk about the mountains went on for a while, and then he wanted to know about their plans for the future. Were they going to stay in Zürich or return to France?

Kate looked at Ethan. 'We're going to spend the summer in Zürich. Then, who knows?'

'Any chance I can talk you two into forming a business partnership with Luca and me?'

'What kind?' Kate asked him.

'An associate of mine saw a very fine Cezanne last summer in a private home in Malaga. Reasonable security, but nothing the two of you couldn't get past.'

'We are out of that line of business for good,' Kate told him.

This raised a curious eyebrow and Bartoli turned his gaze on Ethan. 'My fault again,' Ethan said. 'I finally figured out stealing things was probably not the safest way to make a living.'

'Well, I can't say I disapprove,' Bartoli told him, his eyes cutting back to Kate. 'There comes a point when the risk is greater than the reward. I suppose if you have earned enough to be comfortable it's time to get out.'

'We appreciate the offer,' Ethan told him, not daring to look at Kate, who he feared would be interested. He had lost his taste for stealing after their last job and had even told Kate they either stopped or he was leaving. To his surprise, she took him at his word. His fear at this point was she had accepted his ultimatum with the idea that she could change his mind eventually.

Kate turned to Ethan. She hated to say it, but one of them probably needed to make sure everything was all right inside. Did he mind?

Ethan turned to Bartoli. 'We could all three go in, if you want. Have a look at the collection Roland put together. . .'

Bartoli said he was going to have to take off soon. Besides, he was familiar with most of Roland's collection. He had only wanted to stop by and wish them well. He added that if the two of them ever wanted to visit him, all they had to do was give him a call. He would make time for them no matter what.

The two men shook hands and then Ethan headed back for the house.

*

Without taking his eyes from Ethan as he walked away from them, Giancarlo told Kate, 'I like him.'

'I like him, too.'

Bartoli turned and looked at her with his steady gaze. He did not say it, but he seemed to wonder if that was all she felt. 'I'm glad he has convinced you to give up the life, Kate.'

'There was a time when I needed it. It was the only thing that really made me feel alive. Even now, I can't say I don't miss it.'

'When one is good at something, it *is* hard to stop.' He let this settle, before asking, 'I assume you have told Ethan what happened on the Eiger?'

Kate turned toward the lake and crossed her arms. She had known this was coming, but she was still uncomfortable with the subject. 'I told him after we were married. I was tired of keeping secrets from him.'

Giancarlo was quiet, as if considering the implications. 'You promised me you would tell no one.'

'And you promised me you would find out who sent those men to kill Robert.'

'I told you I would try.'

'No,' Kate answered. 'You told me you would never stop looking for Robert's killer.'

'I was upset. Robert was my friend, too.'

'Robert was not my *friend*, Padrino. He was my husband.'

Giancarlo gave a thoughtful look in the direction of the house. 'Are you willing to lose another for this passion of yours?'

'That sounds like a threat.'

'You know better than that. I just meant that it was a mistake to tell Ethan.'

'I don't think it was.'

'I expect he is determined to help you find Robert's killer.'

'Is there something wrong with that?'

Bartoli fixed his gaze on the churning water. 'You risked your life to find out the truth, Katerina. I told you that eleven years ago, and you said you didn't care. You said there was nothing you would not risk. I am simply wondering if that is still the case.'

'Nothing has changed.'

'Perhaps it ought to. Life goes on, you know. What you feel now is a raw nerve. If you will only quit irritating it, the pain will grow dull.'

'Someone paid those men to climb the Eiger and find Robert.'

'You have made some very dangerous people *uneasy*, Katerina.'

'Have I really?'

'This is not something that should please you. These are the kind of people who come out of the shadows and you are dead before you understand how close they are!'

'You seem to know a great deal, Padrino. Does that mean you can give me a name – the person responsible?'

'If you push to know the truth, Katerina, I simply cannot protect you anymore. . . or Ethan.'

'Who is going to hurt me, Padrino? You can tell me that, can't you?'

The old man shook his head. 'Robert was involved in a great deal more than you know.'

'So you have been keeping things from me?'

Bartoli shook his head sadly. 'You are not hearing me.'

'You are telling me you know who killed Robert.'

'I said nothing of the kind.'

'Tell me this. Are *you* protecting someone?'

'I have always tried to protect you, Katerina, but I am afraid you are making it impossible.'

'How long have you known about these *dangerous people*, Padrino?'

The old man met Kate's gaze. He seemed to be wrestling with how much he wanted to tell her. Finally he said, 'A great many years, I'm afraid.'

'So you were lying to me when you said you had not given up?'

'I was protecting you, but it seems now that you have found someone who thinks he can find Robert's killer. . .'

'I am going to find out the truth, Padrino, and these very dangerous people had better understand one thing. I swore an oath to God that nothing was going to stop me, and I meant what I said.'

'Then pray God helps you, Katerina, because I cannot.'

The moment Giancarlo Bartoli returned to the limousine, Carlisle greeted him in Italian. 'Is she involved?'

A few years shy of fifty, David Carlisle was tall and handsome with a silver mane of hair and sun-darkened skin. Bartoli settled himself opposite Carlisle and stared at the house that had once belonged to Roland Wheeler. He was not a happy man. 'It is exactly as you thought,' he said at last.

Their car pulled away from the kerb and entered heavy traffic at the top of the hill. 'I suppose you told her to let go of her feelings?' Carlisle asked. There was an edge of sarcasm to this that Bartoli did not care for, and he fixed his eyes on the younger man.

'I do not mean to tell you your business, David, but Kate cannot find you without Thomas Malloy's resources. Eliminate Malloy, and you are safe again.'

'I listened to you once about what I should do with her, Giancarlo, and you see where it has got me.'

Bartoli gave his friend a curious look. 'So you are determined to kill all three of them?'

'I don't really think I've been given any other choice.'

Bartoli offered him a sardonic smile. 'You might give the matter some thought before you try something that you could end up regretting. As I recall, the last time you decided to murder her, Kate tossed your assassins off a mountain.'

Carlisle laughed pleasantly as if he had heard a fine joke. He turned to watch the streets of Zürich as they slipped past. 'This time she won't see it coming.'

'I told her that. She doesn't seem to care, David, and from

the look in her eyes, I am thinking you are the one who might not see it coming.'

'She thinks she is close to finding out what happened. That's Malloy's doing. He imagines Jack Farrell can be made to talk.'

'Are you so sure he can't?'

'Quite positive. But tell me something I don't know, Giancarlo. You met Kate's new husband. Do you think she is in love with him?'

Bartoli turned the palms of his hands up and lifted his shoulders. 'A woman arrives at a certain age, David, and suddenly she understands love quite differently. If she is honest with herself, she knows there is only one man she ever truly loved. It is why her husband is so eager to help her with this. He wants to take the place of his predecessor. He wants all of her love. Of course, he knows he can never have it, but he persuades himself that if he helps her that somehow he will be closer than before.'

'Lord Kenyon, I think, was a very fortunate man.'

Giancarlo Bartoli reflected on this observation. 'More than he knew, I expect.'

'A shame he had to die so young.'

'I have always thought so.'

Kate found Marcus Steiner as he was leaving the party. She spoke to him in High German, using the formal *Sie* of strangers as she shook his hand instead of kissing his cheek as an intimate. To her thinking, Marcus Steiner was the quintessential Swiss, charming, reserved, diplomatic, and true to his word – especially in his criminal enterprises. 'Did you enjoy yourself, Captain?'

'Very much, thank you, Mrs Brand.'

'By the way, I'm curious. Are you still. . . ?'

A look of recognition, a pleasant shrug of the shoulders. 'Nothing has changed since you have been out of the country,' he said.

'Is my credit any good?' she asked sweetly. 'Or will you need cash in advance for my order?'

'If anything it has improved after today.'

'I'm sorry I haven't given you much notice, but I am going to need something very soon, I think. I've put a wish list in your coat.' Marcus Steiner looked at his coat in surprise. 'Over your heart,' she told him, taking the lapel and laughing as if it were a fine joke.

'Did you want anything exotic?'

'Nothing too extraordinary.'

'Will you want everything in the garage at your old flat, the way we used to arrange it?'

'It's being watched, I'm afraid.' Marcus gave her a curious look. Not by the police, he knew, but then she didn't really concern herself with the police. She was too well liked to worry about secret investigations – especially after today. 'Ethan and I have a new place – close to the Gross Munster. I put my address at the bottom of the list. Just leave it all in the main room if we aren't there. I'll put enough money in an envelope to cover the debt and trust you to assign the rest to any future needs.'

'That works for me. Will I need a key to get in?'

Kate smiled. 'A man of your talent?'

Chapter Three

New York, NY
Thursday March 6, 2008.

Thomas Malloy stepped off the subway at the 86th Street exit and joined a late afternoon crowd heading south on Fifth Avenue. He wore black loafers, dark, pleated wool slacks, a grey sweater, sunglasses and a black windbreaker. A few out-of-towners gave him a second look. They were trying to decide if he was someone important. They usually decided he wasn't but not always. Malloy caught his reflection in the glass of a building, indulging in a bit of vanity.

His hair was over his collar, going to grey at a leisurely rate. The style was a bit artsy: actor, architect, freelancer writer. He was tall and slender, reasonably handsome by his own estimates. It was not the best face for someone who preferred to be unnoticed as he went about his business, but it was a versatile one. Change the clothes, move the hair round a bit, add or reduce a few mannerisms, change the voice, and he could be different types – French, German, Swiss, English, and of course three or four brands of American. He usually travelled abroad on a Swiss passport with one of four identities, but he had four American names, two German, and even a French passport – just in case.

Through most of his life Malloy had worked as an intelligence officer without official cover. That meant he was vulnerable to arrest and prosecution in most countries, immediate execution in others. It was the kind of life that had taught him to cultivate the friendship of criminals – people with the skills and resources to get past the usual barriers governments imposed. They were sometimes freelance thieves or assassins, sometimes traitors to their countries, sometimes patriots with an agenda. Many just wanted to get rich or do the right thing or they liked him and did him a favour because he was, above all else, a persuasive individual.

With a couple of brutally violent exceptions, Malloy's professional life had been a quiet one. The worst had come when he was a fresh-faced operative in training. He still wore the scars of that one – a nest of wounds on his chest. At the height of his career he had penetrated deep into the Swiss banking conglomerates as well as a number of the major European crime syndicates – all through contacts he had developed. In the process he had managed to stay invisible and far beyond the reach of the violent people he tracked. In the late 1990s an old nemesis within the agency named Charlie Winger reached the semi-divine position of Director of Operations and celebrated his promotion by calling Malloy home from Europe and chaining him to an analyst's desk at Langley. The move was supposed to lead to further administrative assignments, but that was just Charlie's spin on it. In fact it was payback for unspecified wrongs at the Farm – when they were both still boys.

Malloy had stuck it out as an analyst long enough to finish his twenty years and secure a pension at half-salary. After that he walked. The September 11 attacks happened a few months afterwards and he ended up pitching in as a contract analyst in the aftermath. But at least he was able to carry it out from his home in New York. During the past year or so Malloy had reactivated a few of his old networks and had started travelling on his various passports again. He was a decade out of the field and sometimes felt that he had lost his edge in an unforgiving game. Worse still, his contacts had all grown old and got nervous. They didn't care for the giddy risks they took in their youth. So he had started with the next generation and did what he could to get back in form.

With his occasional research for the agency, his pension, a family inheritance, and some modestly ambitious investments, Malloy made a decent income and always had. It had just taken him a few years to remember the wisdom of his youth, but as he came toward a head-on collision with fifty, he got it firmly in his grasp again: he could do whatever he wanted. He had only to be ready to pay the price. It wasn't a profound point. He had believed it all his life, but after he lost what he once considered his life's work and had been plunged into the despair of retirement at the tender age of forty-two it had taken a bit of time to get past the idea that Charlie Winger had done him in. The truth was it had been time for him to move on. He needed the freefall and so he had let it happen. Now he needed the work – even if it was work of his own making – and so he was up to his old tricks.

At the Met, Malloy took the broad steps stretching across the front of the building without hurrying. Pure habit. When you go to an urgent meeting, never look like that is what you are doing. He checked out the students and tourists lounging on the steps as he went. He was a man enjoying a glimpse of youth on a blustery spring afternoon. The kids sprawled across the stone steps in an attitude of leisure only kids can master. He liked to think he had been different when he was young, but he knew the truth. He had not imagined the wealth he had owned with his empty pockets and guileless smile anymore than they did. Oh, but what he could do with that innocence now!

Waiting for his turn to purchase a ticket, Malloy studied a flier about an upcoming exhibit his wife Gwen wanted to attend. Gwen knew very little about Malloy's professional life, having met him soon after his retirement. She was aware that he had worked overseas for a number of years. He had led her to believe he did contract work these days for the State Department as a forensic accountant. Admitting to being an accountant, he had learned from long experience in the game, usually ended all queries about his professional life. The forensic aspect excited Gwen's interest a bit, but that was fine. He didn't mind his wife thinking of him as a detective of sorts. The rest was probably a bit more than she was ready to believe anyway. She asked him once about his wounds. 'A visit to a bank in Lebanon,' he told her, which was true, 'a case of mistaken identity,' which was not. It had been Malloy's first assignment. In the course of an afternoon he had lost all of his assets, the people he had recruited in other words, and learned as no lesson before or since never to tell the truth about anything to anyone.

Gwen was a painter, lately a very successful one. In her world what she said was true and the people she associated with she either liked or avoided. She knew her husband kept weapons and was trained in their use, but she wouldn't touch them and preferred actually never to see them. That was fine. With Gwen, Malloy could be. . . well, not exactly himself, he was only himself when he was working, but at least content. Call it what it was: with Gwen he was happy.

Gwen was a good soul with a streak of disobedience toward authority that he shared. He liked to think he had worked through his transition on his own, but he knew he had only made it back to his own two feet because Gwen loved him. The shame of it was she never really knew how much she had done to make him a man again. But that was his only regret.

Having bought his ticket, Malloy meandered through the Greek and Roman sections, stopping occasionally as if to consider the stone visages but in fact memorizing the living faces within the hall. When he moved on he wanted to be sure no one was following him without his knowledge. Good guys, probably, but nothing irritated him more than letting anyone know what he was doing.

He saw a pretty long-haired girl in a short skirt studying a mosaic featuring long-haired naiads, and took a moment to reflect how little had changed in two thousand years, at least with regard to hair styles, young girls, and the eternal erotic in the fantasies of the male of the species. In the next hall the girl showed up again and studiously avoided eye contact again. He could imagine it was coincidence if he believed in such a thing, but he knew better and lost her after a fast turn.

She was waiting with just a hint of a blush at having been shaken so easily when he came to the centre of the museum's labyrinth, the Metropolitan's impressive medieval collection. The hall was mostly empty except for the long-haired girl and a tall blonde in her thirties, who studied a Byzantine triptych with far too much earnestness. Jane was employing children! But then, as he recalled only too well, she had hooked him at a tender age as well, bullet-riddled and desperate for a second chance.

Jane was good. She ran operatives the way the best operatives ran their assets – pay, coddle, cajole, pay some more, and have a heart, as long as it served a purpose. In two or three more years the young girl would go to the ends of the earth for Jane and probably wouldn't get spotted doing it. The one in her thirties was already there and might well have followed him without his knowing. If Jane had wanted Malloy dead, this one would have accomplished that too and without a flicker of conscience. It was something to keep in mind.

A guard sat contentedly at the far end of the room, probably not one of Jane's people. When two boys ran through the hall, their shouts awakening his attention, he wandered dutifully after them. The kids might have been Jane's doing. The girl with the long hair now walked toward a smaller room, and Malloy followed her as if to a tryst.

Jane Harrison was contemplating a Byzantine fibula crossbow, a weapon that could be held in one hand like a pistol and was good for killing at a range of no more than about two or three metres. Naturally, it was not only deadly, but quite ornate. Malloy had never warmed to Byzantine art. It was too formularized for his tastes, but he thought their weaponry showed real imagination – the true art of that gold-laced god-driven culture.

Jane was in the spirit of things. She didn't want to be seen, so she had come frumpy: large square glasses with a good smudge or two, no makeup, and even a bit of an old lady totter. Her hair was slightly frazzled, giving her the look of a slightly off balance schizophrenic with an expression that said, 'Talk to me, I dare you!'

She had finished her composition with shoes that were scuffed and breaking down at the heel, because pros always looked at the shoes. Jane believed frumpy old women in frumpy overcoats were invisible to the human eye – the prototype of stealth bombers – as she had put it years ago. She claimed actually to have run some experiments to prove it. Put fifteen people in a room and ask trained agents to recall each individual in detail. The frumpy old lady not only didn't get a colour of hair or exact height or weight, she actually vanished sixty-two percent of the time – or so Jane said. Jane had Malloy's failing. She lied so earnestly and constantly you never knew what was true. The fact that a statement wasn't important had no relevance. Lying was an art one employed for all occasions because a time might come when it would keep you alive or get you killed. It paid to be good at telling a lie and even better at reading one.

In this case, if it wasn't the truth, it ought to have been. Except she wasn't invisible to Malloy. To him Jane was simply amazing. Malloy had admired very few people in his life: his father, his mother, Gwen and Jane Harrison. He trusted a few more than that, but oddly enough, both his father and Jane failed to make the cut on his 'trust' list.

Looking at her costume it was hard to imagine Jane was currently the deputy director of operations at Langley, nearly impossible to believe she had started her career with a field assignment inside the Italian terror cells, spouting Marxist tripe and making love by the numbers.

'A thousand Madonnas,' Malloy muttered, 'and I find you admiring the only weapon in the room.'

'There aren't a thousand Madonnas here, T. K.'

Malloy looked around at the stiff Madonnas holding their miniature men wearing halos and giving the old hippy peace sign. 'Feels like it,' he said.

'Not a fan of Byzantine art?'

'They made nice weapons.'

Finally she smiled. 'Didn't they?'

Jane turned and walked toward an especially primitive painting of the Crucifixion. Malloy followed via a Madonna and child. As he passed by her for the sake of a slightly more interesting Crucifixion, Jane said, 'What have you gotten me into, T. K.?'

Malloy inspected the second Crucifixion. The spear of Longinus had just pierced the flesh of Christ. The blood spurted out like a fountain. A man in silk robes stood at the foot of the cross catching the blood in a gold chalice. It was bad science – Christ, being dead when struck by the spear, wasn't going to bleed like that – and bad art certainly, but what struck him was the notion of the blood itself. The medieval mind had believed in its power beyond all else. It was the blood staining the spear, the Chalice, the thorns, and the Cross, that made those relics the most prized possessions of the faith. It was not the same as the 'blood' of the Eucharist either. Not for those folks. For even the hint of a stain of the Saviour's blood they had been known to trade away whole kingdoms.

'You're talking about Jack Farrell?' he said with a touch of well-rehearsed surprise.

Jane stood slightly behind him now, just off to his side as if she too wanted to examine the arc of blood from the hanging corpse to the cup. 'This was supposed to be a quiet operation, T. K.'

'What can I say? I didn't think he would run.'

'It wasn't the running that got the media's attention. It was stealing half-a-billion dollars before he took off.'

'Taking his secretary along didn't help.'

'The secretary was a nice touch – from the media's stand-point.' Jane sounded tired, frustrated and justifiably pissed off.

Jack Farrell might have caused the problem, but she was blaming Malloy.

She walked toward another painting whilst Malloy continued to stand before Longinus and his spear. The Holy Lance, if one thought about it, was a curiously ambivalent symbol. Normally an instrument of violent death, its use on a living man being crucified would have been an act of mercy. Understandably, it was the most popular relic of Medieval Europe – a weapon everyone knew and understood. By modern times, the popularity had grown into the notion that whoever possessed the True Lance held in his hand the destiny of the world. Hitler had apparently been fascinated by this notion and had brought what he thought was the True Lance out of Austria once he had subjugated that country in 1938. He had kept the relic in the cathedral of Nuremberg to the end of the war, according to some, the supreme treasure of the Third Reich.

'You told me you could make Farrell an asset.'

Malloy resisted confessing he was wrong. Confessions, even genuine ones, only antagonised Jane. She had disliked the idea of recruiting Jack Farrell from the beginning. As far as she could see, Farrell was too big, too public. Besides if he was really connected to European crime families she ought to put someone else on it. Malloy was more valuable to her working black ops. The truth was Malloy had wanted Jack Farrell for his own reasons and so had claimed, without offering proof, that he was the only person capable of turning the man.

Jane had got to be an old woman by trusting no one – especially her best operatives. 'There's something you are not telling me,' she had answered. As usual there was a great deal he was not telling her, but what Malloy had said to her was this: 'If we go after Jack Farrell, I think we could end up inside the largest crime families in Europe.' That got Jane's attention. Was Farrell really so dirty? Malloy had lied to her with utter conviction: he was sure of it.

Jane had people on the ground in most of the major

European cities. She knew the key families and the politicians who protected them. She had a reasonable idea of the nature of their activities and a good estimate of the kind of money involved. What could Jack Farrell give her beyond that?

'With Jack Farrell,' Malloy told her, 'I'll have the bank account numbers of the bosses.' This had led to a series of questions. How had he settled on Jack Farrell? Interesting fellow. Jane had laughed at him. That was no answer. What did he *like* about Farrell? His old friends – the ones he avoided these days. Anyone she knew? Malloy dropped a few names. The more pertinent question was how much Jack Farrell really knew. Did Malloy have any idea what his role was inside the various syndicates? What did he do? What did he know? What piece of information was going to take them inside? How did he intend to turn the guy? What did Malloy know that someone else could not learn and use? Why did he have to be Malloy's asset? And her greatest concern: what if laundering funds was the extent of his involvement? 'We go to a lot of trouble and get nothing but intelligence we already have – and I've called in markers. . . for what?'

'Jack Farrell knows things we don't,' Malloy told her.

Was she supposed to take that as an article of faith? Why not? Well, for one thing, he had no criminal record, no known contacts with any of the crime families. . .

Not exactly true, Malloy had told her. He had business dealings with various companies connected in one way or another to Giancarlo Bartoli. Jane had answered this with the obvious: most international companies had dealings with Bartoli, like it or not. Besides Bartoli was grey. He was also international. If you dealt with Italy – if you dealt with Europe – you brushed up against him. Malloy had countered with the observation that Bartoli was considered mostly legitimate because of a lack of good intelligence. With Jack Farrell as Malloy's asset, Giancarlo, his son Luca, and their whole syndicate would come tumbling down.

Jane had offered to see what she could do, but Malloy told

her that wasn't good enough. A cursory look, even a long steady examination, wasn't going to work. In the end Farrell was going to be too clean to prosecute. What Jane needed to do was get the SEC to pursue every violation his company had made no matter how insignificant. Once the U. S. Attorney had indicted him, Malloy said he would have a talk with Farrell. 'If he cooperates, we can give him a pass. If he plays tough, he gets to see if country club prisons are all they're cracked up to be.'

'If he's clean and I persuade the SEC to go after him, someone this prominent, I'm going to feel some pressure.'

'Trust me,' Malloy had answered. 'Jack Farrell is dirty and he *will* talk.'

'If you're wrong about this, T. K. . . *trust* me, I'll take your legs out from under you.'

As Malloy had predicted, the Securities and Exchange Commission investigators had found very few irregularities in Farrell's company practices, but there were enough dubious circumstances to persuade an especially naive grand jury to hand down a seven count sealed indictment, including two counts of perjury and three of obstruction – all arising from his claims of innocence. Immediately before his arrest was to take place Farrell had got wind of the proceedings and made a run for it. That hadn't excited anyone particularly. Farrell was well known in a small world. He had dated a number of B-list celebrities for a time, getting some tabloid attention, but he was hardly a household name. All that changed when the press got word that Farrell had run off with one of his administrative assistants *and* his corporation's most liquid assets – an amount close to half-a-billion dollars. *That* was a story.

Within two days the FBI tracked Farrell to Montreal, but he was already gone, on a flight possibly to Ireland or possibly not. By the time the administrative assistant surfaced in a Barcelona hotel, Jack Farrell was still an American story – more oddity than anything else – but after Barcelona the media converged on the story en masse. The scandal sheets began to love him even as a hardcore group of professional financial writers were beginning to question the SEC's decision to go after Farrell in the first place. The indictment stank, to put it mildly. No one had whispered the infamous letters C-I-A but people at the SEC were starting to run for cover, and it was only a matter of time.

The evening before – midnight in Hamburg – the Hamburg police had received an anonymous phone call about Farrell's location. The police converged immediately on a five star hotel in the heart of the city. They missed Farrell by a matter of minutes. The media storm in the aftermath of the raid had started on the East Coast in time for the prime time news programmes. The morning talk shows had already turned Jack Farrell into an instant American folk hero, dubbing him the Runaway Billionaire.

'They're going to get this guy,' Jane muttered, 'and he's going to come back and stand trial. When that happens the media is going to drag the agency into the middle of this, and when they do that, the Director is not going to have any trouble finding where to put the blame – and neither will I.'

'Tell me what you want me to do.'

'I want you to make Jack Farrell go away.'

Malloy let his head tip back as he took a deep, thoughtful breath. '*Away?*' he said, finally.

'Dead, gone, or locked up for good in a German prison. Take your pick. Just don't let him come back to New York – or any place that is willing to extradite.'

'I can do that, I guess.'

'Farrell left two different passports in his hotel room. He was using one. The second was presumably his backup. He won't try leaving the country without a new ID, and my source in Hamburg tells me he's looking at a minimum of three days, probably closer to a week before he can get something that can pass. We don't know if he's still in Hamburg, of course. He could have moved to Berlin, but hunkering down right now is the smartest move he can make, and so far he's been making smart moves. Hamburg gives him a lot of cover. He takes a week, gets a new ID, and crosses the border someplace easy.'

'I'll get a flight to Hamburg tomorrow and see what I can do.'

'Your plane leaves tonight. We have to move on this thing, T. K. If the Germans get to him before you do, they'll send him back to us out of pure malice. If that happens you and I are going to suffer the consequences.' Malloy looked at his watch. A flight out that evening was pushing things a bit. 'And one more thing,' Jane told him. 'It's not out yet, but it will be for the evening news. Jack Farrell's new travelling companion is Helena Chernoff.'

Malloy blinked. He knew the name but hadn't thought to link it to someone like Jack Farrell. 'Number seven on Interpol's Most Wanted list?'

'Big fan, are you?' Jane asked.

'Some people check out the best sellers, I watch the FBI and Interpol Most Wanted lists.'

'What do you want to bet she moves up a couple of notches in the ratings next week?'

'What's an assassin doing with Jack Farrell?'

'Sleeping with him, according to the Germans.' When Malloy had nothing to say to this, Jane let one shoulder kick up in resignation. She was too old to question human nature's capacity to surprise. 'She works for money, T. K., and Jack Farrell has a lot of it. Also, she knows Hamburg.'

'So Farrell can sit it out for as long as it takes?'

'Interpol has been looking for Chernoff for close to two decades without any luck. I think she knows what she's doing.'

'Well, now she's got the FBI interested.'

'They've been interested for quite a long time, but that's another story. Here's the thing, T. K. We've got two FBI agents on the ground in Hamburg. They were in Barcelona interrogating Farrell's girlfriend and flew to Hamburg as soon as they heard about the near-miss. I'm guessing they're feeling a little over their heads at the moment, especially as neither of them speaks German. I went through a friend at State and arranged to give them some help.'

Jane passed behind him as he studied the naked breast of a Madonna placed a bit too close to the shoulder – medieval erotica.

'The best possible situation would be if the Germans keep Farrell. We raise a fuss, kick and scream, and Farrell doesn't see an American courtroom for ten-to-fifteen years. By then I'm retired and you've been shot to death by a jealous husband. Trouble is once the Germans understand how flimsy this indictment is, they're going to cooperate just to watch the show.'

The pretty girl walked into the room, and Jane said, 'We're out of time. Get with Dale Perry in Hamburg.'

'I know Dale.'

'I know you do. I introduced the two of you, remember?' Malloy tipped his head. In fact Jane had sent Dale to Zürich for six months when Malloy was operating there, but in the trade he supposed that amounted to an introduction. 'If Chernoff and Farrell are still in the city, Dale has the best chance of finding them. Just keep him out of the spotlight. I can't afford to expose him – even for something this big. You'll go in on your State Department ID, by the way. With the financials the Germans have turned up that shouldn't raise any eyebrows.'

'Anything in the financials worth looking at?'

'*Nada.*'

The girl handed him a business card as she passed him. Checking it, Malloy saw only a number.

'Remnants of your old slush fund in Zürich I just reactivated,' Jane told him. 'For incidentals.'

'What's my limit?'

'Whatever it takes.' And then she was gone.

Malloy walked back to the main hall, where the woman in her thirties approached him carrying a site map of the Met. 'Excuse me,' she said, and extended her map, 'Do you know where I can find the Impressionists?'

Malloy palmed the airline ticket she handed him as he touched her map and then shook his head. 'Sorry,' he told her, 'I'm lost myself.'

Malloy returned to his Ninth Avenue apartment an hour later. Gwen was out and not answering her cell phone. He wrote a note, packed his bag, and then started shifting files to one of his travel laptops. As he was finishing up, he called Gil Fine. Gil had been an analyst with the agency when Malloy was overseas. After the shake up in 2002 Gil had caught an updraft and floated into Homeland as a senior analyst. For the past several years Gil had provided Malloy with raw data which Malloy processed and summarized and filed with various intelligence agencies. The work kept his hand in the game and gave him a little bump in his income, but of course it was indescribably dull.

When Gil answered, Malloy said, 'Do you know who's sleeping with Jack Farrell?'

'Should I?'

'Hamburg police are saying he was in bed with Helena Chernoff last night.'

'The media is going to go ape on this guy, T. K.'

'What have you got on the lady, Gil?'

Malloy heard the clacking of computer keys, then, 'About six gigabytes. Pics, police reports, intelligence summaries, biometrics, video. . .'

'You have her on video?'

Malloy heard more key-tapping. 'Several, actually. You kill people in hotels and that's what happens. Got a gunfight in a parking garage. . . footage of her shooting a man when she was working for Julian Corbeau. . . a ton of stuff actually.'

'She worked for Corbeau?'

'The only one left standing as far as I can tell.'

'I'm going to need everything you have on this woman, Gil – not just summaries.'

'Sorry. Can't do it. Only a handful of people are authorised to access most of this stuff.'

Malloy looked at his watch. 'What's the problem?'

'Jurisdiction. There's possible activity inside U. S. borders; so we can't send that to you without formal requests and high level approval.'

'Give me the broad strokes.'

'You're on a secure line?'

'You, me and Big Brother.'

'Main case is Senator Brooks. From the 2004 election?'

Malloy didn't place the name immediately. 'What was his story?'

'Plane crash.'

'Right. Won the election anyway.'

'But the governor got to make the appointment.'

'Right. He tapped someone in the other party. Democracy at work. What's Chernoff got to do with it?'

'They were calling it a pilot error on the news, but there may have been tampering, and FBI found some footage on a security camera somewhere that might have been our girl.'

'I thought Chernoff worked mostly in the old East Bloc countries.'

'That's where she got her start. In the past ten years she has been working in the West – but *very* quietly and mostly against politicians and legitimate businessmen.'

'I've got to have this stuff, Gil. Get your supervisor to call Jane Harrison if you have to.'

'Teaming up with the Iron Maiden again, are you?'

'Catching Farrell has become a priority. Right now Chernoff is the only lead.'

'With Chernoff's track record, T. K., that's no lead at all.'

Malloy grimaced. He was working long odds on this thing and didn't care to have that fact thrown in his face.

'I'll tell you what I can do. I can send it without authorization to Dale Perry. He's probably got most of it, anyway. I assume you've arranged to contact him?'

'I'm meeting him tomorrow night. While you're moving files, can you send him everything the FBI has on Farrell's flight? I've got deep background on the guy, but since he ran I've only got what the news is telling us.'

'I've got the summaries I can send you right now. The rest I'll pack into the files I send Perry.'

'Great, but make it quick. I've got to be out the door in five minutes.'

'No problem. Hey, T. K., I just thought of something.'

'What's that?'

'You know Chernoff used to sleep with some of these Russian mobsters before she took them out?'

'What's your point?'

'With *that* lady in his bed, I'm just thinking Jack Farrell might want to think twice about going to sleep afterwards.'

Malloy shot out a couple of coded e-mails to contacts in Europe and then tapped into Jane's black ops fund. He moved ten thousand Swiss Francs into a Swiss Post account he kept under one of his aliases. This he could access as Euros via any postal machine from Germany. He checked his mail and got the FBI summaries on Farrell. That finished, he started for the door.

As he did, the elevator pulled down to the ground floor. The building renovation wasn't completed, but he had brokered the sale of two flats, each taking up an entire floor. Both individuals spent about three months a year in the city, the rest in the sunshine somewhere or other. Neither resident was in New York at the moment. So it had to be Gwen. The old freight elevator came groaning up to the top floor and opened.

Gwen had short dark hair and dusky skin, a slender frame, and large brown eyes that Malloy had simply never been able to resist. They had met shortly after Malloy had left the agency and floated along together for a few years before getting married. Marriage had happened about a year ago. The honeymoon should have been over long since, but they still flirted and teased like a couple of kids. Malloy wasn't complaining. It was the only innocence he knew and he hoped, actually, it would never stop.

When Gwen saw the suitcase set out she said, 'You're leaving me for another woman?'

'I'm too old to start over, Gwen. I just need to chase one for a few days.'

Gwen stepped off the elevator and gave him a wry smile. 'The romance just never stops with you, Thomas.'

'I caught some work overseas. I left you a note. Sorry for the rush but—'

'Where overseas?'

'I'll start in Hamburg and see where it takes me.'

'The Runaway Billionaire?'

Gwen didn't watch the news or read anything other than the arts, food and travel pages in the paper. She claimed it was the only way to stay sane. 'You know about this guy?' he asked.

'Wake up, honey. Jack Farrell is big.'

Malloy suppressed a groan and tried to downplay his assignment. 'State Department has loaned me to the FBI for a few days. They want me to see if I can track the credit cards they found back to the source.'

'They've got all that!'

Caught in his lie Malloy rumbled on, 'Well, good. Then it won't take too long. As soon as I find out where he stashed the half-billion I'll be back. They haven't found his money yet, have they?' He cast a reproachful look at the darkened TV.

'No sign of the money or Jack, but they got his DNA and the DNA of an unidentified female companion – *not* the secretary. She's still in Barcelona. I'm telling you, this guy is something with the ladies. Are you really going to get in the middle of this?'

Gwen was excited. Malloy tried to look bored. 'In the middle of the money, if I can get a handle on it.'

Her eyes widened as a thought struck her. 'You're not going to be in any danger are you?'

Malloy laughed and shook his head. 'The guy is an embezzler, Gwen. I doubt he has ever touched a gun in anger. Besides, I'm not going to be doing anything other than sitting behind a desk and talking to bankers.' A tired smile, 'Same old same old.'

'I think it's exciting anyway. I mean this guy is *primetime*!'

'They want me on the next plane to Hamburg, Gwen. I've got to go.'

'No time for a proper goodbye for my crime fighting forensic accountant?'

Malloy looked at his watch, 'They get real touchy if you're not there two hours early.'

'You want the airline mad at you. . . or your wife?'

Chapter Four

Carcassonne, France
Summer 1931.

'I invited a young man to meet us for drinks in the lobby bar. I hope you don't mind.'

Dieter Bachman spoke to his wife from the bathroom through the half-opened door, but her husband's offhanded manner excited her curiosity. 'What sort of young man?'

'His name is Otto Rahn.'

'A German?' Elise was vaguely disappointed. She had come to France for new experiences. Bachman, on the other hand, could find a fellow German in Mongolia.

'German or Austrian is my guess, but to tell you the truth I'm not sure. His French was so good I could not place the accent. Magre introduced us.'

Maurice Magre was a novelist of modest reputation they had met on the previous day through a fellow German's introductions. Magre played the celebrity to cadge drinks from the tourists. 'And how does Magre know him?' she asked.

'I didn't ask. All I know is that Magre told me after he had gone that Herr Rahn is a treasure hunter.' Elise was not impressed. Adventurers were as common in the Languedoc as aspiring writers in Paris, all of them looking for Cathar gold and a free drink.

Elise picked up an apricot-coloured dress and held it beneath her chin as she turned to face the foggy hotel room mirror. She was not sure about it. The colour seemed to accentuate her tan. She actually liked the effect with her black hair and dark brown eyes, but Bachman had begun to complain that she was soon going to be mistaken for an African. If he had his way her skin would be as pale as snow, her hair white-blonde, her eyes crystal blue. She had asked him once why he had proposed if he did not care for her colour. Her colour was fine, he told her, but if she must know he proposed because he had fallen in love! She had not bothered responding to that. Their marriage had been about money and family. Whatever love there might have been had long ago turned into a comfort friendship.

She tossed the dress aside. Too many wrinkles, anyway. 'And why did *Monsieur* Magre think we would like to get to know this young man? I hope it wasn't because he's German. We can see all the Germans we want when we're back in Berlin.'

'*I* thought we might enjoy getting to know him, actually.' Elise cast a speculative glance at her husband. He was still standing before the bathroom mirror, razor in hand. Bachman was a tall man with slightly hunched shoulders and a bit of a paunch. He had a round common face with thick cheeks and dark eyes. He had favoured a moustache since she had known him, but had decided to cut it recently, thinking he looked younger without it. His hair was already thinning and touched with grey, but the moustache had to go! She had been kind enough to lie and tell him he looked much younger without it. What had instigated the removal was a remark by a Swiss woman a few days ago in Sète. She had mistaken them for father and daughter. They had all laughed self-consciously at the mistake. Bachman asked if his wife really looked so young, but Elise had not been the source of the woman's confusion. Bachman was thirty-eight, a decade older than she, but he looked like a man pushing fifty. What was worse, he acted it as well.

'Tell me,' Elise said. 'Have you properly enquired into Herr Rahn's political sympathies?'

Bachman managed a smile as he came into the room. He was holding a towel in both hands. He knew Elise was teasing him, which he hated desperately, but he tried not to show his frustration. In Berlin Bachman endured no one who did not share his opinion with respect to political matters. In France, for the sake of a bit of sun, he was more liberal.

'From what Magre tells me Herr Rahn is not at all political. Too young really to know anything about the War, I suppose, and from what little he managed to say about himself, I take it he has been working in Switzerland the past couple of years.'

'Well then. . . drinks with a youthful adventurer who has absolutely no opinion about anything? It sounds as if you have planned a delightful evening for us, darling!'

Otto Rahn *looked* the part of a treasure hunter, Elise thought when she saw him from across the room. He was as tall as her husband, easily over six feet in height, but unlike Bachman he was lean and muscular and deeply tanned. Exactly as a man ought to look who had spent the summer out-of-doors scrambling amongst the foothills of the Pyrenees. He had a long, square face and combed his dark blond hair straight back, using oil to keep it in place. The style was common enough, but the effect on Herr Rahn was more pleasing than on most men. It accented his chiselled brow and high cheek-bones. She tried to imagine him as a movie star who had come to France to play the role of an adventurer and thought the image perfect.

When he saw Bachman, Herr Rahn left the bar and walked toward them with an animal grace that stirred something in Elise she had imagined long dead. This was no actor playing a part. He climbed rocks and plunged into caves, and he did it the livelong day! His smile and confidence, which had not a wit of subservience or awe for Bachman or his money, simply left her undone. Otto Rahn was, she decided, an incredibly handsome young man!

Bachman sometimes brought men of a certain type to meet her. They were artists of one kind or another, all penniless and very eager to please a wealthy patron. She had always imagined he was showing off his conquests, at least the ones he hoped to make, but of course she could not be sure. The issue wasn't something one discussed in a polite marriage, and theirs, if nothing else, had always been polite. If that was Bachman's plan on this occasion – with an excuse to send her back to Sète whilst he stayed on a few days more trying to seduce a treasure hunter – he had gravely miscalculated. Herr Rahn liked women. She could see it the moment he looked at her. After only a few minutes together, she was sure of it. He included her in their conversation, and in doing so he would happen to glance at her hands with thoughtful appreciation, then her shoulders. The next time he was looking at her hair. Once, as she left the table, she saw his reflection in a mirror and realised he was studying her manner of walk! It was not overt by any means. He was certainly not uncouth about it. It was appreciative and gentlemanly. Not *exactly* flirtation, her husband was sitting before them after all, but very close to it.

'So you are in Carcassonne for a few days more, I hope?' Rahn asked. Elise imagined he was asking her, but Bachman answered for them.

'Leaving tomorrow, actually. We have a place in Sète we are renting. We have it for the summer, so I expect we had better get back to it and get our money's worth.'

Was there disappointment in his eyes? Elise wanted to think so, but then she reminded herself that Herr Rahn might only be making conversation. Perhaps she was no different than Bachman, seeing what she wanted in a handsome stranger's glances.

'Of course you're welcome to come see us there, if you like,' Bachman added. 'We have plenty of room, and the Mediterranean is especially beautiful there.'

'That is very generous of you. . .' A glance at Elise. No, not just making conversation. He was thinking, in that quick appraisal of her, about his chances if he travelled to Sète for a visit. There were men who only pursued married women. She had friends who had encountered them and had been tempted or at least they had admitted to that much. Some husbands presumably turned a blind eye to it. Was Herr Rahn imagining that was the game here?

She looked at Bachman. He was sometimes hovering and protective about her when a man was obviously interested, but not this evening. Herr Rahn excited him too much to let something like jealousy diminish his enthusiasm.

Politics did not come up until the second round of drinks. Bachman mentioned that they lived in Berlin but had taken to spending the summers away from the city because of the troubles.'

'Is it really so bad?' Rahn asked him with genuine concern.

'Have you been to Berlin in the past few years, Herr Rahn?' Bachman asked.

'It has been a few years, I'm afraid, though I went to university there. I have always loved the city. I hate to see it torn to pieces.'

'You and every other good German! And all because of the Communists! They are determined to ruin everything!'

Bachman hated the Communists only slightly more than the present government. A dozen years ago he had been an aristocrat. Stripped of his title by parliamentary decree in 1919, he had wanted to pretend it was no great matter, but the wound ran deep, and when he found others like him mixing with the Nazis, he joined up. With a fortune at his disposal, he had of course been well received by the party's inner circle, and that was all it took for him to become a passionate supporter of the cause. Elise had seen very pleasant evenings such as this plunge into a violent argument for the sake of an ill-advised remark either against the Nazis or for the Communists. Bachman would accept indecision, even reticence – people needed to be persuaded – but when he found resistance the fight was on. As he had introduced the topic for no better reason than to evaluate Herr Rahn, Elise held her breath.

The topic appeared to make Herr Rahn uncomfortable. He was probably himself a Communist! The worn down heels of his shoes and frayed collar certainly indicated he was poor enough to be one. And why not? Everyone had a political opinion these days, the more radical the better. A middle course had certainly not solved anything! 'Well, of course,' Herr Rahn interposed, 'something has to change. Everyone believes that except the crooks in power, but until it does I don't care to get in the middle of it.'

'Germany finds itself at a crossroads,' Bachman told him. 'Those who stand off to the side now will no doubt be left behind once things take a new direction! For a young man such as you are that is something to consider very seriously.'

Before Bachman could work himself up to a full choleric fit, Elise touched her husband's arm. 'We'll have enough politics back in Berlin, dear,' she said. 'I want to hear about all the Cathar gold Herr Rahn has found.'

'I wasn't aware I was looking for any,' Rahn answered. He gave them both a bemused smile, curious no doubt as to the source of the confusion.

Elise looked at Bachman as she said to Rahn, 'I'm sorry. I was under the impression you were. . .'

Suddenly it came to Rahn. 'Is that what Magre told you?' he asked Bachman. 'That I'm a treasure hunter?' Bachman tipped his head. Such had been his understanding. Rahn seemed astonished and maybe a bit irritated, but after a moment he laughed. He had apparently had some dealings with the Frenchman.

'So what *are* you doing down here?' Elise asked.

'I'm researching a book I intend to write about the Albigensian Crusade of the thirteenth century.'

'Really?' Elise exclaimed. Things began to make sense to her. That he was writing a book explained his natural eloquence and the confidence he wore like a crown. He was an educated man, as she might have guessed! Still, he seemed a bit young for something so. . . well, so utterly stuffy.

'Another enthusiast of the Cathars!' Bachman announced, after taking a sip of his drink. He looked as if he were preparing to repeat some grand remark he had picked up from Magre the evening before.

'I have to tell you something very awful,' Elise said, before her husband could trample over the conversation again. Both men waited for her confession with the curious smiles of men anxious to hear 'something very awful' from the lips of a beautiful woman. 'Last night, I sat through dinner listening to our friend Monsieur Magre explain the Cathars to us, and I still haven't a clue what they believed, or for that matter who they were!'

'Do you want to know why Magre did not make it clear to you?' Rahn asked. He spoke softly, a man with an interesting secret to share with good friends.

'I should love to know.'

'It is because he hasn't a clue himself! If you want to know the *awful* truth,' he added with a smile that pretended to be wicked, 'no one really knows! Neither who they were nor what they believed!' He sat back like a born aristocrat and finished his drink in a gulp. 'Fortunately for everyone,' he announced with quiet authority, 'I intend to change all that.'

Both Elise and Bachman were anxious to know the essence of Herr Rahn's theory about the heretical Cathars, a people that had quite literally been exterminated in the first half of the thirteenth century, but such a topic, Bachman thought, was best handled over dinner, and so they moved to the hotel dining room where Herr Rahn could proceed to sing for his supper.

'The first thing you must understand,' Rahn told them, 'is that the Vatican's attack was economically motivated. The Cathar "heresy" was a convenient excuse for war. There was no movement to separate or purify the faith, no quarrel over dogma. The Cathars were simply oriented toward all things spiritual, much like St. Francis of the same era. They were followers of the teachings of Christ, if you will, but did not overtly reject the authority of the Pope. Vatican priests newly arrived to the region encountered a people of faith, so much so that many of them began conforming to some of the local customs of worship. After the war began, of course, lines were drawn.'

'According to what I've read,' Bachman said, 'the Cathars were Gnostic dualists. . . Manichaeans. . . whatever you want to call it.' He had got that from Magre. 'God and the Devil on equal footing. That sort of thing.'

'A world divided between God and Satan?' Rahn answered with a genial nod of his golden head. 'Two powerful deities fighting for the souls of men and women?'

'Exactly!' Bachman answered. Just as Magre had described it.

'That was the position of the Church in the thirteenth century, not the Cathars.' At Bachman's look of confusion, Rahn continued, 'St. Augustine had guided the Church away from the Manichaean heresy early in the fifth century, but by the eleventh and twelfth centuries the Devil had made a comeback. You have only to examine any medieval text to see the universal dread of the Evil One. If one did not know better, one could almost imagine Christ fared a sorry second behind the Prince of Darkness. People spoke so often of Christ and the angels and the saints that they had transformed into benign spirits who *might* help one in need, but only so long as the sun shined. When night fell a more potent force took over the earth, and absolutely no one was foolish enough to whisper the dread name of Satan, lest they inadvertently summon him.

'The Cathars, by contrast, had no interest in the Devil, not even a healthy fear of him. They understood evil as Augustine had defined it, a turning away from the light of God. For them, that happened whenever one came to be too much in love with the pleasures of the world, which is to say, the pleasures of the flesh. The contest for one's soul amounted to a struggle between the desires of the flesh and those of the spirit. They understood of course that we owe our existence to the physical world, but they knew as well that even our physical needs, what we require for survival, diminish our thirst for the world of the spirit. The notion is natural enough in our own time; even the Church preaches Cathar beliefs today, and we are certainly not reduced to dread that a thoughtless remark might summon a legion of devils, but I can assure you that in the poorly educated world of the thirteenth century the Cathars were the exception. Still, no one thought to call it heresy until the French king began to lust for the wealth of the region.'

'Correct me if I am wrong,' Bachman ventured, 'but the Cathars were against marriage – and sex in particular?'

'That is the first thing anyone will tell you about the Cathars,' Rahn continued, 'and pretty much the last.'

'Magre said as much to us,' Bachman interjected, pleased that he had got something right.

'All perfect nonsense,' Rahn told them. 'The truth is the Cathars invented romantic love. We call it courtly love now to distinguish it from romantic trysts between lovers, but it was hardly the tame stuff of polite society as people these days pretend it was. For the Cathars a love affair was not about adoration and purity and good manners, and it was not platonic. On the contrary, it burned with desire. In fact, its sole purpose was to stir the desire of two lovers to a white-hot pitch. But here is the thing: they refused to surrender to it. Once a knight offered his love and a lady accepted it the two carried on an affair of the heart – quite literally of the heart – for the rest of their lives. It did not come easily. Many knights would vie for the affections of a particularly extraordinary lady, but once she gave her heart, the affair was sealed and sacrosanct. Denied fulfilment at a physical level – sometimes even denied a chance to be alone – the lovers ultimately discovered a profound spiritual bond through their feelings for each other, but it was not friendship, not even the friendship of a comfortable married couple. It was the real, earth-shaking, dynamic of lovers at the moment before consummation, all of it carried out without touch, certainly without a kiss, and it burned for a lifetime – into eternity itself. Or so they believed.'

'What you're saying,' Bachman muttered, 'is that they

celebrated a kind of love that was doomed to failure and disappointment.'

Rahn smiled cheerfully at the assessment. 'To modern thinking, I suppose that is a fair statement. To their thinking such affairs left them inspired. You have only to look at Dante's love for Beatrice to understand the sublime effect of his passion. He did not simply elevate Beatrice to some implausible level of beauty and goodness. He chased after that image until by virtue of his love he became worthy of her affection. Before the Cathars, passion was sin. It ruined marriages, and that in turn had economic and political repercussions. This was a new idea. It offered a socially acceptable romantic intimacy between a man and a woman that did not threaten in any way the practicalities of the institution of marriage. A woman might bear the children of her husband and stand beside him as his political ally and even his confidant and friend, all the while carrying on a correspondence with the one true love of her life.'

'And what did husbands think when their wives enjoyed such affairs under their very noses?' Bachman asked with a tone of quiet indignation. 'I can't believe everyone would celebrate such a condition without. . . well, without a bit of old fashioned jealousy!' He looked at Elise. 'I for one could not stand it if Elise loved another man!'

'What you cannot stand, if I may be so bold as to say it, is the notion that your relationship might change or be lost because of such an affair of the heart. In the world of the Cathars that fear was irrelevant. Romantic love was never expected to lead to anything more than desire. It played out in the eternal realm of the spirit, ultimately taking the participants closer to God, and certainly closer to the ideal virtues of the faith. It taught them by the hard practice of self-denial to be less dependent on the sensory world.'

Bachman smiled but shook his head. He was not convinced.

Neither was Elise, who asked, 'Have you ever enjoyed such an affair?'

At last Adonis lost his confidence. Rahn's eyes focused on the table. The smile grew wistful. 'We no longer live in such a world. Say what we will in praise of the gifts of the spirit and all the rest, we want to taste our food and wine.' He lifted his glass and let the red liquid swirl to make his point. 'We want our lovers close to us and our money closer. We live knee-deep in sensation and as far as I can see we only want more of it.'

'Then it is no longer possible to love in such fashion?' Elise asked.

Rahn looked at Bachman as he spoke to Elise, 'If I allowed myself to write you the kind of letter Cathar knights sent the women they loved, I'm quite confident your husband would shoot me – and be acquitted for it in a court of law!'

'Even if he knew we were never to touch one another?' Her voice quivered as she spoke, and as she finished she too looked at Bachman. It was a moment of curiosity and challenge and maybe even of hope. Could Bachman bear her loving another man – *this man* – if nothing physical would ever transpire between them?

'I don't believe it is possible,' Bachman said at last, almost as if responding to a direct question. 'I think. . . where there are feelings men will act and women will follow!'

'You are talking about people of our own time,' Rahn told them, as if settling an argument amongst scholars. 'We have been corrupted. Not by our desires but by surrendering so often to them. We need too many assurances, too much comfort. We cannot trust to the love someone may have for us without some physical contact along the way to seal the promise.'

'Do you really believe it happened?' Bachman asked him. 'People madly in love without ever having physical intimacy? Don't you imagine that they in fact talked a good game and then when backs were turned. . . well. . .?'

'Some individuals failed. I don't doubt that. It is the nature of humanity. I am convinced, however, that many experienced a joy and depth of love that for all our sophistication we can no longer even imagine. Think of it as the first sensation of profound desire prolonged for a lifetime. Think of the madness and despair and happiness of falling in love – the world itself in the palm of one's hand – and then add to it the sensation of one who will always remain beyond the gates of that blessed place. Such emotions I think must lead us to a higher plain, to humility and patience, and probably even to prayer, but I can't be sure. For me it is an academic exercise. To be in love like that is to take a journey I have never attempted.'

'What do you think of Herr Rahn?' Bachman asked once they were in their room again. It was late, but he seemed energised. He wore a wry smile on his face as he asked Elise this question. It seemed to her he was actually reflecting on the practical aspects of Herr Rahn's theories about love.

Elise blushed guiltily at the mention of Rahn's name, but she answered honestly. 'I don't think I've ever met anyone like him.'

'So much so that you could fall in love with him?'

It was tempting to imagine desire transmuted into something beyond reproach. She wanted passion, but not all that went with a married woman making a fool of herself. She had not had very much excess in her life, but she thought to be madly in love with someone must be a wonderful thing. Enough of polite relations! She wanted to burn! But not if it meant guilt and scandal. Berlin society, after all, was still a tightly closed circle. One watched the reckless wives and coquettes taking chances. It was great entertainment to observe them circle ever closer to the flame, but there came a time when such in-dividuals went too close. And afterwards, as she had seen more than once, they were quietly but surely excluded. As one intimate had said to her quite bluntly, if one longed too much for the pleasures of the street, the street was what one got!

'Tell me,' she said with a look that assured Bachman she was answering his question, 'must we really go back to Sète tomorrow?'

New York-Hamburg
Thursday-Friday March 6-7, 2008.

Malloy made it to JFK an hour before his flight. Because he was flying first class the scolding was gentle. The real concern was his last minute decision to travel. To this query he presented his State Department ID and the officious manner of a government bureaucrat who breathes fire: not a word of explanation.

'Jack Farrell?' the woman asked, her eyes dancing.

Malloy blinked with studied dullness, 'Who?'

'Sorry. I just. . . have a good flight, sir.'

CNN was running Breaking News when Malloy arrived at his gate. They had the Chernoff story. Malloy checked his watch. They had scooped the networks by an hour – no doubt thanks to Gil Fine – and were already showing a vintage file photo of twenty-two-year-old Helena Chernoff in the military uniform of East Germany. She looked good, very good, if you liked pretty girls in military uniforms, and who didn't? A lot like Gwen, he thought. Nice large eyes, short dark hair, a certain hunger, and an abiding innocence. Of course, in Helena Chernoff's case, the innocence was pure artistry.

A man called out from the waiting area, 'Go, Jaaaack!' Several people smiled at this. Next the TV showed a grainy still from security footage of Chernoff walking with Jack Farrell out of Hamburg's Royal Meridien Hotel. Their faces were in shadows, her body covered in a coat and pressed tightly against Farrell. According to the reporter a DNA analysis of the trace elements left in their shared hotel room proved the two were lovers, not just employer and employee.

A shout went up from a group of young salesman-types. 'Jack! Jack! Jack!' Old ladies were smiling.

Chernoff, the report continued, was wanted for questioning in at least. . .' Malloy missed the number, drowned out by the fraternity of good will for the Runaway Billionaire. He heard '. . .Russian and East European businessmen with ties to organised crime.' They said nothing about activities in the West.

He turned away from the screen and took a moment to reflect on Jack Farrell's exalted status. Jane was right. With Chernoff coming into it, the story was getting legs. It wasn't going to fade away after the arrest. The media was going to keep looking for something new, something controversial. A CIA conspiracy to entrap an American icon? That would do the trick.

And when *that* broke, Jane was done – along with everyone riding her coat-tails.

On the flight to Hamburg, via London as it happened, Malloy went through the FBI summaries Gil had sent him.

Farrell had been missing from his Manhattan townhouse thirty-six hours before NYPD contacted the FBI. There was no sign of trouble, just an unmade bed and clothing left lying on the floor. He looked at digital photos of the apartment. Jack Farrell had lived the good life. Malloy skimmed down the material until he came across Irina Turner, the assistant who shared the first few days of Farrell's run. He found her image and bio. She had worked just over a couple of months as Farrell's administrative assistant. Turner was a pretty blonde, age thirty-two, education. . . no information available. A Lithuanian national with American citizenship since 2000. The citizenship came after her marriage to Harry Turner, an American businessman who travelled frequently to the Baltic countries. Divorced four years later. Nothing else on Harry Turner. . .

He went back to the narrative of Farrell's movements. Nothing from his cell phone since the run, though it was missing. No credit card use. Twelve hours into the Missing Person search an FBI support team discovered Farrell had looted the cash reserves of three insurance companies he owned. Curiously, that had occurred six weeks prior to his run. Malloy considered the matter. Seven weeks ago, the SEC was gearing up for interviews and requesting that Farrell provide them with certain of his financial records. Farrell had been starting to feel the pressure, but he should not have panicked. The amount looted was sixty million, serious money, but as it turned out just the beginning.

Less than a week after he tapped the insurance reserves, one of Farrell's trading companies in Europe purchased a little over fifty million dollars of platinum and immediately sold it to a German automaker. This was a routine transaction, but the money received was wired to a newly created cash pool. From there the money bounced into various accounts, then became untraceable. There were more moves like this in the same company over the next two weeks. The same thing happened in some of the commodity companies in which Farrell had controlling interest. Ten here, thirty there. No one was getting overly excited. It was just business as usual and a few million falling through the cracks. It was the kind of theft anyone in business could execute, the downside being it was going to catch up with the perpetrator quickly, unless of course one arranged to disappear.

Malloy had not realised Farrell had been preparing for his vanishing act for weeks. He should have. You don't put half-a-billion dollars in your suitcase or melt down ten tons of gold and carry it off in the boot of your car. And you don't make it all go away with the press of a button. You work at it. You plan out the financial moves. You keep the red flags to a minimum for as long as you can. You take out a loan you don't intend to repay, you miss a payroll, you lose the paperwork on a wire transfer. You send people looking in the wrong places. You create problems with a shipment and withhold payment until the problem is settled and then wire the funds to a holding account. From there on to the Caymans or Panama City or Nicosia or Beirut or Lichtenstein or any other country where banking officials are permitted or encouraged to refuse access to Western law enforcement agencies. Some here. Some there. And all the while the clock is ticking. Farrell's whole world had been ready to come crashing down on him the moment people in his various enterprises began talking to each other about the problems they were suddenly having.

In Montreal Farrell had got new identities for himself and Irina Turner. He then flew a private jet to Barcelona, though the flight was originally scheduled to Ireland. Less than a week after Farrell's disappearance, Irina Turner surfaced and was arrested by the Spanish *Federales* on false document charges. The FBI was invited to Spain to conduct interviews. Malloy didn't have the actual transcripts but he read the summaries. Turner was cooperative and gave enough detail that the FBI could trace Farrell's movement from New York to Barcelona. So they knew where he had been but not where he had got his false documents or, more importantly, where he was going.

Soon after Irina Turner surfaced, the Hamburg Police received an anonymous call from a public telephone telling them Jack Farrell was at the Royal Meridien. The Royal Meridien was a five star hotel in the heart of Hamburg. The police staged a midnight incursion into Farrell's suite minutes after the call. They found steam on the mirrors, moist towels, rumpled and apparently well-stained sheets, a man's wallet on the bureau, passports and credit cards – everything but Jack Farrell. Within hours police had identified Farrell's new girl-friend – Helena Chernoff.

FBI Special Agents Josh Sutter and Jim Randal caught the first flight out of Barcelona and were in Hamburg by noon.

Malloy shut his computer down and tried to get some sleep. It didn't happen. There was too much he didn't like about Jack Farrell's run. By rights he should not even have known about a sealed indictment and the pending arrest, and yet he had run within hours of the indictment. Worse still was the decision to start moving money out of legitimate enterprises and into secret accounts just as the SEC started sniffing around his company's procedures. If CEOs ran every time that happened, they'd all be fugitives!

It made no sense. Besides, if Jack Farrell had truly feared what the SEC was going to find and knew they were looking at him, he ought to have moved someplace where he would be safe from extradition. He had access to at least forty or fifty million in legitimate and relatively liquid funds. With the language and business skills to earn more once he had resettled that should have been sufficient. It happened all the time. There were countries that didn't care about 'minor' infractions and welcomed billionaires and their fortunes, but once stolen money was involved, these same countries were no longer willing to protect individuals from extradition.

At this point Farrell's options were limited and uniformly unappealing. He could engage the services of a rogue nation and take his chances with a lawless dictator, or he could change his identity and settle down in obscurity somewhere in a second or third world country. Why, Malloy wondered, would an intelligent man put himself in such an unenviable position?

The Languedoc
Summer, 1931.

Dieter Bachman found Rahn at his pension quite early on the morning after their dinner together. Bachman seemed like a man about to make an unsavoury offer, but in fact simply enquired of Rahn if he would be willing to act as a guide for a few days. Rahn, not sure he understood what was expected of him, hesitated.

'There is such a lot to see,' Bachman added with an awkward smile, 'and to be blunt about it we really had not planned to tour the region, but you have ignited our interest – in the Cathars, I mean!' He added that he would pick up all of Rahn's expenses, and naturally pay Herr Rahn for his trouble. The amount he offered was well above the rates the locals charged, and Rahn took a moment before responding. One did not want to appear too eager, after all.

'There are plenty of guides about,' Rahn answered. 'Have you enquired as to their rates?'

'If one is pleased with superficial accounts, one can get a discount, I am sure. I understand that, Herr Rahn. We are not interested in that sort of thing, however. I am thinking a week or two, as your schedule allows. Some of the castles and a few of the grander caves, a bit of the history along the way, and over dinner something with an academic flavour to it so we might take something away from the experience.'

'I suppose I could do that. Certainly. It sounds like it might be a great deal of fun, actually.' And with that they shook hands.

Alone, Rahn considered the exchange. Herr Bachman's words had suggested nothing untoward, but his manner had seemed awkward, as if he were proposing a bit more than a tour through the Pyrenees. Despite his instincts toward caution, however, Rahn dismissed his concerns. Bachman was clearly not the sort who might enjoy his wife's infidelity. He was very careful of her, actually. Maybe he just wanted to become acquainted with the sensation. Flirting with disaster, so to speak. Not that a flirtation with Frau Bachman would be hard work. Not at all. Frau Bachman – Elise – was extraordinary. A dark beauty, taller than average, with a lean, athletic build, and the saucy smile of a woman who is still alive to the pleasures of the world. Not hard work, by any means! Plus she had seemed interested in everything he had said – no pretty face and empty head, that one. She was probably his age, he decided. Born in this century, at least, with the Great War being only a childhood memory. Years, maybe even a couple of decades younger than her husband, who wasn't really a bad sort, only a bit pretentious.

He had gathered from certain remarks that they had been married a few years. They were not newly-weds. More likely, they were looking for the spark that could bring back the honeymoon. As he thought about it, Rahn found himself wondering if she had married for love, security, or comfort. He knew it had not been for the sake of their passion. Dieter Bachman came from old money from what he had indicated. That was something the rich always seemed to get across as quickly as possible. Had she been a poor girl who caught his eye? Or had she come from the kind of people who had money and wanted a better family name?

Rahn had worked hard for his summer in the French Pyrenees. He lived on a tight budget, hoping to stretch a few weeks into a month or two. Magre had tossed him a morsel with the Bachmans. After a pleasant evening of talk Rahn had managed to turn it into something of a banquet. With the money Herr Bachman had offered him, a week of work would buy him another month of study, not to mention a free ride to every ruin and medieval fortress in the region.

Along the way if a bit of flirtation with Frau Bachman developed, what was the harm? As long as no one got too serious everyone could have some fun!

'We can all fit, I hope.'

Dieter Bachman pointed toward a 1930 Mercedes-Benz SSK. The vehicle was a long sleek convertible set low to the ground. Its curving front fenders looked like giant sleds to either side of an engine that ran two thirds the length of the automobile. The tiny boot could hardly provide enough space for their combined luggage, but Rahn managed to tie his own luggage across the rear bumper, and then found himself sharing a seat with the delicate Frau Bachman nearly on his lap. Herr Bachman made a joke about trusting Herr Rahn to be a true Cathar and all three of them laughed with the giddiness of adolescents starting off on a road trip.

Bachman liked to drive fast, so they tore through the countryside with Elise, Frau Bachman, jostling against Rahn until he could think of nothing but her, the fine scent of her lustrous black hair, the sweet dusky skin so close to his lips, the delicate neck, the dark, enticing eyes. She asked him once, without the slightest insinuation that she was aware of her effect on him, if she was making a nuisance of herself. He answered bravely. Not at all!

They stopped to stretch once along the way, and before they got back in Bachman asked him purposefully, 'My wife isn't making it too hot for you, is she?' He seemed to be enjoying himself.

Rahn had directed them to the village of Ussat-les-Bains, where he had decided to show them one of the great caves of Europe. He suggested they have lunch at the *Des Marronniers* before their descent, and they sat outside in the shade of a grove of chestnut trees – after which the hotel had been named. They enjoyed roast duck and a bottle of Languedoc Merlot. As they dined Rahn described certain of the key families of the region in the years leading up to the Vatican's crusade into the territory. As in much of Europe at that time, the marriages crossed borders, even languages and culture. To speak of the Cathars as a people was rather a misnomer. They were more precisely a culture. Rather than being a rural, mostly im-poverished mountain region as the area was today, he told them, the south of France had actually been far in advance of most of the rest of Europe: politically stable, economically prosperous and in general at peace with its neighbours. That, he assured them, had been a rarity in feudal Europe.

'Given the advanced state of political and economic con-ditions,' he said, 'it was natural that they turned its attention to those things we associate with civilisation: music, poetry, the arts, and good manners. And what started here, especially the notion of romantic love, began to sweep through the courts of Europe – along with the legends of the Grail.'

Over coffee Elise asked him how he had first got interested in the study of the Cathars.

'For me,' Rahn told her, 'everything goes back to Wolfram Eschenbach's story of Percival.'

'The knight searching for the Grail?' she asked.

'Percival was the first of many and the only one who actually saw it.'

'It has been a while since I read Eschenbach,' Herr Bachman said.

'The gist of it is that Percival found his way to the Castle of the Fisher King. At a banquet, Percival witnessed a procession of knights and ladies carrying an ivory lance and a gold chalice through the great hall. Blood dripped from the tip of the lance continuously, but all of it was caught by the chalice. As Percival watched he was fascinated, of course, but he had been warned about talking too much, since he was such a young man, and so he was afraid to ask about what he had witnessed. That was his undoing. If he had only made enquiry about it, the Grail would have been his, the Fisher King would have been healed of his lameness, and the dying kingdom would have bloomed with life again. As he failed to do that, he fell asleep and awakened some-time later utterly alone in a wasteland.

'Once I realised Eschenbach's story was not a fairytale set in a far-away land but was actually an allegory about the fate of Cathars – who had not yet perished but were on the verge of extinction when Eschenbach wrote his story – I began to read about the local families, and realised the Grail Castle of Eschenbach's romance was Montségur, the last fortress of the Cathars still able to resist the Vatican's army. At that point I had to come here and see everything for myself.'

After lunch Rahn took them into the *Grotto de Lombrives*. With its jasmine-coloured columns and glistening crystalline stalactites hanging like the teeth of a shark, the cave was one of the great treasures of southern France. Deep inside they found the Cathedral, a subterranean vault that was larger than Europe's grandest cathedrals.

'The Iberians worshipped their sun god here, long before the Greeks arrived,' Rahn told them. 'After the crusade began in 1209, the Cathars in the Ariege valley gravitated here for their services, since the Church had reclaimed all their churches and replaced the sympathetic priests with Dominicans – the Order which conducted the Inquisition.'

Later in one of the side vaults he showed them a faded painting of a lance dripping blood into a cup. 'It is the Blood Lance that Percival encountered in the Grail Castle,' Rahn told them. 'The image was more popular amongst the Cathars than the Cross and for good reason. It represented knighthood and had no equivalent within the church. So it became their emblem of faith.'

'If the Lance always bleeds,' Elise observed, 'and yet the cup is never filled, it must symbolise the eternal and unrequited passion between the lovers.'

Rahn looked at her with interest. 'I had not thought of that,' he said, 'but it is certainly something to consider.'

'But would they have understood the symbolism of the male and female in the cup and the lance?' Bachman asked. 'I mean isn't that sort of thing a modern concept?'

'I expect for a Cathar the power of the image was the blood itself, not the Lance or the Cup. They would have understood the image as an expression of continual renewal and potency.'

'Like their passions,' Elise whispered.

The French Pyrenees
Summer, 1931.

There was no explicit understanding, certainly no pact, between the three of them. No one, least of all Herr Bachman, attempted to established boundaries or even to discuss the nature of what they were pursuing. But in the days that followed all three of them became increasingly comfortable with their evolving relationship. The Bachmans were good travellers. They were curious about the countryside and local customs, even the dialect, which was peculiar to the region. Herr Bachman asked numerous informed questions about the fortresses. He had fought in the war and had briefly attained the battlefield rank of major before his discharge. Elise was more affected by the love affairs, and followed the marriages and the families and the affairs of the heart with the enthusiasm of a woman addicted to nineteenth century French novels. Rather than growing jealous of his wife's obvious affection for their guide, Bachman would sometimes take occasion to leave them alone. Not for long and rarely in perfect privacy, but he seemed to give them their freedom at least to talk for a few moments. As the days passed Rahn was frequently tempted to say something during these moments of solitude – to ask about visiting her in Sète or perhaps coming to Berlin the following winter. He was desperate to know if her interest was something more than flirtation, which even her husband now seemed to encourage. The truth was he was falling in love, and though he knew he had no hope of persuading her to leave her husband's fortune, he was willing to do anything in order to have an affair with her.

Still, one word too far and it could all be ruined. He had no idea if she understood what she had inspired, nor any notion of how seriously she took their flirtation. She certainly enjoyed his company, but that was not the same thing as meeting him after she was sure her husband had fallen asleep! If something was going to happen, he was determined that she must first give a signal, but no signal came. She was happy talking with him alone or in the company of her husband. She grew comfortable settling quite squarely on his lap and letting the miles roll by. Sometimes she leaned back against him, her lovely hair blowing over his face. He was a fantasy for her; that much he had determined. How seriously she took the fantasy, he could not decide. Sometimes it seemed she would fall into his arms if he only had her to himself long enough. Sometimes he was sure she would protest violently if he were even to ask for a kiss.

At dinner one evening following a day scrambling over the splendid ruins of Minerve in the north of the region, Herr Bachman suggested they dispense with formalities. They were going to be travelling together for a few more days and it was silly not to relax a bit. They had become friends, and they weren't still in the nineteenth century, after all! He was Dieter. His wife was Elise. Rahn answered that he liked to be called Otto.

There followed, as custom demanded, a toast to their new friendship – and the pleasant shifting of grammar from the *Sie* of strangers to the *Du* of intimates. They made a night of it, Bachman losing his habitual stiffness and seemingly pathological fear of impropriety. Elise as well was less cautious, more prone to laugh. With the shifting of grammar and the use of personal names, it became obvious to all three of them that the tour must end, but their friendship ought not. They must stay in touch! A visit now and then, letters to keep informed. It was only natural amongst friends!

Very late in the evening, the waiters hovering in the shadows to encourage them to finish their party, Bachman said, 'If you are falling in love with my wife, Otto, it is perfectly fine with me.' At Rahn's look of surprise, Bachman added, 'I mean it! Only do not make a fool of me! I will not be any man's fool!'

'That goes without saying,' Rahn answered cavalierly. He shifted his gaze to Elise. 'The real question is whether Elise has any interest.'

'I cannot help you with that! Women are impossible to comprehend! Are you interested in his honourable affections, my dear?'

Mortified at her husband's crass behaviour, Elise fixed her gaze on her wine glass. 'You are quite drunk, Dieter. I think we had better get to our rooms.'

But Bachman was in no mood for his bed. He went on for a while about the custom of the Cathars to write letters to their lovers pledging their eternal passion. It wasn't really such a bad idea so long as it left marriages intact. He did not mind at all if they were in love with one another so long as it remained pure! 'Eye batting is another matter,' he muttered with less humour. 'That much has been going on from the start between you two!'

*

Later, on the stairway, Bachman nearly toppled over, and Rahn had to help Elise get her husband up the last steps. Once inside the darkened room he asked if she needed help getting him to bed.

'If you don't mind! He's already out, I think!'

She was furious with Bachman, who was usually better than this, and maybe irritated as well that Herr Rahn had not protested at Bachman offering her affections like a market place panderer – *pure intentions* or not! After they had dumped him on the bed, Rahn bent down on one knee and started untying his shoes. It was a very decent thing to do, she thought, but slavish as well. He was their guide not a valet! 'I'll take care of him,' Elise said.

Rahn looked up at her. 'It is no problem. I have had a night or two like this myself, and it is really best to get one's shoes off.'

Elise was breathing hard from the exertion of wrestling with Bachman, but it seemed to her suddenly as if it was from the excitement of their being finally and completely alone. 'Let me get that!' she said, and brushed his shoulder with her breast as she bent to remove Bachman's second shoe. She had not meant to do it, but for a moment she did not pull back.

Bachman forgotten, Rahn pulled his arm away but only so that he could touch her hair, pushing it back from her face to a have better look – or to kiss her, she could not be sure!

Elise dropped her husband's foot and stood up as if scalded by his fingers. 'Go to your room, Herr Rahn.'

He stood, but he did not retreat. He faced her squarely, his smile not nearly so drunken as she had imagined. 'Will you come with me?'

'Go! Or I will tell Dieter how you have behaved!'

'I don't think you will.' He took her hand, and though she shook her head as he held it, she could not force herself to pull away from him. 'I think you want to come with me,' he said. He moved closer, meaning to kiss her if she would let him.

'Maybe I do,' she said, dropping her chin away from his advance. 'Maybe I want you more than you can know, but what I want and what I will do are two different matters entirely. Now kindly leave!'

Rahn smiled, convinced at last, and turned toward the door. 'I expect a great many people envy your husband his wealth.' He stopped at the door and leaned against the doorjamb quite comfortably. 'I know almost any man would envy him for having such a beautiful wife, but do you want to know why I envy him?'

'I haven't the slightest idea, nor do I care to hear your nonsense.'

'It is the loyalty you show him. If you were mine I would not risk—'

'But I am not yours.'

'Not tonight.'

'Not ever, Herr Rahn.'

'It's Otto, or have you forgotten already?'

'Go!' she whispered, 'and close the door behind you.'

Alone, Elise did not sleep. She thought instead about the young man in the next room. She heard him moving about, then undressing. She heard the springs of his bed, and thought, 'I could be there instead of here. I could have all that I want as easily as knocking on his door. And no one need ever know. . .'

Why she didn't go she could not have said.

Hamburg, Germany
Friday March 7, 2008.

Malloy's plane landed in London. Three hours later he was in the air again and headed for Hamburg. By mid-morning he passed through customs and saw a well-built sandy haired American holding a sign for Mr Thomas. The man was in his late thirties and had an open friendly face, broad shoulders, a trim waist, and a wedding ring that looked welded in place. 'I think you're looking for me,' Malloy told him.

91

'I'm Josh Sutter, Mr Thomas.' Sutter passed his business card, which Malloy took without offering his own.

'It's T. K. Nice to meet you.' They shook hands.

'My partner has got our ride at the kerb.'

The ride was a bright red SUV they had rented the day before. The partner was Special Agent Jim Randal. Randal was polite but more suspicious than his partner. He wanted ID. These were presented on all sides, two badges and Malloy's suitably worn and faded State Department ID with his title, Certified Public Accountant.

Randal was probably Sutter's age, but he looked older and certainly more jaded. He carried some extra weight and was losing his hair. After a few sentences about the weather and Malloy's flight, Malloy was willing to bet Randal was New York born and raised. Sutter's accent had touches of New York, but it originally came from the Midwest, some-where north of Chicago, he thought. Wisconsin, maybe. Sutter certainly had the manner of an honest hardworking farm boy who has moved to the city. Despite their overt differences Malloy could see these guys were long-time partners and good friends.

'Royal Meridien okay?' Josh Sutter asked.

'Is that where you two are staying?' Malloy asked.

'The German detective who's working with us got us a discount.' Big smile at this. Who didn't like a five star room on a government per diem?

'Nice rooms?'

'They're great!'

'Sounds good.'

Having bugged the FBI agents' rented SUV a matter of hours after they had landed in Hamburg, David Carlisle knew that a Mr Thomas from the State Department had been dispatched from New York. Carlisle had assumed Mr Thomas was an alias of Thomas Malloy and proceeded to the airport for his first look at the man. Carlisle followed at a discreet distance as

Malloy and Sutter left the area and joined Agent Randal, who was waiting in the SUV. Once their vehicle pulled away from the kerb, a taxi slipped forward and Carlisle climbed into the front seat beside Helena Chernoff. 'Is it definitely Malloy?' he asked her.

'In the flesh,' she told him.

Carlisle smiled.

An automated female voice directed Agent Randal in British English as they drove back to the city. 'In Barcelona,' Randal said, 'we couldn't get GPS and we spent half our time there trying to read a frigging map. We come here and get *this* gal's voice – I mean sometimes I take a wrong turn just so she'll scold me!'

Embarrassed by his partner's patter, Josh Sutter said that the good part about being lost all the time in Barcelona was they got to see a lot of the city.

'You speak any German, T. K.?' Jim Randal asked.

Malloy's parents had moved to Zürich when he was seven. By the time he was fourteen he was fluent in Swiss German and beginning to understand the nuances of High German, the written language of the Swiss. Two decades working in Europe had pretty much turned him native, but of course the FBI didn't need to know all that. 'I can order a beer or a cup of coffee,' he said.

Sutter thought about it. 'They're like. . . the same word. . . right? Coffee and beer?'

Malloy answered with what he hoped was a disarming smile.

'We learned that much yesterday – I mean get the essentials, right?' This from Jim Randal. 'Toilet is toilet. Beer is beer. Coffee is coffee. I figure out how to ask for a steak and I could pretty much live here.'

'I tell you what. I thought I knew a little Spanish,' Josh Sutter announced, 'but we got to Barcelona, and I didn't even understand their English!'

'The cops treating you all right?'

'They're great!'

'Total professionals,' Randal nodded. 'Especially the Germans.'

'To tell you the truth I was surprised at that. I mean, you know, you see these old war flicks with the Germans and everybody's throwing their arms out and shouting *Heil Hitler*. So. . . we get here and we're ready for the Swastika armbands and goosesteps, but they're like smiling and friendly—'

'Efficient!' Randal offered with a nod. 'First thing you see, their offices are like *clean*. They got no papers or files sitting around, no stained coffee cups. Everything is like an operating room! You go into an NYPD precinct, you know what you see?'

'We got in yesterday,' Sutter said, cutting off the litany of what one would see, 'and they're handing us reports that are already translated. And they like give us this guy—'

'Hans!' Randal said from the driver's seat. He liked Hans.

'Hans,' Sutter agreed. 'Some last name you couldn't say if someone put a gun to your head! But he like went to school in South Carolina so he's got this like German-South Carolina thing going on, but his English is like better than mine!'

'*Way* better than mine!' Randal added.

'They're embarrassed,' Malloy said in a matter of fact tone.

As he expected, both agents got quiet. Finally, Sutter bit. 'Embarrassed about letting Jack Farrell get away?'

'The Germans study us and then do what we do – only they expect to do it better.'

'Well, *we* lost the guy, too!'

Malloy let one shoulder kick up, 'We're not as efficient.'

Randal's eyes caught his partner's gaze through the mirror. They were evaluating Malloy, not what he was telling them. That was okay. That was the first step to getting them on his side.

'They're going to bury you in paperwork to show you how efficient they are.'

'I don't care why they're doing it,' Sutter said with a laugh, 'it's just way better than what we got in Barcelona.'

'In Barcelona,' Randal added, 'they never heard of English! They brought some translator in and we couldn't understand a word she said either. And the reports! All Spanish. We had to like fax them to New York for a translation.'

'And we're *still* waiting on the DNA from the bed sheets there,' Josh Sutter added. 'The Germans had DNA by the time our plane touched down. That was like twelve hours after they got the evidence!'

'I understand you talked to Irina Turner in Barcelona.' Malloy said.

Sutter nodded, his face showing frustration, 'Nothing there. She's this. . . secretary I guess you'd call it—'

'Sex-a-tary.'

Malloy looked at Randal, then back to Sutter. Josh Sutter shrugged in his farm boy manner. 'Girlfriend-slash-administrative-assistant. I guess it was like blow jobs at the office and three or four other assistants around to move the paper and set up the meetings.'

'Russian girl?' Malloy asked.

'Lithuanian.'

'Right. . .'

'In way over her head,' Randal grumbled.

'Barcelona still holding her?'

'I don't think they really want her,' Sutter said. 'She was travelling on a forged passport, but that's all she did.'

'Countries frown on it,' Malloy answered.

'She didn't sign anything, didn't talk at Immigration. Farrell handled the documents. She gets a good lawyer she can say she thought the passport Farrell gave them was hers.'

'Just doing what Farrell told her to do.' Randal said.

'She said they hit Barcelona and like the only English on TV was CNN. They were hanging out in this hotel watching CNN all day long. They go out, Farrell's talking in Spanish. She's like . . .isolated. She gets on his case, says they got to go some place where she can understand people. Like Russia, only *he* doesn't speak Russian.'

'Anyway,' Randal picked up the thread of his partner's narrative, 'Farrell sends her downstairs to dinner one night. Tells her he'll be right down. . .'

'And skips!'

'Tired of the nagging,' Randal added.

'She waits around all night,' Sutter continued, 'and next morning she goes down and turns herself in. She's got nothing – no ID, no money, just a frigging hotel bill she can't pay.'

'And a lot of questions in Spanish she can't even understand.'

'Tough,' Malloy answered.

'I asked her,' Sutter said, 'what she thought it was going to be like where she couldn't speak the language. All she said was, "Not like this."'

'Good looking woman,' Malloy offered.

'Take the makeup off and put her in a jailhouse jumpsuit she's pretty plain, you come right down to it,' Sutter said. Josh Sutter liked his women dolled up, Malloy decided. Probably hadn't seen his wife without her makeup until a year or so after the honeymoon.

'What it is,' Randal explained, 'she's like. . . this submissive. Like whatever Farrell wanted her to do, she was ready.'

'I wish my wife was a little bit more that way,' Josh Sutter said. 'I mean she's great! But sometimes. . .'

'I keep telling you, you carry handcuffs, use 'em!'

'This from the guy with two divorces and a string of ex-girlfriends.'

Jim Randal smiled and shrugged his shoulders. His women apparently took orders whilst they lasted.

From the back, Sutter said, 'Hans was telling us a lot of these girls from the former Soviet Union get into the West any way they can, and then they get married to the first guy with money that comes along – you know, to like an older guy that doesn't want any hassles. They basically do what they're told, and they get to live in the West.'

'A lot of Germans hate the Russians,' Malloy answered. 'It's hard to believe, but it goes back to the Second World War. There were atrocities on both sides, but you know when something happens to people in your family you don't see it objectively and you don't forgive and forget because fifty or sixty years have passed. With us the thing with the Russians was ideological. With the Germans it runs deep in the blood. Plus the Cold War tensions kept it in their face. Put it all together and you find otherwise decent people jumping at the chance to say something like that. You know, the Russian men are all drunks. The women are all whores. That kind of thing. You want to be careful about accepting those kinds of judgments as fact. Irina Turner could be anything.'

'One thing she ain't is smart,' Randal told him, his Queens accent coming on strong.

Sutter shook his head. 'Give you an idea what the interview was like. We ask where Farrell was planning to go. She says maybe Italy. We ask if he mentioned a city in Italy. She says, "Geneva?" '

'Met her first husband in St. Petersburg. He's some American businessman who doesn't mind a good looking woman living with him, but he sets up this pre-nup that gives her nothing – I mean nothing – when they get a divorce. He gets a little tired of the Russian accent and she's on the streets with like the clothes on her back.'

Josh Sutter finished his partner's story: 'Sees this ad in the paper for a party hostess and ends up at one of Jack Farrell's Long Island bashes. She's like the queen bee at the orgy, so the next week Farrell hires her as his assistant.'

Malloy laughed. 'Okay. Sounds like Hans might be right about this Russian.'

'You're some kind of forensic accountant?' Jim Randal asked with his Queens accent. As he spoke his eyes cut to the rear view mirror. He and his partner had been speculating.

Malloy nodded. 'The thinking is if we find his money we can wait for Farrell to come to it.'

'Oh, I know the thinking,' Randal answered with just a touch of condescension. 'We've got guys like you that have been on the job fulltime since we got called in. What I can tell you is this: the money is gone. We get these credit cards and they're just piddling little bank accounts in the middle of nowhere.'

'But the money comes from somewhere.'

'Sure it does. A place called Montreal. First thing Farrell did, he opened an account in Montreal with cash. Did the same with a Barcelona bank – fifty thousand cash in each. They're falling all over themselves passing out toasters and credit cards. Meanwhile, the big stuff, what he wired to different accounts before he ran, that's all been routed through banks that won't give us any information. We're talking places like—'

'I get the idea.'

'And you can follow it?' Josh Sutter asked. He was willing to believe Malloy could walk through walls because he *wanted* Jack Farrell. Jack Farrell's arrest and extradition back to the U. S. was his next promotion.

'That's what I'm here to find out,' Malloy answered.

They were quiet, mulling it over, but they both were thinking *spook*.

Chernoff and Carlisle listened to everything said between the two agents and Malloy on the ride into the city. Once the three men had left the SUV there was no more audio, but Carlisle tracked the two agents on Chernoff's computer monitor through their cell phone signals. The two men entered the hotel, Malloy presumably with them.

'What do you think?' Chernoff asked. She was a small woman with dark eyes and a creamy white complexion. They had been lovers some years back, but it had been the sort of affair where you kept your eyes open when you kissed, and they had finally settled with a working relationship. After a time they had not even bothered with pleasantries. Chernoff assassinated people. For that she took a great deal of money.

Once he had finally understood that she did not care what he thought of her, making conversation was rather pointless. In his considerable experience with killers of every ilk, Helena Chernoff was the coldest creature he had ever known.

She seemed never to tire of the game she played, never to reflect on the choices she had made in her youth. She planned ahead and she put away her past as easily as throwing out old clothes. There was simply no pleasure in the woman's existence unless it came in those intimate moments when she cut away a man's genitals as he watched her doing it. She ate food with indifference. She drank wine if you put it in front of her. She could survive without food or water the whole day through and then take a modest amount at the end of the day without caring for its flavour or even the relief it provided. She lived constantly in the shadows, and had learned to make love like a well-paid escort. She was competent and businesslike about it, as intimate afterwards as a streetwalker.

David Carlisle, on the other hand, considered himself a creature of the sun. He could endure pain and do without almost anything, if he had to. He was a soldier, trained to suffer hardship, but when he had the choice he was a sensualist. He liked spending money lavishly. He liked women, all kinds – even hard cases like Helena Chernoff on occasion. He loved wine and could talk all evening about the nuances of flavour it offered. He liked travel, liked seeing the colours of the world, and he loved good food. Spending a day with Helena Chernoff was like sitting beside a ghost. In answer to her question, the first comment she had made since identifying their target, Carlisle offered a dry laugh. 'I think we might have overestimated our Mr Malloy. I'm not sure he's smart enough to find you.'

Chernoff kept her eyes focused on the road as they passed between the hotel and the lake. 'He found Jack Farrell,' she answered.

'He had help.'

'It's not a problem,' she said. 'If he can't find me, I'll find him.'

'If I just wanted him dead, I could have taken care of it in New York.'

'I know,' she answered, 'but sometimes people just get killed.'

'Not people like Malloy. If *he* falls there has to be a reason. If we don't create a convincing one, he has the kind of friends who are going to keep looking until they understand exactly what he was doing, and suddenly I'll have a great many more problems than before.'

'It's simple. He came here looking for me, and I found him.'

Carlisle said nothing to this. She was right, it would work, but he liked the original plan better, because he was sure Malloy would bring Kate and Ethan Brand to help him. That meant one crime scene for all three and no bothersome questions. 'Anything happening with the Brands?' he asked.

'Still off radar.'

As they had been since the party at the foundation. As if they knew he was coming for them. 'So they could be in Hamburg?'

'They could be in your rear view mirror for all I know.'

Carlisle looked in the mirror reflexively, then at Chernoff. Was she smiling?

'Are you sure Malloy will get them involved?' Chernoff asked.

'He's doing this for Kate, and he is going to need something more than those two FBI clowns if he intends to go after you. I don't *know* that he'll call them, but I know *I* would.'

'You want someone waiting at the airport?'

'Let's concentrate on Malloy. If he moves, I want to know where he is. Get someone inside his room as soon as you know it's safe, watch to see if his new FBI friends call him on his cell phone. If we get his cell phone number, we can monitor the calls he gets – maybe get a location on the Brands as well.'

Neustadt, Hamburg.

At the Royal Meridien Malloy took a room at the cop discount and told agents Sutter and Randal he would meet them at the hotel bar at around eight and they could get dinner together. 'Right now,' he said, 'I'd like to take a shower and get some sleep.'

They looked at one another. 'We thought maybe you'd like to meet Hans this afternoon.'

Sutter checked his watch and added, 'Maybe you can get a quick nap and we can drive over in a couple of hours?'

'Could you set a meeting for tomorrow morning?' Malloy asked. 'I tell you I was up all night. I'm just flat beat.' The last thing he wanted was a face-to-face with Hans.

'Sounds good,' Randal answered without enthusiasm.

As the elevator doors closed, Malloy watched the agents conferring. They were wondering what kind of hotshot forensic accountant arrives and wants to take a five hour nap. Malloy got out at the mezzanine, found the back of the building and asked an assistant concierge to get him a taxi. Ten minutes later he was in heavy traffic.

He got dropped off a few blocks north of the harbour in the Neustadt – the New Town – and rented a room in a small, family-run hotel. Just to be on the safe side, he used the name Imfeld at the desk, one of his Swiss identities, and paid in advance for a full week.

Once in his room Malloy unpacked, pulled the blinds, and got himself a good three hours of sleep. He took the underground to the train station, got cash from a machine, got a suitcase and some cheap clothes, bought a three day travel pass and made a couple of phone calls on a payphone. He then took a taxi to the Royal Meridien. By a quarter-to-eight he was at the hotel and went to his room. He left his freshly purchased suitcase open with the clothes and toiletries out in the usual chaos of travelling. He called the desk and asked them to hold all his calls during his stay and then went down to the hotel bar, where he got a beer and charged it to his room. Dressed in jeans, a hooded sweatshirt and a leather jacket, he looked nothing like the accountant the FBI agents had picked up earlier in the day.

Because he was in the shadows of the bar reading the *Herald Tribune* Sutter and Randal walked right past him when they entered a few minutes after eight. 'Guess he overslept.' Randal quipped.

Malloy stood up and walked in behind them. 'I got us reservations at a Chinese restaurant close to the harbour—'

'Jeez!' Randal jumped in surprise. 'I didn't see you back there!' He was blushing, trying to figure out if Malloy had heard him. Both men were looking at Malloy's costume. He didn't look like a guest at the Royal Meridien anymore.

'The place is supposed to be top notch,' Malloy continued. 'My treat.'

'Hey T. K.,' Josh Sutter answered with the easy-going manner of a Midwesterner, 'we're all on a per diem here. You don't have to spring for dinner just because you're the new guy on the block.'

'They're a little more relaxed at State about expenses. It'll be my pleasure. It's the least I can do to say thanks for your picking me up today.' Both men let their eyebrows slip up in surprise but they agreed. Why not?

Randal wanted to programme the automated voice for their destination, but Malloy told him he knew the way. Both men were surprised. 'I had a chance to study the map on the flight over,' he told them. 'I've got the city memorized.' This raised eyebrows but didn't get a comment.

As they drove along the shoreline of the Aussenalster, the larger of the two artificial lakes in the city, Sutter asked Malloy about his room.

'It's great,' he said.

Sutter nodded, beaming with boyish excitement. 'You get chocolate on your pillow tonight.'

As they were crossing between the lakes on the Kennedy Bridge they had a wonderful view of the low, ornate Hamburg skyline at night. 'I tell you what. This city is nothing like what I was expecting,' Josh Sutter said.

'What were you expecting?' Malloy asked.

'Well, you know, Barcelona has this reputation, but Hamburg's. . . what?'

'Industrial,' Jim Randal said.

'Exactly. So I'm thinking like. . . Newark or something.' He gestured toward the ornate late-nineteenth century architecture beautifully interlaced with the flat, clean lines of the late-twentieth century buildings. 'Not this.'

'Hamburg's got more rich people per capita than any city in Europe,' Malloy answered. 'And more bridges than Venice.'

'They got a lot of water,' Randal answered.

'Why so many rich people?' Sutter was mystified.

'The harbour. It's sixty miles from the ocean and feeds right into the heart of central Europe. You've got Berlin less than three hours away, with Poland just beyond that. The money's been pouring through here for three, maybe four centuries, and the Germans – especially the people in Hamburg – are good about keeping it.'

'I read where eighty percent of the city was destroyed during the war,' Randal answered. 'I mean. . . look at this!' He pointed at a stately eighteenth century house in the middle of town. 'You see buildings like that *everywhere*!'

'After the war the Germans put one rock back on top of another, everything exactly the way it was.'

'With American money!' Randal barked.

Malloy tipped his head and offered a sardonic smile, 'Could be the only example of American aid actually going where it was supposed to.'

Both agents laughed. That *would* be a first!

They found a parking lot at the harbour, had a look at the big ships docked up and down various channels of the Alster, the shipbuilding and brightly lit cranes. Then they walked north a few blocks into the heart of Hamburg's red light district, packed with tourists, colourful locals, and a staggering number of prostitutes of every description.

Randal gave a nervous laugh, 'Where are you taking us, T. K.?'

Malloy pointed at the street name. 'You ever heard of the Reeperbahn?'

Randal shook his head.

'It's the Bourbon Street of Europe – a quarter mile of pure decadence.'

As if on cue a transvestite gave Malloy a coy look and asked him in English what he was doing later. A woman walked up to Josh Sutter and said in English, 'Glad you left your wife at home, honey. You and I can have a good time and she'll never know about it.'

Sutter stopped, but Malloy pushed him along. 'He's not interested,' he said in German.

She answered in German, 'He looked interested to me!'

They kept moving, the light of the clubs and restaurants, the mass of people energizing them. 'The more you talk to them,' Malloy told Sutter, 'the harder it gets to move on. You get too involved and you might as well just hand over some money, because they're not going to let you go without a scene.'

More women called enticements in German and English. One even tried French on Randal, who had settled down and was looking fairly relaxed. They found a policeman standing quietly in the midst of a clutch of prostitutes whilst a group of young men staggered by, drinking beer out of cups and window-shopping the girls.

A transvestite swooped in on Sutter. 'They know what you want, honey. I've got what you *need*!' Sutter kept walking, but he looked like a man who had just had a gun pointed at his face. Two girls dressed in American cheerleading outfits whistled at Jim Randal, throwing kisses and naming prices in dollars. They worked *together*, they told him.

'I always wanted to have a cheerleader,' Randal told Malloy once they were past the girls. 'Only thing better would be two!'

'There goes the old per diem,' Malloy told him.

'This place is crazy!' Josh Sutter shouted. He was grinning like he'd had a few beers.

'I take it Hans didn't bring you here?' Malloy asked.

'Oh, man, Hans took us out last night to some *nice* place. Not a word about this! What's this place called again?'

'I give a group discount, boys.' This from a tall brunette beauty who may have been of either or both genders.

Josh Sutter turned and smiled at her. 'Sorry, married!'

'She can come too!'

'I notice the cops don't seem to care,' Randal muttered.

'It's all legal.'

Randal turned to Malloy in surprise. 'You're kidding me! I thought that was only in Amsterdam.'

'It's been like this for centuries. Second most popular tourist destination in Hamburg.'

'What beats it?' Sutter asked.

'The harbour. . . or so they say.'

Randal shook his head. Legal prostitution defied his sense of a well-ordered universe.

They crossed the street halfway down the Reeperbahn, descended a set of steps taking them below street level, and entered Yuen Tung. When Malloy had called ahead for reservations he had asked for a table at the back, where he hoped they could talk freely.

Whilst the three men sipped their drinks and waited for their food, they talked about the street life they had just encountered. Sutter wanted his partner to find some action – since he was the only single man in the group and it was legal – but Randal turned out to be a true puritan. Sex was fine. Spending money for it was the sin.

Once their meals arrived, Malloy turned to business. 'What's the word from Hans?' he asked.

'We're set for nine tomorrow,' Josh Sutter answered cheerfully. 'Says he'll cooperate any way he can.'

'Does he have anything I can use?'

The two FBI agents looked at each other. 'To tell you the truth,' Josh Sutter said, 'they've got the physical evidence they pulled from the room, including the credit cards and passports

Farrell and Chernoff left behind, but we processed it yesterday. All the money and cards come out of Montreal and Barcelona banks. The passports and identity cards are probably European forgeries, but it's hard to get more specific than that.'

'They find the anonymous caller?'

'They printed the phone booth and they've got a recording of her call, so if they ever find her they can verify she's the one. For all the good it does.'

'You hear the voice?'

'Saw some kind of summary. But I mean she was talking in German so it wasn't going to give *us* anything.'

'You didn't see a translation of the transcript?'

They looked at one another and then both agents shook their heads. But what was there to look at? The woman had just seen Jack Farrell walking into the Royal Meridien.

'If you want my opinion' Malloy told them, 'I think the call stinks.' This surprised them, but before they could respond, he continued. 'CNN was saying something about steam on the bathroom mirror and wet towels.'

Sutter nodded. 'Point being they just got out ahead of the raid.'

'But the caller sees them going *into* the hotel and runs for the phone?' Malloy let them think about it. 'How do they get steam on the mirror and then get dressed and run out of the hotel? The way I understand it, the Germans surrounded the hotel inside fifteen minutes of the call.'

'Maybe the caller thinks about it before she makes the call,' Josh Sutter answered.

Jim Randal, using chop sticks, fed himself a large chunk of chicken. 'What are you saying?'

'Did you look at the hotel security tapes?'

'They showed us a still. The rest they said you couldn't really see the faces.'

'The copy I saw on CNN didn't give much.'

Randal nodded. 'The woman. . . I mean she could be my first wife.'

'But that wasn't the night of the call?' Malloy asked.

'The one we saw was taken while they were checking in,' Sutter answered. 'Hans said it was probably the best one they had.'

'I'm lost, T. K. Where is this going?'

'They've got security cameras on every exit. They know down to the second when Farrell and Chernoff entered and left the hotel. I'm just asking if they gave you that information along with everything else.'

Both men were curious now.

'Hans is keeping things from you for a reason,' he said finally.

They sat back. Sutter dropped his fork. Randal was still clutching his chop sticks. They liked Hans, and they didn't especially care for Malloy – Reeperbahn tour or not. But Hans was maybe a little too nice. They were cops after all, and everyone lies to cops, even other cops.

'Why? What do they get by lying to us?' Randal asked.

'If they had the call and the exit figured out, you'd have the evidence – nicely translated. They didn't give it to you because there's something not right about it, something they can't explain, and they're afraid you'll figure it out and make them look bad.'

'So they don't like looking bad?' Randal said, going back to his dish. 'Tell me who does.'

'Do you have the telephone number or a specific location of the phone the caller used?'

Randal shook his head. 'Getting that kind of stuff didn't seem like a priority.'

'They won't refuse you if you ask for something. It's not a conspiracy, but you're going to have to ask.'

'So we ask,' Randal said, taking some rice in his mouth. 'Problem solved.'

'Let's get some good faith tonight. I want you to call Hans and find out the number for the public phone the woman used. See if he'll cooperate that much.'

'What good is that going to do us? It's a *public* phone.'

'They've already printed it,' Randal added.

'Get the number. Push him a little. Let him know we're onto their games.'

The agents looked at one another. They didn't like a stranger telling them what to do. On the other hand, they'd been ordered to pick up 'some VIP from State' and they weren't about to cross him – not just yet.

Sutter got his phone out, an encrypted FBI issue tri-band. The voices could not be intercepted, but it was still a cell phone. If you knew the number and had access to the local provider's software, it was like wearing your own GPS tag. What was worse these guys printed their cell numbers on their business cards.

'Hey, Hans! Josh, here! I was wondering. . .' Sutter finished less than a minute after starting the conversation. 'Hans is at the house,' he told Malloy. 'He'll get it to us tomorrow first thing.'

'Call him back,' Malloy said. 'Tell him you need it tonight.'

'All due respect,' Randal grumbled with only a modicum of respect, 'We don't take orders from you.'

'I was under the impression I was here to help.'

'I don't see how you're helping,' Randal answered.

'It's a phone call for you and another for Hans. What's the problem?'

'The guy's off for the evening.'

'Okay. . . if you want to give Jack Farrell another twenty-four hours. . .'

The two agents looked at one another. Finally Sutter called again. This time Hans said he'd call back.

Josh Sutter looked at his partner, his farm boy face red with embarrassment and anger. 'He's pissed.'

'Sure he is,' Malloy told him, 'but he's getting the number.'

'I don't get it,' Randal answered. 'What does a public telephone number get you?'

'Something to work until a good lead comes along.'

Randal turned his attention to his plate. He was upset. They had been getting along with Hans just fine until this.

Sutter's phone chirped, killing the hard silence. 'Sutter!' He listened, nodding. He wrote out the telephone number and the address, scratching out the German street name as Hans dictated it. That finished, he gushed his thanks. A big help! Still on the phone, Sutter looked at Malloy, but Malloy shook his head. 'Tell you tomorrow morning!'

Malloy took the information and dropped two one hundred Euro bills on the table – enough for the three meals and their drinks. 'I appreciate it, gentlemen. Have a good time.'

'What? Where are you going?'

Malloy looked at his watch. 'I thought I might try to find those two cheerleaders and see if they're as good as they look. Don't wait up for me, guys!'

Chapter Five

Montségur, France
Summer, 1931.

In the distance Montségur seemed like a pyramid cutting into the blue sky, its fortress once crowning the very peak. At the ruins, which were in fact part of a later castle, Rahn explained to them that Montségur had survived over thirty years of war before surrendering in March of 1244.

'They asked only for a fortnight's truce to prepare themselves for their fate,' he told them. 'Rather than fight it out, the Vatican and French forces granted their request for a truce. That much is fact. The rest, I'm afraid, is pure speculation – not that it has stopped anyone from speaking about it with a degree of certainty that to an academic mind is nothing short of astonishing. As the most famous story goes, four Cathar priests slipped over the wall and down the face of the cliff, taking with them the legendary treasure of the Cathars. Depending on who is relating the story that could be Cathar gold, the Shroud of Turin, the original gospel of John. . . or the perennial favourite, the Holy Grail. Where these priests took the treasure is also unknown, but most people like to think they delivered it to their friends the Knights Templar. Of course when the Templars were all arrested half-a-century later no one found anything, but that is explained away by yet another last minute escape.'

'And what is your theory?' Bachman asked.

'I haven't any, but I did hear a very nice story from an old man who could speak nothing but Languedoc French. This happened the first time I climbed the mountain. When he found out I could talk his language almost as fluently as he could, he told me the kids today have no interest in the old stories, but when *he* was a boy the old men in his village passed down a legend about Montségur they swore was absolutely true. I showed some interest and that was all he needed. He told me that the priests who guarded the Grail at Montségur gave it to their Queen, Esclarmonde, on the night before they surrendered. Such was her purity that Queen Esclarmonde immediately transformed into a dove and flew off toward Mt. Tabor and threw the Grail into the mountain.'

'But that is impossible!' Bachman complained. 'I like the story of the four priests much better! One can see the ropes, the desperate dread of getting caught! It's. . . well, it's *credible*! Turning into a dove. . .'

'I agree, and except for the fact that it is a complete fantasy first to last the story of the four priests is wonderful. But let me tell you something that *is* true. On the morning of 16 March 1244, two hundred and eleven Cathars marched out of their fortress. They crossed this meadow and walked into the fire the Grand Inquisitor had prepared for those who refused to renounce their faith. Not one of them stopped to pray or to consider the world they left. Not one of them turned away from the blaze and renounced the faith. No one hesitated – not one. According to the witnesses, they did not even scream until the flames took hold. That is how they died, and that, I would remind you, is the story their *enemies* tell.'

The wind kicked up suddenly and Elise shuddered with an unexpected chill. 'Can one really die with such courage, Otto?'

'To face death so bravely I think we must love something more than our own flesh.'

'I would give all I own to have such courage,' Elise answered.

'Pray instead that you will never need it,' Bachman told her.

Later, as she sat in the grass, Rahn joined her whilst Bachman examined the natural fortifications that would have supported the castle walls. 'I am going to ask Dieter to take us back to Sète tomorrow, Otto. He will invite you to come along as well of course.'

'That's very kind. I should like that very much.'

'I don't think you should accept his invitation.'

Rahn turned to see why, but for once she would not meet his gaze. 'When I am back in Berlin,' she said, 'I want to think of you sitting here, exactly as you are today. I don't want that perfect image of you ruined. I want one thing in my life to remain pure and good even if the rest of it is sullied with the business of life. She leaned toward him, brushing her lips against his cheek. 'And I will be here beside you amongst the beautiful ghosts for as long as I have breath.'

St. Pauli District, Hamburg
Friday-Saturday March 7-8, 2008.

Malloy left the Reeperbahn at Davidstrasse and sauntered down to Herbertstrasse, where a cop was turning away all the respectable women as well as boys under the age of sixteen. This alley was just for men and ladies of the night. A group of prostitutes clustered close to the cop showing off their skimpy costumes under long coats, which they opened for the interested spectators. They were shouting enticements to anyone giving one of them a second look. There was no rent to be paid for standing here, but of course they had rooms close by. Like those who waited in the windows of Herbertstrasse just beyond the graffiti smeared steel barrier, they came in all sizes and shapes, everything from stunning beauties to hard-bit slatterns: something for every taste and prices to fit any budget. Malloy moved with the crowd into Herbertstrasse and was rewarded with a vision of pure nostalgia, the old fashioned show that sailors at the port of Hamburg had enjoyed for centuries. Some women were naked save for a garter or a necklace, but most wore enough to attract the interest of the men crowding the street for the free peepshow.

They worked deals through the glass for all to see, but when the negotiations were finished their customers went inside and the curtain came down.

After the garter and lace gauntlet Malloy continued into a maze of side streets where the more unusual trade usually took place. Here one found strip clubs featuring a single dancer. Tips were welcome, of course, but anyone really interested in pleasing the woman went upstairs with her. That left the stage empty for fifteen or twenty minutes but sometimes even that had a dimension of pleasure to it.

There were sex clubs where men and women could watch the sexual performances of the models. If they got the itch during the show patrons could start their own – as long as it was for free. Prostitution was not permitted inside a sex club. The bright lights of the Reeperbahn were gone. Here people preferred shadows. A girl stood on a street corner smoking. A boy lounged against a brick wall. Whatever you wanted. Malloy slipped into a strip bar, drank a bottle of beer slowly and watched the dancer. He crossed the street afterwards and entered another establishment, this one called *Das Sternenlicht* – The Starlight. In this one Dale Perry stood behind the bar whilst a sickly thin dishwater-blonde danced on a tiny grim stage. Five men watched her without much interest. No one but the dancer gave Malloy a second look. Dale Perry was a forty-something black man with long dreadlocks, a few well-earned scars, and a nice smile when he bothered with it. He had the build of a college wrestler who has added a few pounds of muscle since back-in-the-day.

Dale called out in German to one of the men. 'Take over for a while.' He then headed toward what looked to be a store-room, never giving Malloy a second look. Malloy got a bottle of beer from the relief bartender, but didn't drink much of it. He watched the girl and felt pity. After her set, he placed a twenty Euro note on the stage, good for a heroine fix, and started to turn away. 'Where are you going, honey?' she asked. 'Don't you want a kiss?'

Malloy pointed at his wedding band the way Josh Sutter had done and shrugged his shoulders affably.

'I won't tell if you don't!' Her voice reminded Malloy of breaking glass.

He walked down to a sex show and loitered there as if thinking about going in, but then went on. Staggering a bit for show, if anyone was watching, he walked through a passageway and came into a courtyard at the centre of a city block. The ambient light from various windows illuminated a dozen or so automobiles, a few dumpsters and even a bit of trade going on in the shadows close to the back entrance of an adult bookstore. Malloy made his way to the back door of *Das Sternenlicht* and waited. At precisely midnight Dale Perry opened the locked door and said in English, 'T. K., my man! Come in!' Malloy slipped inside and the two men shook hands. 'Long time!'

'Too long. It's good to see you again, Dale.'

'I have to tell you, when Jane called to tell me you were coming over, I said to her, "I thought that old dog was *dead*!"'

Malloy smiled and let one shoulder kick up. 'It's not like people haven't tried.'

'I hear that!'

Dale had arrived in Zürich twenty-some years ago, a young world-beater Jane had recruited as one of her NOCs, operatives like Malloy working with No Official Cover. He had been through training at the Farm, but his German was a bit wobbly, and he had no street credentials in Europe. A reputation was something you could not counterfeit. You had to earn it. Malloy got him a bartending job at a strip club one of his assets owned, and then sent him on to Hamburg six months later.

Dale's tour was supposed to last three years, but Jane Harrison had persuaded him to stay on for another two. She was good at that. After five years her people were so deeply entrenched they didn't want to come home. Too much power, too much loose money floating about, and way too much freedom to want to relearn conformity. Dale had got married to a Russian immigrant who worked at a downtown law office whilst he was finishing his second tour. They had settled down in the St. Pauli District, a few streets north of the harbour, tourists and streetwalkers. It was a good working class neighbourhood with families and decent schools. Five years became ten. Ten turned into twenty, and now, like Malloy in his last days in Zürich, what he feared most was getting the call to come back to Langley.

There wasn't anything in Hamburg Dale didn't know or couldn't find out, and the beauty of it was that absolutely no one suspected his link to the agency, including his wife. In fact the Germans had arrested him a number of times and had once even sentenced him to two years at a minimum security facility. Dale's key resource was a lively trade in stolen cell phones, though he could turn out fairly decent counterfeit passports and credit cards. Of course anyone doing business with him usually came to his bar at least once. That got a photograph, finger and voice prints. Better still, the merchandise he sold inevitably turned into tracking devices – with the cell phones having the shortest life but giving the most precise information on movements and contacts.

'How about you? Is life good in Hamburg?'

Dale let a shoulder kick up and offered a crooked smile. 'Getting old, T. K. Thinking about leaving the game when Jane retires.'

'Jane is never going to retire.'

'When they fire her then.'

Malloy tipped his head, offering a weary smile. 'At the moment I'm afraid that's looking like a distinct possibility.'

'She told me. I have got to tell you, my friend, you are not her favourite horse in the barn.'

'What can I say?' Malloy answered sheepishly. 'Jack Farrell surprised me.'

'That's not supposed to happen in our business, T. K.'

'Everybody makes mistakes, Dale. It's just that in our business no one admits it.'

'In our business nobody admits anything! Come on,' he said, 'I'll show you my digs.'

A set of wooden steps led up to a storage room, beyond which was the bar. A second set of stairs led to the cellar. At the bottom of these Dale opened the basement door. They walked into a clean furnace room with a steel door cut into the back wall. Dale unlocked this door and showed Malloy into a surprisingly comfortable basement flat.

'It's yours if you need it,' Dale told him. He gestured at the panelling. 'Sound proof, fully stocked with food, medicine, clothing, equipment, weapons, even some cash – whatever you need.' In the office he pulled a rucksack out of the corner that he had packed for Malloy. 'I got you a Glock 23, like the Feds use, an extra clip, a box of shells, a silencer and a shoulder holster.' He tucked this back into the bag and brought out a phone and charger. 'The access code is JANE. Two numbers on the menu – both safe. I'm the first. Jane's the other. Basic encryption. I wouldn't trust it too much, though.' He pointed to the computer. 'That's safe. Anything you need to send or receive is secure from everyone but the agency and God. Password is set on JANE – so you don't have to strain the brain.' He held up a set of keys. 'For the doors and the Toyota you saw at the back of the bar. If you use the car, make sure you lock off the parking area when you leave. Otherwise someone will steal your spot. The car belongs to some lowlife who is spending a couple of months in jail. Prints all over the thing, so use gloves, and if things go to hell ditch it. The *Polizei* will round up the usual suspects.'

Malloy took the keys and asked, 'were you able to download the material Gil Fine sent you?'

'Just getting to that.' He pulled a couple of disks from the rucksack. '*Two* DVD disks. Ton of stuff on Helena Chernoff.'

'Did you look at it?'

'I checked it out to see what I didn't have, saw quite a bit I didn't know about, and made a copy for my files. We don't catch her this time I might find something in that mess that can help, but I expect better minds have tried. You know they think she's doing hits on Western politicians?'

'Gil told me about a U.S. Senator's plane going down in 2004.'

'That and a contender for the Presidency in 2000 – another plane crash. There was also maybe a stroke in 2006 that could have turned the balance of power in the U.S. Senate. But it's not just *our* politicians, T. K. They think she might be linked to three members of the House of Lords in the past ten years – two accidental deaths and one suicide. There was also a scientist in London who was screaming about no nukes in the run-up to Iraq-Two. The official cause of death was suicide, because he was being discredited for his opinion, but Chernoff was in the UK, and they think. . . *maybe*.'

'How do they know she was in the UK?'

'The usual. She blew an alias a couple of years later, and they tracked it back to three different trips to the UK, all corresponding to suspicious deaths.'

'Who's paying her, Dale?'

Dale shook his head. 'Apparently someone interested in changing the political landscape in the West. . . or employed by people who are.'

'So you think she has a handler?'

'The lady doesn't crawl out of the woodwork to contract these deals. Someone is arranging this stuff, maybe even providing the talent she needs for different kinds of jobs – mechanics, doctors, muscle. There's a network somewhere. We just can't find it.'

'She started out by hitting key players in the Russian mafia,' Malloy said. 'Maybe she's still working for them.'

'I don't think the Russians are doing it. They have too many internal problems to worry about the world stage. I was just skimming the stuff, T. K., but it looks to me like she's hitting people with a particular political view.'

'Maybe she has grown a conscience since the early days.'

Dale laughed. '*Right*.'

'So, any idea how a New York financier shows up in Hamburg and hires Helena Chernoff within twenty-four hours of hitting the ground?'

Dale rubbed his fingers together.

Malloy shook his head. 'He had to call someone. He had to have a contact.'

'They got cosy real fast, T. K. Maybe they knew each other in the old days.'

'He had to call someone to get to her, Dale.'

'I can put some of our analysts on calls out of Barcelona and Montreal to Germany over the past week.'

'I might have a better idea. If I remember correctly, you were looking at a businessman or lawyer here in town a few years ago. . .'

'I look at people like that all the time, T. K.!'

'This one was meeting with a neo-Nazi who went by the street name Xeno. No one ever got a last name on the guy. . .'

Dale nodded. 'I remember the deal. You must be doing quite a bit of reading since you retired if you remember that guy!'

'I had a run in with Xeno about eighteen months ago.'

'That was you – the thing with Julian Corbeau? I didn't know you were involved in that!'

'I'm a good Christian, Dale. I never let my right hand know what my left is doing.'

'Meaning you don't write complete reports for Jane?'

'They're complete. They're just not always true.'

'I remember the guy. I was watching Xeno on and off through a couple junkies for about two years, just keeping track of his network. First he had some people hustling dope and running a few home invasions. All small time, low rent kind of activity. This was right after the Wall came down. Then he got some muscle working for him, and then he hired some types who would pretty much do anything he asked – and the competition started falling by the wayside. He was turning into a real player, but I couldn't get close to the guy. He had been trained by the *Stasi* is my guess. Probably one of those people they were looking for after the reunification. Anyway, I was checking a cell phone I had sold a street hood one day and I realised it was in Xeno's pocket.'

'Nothing like dumb luck.'

'We get enough bad luck we're due some good every now and then. He had the thing right up to his death in 2006, so I knew every phone he called and tracked all his movements. After about three months or so I was charting his movements on a city map, and there was one meeting that took place every fourth Monday at dusk in the Stadtpark – same spot every time. So I set up surveillance on the area when the next fourth Monday rolled around, and who should join him on the park bench but Hugo Ohlendorf?'

'That's the guy!'

'He's a political heavyweight in Hamburg, former chief prosecutor, now a partner in one of the big law firms in town. Very clean, very anticrime, very, *very* rich. Ohlendorf is letting his dog run, and Xeno is like this homeless guy on a park bench. Ohlendorf says something and they talk for a couple of minutes. Something about the dog, the weather. Like that. After that, Xeno walks off. Next month, same deal. Like they're total strangers striking up a conversation about the weather.

'Any idea what they were really talking about?'

'Best I could figure, they were exchanging codes, maybe coordinates for drop sites – something like that. For what, I don't know, but this much I do know, Hugo Ohlendorf is dirty. I couldn't imagine he was on Xeno's payroll, but I thought maybe Xeno could have been on his. Maybe like a messenger, maybe like his chief of operations. Something like that.'

'That would explain Xeno's sudden rise from obscurity.'

'I thought so. I ended up watching Ohlendorf for a few months, got his cell number and tracked his calls and movements, looked at his money, his partners, his friendships. It didn't take me anywhere, and if I had pushed harder and asked

Jane to go to the Germans I figured someone would tip him off. He's connected with the cops from his days as a prosecutor – lots of friends up and down the line, from blue collar beat cops to the chiefs – not to mention the people who run things. So I backed off.'

'I need to talk to this guy tomorrow evening, Dale – in private.'

Dale looked at Malloy, as if to be sure he understood what Malloy was asking. 'I can reactivate the trace on his cell phone, if that would help.'

Malloy smiled. 'That should do it. Then if you can give me a call tomorrow evening when it looks like he's home for the night, I'll handle the rest.'

'I can do that for you, T. K. If you want to have a look at his place, the canal tour goes right behind his house. I took it a few times just to see what I could see.'

'What do you have on his private life – the people living at the house, that kind of thing?'

'Wife and one daughter at home. There's a son who is going to school in Berlin, maybe doing an apprenticeship by now.'

'Any live-ins?'

'I never got that close to the guy.'

'Does he move around town with a bodyguard?'

'He's licensed to carry a gun, but I never saw a bodyguard.'

'One other thing. Kind of a long shot, but it's worth a look. You've got someone in the phone company, I take it?'

Dale Perry chuckled. 'I *own* the phone company, T. K. What do you need?'

'I've got the number of a public telephone. I want to know all the calls from it that were made to cell phones in the past seven days.'

'What is that going to give you?'

'It's the pay phone that was used to call the police about Jack Farrell. I'm thinking the caller should have given her name so she could claim her reward. Since she didn't, I can only speculate that she was part of Chernoff's network.'

120

'A double-cross?'

'Could be. Could be something else.'

'Like what?'

'I don't know. Like Chernoff had someone make the call.'

'Chernoff *wanted* a police raid?'

'Who knows? Maybe she was having trouble controlling her client. Maybe she wanted more money. The thing is if her people are using public phones to make their calls, maybe someone got sloppy and used the same phone to call Chernoff's cell phone at some point when she was inside the hotel.'

'And if we can get Chernoff's cell phone. . .'

'We've got Chernoff's present location.'

Dale smiled, 'Assuming she hasn't ditched the phone since the raid.'

'Even if the phone is gone, as long as we know Chernoff owned it, we can find out where she went and who she called. Worst case scenario, we blow another alias and maybe find some people willing to tell us what they know.' Malloy turned his hands up and lifted both shoulders. 'I mean it's a long shot, but if it works maybe I won't have to interview *Herr* Ohlendorf.'

'You're really going to kidnap this guy, T. K.?'

'My doctor tells me I should be getting more exercise.'

Dale laughed. 'Say you don't get killed or arrested snatching this guy. How are you going to get him to talk? If he can tell you anything about Farrell or Chernoff he's not going to spill his guts just because you ask him!'

It was Malloy's turn to laugh. 'He will, if I ask him nicely.'

Neustadt, Hamburg
Saturday March 8, 2008.

Malloy caught a tram at the Reeperbahn station and rode back to the Bahnhof. It was past midnight, but there was still a crowd. A lot were young people there to have a good time, but there was a hardcore group off in the shadows drinking, smoking dope, shooting up, soliciting, and looking for easy marks. Malloy got some interest on this last count when he used one of the pay phones close to the shadows, but their instincts apparently warned them off. A man dressed as he was could be packing a weapon and you'd never know it until you were on the pavement bleeding out.

He dropped several coins in the telephone and then dialled a cell number. When Kate Brand answered he said, 'I thought we might take a look at how the other half lives tomorrow. Are you up for it?'

At his hotel Malloy brewed some tea and started through the DVD files Dale Perry had given him. He spent the first two hours looking at Helena Chernoff's known associates and affiliations. When he came to Dale Perry's summaries on Xeno, Chernoff was mentioned in passing, but there was no direct link to either Jack Farrell or Hugo Ohlendorf. He moved on to the deep background on Chernoff, just to get an idea of what he was dealing with. Chernoff's early work displayed audacity and ingenuity. She got to men who surrounded themselves with bodyguards. Her first three victims she took in their beds using a razor. The next two were long shots with a scope and rifle. Then there was another close encounter, this one a pickup at a sex club in Amsterdam, the kill taking place in an alley behind the club.

A year or so later a hit in St. Petersburg was caught on a security camera in an underground parking garage. Malloy watched the video after reading the narrative. Chernoff's target was an American businessman who was trying to build a hotel in the city. He had paid one of the Russian mobs for protection and was apparently only supposed to be with a driver. As Chernoff approached her target a team of bodyguards drove in. Some of the fire fight which followed was caught on camera. Most was off screen. The thing lasted about ninety seconds – an incredibly long time for an urban gunfight. The quality of the security film made it difficult to tell what was happening, but one thing was clear: at the end Helena Chernoff was the only one still standing. It was from that incident that law enforcement had finally got reliable blood and DNA samples on the woman.

From surveillance cameras at Julian Corbeau's estate Interpol had pieced together a composite of clips that featured Chernoff – some with excellent voice samples and the best photographs of the woman in years. Whilst it was haunting for Malloy to see a gun battle in which he had been involved, the most disturbing clip showed Chernoff talking about him with Corbeau in three separate encounters. What she said was not especially informed, but the context of the exchanges suggested familiarity with him that he had not realised existed. Given Corbeau's resources and the way he had arranged to eliminate Malloy, it seemed to him Chernoff must have seen surveillance photos of him and could therefore recognise him.

Until Gil Fine had mentioned the video recordings of Chernoff at Julian Corbeau's estate, Malloy had not realised she had been involved. He could not accept the idea that her showing up with Jack Farrell was some kind of improbable coincidence, but he was not sure what he should make of it. It was tempting to imagine that Farrell had sought Chernoff's assistance precisely because she knew Malloy on sight and had gone up against him, but he was relatively sure Jack Farrell had no idea Malloy had instigated the SEC investigation. That meant a third party must have informed him of Malloy's involvement and even arranged for Chernoff to help. But help how? Chernoff was an assassin, not a bodyguard or a smuggler of human cargo. Too much information was missing for Malloy to try to guess at the truth, but this much he knew: his cover had been exposed. His face was known.

Malloy spent some time looking at the images of Chernoff that different agencies had collected over the years. She had distinctively Slavic features, but possessed the ability to alter her appearance radically. Weight gain and loss, hair colour, and even age made her seem like something of a chameleon.

Finishing the slide show, Malloy stood and walked to the window of his hotel room and stared out at the last hour of night. Despite what Malloy had told Jane Harrison he was fairly sure Jack Farrell's criminal activities were limited to some overseas financial irregularities, usually in partnership with one of Giancarlo Bartoli's enterprises, most involving bankruptcy scams. The most notable example of such a partnership was the purchase of a high tech company in Milan that Jack Farrell and Giancarlo Bartoli had bought and then bled dry. The programme for such bankruptcies was to recover a great deal more than one invested and then file for bankruptcy, leaving others to incur the financial loss. On this occasion they had gutted the company and then sold it to their good friend Robert Kenyon.

What Jack Farrell had told Lord Kenyon about the enterprise Malloy had no way of knowing, but on paper, and with the benefit of hindsight, the deal looked like financial suicide. For some reason, Kenyon had loved the idea of acquiring this company and ended up burying himself in debt to finance the acquisition. Within a month of the deal's completion Kenyon was dead somewhere on the Eiger and the company was headed to bankruptcy court. Kenyon's widow, Kate, who had put ten million pounds of her own money into the venture, lost everything. The tally ran close to a tidy seventy-five million pounds against Kenyon's estate and required complete liquidation.

At the time of the purchase the company may have seemed to have had potential, or Robert Kenyon might not have understood some of the debt structure or vendor contracts. For Malloy these were red flags, especially as most of the vendor and service contracts connected in one way or another to companies in which Giancarlo Bartoli had a controlling interest. Add to this the company was top heavy with people who drew enormous salaries and were under ironclad contracts of employment – all known associates of Bartoli.

Kate Brand had never really understood the mechanics of the company's demise. She hadn't any experience in business at the time and precious little since. Aggravating the situation she had been in mourning and was of course still in shock at what had occurred on the Eiger. For an explanation of the financial disaster she had naively gone to her godfather, Giancarlo Bartoli, who apparently convinced her that certain pending contracts had fallen through because of Kenyon's death and for this reason the company was unable to survive. Bartoli's explanation fell short of the truth in nearly every respect.

Just over a year ago, whilst Kate and Ethan had been living in New York, Kate had approached Malloy and asked him to look into Kenyon's death. Malloy had met Kate and Ethan in Switzerland when the three of them had suddenly found themselves targeted by Julian Corbeau. With an eye to developing assets in Europe that would make him indispensable to Jane, Malloy said he was happy to have a look. At his request Kate presented him with all of the financials leading up to the bankruptcy, a rundown of Kenyon's friends and associates, his general business dealings, and even Kenyon's travel itinerary during the last year of his life. Much of the information came from private investigators who had failed to find a lead. Some came from Giancarlo Bartoli himself – elaborate and very professionally written reports from his company-owned security people. Some information came from Robert Kenyon's solicitor in London, the gentleman who had handled the liquidation of Kenyon's estate.

It had not taken Malloy long to settle on the motive for the murder: Kenyon's friends had swindled him out of his fortune and then murdered him before he realised the folly into which he had stepped. As far as he could see there were really only three suspects: Giancarlo Bartoli, Bartoli's son Luca, and Jack Farrell. They had all apparently profited from Lord Kenyon's investment, and they had all been in grave danger if

Kenyon had lived long enough to understand what they had sold him.

When Malloy had made his preliminary report to Kate he was surprised at her response. She wasn't prepared to believe it. She wasn't entirely irrational about the matter: she knew what Giancarlo and Luca Bartoli were all about, she freely admitted to him that she had earned her way back to financial solvency after the bankruptcy through her association with Luca – making a fortune in stolen paintings. She insisted, however, that Robert Kenyon had been like a son to Giancarlo. As for Jack Farrell, he was not only a friend, he and Kenyon were first cousins, only children of two sisters who had managed to spend most of their summers together whilst the two boys were growing up. One summer would pass in Berlin. Another they might spend at Falsbury Hall in the West Country of England. For two summers they camped at the Farrell estate on the Gold Coast of Long Island. Another was spent in Paris where, at the tender age of thirteen, they had studied French each morning and haunted the Louvre in the afternoons. Their time together continued even after they had entered university, the most notable being a summer in Italy – this time without their mothers. It was on this trip that they stayed with Luca Bartoli at one of the Bartoli retreats. For Jack Farrell, whose father was a close friend of Giancarlo, this was the start of a friendship that would become a lifelong business partnership with the Bartoli family. For Kenyon it was the beginning of a casual but ongoing flirtation with the underworld.

The friendship of Jack Farrell, Robert Kenyon, and Luca Bartoli that began that summer continued until Kenyon's death. In fact all three young men had inherited a seat on the board of directors of a humanitarian organisation that called itself the Order of the Knights of the Holy Lance. Until those last few months, Kenyon, by far the poorest of the trio, had always kept his finances separate from the other two. Why had Kenyon suddenly decided to jettison the safe dull investments that had supported his family for years to buy a high risk company in a high risk field? Kate could not say. She only knew Kenyon was excited at the prospect of 'turning the thing around' and had not seemed especially concerned about his ability to do so. He certainly profiled as someone addicted to risk in other aspects of his life. Maybe he had come to a point in his life where he wanted more and imagined that by succeeding with a shaky business venture he could earn the respect of his peers. His fortune, after all, was only substantial to someone who hadn't very much. In the circles in which Lord Kenyon ran he was poor relations – a man with more blood than money. He was starting a new life with a beautiful bride. His father-in-law possessed twice the fortune he had – all of it earned in the most dangerous business of all. Just maybe, Robert Kenyon had grown weary of life on an allowance, even a very generous one, and developed some raw ambition. If that was the case his old friends had used his ambition against him.

Kate wasn't buying the theory – not without proof. She insisted that both Jack Farrell and Giancarlo Bartoli had already had a great deal of legitimate money and were enjoying tremendous profits at the time – record-breaking profits, in fact. The amount of money involved in the alleged scam against Kenyon, seventy-five million pounds, was not a staggering sum to them, but it represented Robert's entire fortune. Robert was a man with influence. He had friends in high places. As a decorated war hero and an English peer, his influence could prove valuable to his friends, and that, she thought, was worth far more than seventy-five million pounds.

Malloy had never met anyone who had enough money, but Kate's argument had *some* validity. Besides, he could not understand why Giancarlo had included Kate in the assassination. She was Bartoli's goddaughter – his favourite, as it seemed. Her father and Giancarlo were not just business associates, they were old friends. *If* Bartoli had wanted to kill Robert Kenyon for some reason why not arrange it without involving Kate? That question led him to modify his theory.

Perhaps Giancarlo Bartoli was innocent. Perhaps Luca and Jack Farrell had arranged the swindle and murder. Luca had handled the romance and marriage of his 'sometime-girlfriend' with exceedingly good grace – perhaps with too much of it. Maybe there were emotions he did not care to show. Kate didn't believe this either. They had rekindled their affair briefly after Kenyon's death, she said, but it was mostly business between them. *Mostly* was a curious word, but Malloy had not pursued it. Besides, he had had a few of those kinds of affairs when he was a young man – and had lost a marriage in the process. Luca was married when all of this had taken place, and Kate had told him Luca was the kind of Italian who married for life. Kate said she had been a passing fancy, nothing more. And when Robert Kenyon came along, Luca stepped aside happily for the sake of his friend. Afterwards, living at the Bartoli farm in Majorca with Luca for several months to learn her trade, there had been 'a few nights', but nothing too serious. Malloy couldn't imagine it. Kate was anything but the kind of woman one enjoyed casually. Of course she had been younger then, something of the proverbial party girl with more money than good sense, and hardly more than a child. It was the Eiger that had made her the woman he knew – Eiger and a decade of risk-taking.

By now Malloy was over a year into his 'favour' and he had nothing to show for it but missing pieces of a puzzle that were still too plentiful to count. He kept circling back to the financial angle. It was the only thing that made sense. What he did not understand he was sure Jack Farrell could explain – if he could only arrange to have a quiet talk with the gentleman – but of course that had blown up like every other lead, and he found himself suddenly in Hamburg trying to clean up a situation he had not been able to anticipate. With Helena Chernoff in the middle of it.

His instincts screamed for him to retreat, that he was walking into a trap, but falling back at this point might not be good enough. Given Chernoff's presence in all of this, there might be no way out but to grit his teeth and push through to the finish.

Malloy thought about looking at a few more files but decided to get some sleep. He caught a few hours and got downstairs to breakfast just before they closed the service. It was typical German breakfast fare: coffee, juice, bread, jam, cereal, a couple pieces of fruit, a smorgasbord of lunch meats, and cheeses. He found himself missing Gwen – breakfast being one of the things they always did together – and he wanted to call her, but of course it was the middle of the night in New York.

He used a pay phone at the Bahnhof to call the Royal Meridien and leave a message for Josh Sutter. He said he could not make the meeting with Hans that morning – he had over-slept – but he wanted to meet both agents at the hotel bar at eight that evening – *very important*.

After that he headed for the docks at the Aussenalster. The canal tour sailed at noon.

Altstadt, Hamburg.

David Carlisle got a call from Helena Chernoff Saturday morning. Malloy and the two FBI agents, she reported, had gone out to dinner as planned. Inside the SUV Malloy had played the tour guide. They had walked along the dock looking at the sights and then went to the Reeperbahn and entered a restaurant. At dinner Agent Sutter had made two calls to his police contact and then received a call back from the same phone.

'What did he want?' Carlisle asked.

'We couldn't tell at the time, but Sutter and Randal were talking on the drive back to their hotel, and it turns out Malloy wanted the pay phone I used to call the police.'

Carlisle smiled. 'Then he is taking the bait.'

'He's at least looking in the right direction. Let's just hope he is thorough.'

Carlisle walked to the window and looked down at the quiet

neighbourhood where he had ensconced himself since following Malloy from the airport.

'After the third call,' Chernoff said, 'Malloy left the restaurant and disappeared a few minutes later in the crowd. The only thing I know for sure, he didn't go back to the hotel.'

'He was probably meeting his contact in Hamburg.'

'Or the Brands,' Chernoff answered.

Carlisle looked at his watch. 'He's still not back at the hotel?'

'No sign of him.'

'What are Agents Sutter and Randal saying about our man?' Carlisle asked.

'They're disillusioned. They were supposed to have a meeting with Malloy this morning and he stood them up.'

'Okay, call me when he turns up again.'

'You'll know about it when I do. Are you all right? Can I send anything over?'

'I'm a little stir crazy.'

'I can send a woman over if you want.'

Carlisle gave the matter some thought. 'Why don't you come over?'

Chernoff didn't answer right away. Finally, she said, 'Do you think that's a good idea?'

'Actually, I can't think of a better one.'

The Aussenalster, Hamburg.

The day was overcast and blustery, perfectly awful for a cruise. That was good. Even on a Saturday, when the ships were usually packed, it served to keep the crowds away. Malloy boarded early, got a cup of coffee and a croissant and made his way to the sparsely populated upper deck. As the crew was starting to pull the gang plank away a young couple dashed breathlessly across the open plaza and onto the ship. Malloy watched them until the young man noticed him. He then retreated to a bench and waited.

The couple appeared a few minutes later. They were dressed casually for their outing, wearing stocking caps, sunglasses, bulky knit scarves and heavy jackets. They sat across the aisle from Malloy without acknowledging his presence and watched the receding shoreline as the ship left dock.

The few people on the upper deck lasted only a few minutes before the cold wind drove them inside. When only Malloy and the young couple remained Malloy asked in English, 'Any record of the two of you coming into the country?'

'We're good,' Kate answered.

'Sorry for the short notice, but we are going to have to find Jack Farrell before the German police arrest him.'

'Whatever we can do to help,' Ethan said.

'I thought we might start by kidnapping Hugo Ohlendorf.'

Ethan's eye came into sharp focus. Ohlendorf's contact with Xeno was a detail Malloy had mined from his research, but Hugo Ohlendorf was Ethan's find. Ohlendorf represented the interests of four elderly individuals who sat on the board of directors of the humanitarian organisation calling itself The Order of the Knights of the Holy Lance. At the time of Robert Kenyon's murder the board, which called itself the Council of Paladins, had included Ohlendorf, Jack Farrell, Farrell's father, Luca Bartoli, Giancarlo Bartoli, and Robert Kenyon. Since Kenyon's death, David Carlisle and Christine Foulkes had replaced Kenyon and Jack Farrell's father. Having the vote of four paladins Hugo Ohlendorf was apparently a considerable force – though clearly a minority block as long as Kenyon was alive.

The Knights of the Holy Lance had been formed in the immediate aftermath of the erection of the Berlin Wall in the summer of 1961. At that time the Order's sole purpose was to raise consciousness in the West about the desperate plight of West Berlin. As the immediate peril had receded, the Knights of the Holy Lance had worked first for fewer restrictions against travel into East Germany and ultimately for a united Germany. Along the way, if not from the very beginning, the paladins had also worked covertly with various intelligence agencies in the West to destabilise various regimes behind the Iron Curtain.

After the Wall came down the Order had redirected its focus to the support of humanitarian causes in war torn countries, beginning with the various Balkan Conflicts in the early and mid-1990s. Ethan and Malloy both believed it was likely that the humanitarian efforts of the paladins might have provided an excellent cover for continued covert activity. They had certainly the networks in place in the old East Bloc to make themselves useful, but exactly what they were doing and on whose behalf remained unclear.

Because all the players involved in Lord Kenyon's bankruptcy were also paladins, Ethan had long held that Kenyon's murder was politically motivated – a coup of sorts. On the face of it, the theory made sense. Assuming some kind of schism, the Farrell-Bartoli faction might have moved against Kenyon. What did not make sense was Kenyon's failure to notice a problem. If he had been at odds with his former allies, why risk his entire fortune on a business venture with them?

At Malloy's matter of fact statement concerning Hugo Ohlendorf, Kate smiled cheerfully. 'You want to kidnap the local prosecutor?'

'*Former* local prosecutor,' he told her.

'Do you think he can tell us anything about Farrell?'

'That's what I need to find out. He's connected to the Hamburg underground, so he could be the link between Jack Farrell and Helena Chernoff, but I don't have any evidence to support the theory, so I just don't know.'

'If we talk to Ohlendorf, maybe we can forget Jack Farrell,' Ethan offered. 'I mean the point is to find out what happened to Kenyon.'

'We can ask him,' Malloy said, 'but at this point the situation has changed. I'm going to have to find Farrell before the Germans do. So the first order of business is to find out if Ohlendorf can tell us how Farrell hooked up with Chernoff.'

'How do you want to do it?' Kate asked.

'As soon as we know Ohlendorf is home for the night, we'll move in on his house and take him. I'll leave it to you two to figure out the best way to handle it. I've got a place ready in the St. Pauli district where we can interrogate him for as long as we need, but the hard part is getting him there.'

Ethan pulled out a handheld GPS navigational system and asked if Malloy could give him the addresses on Ohlendorf and the safe house. Malloy gave him the information. Whilst he was at it, Malloy gave them his Neustadt hotel and the room number, then handed Kate a key.

'How are we going to deal with the wife and kids?' Ethan asked. He kept his eyes on the screen as he spoke. He looked like he was shaken by the notion of kidnapping someone like Ohlendorf, Malloy thought, but was trying not to show it.

'You tell me,' Malloy answered. 'Here's what I know, there is a wife and daughter at the house. If we're really unlucky, the twenty-something son in Berlin could be visiting for the weekend. And there could be live-in help.'

'Not good,' Ethan told him, his eyes cutting to Kate to see how she was handling this. 'That's too many variables to handle. We don't even know his routines.'

'We're going to have to deal with whatever we encounter,' Kate said.

Ethan nodded, but he was not happy.

After a couple of stops the boat left the lake and followed a canal into Hamburg's wealthiest enclaves. Here mansions of various sizes and styles lined the waterway. Most of the homes had some kind of dock on the canal. Some of these sported boats that were suitable for the relatively shallow Aussenalster, but most were speedboats that would run on the deeper Elba. Not long after they had entered the canals, Malloy nodded toward a white palace tucked neatly into a Spanish-style garden. The property was surrounded by a high, heavy wrought iron fence. A thirty-four foot Bayliner yacht was tethered to the canal dock. 'Ohlendorf's place,' he said.

Neither Kate nor Ethan responded. They simply stared at the property as the ship motored slowly by. Afterwards, Malloy asked what they thought.

'He's got a dog or maybe two,' Kate answered, 'a camera at the dock, probably another at the front gate. Otherwise, basic security. The safest way to break in, given the time we have to organise this, is to ignore the alarm and just get in and out before the police can respond.'

'With a house that size,' Ethan said, 'you've got a good chance there's a live-in maid. If it's a couple, the man could take care of the property and maybe double as security.'

'The one thing we can't afford is to spend time inside the house securing the place,' Kate added. 'We could have a real problem if the son is there or if Ohlendorf keeps someone at the house who's trained to deal with home incursions.'

'What about a panic room?' Malloy asked.

'Once we cross the property line there's going to be a warning from the alarm. If we don't enter a code within a few seconds the alarm is going to go off,' Kate told him. 'Let's say we're looking at an alpha male ex-prosecutor and a bodyguard who doesn't care to look cowardly before his employer. I'm guessing if they've got a panic room, the wife and kid go there and the boys go for their guns.'

'Probably the same situation if Ohlendorf is by himself,' Ethan said. 'From what I've put together on him, he's a gun nut – belongs to a couple different shooting ranges. He's also something of a police groupie, so he's not going to let his buddies pull him out of a panic room.

'This far out,' Ethan added, 'the cops aren't going to be that quick to respond.' His eyes focused on the virtual map in his navigator. 'Rough estimate, you've got eight-to-fifteen minutes between the alarm and when they start showing up.'

'That's not much time to neutralise a man with a gun in his own house,' Malloy answered.

'That's not going to be the problem,' Kate said. 'The problem is getting away.'

Ethan nodded. 'The roads aren't good,' he said. His eyes were still on his virtual map. 'You can go a long way but eventually you get trapped with bridges and canals. There are only a few breakout points, and the cops are going to know about them. I mean, these are the people they're paid to protect.'

'Can we take him out by water?' Malloy asked.

'We'll be looking at police boats coming across the lake,' Kate answered. 'If they see us – and we'll probably be the only ones on the lake – that could be worse than the roads.'

'You've got at most six minutes from the house to the first dock,' Ethan told her, his eyes never leaving his handheld. 'Say . . .four minutes inside the house. . . we might be off the lake before they ever hear about it.'

'If we leave by water, I don't want the first dock,' Kate said. 'I want to get closer to downtown, with a car waiting – so we can get lost in traffic. And we need it to be on the west side of the lake so we don't have to deal with any bridges. St. Pauli district, you said?'

Malloy nodded.

Ethan tapped the screen. 'Here, the dock at the Alte Rabenstrasse.'

Kate looked at the screen. 'Should be a good area at night,' she said, 'but we could still be looking at a police boat coming in fast. If that happens, we're looking at every cop in Hamburg hearing about our position.'

They were silent, thinking about it. Finally Ethan said, 'I think I can get a police boat headed in another direction.'

'How?' Malloy asked.

He smiled. 'I'll take care of it, but what we're going to need is a clean car that can get us from the dock into the city.'

'I've got something we can use,' Malloy answered.

'So you put a car at the dock this afternoon,' Ethan told him, 'and I'll take care of the police on the lake.'

'How are we doing for equipment?' Malloy asked.

'We should be good,' Kate said.

'What about a boat?' Malloy said.

'If you're getting the car for the way out, we'll take care of getting to the lake and finding a boat,' Kate told him. 'Boats are easy.'

'Meet at the Neustadt hotel around ten?' Malloy asked.

'We'll probably get there around four, if you don't mind,' Kate said. 'I want to try to get some food down and maybe a couple of hours of sleep before we go out. You know, just in case it turns out to be a long night.'

Berlin, Germany
Fall 1931.

Rahn wrote Elise letters almost every day. He talked about the Languedoc, the sky, and the mountains. He described the lives he had unearthed in some dusty library. He named ruins that had once been cities – so many more than he had been able to show her. He spoke sometimes about the lovers whom history had recorded, always married to others, always yearning for what could never be, and yet staying true to their pledge to the end of their lives. He said that until he had met her, the pain they described had seemed like poetic artifice, a sumptuous emptiness passing itself off as true love. Now he knew what they wrote was genuine. He asked her if there was anything more beautiful than the hope that came each day of getting a letter from her. Was anything more pure than the memory of her kiss at Montségur which he said would stay forever burned into his soul? And yet with those feelings came the gnawing hunger of unsated desire, the feeling of being bullied and beaten and left for dead. Could they not see one another at some point in the future? Could he hope for at least that much?

It did not seem possible to live without her, and yet, he wrote, the days passed somehow. When he was exploring a cave, he would imagine that she smiled upon his endeavour and that gave him comfort. When he read or reread the accounts of battles or listened to some old man tell yet another story no one had ever recorded, something the old man himself had heard from old men fifty years earlier, he no longer considered how he might fit the thing into his book. Instead, he measured its value by this: would Elise enjoy it?

She had been right to refuse him that night, he said, though without referring specifically to the night in question. He had been wrong to ask her to betray her oath of fidelity, but if she knew how much he had wanted her she might find it in her heart to forgive him. She answered this sort of letter with assurances that she had nothing to forgive. On the contrary, she spent each day regretting what she had said to him that night. All she had ever wanted was to please him, and she knew she had failed him when it would have been so easy – just that once – to give them both what their hearts desired. Though she burned in hell for even thinking it, she wished she had gone with him to his room when he had asked.

He answered this with praise for her virtue. She had risen above her desire. He wished he could be as she was, but the world and his own flesh tore at him. He wanted more than a fantasy on top of a hill. Had they given in to temptation the world itself would have objected, he knew that. The world always did! Right as she was to refuse him, he would endure anything for her touch, her kiss, her surrender. Nor did his feeling lessen with time. It was exactly as she had said it was: the lance never ceased to bleed, the cup was never filled!

Once he wrote about Dante's lovers – those two who had surrendered to temptation and then spent eternity circling one another without ever coming close enough to touch. Those who had resisted temptation, he said, the true lovers, found their reward in eternity! But for an hour with her he would surrender this life and the next, as long as he knew she could be spared divine wrath. . .

The letters became an extended conversation of intoxicated desire and strange theology. They were by turns futile, desperate, and full of affection. 'I am no Cathar!' Rahn wrote in one letter. 'I am a man of the twentieth century!' In the next he said Elise was Esclarmonde, the light of the world, the bearer of the Grail, the Queen of the Pure Ones. If ever he found the Grail, he would take it at once to her and lay it at her feet. . .

Elise felt her heart quicken each time she saw his letters. She felt herself giving over to desire when she finished reading his words. It would have been the same sensation, she thought, if she had kissed him goodnight after an evening of courtship. It was the thrill of a young girl who realises, *he loves me!* She inevitably wrote back at first opportunity. She described her garden in the city, her dreams from the night before – especially if he had sat close beside her at the ruins of Montségur. She wrote about the book he was writing. She promised him the world would go mad about it when it was published!

Berlin, she said in one letter, had turned rainy. She was miserable. The city was unbearable with its riots and gunshots and anarchy. She could not imagine any other city in the world supporting so many newspapers, every one of them as certain as the political faction they supported that something was wrong, very wrong in Germany. She had rather climb a mountain in the sunny south searching for the lost Grail of the Cathars. In such a mood, she said, robbed of the opportunity to be with him there, the only solace was to pull his letters out and reread them.

Not once in all their correspondence did either of them mention Bachman. Bachman sometimes brought the letters to her, however. He never asked what was written, and she kept them under lock and key. It would have been easy for him to break into the box where she kept them, but afterwards she would have known he had done it, and by some feat of unimaginable discipline he resisted the temptation. He watched her though. He studied her moods. Once, late at night, after having consumed too much wine, Bachman asked her if she was going to leave him for Rahn. She told him, 'You are my husband, Dieter. I will never leave you.' Other times he asked about her private talks. Had Rahn ever asked her to sleep with him?

'Never,' she said and blushed at her lie.

'Would you have been tempted, if he had?'

'My feelings are my own, Dieter.'

'But you are in love?' Bachman pressed.

'It is not a choice one makes,' she told him. 'It is certainly not like being married to someone. We choose marriage, and we make a sacred vow before God.'

Her one lie to Bachman tainted the purity she felt for her lover, and so she hated her husband for asking and pestering her for every word Rahn had spoken to her. He had kept track it seemed, maybe even had taken notes! She told him honestly that she did not remember some of the conversations. What did it matter, anyway? Nothing happened!

'Are you disappointed that he did not at least try?'

How could she confess such a thing to her husband? How could she take pleasure in her memories when they were all subject to interrogation? She had no glimpse yet of spiritual ecstasy, if that was the goal of a love affair such as this, but this much she knew, despair had become an old friend.

Sometimes Bachman spoke with great affection about her beauty and her goodness. He was lucky to have such a wife. He knew some men who had no wives. As they got older they had nothing at all! He did not want to be like that! He came to her bed once after a fit of adoration. It had been years since they had made love. It had staggered to a close in such an uncertain way she could not remember the last time. Instead of the kisses and courtship of lovers, Bachman told her she could think of *him* – no name given. It was perfectly miserable.

'Does Otto know. . .' began any number of conversations that winter. And she would tell him she was not sure or did not know. He told her to ask him about the matter, usually some piece of politics she knew Rahn would not understand.

Another time he had some new theory he had encountered about the Cathars, he was a voracious reader about the Cathars now, some odd piece of information Rahn might enjoy.

Her solace came one night when she realised that only Rahn could understand what she endured, because he endured it as well. She did not live in Bachman's world when she wrote to her lover or read his letters. She was not married, not rich, not lonely, not virtuous. In the letters his bedazzling smile and tanned handsome face was forever before her, so close it seemed they might kiss. In such a state she could be, for an hour or so, absolutely fearless and free. She could imagine their intimacy in every detail. Later, leaving her room, she inevitably bore the fresh, flushed complexion of a newlywed.

Rahn came back to Germany that spring and sent a note to her to say he was in the city for a few weeks. He wanted to see her. She wrote back to him at his hotel, refusing to see him, begging him to stay away. He came to her door anyway. She sent her maid to tell him she was unable to see him. He tried twice more, demanding she tell him to his face that she had no desire to see him. Alone, waiting to hear how he had taken her refusal, Elise wept. No man would endure such an insult. It was over.

There were no more letters after that. It was a death of sorts, going without his words, living without writing letters in response to wild flights of passion and fancy. Before Otto Rahn had appeared in her life, Elise had been vaguely content and called it happiness for want of a better word. Desire slept in her soundly as she busied herself with life. After meeting him, she felt isolated and the world seemed unbearably cruel. Only when she sat with him in the mountains of her imagination could she find some sort of peace, but once the letters stopped she found it increasingly difficult to see him as he had been on that glorious day on Montségur.

It was not long after that before her entire summer in France began to fade.

*

Bachman told her one evening over dinner, 'Otto wrote me. Did he tell you?'

'What did he say?' Elise asked. Her heart pounded. It was not desire that quickened her pulse this time. It was fear, though she could not understand why a letter to Bachman should inspire it. Perhaps it wasn't the letter, she decided. Perhaps it was the smug look on Bachman's face.

'I have created a business opportunity for him and he wanted to thank me.'

'What sort of opportunity?'

'I have persuaded some associates of mine to take a ten year lease on *Des Marronniers*. Do you remember it?'

Of course she remembered. That was the hotel where they had had lunch before their descent into the *Grotto de Lombrives*. 'I have arranged matters so that Otto will be the owner of record, and he wrote to say he is delighted at the prospect of managing the property.'

'But he is a writer, not a hotel keeper!'

'He's very excited, Elise. I think you ought to be excited as well.'

'And why should I be happy about your ruining a man's life with a shady business deal?'

'Because we are going to spend the summer in Otto's new hotel!'

'You can't be serious.'

'I thought you would be happy!'

The Royal Meridien, Hamburg
Saturday March 8, 2008.

Malloy left the ship at the Alte Rabenstrasse dock and with the help of a city map found an underground station less than a quarter of a mile away. From there he headed back to the Royal Meridien and caught a couple of hours of sleep. Late in the afternoon he went to the courtyard behind *Das*

Sternenlicht and picked up the Toyota Dale had arranged for him to use. The sun was setting, but there was enough light to get a clearer picture of the area now. Like Dale's one dancer bar, the lot itself was a grim piece of work: lined with the backsides of hotbed hotels, sex clubs, three stool bars, strip joints, and adult bookstores. The buildings, however, were actually well made. Directly across from the back of *Das Sternenlicht*, for instance, the upper storeys were made of palatial stone blocks running all the way to the roof. In any other part of town the flats and offices here might have appealed to an affluent set.

There were two passageways into the courtyard. One was adjacent to *Das Sternenlicht* and was not much more than a walkway, though it could fit a small car. The other was large enough to accommodate delivery trucks. There were a few parking spaces in the middle of the square, but most of the parking slots were lined up close to the various buildings.

Heading north by a series of side streets, Malloy passed through St. Pauli's working class neighbourhood. From there he worked his way as far as the Aussenalster. He parked the Toyota on a side street close to the Alte Rabenstrasse dock and walked ten minutes to the underground station. He was back at the Royal Meridien by eight.

Jim Randal and Josh Sutter were in the hotel bar sipping on a couple of draft beers. They were cool, clearly disenchanted with their State Department accountant. 'Missed you this morning,' Josh Sutter told him without meeting his gaze.

'Late night.'

'Whatever.'

'What's the problem, guys?'

'We can't figure out what you're doing,' Randal said, his rough Queens dialect ripping out of his throat. 'You don't want to talk to the investigators. You don't tell us what you're up to. You want this telephone number and then, when you get it, you take off to buy yourself a threesome!' Randal had been rehearsing this.

Sutter, the good cop to Randal's bad, leaned forward, his elbows on his knees, and rubbed his hands together. His tone was conciliatory. 'Look, T. K., the thing is we're getting a lot of questions we can't answer.'

'From the Germans?'

'From our supervisor in New York. It's like. . . are you really *here*, are you working this thing? I mean what's up?'

'Jack Farrell has put himself in Helena Chernoff's hands.'

'Tell us something we don't know,' Randal grumbled.

'Once I find out how he made contact with her I'll have Farrell *and* Chernoff, but this much I guarantee: Hans isn't going to be able to help me with that.'

Randal wasn't satisfied. 'What about the money? I thought that was your *specialty*. Forensic accountant, right?'

'What if I told you I've got a chance to find Farrell tonight, maybe even take him down?'

Josh Sutter's face lost its tension. Jim Randal wasn't as confident. 'You don't play that card without giving us something real. Tell us what you're doing. Have you got something or is this just another Chinese dinner?'

Malloy shook his head. 'It can't go on paper, gentlemen.'

Malloy waited for the agents to look at one another, but he was disappointed this time. They were both staring at him as if he had just committed blasphemy. In their world everything went on paper.

'You think you can find Jack Farrell tonight?' Sutter asked. A vein started ticking in his neck. The spook had something, and he loved it.

Malloy nodded but said nothing else.

'What's the catch?' Randal asked.

'The catch is I don't want the Germans involved.'

Sutter laughed. 'Seeing as how we're in the middle of Germany that might be kind of hard to do!'

'You want to take the guy home or leave without him?' Malloy asked.

Randal swore as his eyes swept round the room. 'Who are

you working for, T. K.? Because I'm sure not buying this accountant nonsense!'

'Listen to me. The Germans aren't giving up Jack Farrell. If they arrest him, they'll keep him.' It was a cold-blooded lie, but Randal and Sutter didn't know that. From their perspective losing Jack Farrell to the Germans was nothing short of disaster.

'Hey,' Randal answered, hot suddenly at someone besides Malloy. 'Farrell is *ours*!'

'If the Germans get involved he's theirs.'

Josh Sutter shook his head. 'Hans told us—'

'The minute they arrest Jack Farrell *Hans* is going to disappear. You'll be meeting with guys who don't understand English. To make a long story a sad one, you'll fly home without Jack Farrell and the U.S. Attorney will get an earful about all the German laws Farrell broke when he came into the country under an alias.'

'Why would they want to keep the guy?' Josh Sutter asked.

Malloy smiled, 'I can give you half-a-billion reasons, but the short answer is because they can. It has happened before, and you both know it.'

'But Hans said—'

'Hans is telling you what his handlers tell him to tell you.'

They were both suddenly angry, but they believed him. They didn't want to, but they did, and they also knew there wasn't anything they could do about it if the Germans wanted to charge Jack Farrell in a German court of law.

'On the other hand,' Malloy told them, 'you pitch in with the take-down when and if it happens, and I'll get your man on American soil before the Germans even know we've got him.'

Josh Sutter took this one. 'How? How are you going to do that, T. K.? Are you going to put him in your suitcase?'

'We've got over a dozen U.S. military bases a few hours south of here. U.S. soil, gentleman. We get Jack Farrell to one of those and he's *ours*.'

'*Tonight?*' Sutter asked.

'Maybe tonight. Maybe at dawn. Maybe tomorrow night. Right now I'm still a step away. Nothing is certain. But if something breaks it's going to be after midnight, and I am going to need to know if I can count on you or not.'

'What are you talking about?' Randal asked. 'I mean what exactly are you asking us to do?'

'I have two people I'm using for the extraction and one person watching our backs. I'm not sure one person is going to be enough for that. What I'm worried about is we go in to get him and Chernoff brings a second line of defence in behind us. I need you on the perimeter to let us know if that is happening and how bad it looks. We'll handle what they throw at us, I don't need fire power, but we need some advance notice if they are coming. And that will be your job.'

The two men looked at one another. 'How solid is your lead?' Jim Randal asked.

'It's promising. Worse case scenario, it comes to nothing, but if something good happens, and I think it might, I'm not going to have time to explain myself. I'm going to need you two – or I'm going to have to do this on my own and hope I don't get sucked into a trap. If that's my only option, so be it, but you're not going to take credit for the arrest. On the other hand, if you pitch in, I'll crawl back into the woodwork and you two can take all the credit.'

Jim Randal looked at his partner again and then at Malloy. 'I appreciate your levelling with us.'

'I'm glad you do, because I just put you in the middle of a criminal conspiracy.'

Both men looked as if they had been tapped in the jaw.

'If you want out, you had better call Hans and tell him what I just told you. Otherwise, you are a part of this, whether or not you do anything tonight.'

'Nobody is calling Hans,' Sutter answered.

'If we get Farrell,' Malloy told him, 'and the Germans figure out what happened, which they will once they have enough time to look at the situation, they'll ask for you both to be extradited and brought back here to stand trial. Of course in New York you two are going to be a couple of heroes and absolutely no one is going to want to give you to the Germans.'

They looked at one another, weighing the risks against the rewards. It was dangerous work and Malloy didn't care for them to get halfway into the thing before they realised this was a criminal matter. 'What are the Germans going to do if they bust us?' Josh Sutter asked.

'They'll make a lot of threats – you know how cops are – but if you give them what they want, they'll let you go home. Of course they won't ever let you come back. . .'

'I can live with that,' Randal answered. 'What are they going to want?'

'Me. But that's fine. If the police end up in the middle of this thing, it will be my fault. You can tell the Germans everything you know and no hard feelings.'

'What are they going to do to *you*?'

'Don't worry about me. I do this for a living.'

They looked at each other again. No way were they going to flinch – not if they could take Jack Farrell back to New York in handcuffs. 'We're in,' Randal said.

'What I need from you tonight is to be ready for a call. Sometime between midnight and dawn – be dressed and ready to move the minute you hear my voice. He handed Randal a slip of paper with an address and cell phone number. Come to that address. It's a bar. One of you come inside and sit down and have a drink. The other needs to stay in the car and keep it running. Are you both armed?'

'We've got a provisional license,' Randal told him, 'but Hans said it's like our ass if we actually have to draw our weapons – unless it's really a life-threatening situation.'

'If we get into that kind of trouble, we're not going to be explaining it to the Germans. We'll take care of business and then go underground and wait for the cavalry. And if anything happens to me. . .' Malloy tapped the cell phone number he had written down on the slip of paper he had given Randal, 'call this number. The person who answers will get you out of the country.'

'Does he have a name?' Randal asked.

'Sure she does, but you don't need to know it. Just call her if you're on your own and do exactly what she tells you to do. For now, get something to eat and try to get some sleep before midnight. . . and be ready to leave everything behind if it comes to that.'

'You mean our luggage?' Josh Sutter was concerned.

'I'll reimburse you for everything or I'll have it retrieved if it's possible, but if you've got something you don't want to lose get it down to your car now. And. . . it's probably a good idea to switch your plates with someone else in the parking garage.'

'That's a felony,' Jim Randal told him.

He wasn't joking, but Malloy smiled and stood up to leave, 'Think they can extradite you for it?'

Neustadt, Hamburg.

Malloy had two helpings of spaghetti at a mom and pop Italian restaurant and a couple of glasses of red wine to take the edge off. He didn't bother with coffee afterwards. On the walk to his Neustadt hotel, Dale Perry called. 'The lawyer was in town this afternoon – at his office for a few hours,' Dale said. 'He's been at the house all evening.'

'Great. I'll get by to see him in a couple of hours. Did you find anything on those phone numbers I asked you to look into?'

'I'm still waiting to hear from my contact.'

The Do Not Disturb sign was hanging on Malloy's door, exactly as he had left it, but one corner had been bent down, so Malloy knocked. A moment later Ethan opened the door. Kate was sitting on the bed. She had obviously been asleep and was trying to come awake. Ethan looked like he hadn't slept for a couple of days.

They were dressed in black jeans and dark sweaters. Malloy

took a peek into one of the two black canvas bags they had tossed on the floor. He saw three AKS-74s, the airborne model of the classic Kalashnikov with the side-folding triangular metal stock, three hand grenades, the butt of an Army Colt and an assortment of ammo and clips, armour, NVGs and tools.

'Where do you get this stuff?' he asked Kate.

She yawned, 'I've got a friend in Zürich.'

'I probably know the guy.' Malloy was a close friend of the Zürich crime boss, a man named Hasan Barzani. He had in fact helped put Barzani at the top of the heap. Barzani was the only person in Zürich he knew who kept this kind of weaponry ready for sale.

Kate smiled. 'I doubt you know *my* guy.'

'I bet I know his source.'

'You probably do, but not my guy. My guy is. . . special.'

'Just so Giancarlo or Luca Bartoli don't know about it.'

'I haven't dealt with them for a long time,' she said and bent over to put her shoes on. 'And definitely not for this.'

Ethan was moving around the room as they spoke, cleaning prints off surfaces. Finished with that, he opened one of the canvas bags and started handing out equipment. He started with gloves and night vision goggles. After that ski masks, Cobra vests, and loose fitting rain slickers to cover them. Finally he handed out Taser stun guns, handcuffs, a few lengths of rope and headsets. The headsets provided basic send and receive communication between the three of them for distances up to three or four hundred metres. They were high quality and picked up a whisper or a breath. They could be turned on or off with the touch of a button on the ear piece.

'Did you get us a car?' Malloy asked.

'There's a parking lot around the corner,' Ethan told him as he grabbed both bags. 'Shouldn't be a problem.'

The hotel entryway was dark as they left. It was just after ten o'clock. The street outside was quiet. At a public parking lot a couple of blocks away Ethan found a car parked in the shadows and slipped a long flat blade down between the driver's window and the side of the door. He hooked a wire deep inside the door and gave a slight tug. The lock jumped up, and he opened the door. Kate and Malloy climbed in. Ethan pulled some wires out from under the dash, cut away the rubber coating on a couple of them and then rubbed the raw ends together. The engine groaned and then kicked to life – the whole thing accomplished in an impressive thirty seconds.

From the backseat Malloy said, 'I'm guessing that wasn't your first time.'

'I hate stealing cars,' Ethan told him. 'Too many things can go wrong.' As he said this, a cop car rolled by the entrance to the parking lot.

'I see your point,' Malloy answered.

They worked their way north through the neighbourhoods. Not far from the Krugkoppel Bridge, at the northern end of the Aussenalster, Ethan pulled into a small parking lot. At the dock Malloy could see several boats out in the water. 'Masks down,' Kate said. 'Could be cameras anywhere from here on.'

'Which boat?' Malloy asked as they walked down the plank.

Kate pointed at one anchored some thirty metres off shore. 'The pretty one.'

Chapter Six

The Aussenalster, Hamburg
Saturday-Sunday March 8-9, 2008.

The boat was a twenty foot 1930s era Chris Craft speedboat. It was long and rode low in the water. With only a few easily disabled running lights it would be virtually invisible on the lake.

Ethan took a pair of bolt cutters out of one of the bags and cut a small dinghy free from its anchor close to shore. He rowed out to the Chris Craft, cut the wire securing it, hotwired the Chrysler engine, and pulled the boat to the dock. Malloy and Kate tossed in the gear and climbed aboard.

The boat was made of mahogany and trimmed in chrome. Once out on the water Kate switched off the running lights. Ethan fished out his navigator and began directing her upriver and into the canals.

It was nearly eleven o'clock by the time they came to Hugo Ohlendorf's house. Except for a single security light at the dock the property was dark. Before they moved, Kate settled their craft in the shadows opposite the property.

'Looks quiet,' she whispered.

Ethan pocketed his navigator, climbed out of his seat and opened one of the canvas sacks. He handed Malloy one of the Kalashnikovs and took one for himself. He then grabbed one of the two tranquilizer guns. 'Once we're on the property,' Ethan told them whilst he strapped down his weapons, 'I'll deal with the dog. T. K., you hold the centre of the yard until I call you in. When we take the back door, I want to come in loud.'

'You two are the diversion,' Kate explained. She picked up the second tranquilizer gun. 'I'll be primary on the take-down.'

Ethan pulled out a sledgehammer and some bolt cutters. 'From here on,' he told them, 'no names.'

Kate kicked up the idle and turned the wheel sharply left. Their boat moved in a slow arc through a one hundred eighty degree turn, coming finally to the portside of the Bayliner tied to Ohlendorf's dock.

The moment the two vessels collided, a warning beep sounded from the alarm pad at the gate. 'Go!' Kate said.

Malloy climbed out of the Chris Craft and up across Ohlendorf's yacht. Kate followed nimbly. Ethan tossed the sledgehammer and bolt cutters up to her and then began tying the two vessels together fore and aft.

He was finishing the second knot when the property lit up and an alarm pierced the silence. Ten seconds. Malloy felt a moment of dread. They were still in the canal some forty metres from the house with an iron fence between them and Ohlendorf. The alarm had sounded. Ohlendorf was no doubt moving. Despite this, Ethan finished tying the two vessels together whilst Kate watched patiently.

When he had finished, Ethan sprang up to the larger craft, took the sledgehammer and jumped down to the dock. Malloy climbed down in deference to his aging knees. Kate set the bolt cutters next to the wire anchoring the Bayliner. Ethan walked to the gate and swung the sledgehammer.

The lock broke on the first blow and all three of them started running for the house.

Ohlendorf's German shepherd came out of the shadows without making a sound. He was a trained guard dog, not the family pet. Ethan took the animal with the dart rifle at ten metres, then dropped the dart gun and drew a combat knife. The dog flinched when it was hit but kept coming, fangs bared. Ethan held his left forearm out in a defensive posture. When the animal lunged for it, he caught its jaw with a right hook. The dog yelped and went down like a sucker-punched brawler. It struggled briefly to rise, but then seemed to lose interest and lay back sleepily in the grass.

Ethan sprinted toward the house, stopping just short of the wall, and turned to face Kate. Kate trotted behind him like a high jumper gambolling toward the bar. She stepped on Ethan's out-turned thigh with her right foot, his shoulder with her left. Without ever losing her upward momentum she sprang easily toward the second storey. Ethan ordered Malloy in whilst Kate scrambled across the roof.

Malloy got to the house just as Ethan kicked open the door.

Hugo Ohlendorf and his wife were reading in bed when they heard the alarm and saw the floodlights suddenly illuminating their property. His wife swore softly and asked what was happening. 'Stay here,' Ohlendorf told her. 'I'll find out.' He set his bookmark in place, and then laid the book on the bedside table as he sat up. He retrieved his stainless steel Beretta 92FS and a loaded clip from the bedside table. Jacking a shell into the chamber of the gun, he slid his feet into his slippers, and stood up.

'Should we call the police?' his wife asked.

'They are on the way,' he answered.

Ohlendorf had enjoyed a lifelong love affair with handguns and shot in competition once or twice a month. At fifty-three he was no longer a contender for the highest marks, but he considered himself a solid performer. He had in fact been to his favourite club's shooting range on the previous evening – scoring sixth out of some thirty-six individuals. A good finish, considering the competition, but not his best.

Despite this the gun felt odd in his hand. There was a strange taste of dread in his throat. *Kids*, he told himself. He tried to imagine a group of teenagers driving by as they threw something at the gate, but his body was telling him something else.

He had talked to cops about just such moments as this. They

told him the first emotion was raw fear. The next was denial. So far, he thought, he was staying with the programme. Opening his bedroom door Ohlendorf saw his seventeen-year-old daughter standing in the hall with a look of curiosity. 'Get back inside, Michelle,' he told her.

She stared at the gun in his hand.

'Go back to your room!'

Michelle blinked. 'What's happening?'

'Probably kids at the front gate, but I'm going to make sure.'

'I heard glass breaking,' she told him.

He did not ask her where she had heard the noise, but said again, 'Get back in your room!'

When her door had closed, he proceeded down the darkened hallway. The phone began ringing. The security company. If he did not answer quickly, they would call the police. Let them make the call, he thought. His hands were wet with fear and his chest was tight. Broken glass. That meant they had crossed into the property. The coppery taste of adrenalin was strong now, and the darkened house, his private retreat from the world, seemed a terrible and frightening place. He wanted the police. More than anything he yearned for some calm professional to tell him everything was fine, but for the next ten or fifteen minutes he was on his own.

He whispered again the reassuring denial, *kids*, though now the imaginary kids had got older and bigger and far more dangerous. He recalled what his police-friends had told him. After the initial fear and denial, you start thinking about what happens if you shoot someone who isn't armed. . . or you wonder if your muscles are going to freeze up. They told him sometimes just lifting his weapon or taking a single step forward was more than a man could handle.

Ohlendorf had never known that kind of fear and had no idea if he could actually get past it. He was standing several steps beyond his daughter's bedroom door and suddenly getting as far as the stairway seemed impossible. His chest ached and he stank with fear. Then, at the sound of the back door splintering, a strange thing happened. He felt the next emotion: anger. Sometimes you freeze, they told him, but sometimes you lose your fear and you move forward because you don't like it that someone is in your house!

He settled on one knee at the top of the stairs without remembering taking the steps to get there. He braced himself against the plaster wall and peeked through the banister. He heard crystal breaking in the dining room, a chair tossed across the floor. He waited for them to come to him and thought about target practice. Then a new fear pierced his hard emotional shell, a strange fear, all things considered. He was, he thought, going to have to kill someone! It was curious how his body reacted to the thought of doing that. It was not at all like arranging someone's death. When he did that he invariably felt an erotically charged sense of power. Say the word, wire the money to an account and a life was extinguished – sometimes a very important life! There was nothing like it, but this was going to happen right in front of him. He was going to have to pull the trigger and see the blood, explain himself to the police, and watch his wife and daughter dealing with it! No anonymity here. No matter what happened in the next few seconds he was going to answer for it.

There was more breakage below. At least two men from the sound of it. One of them came into view – a black figure from head to foot. He wore a mask and carried a Kalashnikov. At the sight of the gun, Ohlendorf hesitated. A Kalashnikov was capable of firing ten rounds *per second*. If the other man was also carrying such a weapon the moment he fired one round from his Beretta they were bound to open up on his position. Ten rounds per second for three or four seconds would take the wall out – and him with it. His only chance was to wait until they both came into the open. Whilst he waited, hoping as he did that he could take them down before either man could respond, Ohlendorf felt something sting his back. He tried turning to discover what had happened, but he was immediately dizzy. He tried to swat away whatever was stinging him and then he began tipping forward.

He was dreaming as he hit the first step, out cold before the next.

Ethan saw Ohlendorf tumble toward the landing on the stair-well and moved up fast to break his fall. Ethan checked the pulse and then lifted Ohlendorf over his shoulders.

'You lead, Man,' Kate whispered as she came down the stairs.

Malloy went out the way they had come. At Kate's command he stopped in the middle of the backyard, turning to cover their retreat. There was no sign of a second individual coming for them. No more lights had come on inside the house. From the dock Kate called to him over the headset. 'Get to the boats! GO!'

Malloy sprinted toward the dock. Kate covered his retreat but there was no need for it: though the lights were still on and the alarm still rang, nothing at all moved in their wake. Kate cut the wire holding the Bayliner and jumped onboard. Ethan waited on the Bayliner's portside with Ohlendorf on his shoulders. 'Help me get him over,' he said.

Kate dropped to the Chris Craft, Malloy climbing down after her. Together he and Kate took Ohlendorf's body into the smaller of the two vessels. Kate sat at the wheel whilst Malloy settled Ohlendorf's unconscious body on the floor.

'Everything okay?' Kate asked.

'Got it,' Ethan answered over the headset. He was still inside the Bayliner. Its twin engines rumbled and then the two boats moved away from the dock together, the Bayliner's lights blazing.

Once they had entered the lake Ethan tied off the steering wheel. He set the Bayliner on a southeastwardly course that would let it run the length of the lake before colliding with the shore. He then swung down into the Chris Craft and cut free of Ohlendorf's yacht. The Chris Craft tipped left, dropping behind the Bayliner, and then turned right, cutting across the wake like a dark shadow on the water.

Seven minutes after the alarm had sounded they heard the first police sirens heading north along the road. A minute or so later they saw a police boat breaking across the Aussenalster making a run at the brightly lit Bayliner. Three minutes later they saw the police boat running alongside it, whilst the Chris Craft slid quietly into the Alte Rabenstrasse dock. Kate and Ethan wrestled Ohlendorf up to the dock. Ethan then carried him to the parking lot. Malloy jogged ahead and got the car started.

They rolled into the street thirteen minutes after the alarm had sounded.

St. Pauli District, Hamburg
Saturday-Sunday March 8-9, 2008.

They turned onto a quiet street and saw a cop car coming in the opposite direction. It was moving fast without lights or siren. Malloy let his car drift toward the kerb. When it turned out that the cop was not interested in them he rolled back to the centre of the road and watched the cop in his rear view mirror.

'They're closing off the roads,' Ethan said. They came to a stoplight and saw another cop car slowing through the inter-section, then roaring on – again no lights, no sirens. They turned onto a major artery and found a bit of Saturday night traffic. Close to the Reeperbahn, traffic slowed to a crawl and Malloy took a series of side streets until he turned into the courtyard parking area behind Dale Perry's bar.

Kate grabbed their two canvas bags. Ethan got Ohlendorf out of the backseat and dropped him over his shoulder. Malloy led them into the back of the bar and down the stairs.

Ethan placed Ohlendorf in a straight-back wooden chair in the centre of the room and began tying him to it by his wrists and ankles. Kate found a coffee machine in the kitchen and made some coffee whilst Malloy turned on his cell phone and saw a message from Dale Perry.

'Did you get the lawyer?' Dale asked when Malloy called him.

'We just got back. Why, did you find something?'

'I think so,' Dale said. 'Where are you?'

'Downstairs at your place.'

'I'll be at the backdoor in a couple of minutes.'

Malloy told Kate and Ethan he might have something and then went outside. Almost five minutes passed before a Land Rover came into the courtyard parking lot. Dale parked behind the Toyota and stayed in the vehicle.

'My contact got back to me after dinner,' he told Malloy. 'I've been tracking cell phones one at a time for the past four hours or so.'

'You found Helena Chernoff?'

'Actually I didn't get anything from the phone you gave me, but when I looked at the calls from the other phones at the same location I found something interesting. It turns out that two days before the police raid on the Royal Meridien there was a call to a cell phone that was inside the hotel. That same cell phone was carried into and out of the hotel a number of times before the raid, but since the raid it's been at an apartment in the Altstadt.' He handed Malloy a slip of paper. 'That's the address.'

'What do we know about the phone?' Malloy asked him as he pocketed the address.

'That's where it gets good, T. K. The phone receives one call a day, usually at the same time, always from a pay phone that's also inside the city but always a different phone. The cell phone never leaves the apartment building.'

'You think Chernoff and Farrell are holed up and someone is running her errands until they get new passports?'

'Looks that way to me.'

'What do you have on the phone account?'

'Activated locally while Farrell was still in Barcelona. It's registered to an H. Langer, funded by a Zürich bank. Jane has put someone on the alias and the bank in case we don't get her tonight.'

'Have you checked the place out?'

'I just did a drive-by. You've got a semi-detached six storey apartment building with what looks likes two apartments per floor. The place has an entrance on the south side of the building. Only other way in or out is through one of the windows or over a balcony.'

'Can we find which apartment she's in?'

'Not with the software that tracks a cell phone location. I'm only accurate to about thirty metres and I'm no good for vertical placements. The phone could be on the first or sixth floor, and I wouldn't see the difference, but I'll swing by the house and pick up a thermal imager. That way we're not going in blind.'

'I'm going to need you to run a perimeter team, so we don't get people coming in behind us. Is that going to be a problem?'

'I can do whatever you need,' Dale answered.

'The FBI agents have volunteered to help keep an eye on things – so there shouldn't be any surprises. How much time are you going to need to get a good look at things?'

'Why don't we meet there in thirty minutes?' Dale responded.

'That's good. I'll give you a call when we're rolling.'

Malloy dialled the desk at the Royal Meridien as Dale circled his Land Rover back the way he had come. He asked for Jim Randal's room. When Randal picked up, he said, 'You need to move now.'

David Carlisle was asleep when his cell phone rang. 'Yes?' he said, struggling to come awake and sitting up in his bed.

'Somebody just kidnapped Hugo Ohlendorf.'

Carlisle looked up at the ceiling and swore. 'When?'

'Just before midnight.'

'Malloy?'

'Police are still putting the thing together. I don't have any details – except that Ohlendorf is gone and nobody has a clue where he went. The other thing is Malloy just called Randal. I have no idea what he said, but Randal called Sutter and said they had to move.'

Carlisle smiled. 'So they're coming?'

'I'll call you when I know for sure.'

Malloy signalled to Kate and Ethan to follow him to the bedroom. Closing the door he told them, 'We might have found Chernoff and Jack Farrell.' Malloy brought out the slip of paper and Ethan used his GPS navigator to find the address.

'The Altstadt,' Ethan said, showing the electronic map to Kate and Malloy. All three of them took a moment to look at the street layout. Depending on traffic, which was still fairly heavy at the moment but would begin to thin out, it was actually less than ten minutes from their location.

'So what do we do with Hugo?' Kate asked.

'We've got fifteen-to-twenty minutes. Let's find out how many people she's got working for her on this.'

'That's not a lot of time,' Ethan answered.

'We don't want to break him. We just want the basics. Now listen, if I need to get his attention, Ethan, I want you to slap the back of his head or thump his forehead with the heel of your hand. Don't hurt him. Just get him to focus on his situation. Let him understand you would love to do more, but that I'm holding you back. Malloy pointed at Kate. You're the X-factor. When you don't like something, start pacing. Be impatient. You want your chance at the guy – because you know how to get the information.'

Kate nodded.

'Let him see you. Then go behind him. Dressed like this, with the ski mask in place, he's not even going to be sure if you're a woman, so don't say anything if you don't have to. Let him worry about it. Let him wonder what your role is in this thing.

When I tell you to do something don't hesitate. Make it look like what I am asking is exactly what you wanted to do in the first place.'

In the front room Malloy sat down in a hardback chair like the one in which Hugo Ohlendorf sat. His knees were almost touching Ohlendorf's, and he used a cold towel to wipe Ohlendorf's face.

'What do you want?' Ohlendorf asked him in German. He was well tanned. His dark hair was thinning at the top and had some flakes of grey at the temple. A few years past fifty he looked to be in good shape. In any other circumstance Malloy was reasonably sure he would be charming and quite sophisticated. In his pyjamas and slippers, his eyes dilated, his hair tousled, he looked like a man who needed to be institutionalised.

'Do you want some coffee?' Malloy asked him in High German. He used a Berlin dialect with a bit of a Russian intonation behind it. He wanted Ohlendorf to imagine the worst.

'I want to know what's going on!'

'Keep your voice down,' Malloy told him calmly, though he really didn't care about the noise.

Ohlendorf swore at him loudly and Malloy gave Ethan a look. Ethan moved in and slapped the back of his skull. He then cocked his fist, waiting to see if Ohlendorf needed less subtle persuasion. Malloy waved him off. Ohlendorf stared at Ethan's masked figure defiantly but he said nothing more. Ohlendorf's response was instructive. He was not a man to take orders and he was not easily frightened. With a professional life spent in the criminal courts and conspiring with the likes of Xeno and Helena Chernoff, he no doubt considered himself capable of dealing with felons, and of course the first rule of that particular jungle was to show no fear.

'Do you want some coffee?' Malloy asked him again.

Ohlendorf thought about it a moment and then said, 'Yes.'

Malloy nodded at Ethan, who went to get him a cup. Whilst he waited, Ohlendorf looked round the room. A single lamp lit the room keeping most of the room in shadows, but it was easy enough to see the place was nobody's idea of home. It was too sparsely decorated. There was a couch and chair in one corner of the room with a coffee table between them. In another area was a desk with a computer. Next to it was a bookshelf with novels, books, and magazines in different languages.

'I want you to understand,' Malloy told him, 'we aren't here to hurt you, but we need information and we'll do whatever is necessary to get it.'

Ohlendorf's eyes brightened in curiosity but he resisted asking the nature of the information, resisted as well the impulse to claim he knew nothing. For the moment his experience as a trial lawyer gave him some confidence. Ethan came back with a cup of coffee and held it for Ohlendorf as he took a sip. 'More?' Malloy asked. Ohlendorf nodded and took another sip. Ethan stepped away and put the cup down. Ohlendorf looked at Kate, his curiosity registering for the first time.

'We want to know about Helena Chernoff,' Malloy said.

For just an instant Ohlendorf's eyes came into sharp focus. 'What are you talking about?' he asked.

'Don't be stupid,' Malloy told him. 'Nobody wants to see you in pain. Chernoff is our target, not you.'

'Who sent you?'

'An old friend of one of Chernoff's victims.' Malloy's allusion to the Russian mafia had its desired affect. Hugo Ohlendorf's voice changed register and his speech grew more rapid. 'I don't know this person! I don't know what you're talking about!'

'Give him some more coffee.' Malloy said.

Ohlendorf watched Ethan's approach as if he expected to be scalded. When Ethan offered the cup to him, Ohlendorf asked, 'What is in it? Why are you making me drink this?'

Malloy signalled Ethan to set the cup aside.

'We need to get past this attitude, Herr Ohlendorf. I've been given only so much time. After that. . .' he looked purposefully at Kate, '. . .we try a different method. Now tell me what you know about Helena Chernoff.'

'I only know you have got the wrong man!'

'Tell me about Jack Farrell.'

'The American?' The mention of Farrell seemed to confuse him.

'Meet me halfway,' Malloy said. 'I know you know who Jack Farrell is. All I want to know is how he got Helena Chernoff to work for him. No problem in doing that, is there?'

'How would I know anything about this man?'

'Look. . . nobody wants to read about the torture and murder of a prominent Hamburg attorney. It makes life difficult for everyone.'

'I don't know Farrell or this other person. What was the name?' When Malloy did not answer his question, he added earnestly, 'I tell you, you have me mistaken with someone else.'

Kate, who had been leaning against the wall closest to the kitchen with her arms crossed over her chest, suddenly began pacing. Ohlendorf's eyes cut to her. She frightened him with her hood and petulant silence.

'This isn't working,' Ethan said. His German was good enough not to sound like an American. 'He's lying to us!'

Malloy held his right hand up, as if to ask for patience. 'Give him another chance,' he said. Kate crossed her arms over her chest again.

'I don't know what you want from me!' Ohlendorf protested. 'I tell you, you have the wrong man!'

'Tell me how often you met with Xeno.'

A look of surprise crossed Ohlendorf's face. For the space of several seconds he said nothing. It was as if the mention of the man caused him to recalibrate things. Finally, calmly, he said, 'I don't know anyone named Xeno.'

'I asked you how often you met with him.'

Ohlendorf glanced at Kate. He was trying to decide her role in this. Was she running it or was Malloy?

'We know about the meetings in the Stadtpark,' Malloy told him.

This shook him and the blood drained from his face. 'I don't know what you're talking about!'

'We know you have been an associate of Jack Farrell's for a number of years.'

'I don't know Farrell!'

'You sit on a board of directors with the man!'

'No. I don't know him.'

'Tell me about Helena Chernoff.'

'I don't know her!'

Malloy stood up, seemingly in resignation, and looked at Kate. 'You were right,' he said. 'Go ahead. Cut his nose off.' He said this calmly, a man who has done his best.

'Wait!'

Malloy held his hand up as if to stop Kate. 'How does it work? How do I contact Chernoff if I want to employ her for a job?'

Ohlendorf didn't answer him at once. He was using the time to calculate.

'She won't know you told us. Believe me. If you help us, she will be erased from the face of the earth. And you'll be a free man again.'

This Ohlendorf did not believe.

Kate crossed behind Ohlendorf drawing her combat knife so that he could hear the blade leaving its scabbard and see the flash of light on the steel for just an instant. When she had slipped out of his line of sight, Malloy held his hand up, as if stopping her. 'Give him one more chance. He wants to tell us this.' Ohlendorf tried to look at Kate but his bindings held him. His breathing was fast now, his confidence gone. 'How do I contact her?' Malloy asked.

Kate brought the diamond edged blade of the knife under his nose and pressed blade to flesh. Blood appeared at once, trickling now over the blade and across Ohlendorf's chin.

'*She* contacts *me*!'

'You're lying. You arrange jobs for her!'

Ohlendorf lifted his chin to escape the knife. 'No! She tells me to set up a meeting and I take care of it.' He tried to look back to see how Kate was handling his information.

'How does she contact you?'

'The Hamburg *Zeitung* – in the personal ads. If she wants to make contact there is a number I should call. The number changes, but you can always find it under Men Seeking Women. She runs three identical ads and always uses the same key words: *full-figured*, *vigorous*, and *discreet*. The last two digits of the number are reversed to avoid unwanted calls.'

Malloy stood up. He checked his watch. He was running out of time. 'So you call this number and then what happens?' he asked.

'She tells me what she needs.'

'Cut his nose off!'

'I'm telling you the truth!'

Malloy lifted his hand, asking Kate to wait. Ohlendorf's breathing was fast and shallow. His eyes were bulging, his head thrashing back and forth. Kate's knife was poised before his face. Her body braced the back of Ohlendorf's head so he could not pull away from her. 'Last chance,' Malloy told him. 'If you want your daughter to see you after we're done hacking away your nose, just lie to me one more time.'

'I'm not lying!'

'Did Jack Farrell ask you to contact Chernoff?'

'No! I don't know what he's doing!'

'So you *do* know him.'

'I have met him several times. I would not say I *know* him.'

'When was the last time Chernoff needed your services?'

'End of last year. I don't know. . . late December, I think it was.'

'Tell me about it.'

'I need a drink of water.'

He was blinking, stalling, thinking.

'Do you know a decent plastic surgeon?'

Ohlendorf's eyes dropped and cut. Malloy signalled Kate to step back and slapped the back of Ohlendorf's head as he walked behind him. He took Kate's knife and locked the man's head against his torso, bracing the knife under his nose. 'I'll do it myself if I don't get something!'

'She was arranging a multiple assassination. She needed talent! I contacted certain people with the protocols.'

'*Multiple?* Who were the intended victims?'

'I wasn't told. I arrange for the kind of people she wants on a given job. I'm not involved in the rest of it!'

Malloy let his head go and walked around to face him. 'I don't believe you.'

'I cannot help that. It is the truth!'

'Do you know the Langer alias?'

The lawyer was surprised at this and took his time answering. 'She wires money to me through that alias sometimes.'

'You don't pay her, she pays you?'

'I make arrangements for her. She pays me for that!'

'What bank does she use?'

'Sardis and Thurgau. In Zürich.'

'What was Xeno's relationship to Chernoff?'

'He worked for me. He supplied her with people when she wanted them, managed some of her safe houses, provided equipment, weapons. . . phones.'

'Were they lovers?'

Ohlendorf laughed. 'She runs in better circles than that!'

'Does she run in your circles, Hugo?'

When he did not answer, Malloy pressed the point of the knife close to Ohlendorf's crotch. 'Sometimes! Once in a while!'

Malloy slapped his face lightly to keep him focused. 'How many people did Chernoff need in December?'

'I don't know. It depends on the job. . .'

'How many for the December job, Hugo!'

'Eight. Nine! Eight in the city. Plus the. . . the one.'

'*The one?*'

'One specialist, the rest. . . street level talent.'

Malloy walked behind him, handing Kate her knife back. 'You arrange passports for her?'

This surprised him. 'No. That's. . . I don't do that.'

'Who does?'

'I don't know.'

Malloy came around to face him. 'You're lying!'

'She has contacts in Spain. I don't touch identity cards or passports! I run. . . I contact people who get her what she needs.'

'What were you paid for the December assassinations?'

'I haven't been paid.'

'Why not?'

'The contract is open. Look, I have given you what you wanted to know. You said if I told you what I know about Chernoff you were going to let me go.'

'You haven't given me what you know. You're keeping things from me, Hugo! You're lying more than you're telling the truth!'

'No! I've told you everything!'

Malloy left the room to search through the bags and dug out Kate's dart gun and an extra dart. When he came back into the room Ohlendorf's eyes brightened in fear. 'What are you doing?' he asked. 'I told you – no, wait, please! Wait!'

His body recoiled when the dart hit. He tried to speak, trembled, and then his eyelids fluttered. A few seconds later his head slumped.

'Put some kind of a hood on him,' Malloy said, 'and get the gear out to the Toyota. I'll be on the street at the front of the bar when you're ready.'

'What have you got, T. K.?' Josh Sutter asked when Malloy walked into the bar.

'Possible location for Jack Farrell.'

'You're kidding me!'

'I'm quite serious, actually. Come on, let's move.'

They found Randal double parked outside the bar. A prostitute was standing at his door trying to make a deal. Malloy gave her fifty Euros and told her to get lost. Fifty was the right price. She disappeared into the crowd.

'I thought you only liked the cheerleaders,' Malloy said. He was standing by the driver's side window.

Randal smiled and let one shoulder kick up. 'What can I say? I'm sitting here one minute, next thing I know I'm getting the midnight special.'

'We think Chernoff is keeping Jack Farrell at an apartment house not far from here.' The Toyota came out of the alley and turned into their street, pulling up beside Malloy. 'We're staging in ten minutes. Try to keep up!'

Malloy settled into the backseat of the Toyota and hit the speed dial as Kate accelerated. Dale Perry picked up on the second ring. 'Yeah.'

'We're rolling.'

'Three blocks due north of the target,' Dale said, 'there's a BP station that's closed for the night.'

Malloy gave Ethan the location and then checked the back window to make sure Sutter and Randal were still with them. The streets were cluttered with pedestrians and cars, but that thinned out as they left the fringes of the sex district.

'What do you think about Ohlendorf?' Kate asked.

'I think right now he is still picking and choosing what he wants to tell us.'

'You think she's really got nine people working for her?'

'She needs people to run errands, stand lookout, maybe a couple of bodyguards. You figure twenty-fours a day. . . that could be pretty close to nine. What I'm worried about is the specialist. What's his job?'

'I kind of wondered about that too,' Ethan answered.

Ethan was watching the GPS and told Kate to turn.

'What's a guy like Ohlendorf doing mixed up with assassinations?' Kate asked.

'It sounds to me like he runs a talent agency.'

'You think he's working for someone?' Ethan asked.

'Maybe. . . or maybe what we're looking at is a mutual assistance league. Ohlendorf provides Chernoff with freelance talent for a price. If they need passports they go to their friend in Spain. . .'

'Luca?' Ethan said.

'We know Luca deals in passports. We know Giancarlo and Jack Farrell launder money. If Ohlendorf manages talent. . .'

'This is all about the paladins, T. K.,' Ethan answered. 'It's the only thing that makes any sense.'

'I think you're right, but I still have a lot of questions I want to ask Farrell and Ohlendorf.'

'I'm guessing Robert Kenyon didn't like the direction things were going and the others decided there was too much money to be made to let him walk away.'

'What I'm having trouble with,' Malloy answered, 'is the seventy-five million dollar swindle. If they were having troubles, why would Kenyon put everything he had into a dubious investment?'

Ethan had no answer for this. 'I'm curious about that myself.'

'Tell us about the people we're going to be working with,' Kate said. They were close to the staging area. 'I mean. . . do they know what they're doing?'

'The man who found Chernoff for us is Company issue. He's been in Hamburg for something like twenty years. We won't have any problems from his end; just make sure if he asks you any questions about yourselves that you don't tell him the truth.'

'And the guys behind us?'

'Those are the two FBI Missing Persons agents tracking Jack Farrell. They're in a little bit over their heads, but they're trained cops, so I figure they know how to stand lookout.'

'They have any idea how many laws we're breaking?' Ethan asked.

'I didn't happen to mention that we were kidnapping a local politician if that's what you mean.'

Ussat-les-Bains, France
Summer 1932.

The hotel got more than its share of visitors that summer, including a steady flow of German tourists, all of whom stayed at reduced rates at *Des Marronniers* and went about the countryside in search of the Holy Grail and Cathar gold. Bachman, as majority shareholder, took the best room in the hotel without paying for it. He spent a great deal of time with the other Germans. Rahn went with them sometimes to show them various caves or ruins in the vicinity but, more often than not, he stayed close to the hotel and supervised the hotel staff.

Elise would see him frequently, but there was no cordiality between them. They were like school children who had promised themselves to each other in springtime only to discover the summer had turned them into strangers.

'How is your book going?' she asked him once when it seemed they had no choice but to speak.

'It's fine. Some problems, of course, but nothing I can't work out.'

Usually when they saw each other they were as likely to look elsewhere as to greet one another. There were no letters under her door, even when Bachman was travelling. There were no walks together, though he saw her leave the hotel alone many times. Nor were there any late night conversations that might have fixed the wound between them. Only chance meetings, and these all uniformly awkward.

Bachman would ask her about Rahn whenever she had encountered him, so Elise knew Bachman had spies watching her. She began to dread seeing Rahn because she knew she would hear about it from her husband later. One evening she went down to the bar and found Rahn talking to the North African bartender about a trip he had taken to Spain some years earlier. Bachman was away on another of his overnight excursions. Elise perched at the other end of the bar and ordered a brandy when the bartender sauntered down to see what she would like. Whilst she sat with her drink before her, Rahn finished his whiskey soda in a gulp and left the bar without so much as a nod of recognition.

No one else had been in the bar, but Bachman asked her about that night as well.

'Things are not good in Berlin,' Bachman muttered one morning after returning from a walk with yet another of the newly arrived German guests.

'More riots?'

He shook his head. 'Hitler has been passed over. He is not going to be the new Chancellor. He is not even going to be *relevant*!'

Elise felt nothing at this news. What did it matter who was Chancellor? She was sick to death of politics.

'I need to fly to Berchtesgaden,' Bachman announced two nights later. 'I have talked to Otto, and he assures me he will take care of you.'

'I can take care of myself!'

'You know what I mean! The men see a woman like you alone. . .'

'A woman *like* me? Tell me, Dieter, what kind of woman am I?'

'I only meant a woman alone invites attention!'

'And you imagine I am incapable of resisting it?'

'I did not mean that. Look, it is only for a few weeks.'

'*Weeks?*'

'Hindenburg has. . . well, there has been another setback. Some of us are meeting in Berchtesgaden to talk it through.'

'I want to go back to Berlin. I am tired of France, Dieter! Take me with you.'

'When things are settled and I know how we plan to proceed, I'll take you home. I promise. Until then it's not safe.'

'Are you planning another putsch?'

'I don't know what we are going to do.'

For almost a week after Bachman's departure nothing changed. After breakfast, Elise took a walk. In the heat of the afternoon she liked to read. She usually had drinks with some of the German tourists before dinner. At dinner she always sat with one or two couples, listening inevitably to stories about Hitler or his circle. After dinner she liked to turn on the radio for a while and then read a book. With Bachman gone, planning God knew what in Germany, she felt unsettled. One evening she stepped outside to breathe the cool air before she gave over to another sleepless night and saw Rahn coming toward her from the road. He carried quite a bit of equipment, including climbing ropes and picks, a lantern, and a rucksack. 'Have you been climbing?' she asked.

He shook his head and looked back toward the darkness. 'There was a chasm inside the Lombrives I have always wanted to look at, and I finally worked up the nerve to do it.'

'And did you find anything?' she asked.

'A great many bones,' he told her with a smile. Then after a moment of consideration, he asked, 'Is everything all right?'

'Why wouldn't it be?'

'I mean in Germany. I hear that Hindenburg refuses Hitler any role in the government.'

'I don't care about Hitler!' *Or my husband*, she thought.

He hesitated, wanting to speak, but the bright confidence she had seen in his smile the year before had been stamped out. 'I only meant that Dieter seemed upset when he left.'

'What is his mood to you?'

'I was thinking about Germany. The way things are. . . one worries!'

'If you want to know the worst of it, it is seeing *you* running a hotel!' And with that she turned to go inside, retreating to the safety of her room.

Much later there was a knock at her door. *His* knock. She knew it was him and called through the door, 'Go away!' Bachman's spies were everywhere. He must have known that as well but he stood beyond the closed door without moving. Finally, he knocked again. She went to open the door. Rather than speak to her he stared at her night dress which, she realised, had turned transparent in the pale backlight of her bedroom lamp. She crossed her arms across her breasts and watched his eyes sweep down across her belly. She turned and went for a robe, feeling naked suddenly. He stepped into her room and shut the door whilst she wrapped herself in her robe. 'What do you want?' she asked. The shard of fear in her voice surprised her.

Rahn's eyes softened, his shoulders sagged. 'I wanted to tell you I have stopped writing.'

'You. . . stopped? When?'

'Last year. Since I met you, actually.' He shook his head sorrowfully. 'There wasn't much point continuing. What I had put on paper sounded like someone else had written it. I was writing for the approval of my professors – old and formal and stuffy!'

'You write beautifully, Otto.'

'A book cannot be written as one composes a letter.'

'Why not?'

'It just isn't done!'

'You can do anything you like. Why not write a long, beautiful letter about *your* Cathars! They *are* yours, you know! No one loves them as you do! Don't write for your professors. *Their* professors are the same withered old men who laughed at Schliemann's Troy until they saw the gold he brought out of its ruins! Write for people who can still fall in love! Write about your troubadour knights and the ladies they loved. Make them breathe with life as you used to do when you would tell me their stories!'

'I can't write anymore,' he muttered, 'but this. . .' He gestured miserably at the room, but he meant the hotel, '. . .this is killing me! I am not a businessman, Elise.'

'Tell Dieter you want out!'

'I can't! He thinks. . . he thinks it is a great success – which it isn't – and I have my name on a ten year lease. . .' He stared into the awful middle distance of overworked worries. 'I hate doing this more than anything I have ever done, and I have had every kind of job!'

'But you will close in the winter, and you can afford to stay here, can't you? That will give you time to write! You'll be alone, with no one to disturb you!'

His head dropped. He looked like a man who had been told he has only a few months to live. 'I suppose you know Maurice Magre has published another book.'

'Dieter said something about it. So what?'

'Have you seen it?' She shook her head. 'It is about Buddhist influence on the Cathars. Pure rubbish, of course, like all the rest he does. . .'

'You need to write *your* book!'

He shook his head. 'It will change nothing. They were Buddhists. The Frenchman has spoken! Will anyone care what I have to say?'

'Don't *say* anything. You are a *troubadour*! You must sing the story! And if you sing, the rest of us will forget our cares for a few hours and dream about that other time and all the love affairs that were so incredibly overpowering they needed neither touch nor kiss!'

'But I want people to know what happened! The Vatican's crusade was a *crime*, Elise!'

'It was a crime seven hundred years ago, Otto. Now it is only a story. Write about the people. . . and the land. That is what you love. I think of the first letter you wrote to me when I got back to Berlin. . .'

He smiled. 'Do you remember it?'

'Do you?'

'I tried to describe the sky to you – because I knew how dreary Berlin winters can be, how one breathes differently in a city. I wanted you to think about the sun and the colour that is so much a part of this landscape.'

'It was the loveliest thing I have ever read. You could start a book with such words. Let's be honest with ourselves, Otto. I am some fantasy to you.'

'No!'

'I am! This place is what you love. You must love it when you write and then your language will be anything but stuffy. Write exactly as you did last winter in your letters and you will stand alone on Montségur forever!'

'You are not a fantasy, Elise. You are the woman I was born to love. I cannot stop dreaming about you even when I want nothing to do with you! And seeing you. . . all I want to do is take you in my arms. It is as if you have cast some spell over me!'

'I think you had better go.'

A smile flickered, the old confidence resurrecting momentarily. 'Before I do I want to see you.'

'You *have* seen me. Go! Tomorrow you can show me where some Cathar priest was murdered or where a certain knight did not kiss the woman he loved.'

'Take off your robe. Drop your gown. Let me look at you, even if you will never let me touch you. I have loved you for a year. I deserve that much!'

'You know I can't do that. I am a—'

He reached to undo the robe and stopped her speech. It was as if he flicked a switch. Once he had loosened it, he pushed it from her shoulders. It fell in a crush at her naked feet. Now he touched one of the thin straps of her gown, lifting it from her shoulder delicately. 'It is the easiest thing in the world,' he told her. 'Why *can't* you do it?'

Elise wanted to say, because she chose not to do it, but when she tried to speak her throat locked up.

The strap fell off her shoulder. Then he nudged the second

one free. Her hand pressed against her gown, holding it close to her heart.

'No,' he whispered. His voice was thick with desire. 'Don't do that. Show me what I will never have. Show me this once, and I will leave you forever.'

She began to cry.

Taking her into his arms, he said he was sorry. He was terrible. He was a monster. A perfect monster!

That was not why she was crying, she said. She was crying, she said, because this moment would change everything, because they were both perfect monsters.

Altstadt, Hamburg
Saturday-Sunday March 8-9, 2008.

'They're coming.' Chernoff's voice was cool, but Carlisle knew she was excited. 'Malloy is riding with two people – one of them a woman. The agents are following them.'

Carlisle stepped to the window and looked at the dark streets. 'What about Ohlendorf?'

'If they still have him we should be able to find him afterwards.'

Kate pulled the nose of the car against a wall at the edge of the BP lot. Randal pulled his SUV in beside her. Dale Perry had parked his Land Rover across the street and walked over to join them as they got out of their vehicles. Dale was wearing a vest and carrying a machine pistol under a long coat as well as his holstered government issue Glock.

'Everybody here American?' Jim Randal asked. It was probably a joke, but it came out like a bark.

'Close enough for government work,' Malloy told him, his eyes cutting to Kate. He made the introductions casually. He gave the first names of the two agents and Dale. Kate and Ethan he called Girl and Boy. After the handshakes, Malloy asked Dale, 'Did you find out which apartment they're in?'

'There are five people inside the building, all apparently in bed for the night.' Malloy checked his watch. It was almost one o'clock.

'Where are the rest of the renters?'

'People stay in places like this Monday-through-Thursday, T. K. They all have real homes somewhere else. Anyway, of the five people inside, only two are in the same apartment – a man and a woman.'

'Farrell and Chernoff?'

'Looks that way. They're on the east side of the building, one storey up. The apartment across the hall from them is empty. You've got two more people on the fourth floor, separate apartments, and one on the top floor. Most of these buildings don't have elevators. So if we can hold the stairwell, we should be able to isolate the couple.'

'What about a lookout?' Malloy asked. He was thinking a lookout could alert Chernoff and call in as many as five more guns from somewhere beyond the perimeter.

'That's where we get some bad news. You've got quite a few apartment buildings facing the entryway and you've got fairly decent lighting. So going in and coming out, you're exposed to a crossfire.'

'Any way into the building from the back?' Ethan asked.

'That's the best way, if you can manage to get up to the second floor. The ground floor is closed off – no doors or windows – but after that you've got balconies that give you easy access to all the apartments. The street is close, but it's quiet this time of night and mostly in shadows.'

Malloy looked at Kate. 'Your call.'

'We can go in through one of the balconies at the back. If we get Farrell we can leave by the front door and have a car waiting at the kerb. If we have to bail out – we leave the way we came and ride out with the other car.'

'Someone needs to watch the rope to the balcony,' Ethan added. 'That's our line of retreat.'

'I'll take the rope,' Dale told them. He pointed to the FBI

agents. 'You guys decide between you how you want to deploy in the cars.'

'I want to be the first to shake Jack Farrell's hand,' Jim Randal said. 'So I'll take the front.'

Josh Sutter looked like he wished he had called for the front, but he didn't argue. He was a team player.

They got the equipment they needed from the bags in the Toyota's backseat and then locked the extra gear in the boot of the car. Sutter and Randal, armed with a couple of machine pistols Dale loaned them, took a long look at Ethan's handheld navigation system and then drove off to their posts. If either of them saw anything coming, they were to call Dale's cell phone. Dale would contact Malloy.

Dale and Malloy walked in along one street. Ethan and Kate took another.

'What's the story on this Brit, T. K.?' Dale asked.

'No story.'

'One of yours or is she on loan?'

'Girl and Boy belong to Jane. At least that's the impression I got, but I didn't ask. All I know is they're not fresh off the Farm. They've been bouncing around over here for a few years.'

'If they're any good I probably would have heard about them.'

'You're probably right. Unless they're *really* good.'

Dale laughed. 'That would be the kind Jane would recruit.'

'That's what I'm thinking.'

They met under the balcony of the empty flat. Kate, Ethan and Malloy pulled their night vision goggles into place and strapped their AKS-74s over their shoulders – the first round already jacked into the chamber. They turned on their headsets and then Ethan tossed a rubber-coated grappling hook up to the balcony.

Kate went up the rope first. She used a quick hand-over-hand and covered the ten metre climb within a couple of seconds. Ethan followed with the same ease, making the climb look embarrassingly simple.

'So far I'm impressed,' Dale whispered.

Malloy used his legs to hold himself and scaled the rope one deliberate pull at a time. Just under the lip, as he considered the prospect of fighting his way over and maybe falling back to his death if he slipped, Ethan and Kate took him by his armour and lifted him up to the ledge. At least they left him the dignity of climbing over the railing on his own. Whilst he did, Kate pulled the rope up and stowed it neatly away.

The balcony was set off from the kitchen and was only large enough for trash and compost and a few utensils. The door was made of wood and glass, secured with a latch. Ethan used a handheld pry bar and cracked the lock with a single twist of his wrist.

Keeping the lights off and using their NVGs, they examined the floor plan in order to get a better understanding of the layout of the adjacent flat. This was easily accomplished. There were two rooms besides the bathroom and kitchen. From the hallway at the front door they would have visual access to most of the living room and bedroom. The kitchen and bath-room doors lay opposite the bedroom – next to the front door.

After having a look, Kate signalled them back to the kitchen. 'You go in first hard and fast,' she told Ethan, 'I'll come behind and take the bedroom door. T. K. can watch the stairwell.'

'I want the bedroom door,' Malloy told her.

'That's the hotspot, T. K.'

'Have you ever seen a photograph of Helena Chernoff?'

'I can't say that I have.'

'I looked at a few hundred last night. I'll take the bedroom. You hold the stairwell.'

The front door of the flat they had entered could only be unlocked with a skeleton key, but the key itself was missing. Rather than waste time looking for it, Ethan knelt down and began tinkering with a set of lock picks. It was pretty standard stuff and within a few seconds the tumblers rolled and the deadlock snapped open. Like the breaking of the wood at the balcony door, the metal snap of the lock sounded like a gunshot inside the darkened flat. Such noises rarely woke city people, who were accustomed to all manner of nocturnal disturbances, but there were always exceptions. And Helena Chernoff, a fugitive for two decades, was probably one of them. So they went through fast.

Kate settled just outside the door at the bottom of the stairs. Ethan crossed the landing immediately behind her and kicked the outer door open. Malloy followed close behind him. As he moved he got his bearings. On his left he saw an open kitchen door and a closed bathroom door. Opposite the front door was the living room. Facing the kitchen was the closed bedroom door. Malloy, never breaking stride, tapped it with five rounds from his Kalashnikov.

Dale heard the clicking of high heels on the sidewalk across the street even whilst Malloy was still struggling to get up the rope. He got his first glimpse of the streetwalker's pale skin and straw-blonde straight hair when she lit a cigarette at the kerb. She took a moment to consider whether or not to cross the street and then noticed him standing in the shadows.

That would have been enough for a civilian to stay on that side of the street, but she was in the life, and headed right for him. Dale had long ago lost interest in women who sold themselves. Up close to it, as he was, there was no romance or mystery to the oldest profession. Mostly it was laziness and low self-esteem. Sometimes it was hatred in the mask of subservience. And sometimes it was slavery or drug addiction. Take your choice: anyway you looked at it prostitutes of either gender were bad news. This one was in the middle of the street when he realised that under her coat she wore nothing besides a garter belt and stockings.

Impervious or not, Dale Perry was still a man. He pulled his gaze from her dark pubic mound and tried to study her face. He got only vague outlines. Sometimes Hamburg streetwalkers were like street prostitutes the world over, too young to have much choice about their conditions or too old and hard-bitten to afford better circumstances, but sometimes beautiful women worked the streets. This one wasn't young, but she wasn't rough trade either.

There was just a hint of tightrope walking in the swinging motion of her hands, but once she was on the sidewalk and about ten metres from him, he could smell the booze. 'You looking for a good time, honey?'

Saying this she pulled her coat back, in case he hadn't noticed her skin under the glare of the streetlight. Her body was gorgeously tight and enticing, and she knew it.

'Thirty Euros straight. Twenty if you just want head.' She spoke with a hint of *Plattdeutsch*, as if she had originally come from the farm country surrounding Hamburg. 'We can do it right here if you want. I'm not picky.'

'Get lost,' Dale told her.

'What are you doing back here?' she asked, coming toward him. Her spiked heels sank into the soft dirt and she nearly fell. 'You with someone?' She looked round as she caught her balance. 'You with a man?' She giggled and then lurched wildly as the other heel sank into the dirt. 'I'll do you both for forty.' She caught her balance, but she looked ready to faint or vomit.

Dale swore and took a step toward her. He was going to have to get her out of here, and he wasn't sure how easy that was going to be.

'Thirty Euros straight,' she muttered. When he took her arm, she didn't resist, but neither did her arm and body seem quite connected. He could smell cigarette smoke clinging to her coat. The sweet stink of booze on her breath and skin was over-whelming. 'Twenty for. . . anything you want.' She seemed loose and unstable – like a sack of water. How could a woman like this let herself get that drunk?

At the sound of a Kalashnikov discharging from somewhere

inside the building Dale turned instinctively. He was still touching the streetwalker's arm but otherwise forgot her. Then he heard the blast of two shotguns and more automatic fire.

Her muscles did not tighten as she moved. Her free arm simply snaked up toward his neck as her body seemed on the verge of collapsing. Still processing the sounds of gunfire above him, Dale felt something sting his neck.

No. Not a sting. She had cut him!

His first reaction was anger, and he pushed the woman away. Instead of letting herself get tossed to the ground, the prostitute tightened her body and stayed close, her free hand suddenly holding his wrist. It was then he realised she was not at all what she seemed. He tried to cock his wrist so he could fire his Uzi into her side but she held his hand in an iron grip. Held him and looked into his eyes – happy to watch the life in him bleed out. Only as her eyes danced did he understand that blood was pouring over his shirt and armour.

Dale tried to recall her name – the woman who had just killed him – but the only thing that came to his panicked thoughts was the word *Stasi*. The East German police had been gone from Germany almost two decades, but the word itself was still synonymous with midnight raids, torture, terror, and murder. Stepchild of the Gestapo and KGB, they were as relentless as the latter, as efficient and without scruple as the former. And this one, Dale thought, as his knees buckled. . . this was the last of them. But her name eluded his clouded thoughts. If he had had the blood for one more thought he might have wondered how his wife and children were going to handle his death – a lifetime buried in the underground and coming to this ignominious end without their ever knowing it was all just a cover, that he was in fact something far more honourable and decent than they had ever imagined.

As it was he had no time for regret or even a fleeting thought to give to his family. There was no passing memory of his homeland. Nothing at all could crowd past that all consuming idea of the cold, efficient and deadly *Stasi*.

*

The shotgun boomed from inside the kitchen and hit Malloy in the back just as he shot the bedroom door. Ethan turned into the opening with his AKS-74 on full auto. He saw the man who had shot Malloy. The shooter was pumping another shell into the chamber. He was wearing a vest, but it wasn't going to do him any good. . .

Before Ethan could close his finger on the trigger, he got hit in the back with the blast of a shotgun. He only understood what had happened after he had been slammed facedown into the floor – his armoured back and bare right arm hit.

The gunman he had been about to shoot stepped over him. Ethan twisted up to face him. His gun gone from his hands, he reached for his knife, thinking wildly that he might just twist out of the blast. For a moment he did not understand that the chaotic clatter that rang over the shotgun blasts came from Kate's weapon. He saw the splinters of masonry and wood inside the kitchen, then the explosion of the cabinets behind the man who was about to kill him. And then he saw the man's face torn apart.

Rolling to his feet, Ethan saw Malloy was still down. Wounded? Dead? He could not tell. Kate had killed the woman who had been hiding in the living room – the one who had shot Ethan in the back – and now kicked open the bedroom door. Malloy pushed himself to his hands and knees. Kate came back out of the bedroom.

'Clear!' she told them. 'T. K.?' From his hands and knees Malloy tried to look up but couldn't quite manage it. 'Are you hit?' Kate asked him.

Malloy was moving slowly – his jacket torn apart at the kidneys. 'I think I'm okay,' he said. Kate looked at Ethan. Because he was standing she hadn't realised he was hurt. She saw something now and went toward him. 'You're hit!'

Ethan looked at his arm but the NVGs limited his periphery.

'Can you move your arm?' Kate asked, bending her masked face close and trying to see through the NVGs.

Ethan lifted his arm. Not broken – but hurting. Malloy got
to his feet finally. His body swayed. He'd taken a kidney punch
delivered with buckshot. 'I'm okay,' Ethan said, 'but I caught
some buckshot in my arm.'

'We've got to get out of here now!' Kate told them. 'T. K.?
Can you climb?'

Malloy staggered and looked at Kate, Ethan, and the dead
man and woman. 'Farrell!' he muttered.

'Forget him. We're out of here – *now*! Can you climb?'

He bent over like an old man to get his gun and when he was
standing again, he said. 'I'm okay.' It was not a very convincing
statement.

'Boy?'

Ethan nodded. 'I'm good.'

They stepped into the hallway, glancing at the stairwell, and
then went back into the flat across the hallway.

At the sound of the guns, Jim Randal phoned Sutter. 'You hear
that?' he asked.

'I hear it.'

'It's not good.'

'Sit tight!'

'I'm not moving, but I'm saying it's not good.' He clicked off
and looked around. They had set him off half-a-block away in
the shadows but he could be at the kerb in front of the entrance
in a matter of a few seconds. The street was still empty but the
gunshots brought a light on in the window of a flat another
across the street from where he sat. Then he saw a movement
in his rear view mirror. A woman in a long fur coat and high
heels was running in something of a panic down the middle of
the street. Randal scanned the streets again. She was alone,
watching the apartment building as she ran. Her coat was open
and Randal stared in disbelief. She was wearing nothing but
high heels, a garter and hose! He swore quietly at the sight and
at German mores in general, but he could not resist the show
and watched her closely for the few seconds it took for her to

come almost up to his vehicle, seemingly unaware of his presence. He looked away finally, checking the streets. Then he heard her calling out to him in German. When he did not respond, she staggered toward him and pointed in the direction of the gunshots, still screaming in German – something about *sheezie* or *shizti*. Her coat was still completely open, like it was the most natural thing in the world.

Randal was not sure what to do, so the first thing he did was hit his window switch. 'You speak English?'

He decided if she spoke English he would tell her to get lost, and if she didn't he would pull his service weapon and tell her to get lost, but as he was working through how he wanted to deal with her, Randal felt something hot hit his neck. Then he felt dizzy.

Ethan was first over the balcony. This time he used his legs, not really able to put any of his weight into his right arm. When he got to the ground, he saw a shadow and knew it was Dale. 'We've got a man down!' he whispered, pulling his weapon free and getting ready.

'What is it? What happened?' Malloy asked.

Ethan moved to the body quickly and turned the shoulder. 'It's Dale. His throat's been cut.' He spun, searching the shadows with his NVGs. He saw a woman's shoe prints coming and going. Coming there was an odd meandering aspect, but the tracks departed on a straight line. Ethan backed off and set his gun to his shoulder to cover the building whilst Malloy came down the line slowly. He was hurt, maybe seriously wounded. Kate watched the upper balconies from her position on the second storey balcony. For the moment she was trapped and could do very little from her position. Once Malloy touched the ground Kate flipped over the balcony, descending in a rapid hand-over-hand. There was a movement on one of the upper balconies as she finished. Ethan shifted his sights, saw a gun, and squeezed off a burst. He heard Josh coming in with the SUV. Kate ran past Ethan and then turned, firing off several bursts at the building.

Ethan saw Malloy trying to drag Dale out. 'I'll get him, T. K.,' Ethan whispered. 'You cover the building.'

He moved forward and swept Dale up over his shoulders, almost collapsing under the weight of the body and the hot pain in his shoulder. Kate and Malloy continued firing at the building, with Kate backing toward the kerb. Josh was waiting – his SUV now taking fire.

Kate emptied her gun and dived into the backseat. Several more shots hit the vehicle as Ethan rolled Dale's corpse into the backseat and climbed in after him. Malloy emptied his clip and plunged headfirst through the open passenger window in the front. Ethan shouted, 'Go!' but Josh was already burning rubber.

Josh made a hard right turn at the end of the block and came round a second turn to the front of the building. He slowed in perplexity when he did not see Dale's Land Rover. Breaking the lull, a burst of fire hit the windshield. Josh turned a one-eighty, fish-tailing into a parked vehicle as he finished, but he got them out of the kill zone. Kate called directions from the backseat as they roared down the street and soon they skidded into the BP station. For the moment, no one was following and the streets were quiet. That gave them time to move to the Toyota, Malloy and Ethan fitting Perry's corpse into the boot. This time Malloy drove. He pulled out of the lot slowly, not a worry in the world, just as the first police car screamed out of a side street opposite them and went roaring by.

'Call Jim,' Malloy told Sutter, as he tapped the speed dial of his own phone.

It was early evening in the U.S., and Jane let her phone ring several times before she got to it. When she picked up, she said, 'Yes.' She knew it was Malloy. He was pretty sure from her tone she expected good news.

'Dale's been killed,' Malloy told her.

'How?' Jane asked. Her voice was calm, her manner cool.

Malloy could imagine someone was with her, that she could not talk freely, but she was always like that. The rougher the game, the colder she got.

'Somebody got in close and used a knife.' He looked at Sutter who wasn't getting an answer. 'We've also got an MIA – one of the FBI agents on the case.'

'Which one?' she asked.

'Special Agent James Randal.'

'I'll let his people know about it. Can you give me the last-seen location?'

Malloy gave the address of the building and told her Randal had been driving Dale's Land Rover. Ethan recited the license number on the Land Rover from the backseat and Malloy repeated it, wondering as he did how Ethan could remember something like that at a time like this.

'I'll handle it,' Jane said.

'I got Dale's body off site. I'll leave him at his safe house under *Das Sternenlicht*.'

'Where is the second agent, T. K.?'

Malloy glanced at Josh Sutter, who looked stricken and lost. 'He's with me.'

'We need to get him out of the country tonight.'

'I've got my hands full with another problem.'

'Can you tell me about it?'

'Not really.'

'I can send two teams in: one to clean up Dale's operation, the other to get Agent Sutter down to Ramstein. How about you? Are you going to be okay?'

'I'm okay.' Sore, he thought, maybe even wounded, but she didn't need to know that. Not at the moment at least.

'I want you to go after Chernoff, T. K. She's the priority now. With federal agents killed in pursuit, Mr Farrell just lost any sympathy with the media he might have had. Are we clear on that?'

'We took a woman out. It might have been Chernoff, but if not, trust me, Chernoff is mine.'

Once Malloy had clicked off, Josh Sutter asked him, 'What are the chances Jim is still alive?' He was still trying Randal's cell phone every couple of blocks and staring out the window as if he thought he might discover his partner somewhere at the side of the road. When Malloy didn't answer him, Sutter said, 'You think he's dead?'

This really wasn't a question and Malloy let it hang before he said, 'I think you had better be prepared for the worst.'

Josh Sutter started punching out another number. 'I need to call my supervisor.'

'It's being handled,' Malloy told him. When that didn't stop him, Malloy took his wrist. 'You don't need to do anything right now, Josh. Everything is being handled.'

'What about Jim? He's *missing*, T. K.! We can't just assume he's dead!'

'The Hamburg cops are going to be all over this. They've got the crime scene by now and they've got the license plate of the Land Rover.'

'I need to call Hans!'

'Call him. . .' Malloy said, '. . .and you'll do twenty-to-life as an accessory to murder.'

Murder stopped him. 'What are you talking about?'

From the back seat Ethan said, 'If you kill someone while you're committing a felony in the States, don't they charge you with murder in the first?' When Sutter didn't respond, Ethan told him, 'It's the same over here. Only thing is over here they don't have the death penalty.'

'Hans is not your friend, Josh,' Malloy told him. 'Not anymore.'

'No, T. K. *You're* not my friend.'

'Right now,' Ethan told him, 'like it or not, you've got three friends in this country – the people in this car. Everybody else is after your ass.'

Altstadt, Hamburg.

'How bad is it?' Carlisle asked. Jim Randal was bound and gagged in the next room, conscious but groggy. Helena Chernoff had already changed clothes and was strapping on armour.

'No one in the apartment building is responding,' she said. 'The other three got out before the police showed up.'

'So we can get Ohlendorf?'

Chernoff gave Jim Randal a speculative look. 'That shouldn't be a problem. All we have to do is persuade Agent Randal to make a phone call.'

St. Pauli District, Hamburg.

'Better tell Josh about Ohlendorf.' Kate said as Ethan slipped out of the car and unlocked the parking slot at the back door of *Das Sternenlicht*.

'I was just going to do that,' Malloy answered. He looked at Josh who had gone quiet since realising he had no friends. 'The guy who gave us our information is inside.'

'You still trust him?' Sutter asked. This might have been a joke, but nobody was laughing.

'Never did,' Malloy answered and pulled the car forward. 'When you get inside, I want you to go to the back room. Don't let him hear you say anything. We're going to have to let him go later and I don't want him to have any information the police can use to find us.'

Malloy went in first to make sure no one from the bar came back through the storage room and found them. Ethan and Josh Sutter brought Dale's corpse out of the boot of the Toyota and got him to the cellar. Kate brought the canvas bags.

Malloy led all three of them into the bedroom. When they had settled Dale Perry's corpse against the far wall, Sutter said, 'We can't just leave him here like this.'

'A team will come in before dawn. They'll take care of it.' By that Malloy meant they would drop the body someplace and leave it for others to find. Sutter looked at the sterile setting of the bedroom. 'Is this where he lived?'

'No. This is one of his safe houses. He had a wife and kids, a house. . . a real life.' He felt a moment of sorrow taking him and pushed it away.

Kate stripped away her jacket and guns. 'Have you got some kind of medical kit?'

'In the bathroom.'

'Then let's go. I want to have a look at your back.'

'Take care of Ethan,' he said. 'I have to clean up the computer before I do anything else.' After they had left, he told Josh Sutter, 'You might as well get comfortable, Josh. We've got a three-to-four hour wait for your ride home.' He looked at his watch. 'The good news is you should be on a plane bound for New York sometime in the next eight hours.'

'I'm not leaving until I know what happened to my partner.'

'Josh, you don't have a choice. If the police find you, you are looking at multiple charges of murder and one count of kidnap.'

Sutter's face washed pale with fear, but even then he was thinking about Randal. 'So you're saying if the police find Jim alive. . . ?'

'Either way, it's not good, but at least if the cops find him he'll be alive and we can start dealing with the Germans. Maybe get a reduced sentence.'

'What the hell did you get us into T. K.?'

Malloy looked down at Dale, feeling his stomach churning. 'I don't know, Josh. I really don't have any idea.'

Malloy turned on the computer. He had all the relevant files on Chernoff at his hotel room in the Neustadt, but thought he might as well try to search for leads on the Knights of the Lance before cleaning the thing. He tried *knights*, *lance*, and *paladins*. When that failed to turn up anything, he searched for Ohlendorf and found a nest of files, including known associates. He downloaded the material to a two gig memory stick, which he pocketed. He then activated the self-destruct software. The prompt asked for his code. He typed in JANE and the files started disappearing. Whilst the programme ran, he checked the drawers and turned up a bound stack of DVDs, all agency material. There was also another memory stick with two gigs of memory, though he could not read it now. He took these to the kitchen and began breaking them. When the files were clean on the computer, he lifted the hard drive out and went to the kitchen and broke it apart. Then he dumped the hard drive, the broken DVDs, and the extra memory stick into a glass bowl and poured liquid drain cleaner over them – just to be sure nothing survived.

When he tapped on the bathroom door Kate called for him to come in. Ethan was naked to the waist and sitting on the edge of the bathtub. Kate was beside him, straddling the edge of the tub and stitching his wound with a needle and surgical thread.

'How bad?' Malloy asked.

'There's buckshot all through his upper arm. I did what I could to clean the wounds, but he's going to need a doctor to dig them out. This,' she nodded toward the flap of skin, 'needs to be taken care of now.'

Malloy nosed around in the medicine box. 'What did you use to kill the pain?'

Kate took her eyes from her bloody needlework and met Malloy's. 'Guts.'

Malloy looked at Ethan. 'Hurt?'

Ethan's stony ghost-white face gave no expression, but he had enough breath to answer. 'Little bit.'

Kate finished sewing the wound and rummaged about in the medicine kit for bandages. Afterwards she turned to Malloy, 'Your turn, T. K. Strip.'

Without a needle running into him Ethan finally worked up something like a smile. 'Remember when a beautiful woman telling you to strip was a good thing?'

Malloy pulled off the armour and then his shirt. He was

hurting – a deep hollow ache, like his body had just been slammed into a wall a few times.

'Drop your pants, too,' Kate told him.

'Aren't you even going to buy me dinner?' he asked.

'Oh, man!' Ethan said as Malloy turned delicately away from Kate. 'What happened to your chest?'

Malloy glanced down at his chest as he dropped his pants. 'I got those in Lebanon – my first tour of duty.'

'Looks like it should have been your last.'

Malloy grinned. 'The people who found me told me later they didn't give me a chance in hell of making it.'

Kate started poking Malloy's kidneys and he winced, his eyes tearing uncontrollably. From the feel of it he thought she might be using her needle.

'You've been bruised pretty badly here, but I can't tell if there's any internal damage. You need to watch for blood. Kidneys are not something you want to mess with.'

'How bad are the buckshot wounds?'

'It's a bloody mess, but I'll clean it up and bandage the area. What do you like, salt or alcohol?'

'How about Demerol?'

'Alcohol it is.'

Cleaning the wounds hurt more than getting shot, but it wasn't a needle and thread, so Malloy took it without too much whimpering.

'Do you think my wife is going to figure out what happened?' he asked.

'I don't know,' Ethan answered. 'How stupid is she?'

Josh Sutter knocked at the bathroom door and then opened it. His face was pale. He held out his cell phone for Malloy to take. 'There's a woman on my phone. She says she'll only talk to you.'

Malloy looked at Kate and then at Ethan. Finally he took the phone and said in German, 'Who is this?'

'I'm willing to make a trade,' the woman said in German. 'Are you?'

191

He recognised the voice from the video clips he had seen the night before. 'What are we trading, Helena?'

'One FBI agent for one Hamburg attorney.'

'I'm going to need proof—'

Jim Randal's voice broke over his own, 'T. K.! For God's sake, help me!'

'Good enough?' the woman asked.

'Let me talk to him.'

'There's a parking lot at the end of the *Alsterchausseestrasse* – close to the Aussenalster. You can talk to him there, if you bring the lawyer.'

Malloy repeated the street name and then said, 'I'll find it.'

'Good, because you've got twenty-five minutes to get here. After that. . . Special Agent Randal is a dead man.'

Chapter Seven

St. Pauli District, Hamburg
Sunday March 9, 2008.

'Helena Chernoff has Jim,' Malloy told them. 'She wants to make a trade.'

'When?' Kate asked.

'Now.'

'You think she's on the level?'

Malloy wasn't sure, but a trade made sense. 'Ohlendorf obviously knows a lot about her. I expect she's desperate to get him back.'

'How did she know you kidnapped Ohlendorf?' Ethan asked.

'Contacts inside the police force, an accomplice with a police scanner. . . maybe it's on the radio and TV by now. Who knows? Point is she knows, and she wants him back.' He looked at Josh Sutter. 'You up for this, Josh?'

'You couldn't keep me away if you tried,' Josh Sutter answered.

Malloy nodded. He looked at Kate, who looked at her husband.

'We're in,' Ethan said. No hesitation either – and getting nothing for it but all the trouble Helena Chernoff could throw at them.

'I expect the best way to handle this is to make the trade and walk away,' Malloy told them. 'Trouble is I can't do that. I need to take this woman out.'

'She's going to have backup,' Kate answered.

'Then we'll take them out too.'

'Look,' Ethan said, 'she lost people tonight, and she's putting this thing together on the run. She *might* have a couple of people, maybe three still on their feet. It's not going to be like taking out an army.'

'Just so we don't risk losing Jim,' Josh said. He was clearly anxious to get moving.

'I'll drop Boy and Girl about a mile from the exchange and keep you with me,' Malloy answered. 'Once you and I make the trade,' he nodded toward Kate and Ethan, 'they'll take their best shot at Chernoff.'

'That means we lose Jack Farrell,' Kate answered.

'Farrell doesn't matter now. The important thing, after taking out Chernoff, is to get Ohlendorf back. I think he can tell us what we need to know.'

They found a pair of night vision goggles for Josh. Whilst they were looking for a vest for him, Ethan snagged the three hand grenades from his and Kate's arsenal and all the spare ammo clips he had for the Kalashnikovs. They reloaded their weapons, and then got their guns neatly stowed under their slickers.

That finished, Malloy cut Ohlendorf loose, got him bundled up in a coat and then cuffed him. Ohlendorf still wore a hood, but that wouldn't be a problem. Except for some ambient light from various windows the courtyard was dark. Besides, in this district, a man wearing a hood and handcuffs almost seemed a part of the milieu.

Malloy, Kate and Ethan took up their headsets but left them off for the moment. At this point they needed to think about saving their batteries.

'Everybody ready?' Malloy asked. When they had all checked their equipment and nodded their assent, he pointed to Josh. 'You run interference and make sure no one comes through the storage room.'

'How do I do that? What do I say?'

'Flash your badge and say, *Raus*. If that doesn't work, shoot them. Once we back out of the parking spot, lock it behind us, we might need to come back.' He passed the key to Josh. To Kate, 'You're on point. Make sure no one is coming through the passage while we're getting him into the car.' To Ethan, 'I want you and Kate in the backseat. Keep Ohlendorf out of sight.'

Once Josh had secured the stairway, Kate and Ethan followed, Malloy coming up last, guiding Ohlendorf with his voice. Outside they moved quickly to get into the car. Kate was already on the opposite side of the Toyota covering the passageway. Ethan held the Toyota's back door open for Malloy and Ohlendorf. Sutter, as instructed, came out the back of the building and stood at the front of the car waiting for Malloy to pull the car out so he could lock the parking slot.

When Ohlendorf hesitated, Malloy thought the lawyer didn't want to get in the car. He had no idea where he was, of course, and he might have thought by making a scene he could get help. Then, as Ohlendorf dropped toward the pavement, Malloy felt a live round of ammo thump into his armour. There was no sound accompanying the impact. Whilst Malloy was falling, three more rounds hit within an inch of the first.

'SNIPER!' he called as he tumbled back to the pavement.

Kate was on the opposite side of the Toyota when Malloy shouted. Next to her was Dale Perry's second parking slot, empty. Beyond this was a narrow passage to the street. She heard the bullets hitting flesh and armour as Malloy fell with Ohlendorf – hit or finding cover, she could not tell. She saw Ethan jump in surprise and swing his left arm, like a man who had just been stung. Then he dropped as several rounds smacked his vest. Kate dived toward the building, but she was exposed and three rounds drove into her back. A fourth scorched through the right thigh.

With her Kalashnikov trapped under her jacket, Kate had no choice but to draw her .45. She heard footsteps in the passageway and realised they were coming in fast for the kill. She hit the first in the chest and heard the thump of armour. He flinched and spun. The second was aiming his weapon when she rolled and fired three rounds under the blast of his shotgun.

The last was a headshot. She finished her roll and came under the first assailant, who was bringing the point of his weapon down on her. Before he could pull the trigger Kate emptied her gun into his groin.

Ethan saw a man running at him from the centre of the courtyard. With his AKS-74 still trapped inside his slicker and his left wrist numbed with pain, he reached inside his jacket for his holstered Colt.

He heard Kate's silenced .45 punching out rounds, but the man kept coming, then the blast of a shotgun close to her. Ethan rolled as the gunman approaching his position fired his shotgun. He felt the sting of buckshot in his legs and heard the sound of both guns echoing inside the square as he brought his .45 up. He fired once, but the shot was wild. He fired a second time. This drove into the gunman's vest but failed to drop him.

The gunman pumped a new round into his shotgun and was taking aim when Ethan put the sights on the man's head and squeezed off a third round. The shotgun jerked up and exploded harmlessly. The man dropped.

Chernoff hit Ohlendorf and Malloy with two quick bursts from her silenced M-4, weaving the sights in a delicate figure-eight. As both men fell, she released the trigger, dipped the sights into Brand, and then squeezed down again, taking the point of the weapon across to his wife. She finished the clip on the FBI agent, then slapped in a new clip and flipped the selector to single shot.

Everyone was down: wounded, cowering, or dead. Chernoff had warned her people to go for Kate Brand and her husband first, and they moved in even as she was finishing her clip.

Ethan Brand got the man in front of him with three shots. Chernoff was lifting her weapon for the kill shot when she realised the second team was down as well. She turned her scope on Kate, but felt the sting of masonry hit her face. Whilst she was processing this, a second round cracked past her face, colliding with a vent directly behind her. Ethan Brand had found her.

She pulled back before he scored a lucky hit and moved across the roof, coming forward carefully. She heard Kate Brand call out, 'I'm going after her. Cover me!'

Chernoff put her sights on Kate just as Ethan opened fire on her new position. She heard a round crack beside her as it passed. The second bullet slammed into her armour and sent her rolling back for cover.

Malloy came to a seated position as the shotguns exploded. He was still trying to get his Kalashnikov free when Kate dropped her first clip, reloaded her .45 and started running across the lot. As she went she called to them to give her cover.

Watching her move, Malloy realised she had been hit. She took cover at the centre of the lot and then moved on whilst Ethan unloaded his .45 at the roof. Malloy used the cover to check on Ohlendorf. The lawyer was dead. He scrambled toward the front of the car and found Josh Sutter down, breathing hard, and obviously scared.

'I'm hit,' he said.

Kate ran over the boot and across the rooftop of a sports car. She jumped for a piece of gothic trim some twelve feet off the ground and caught a ridge of stone in both hands as her boots slammed into the plaster wall. Above the trim the building offered blocks all the way to the roof. The only problem was that her wound was hot. The pain was starting to drain her strength. She got her fingers over the ridge of the first block and pulled herself up toward the next as she got her feet on the trim.

Whatever nausea she had felt clawing at her she forced away with sheer rage. She reached higher, settling her fingers into a mortar joint between two large stones. She brought her good leg up until she had settled her toe into another mortar joint and grabbed for the next block. She pushed herself up quickly. Chernoff was not going to stick around for the police to catch her, and Kate didn't care to give her another chance at them. Just under the roof, she reached back and grabbed the guttering. This kind of stuff was notoriously fragile. It could sag or break without warning. Still, she had no choice. She had to trust it or retreat. She pulled down hard. It seemed solid enough. The Germans were good about keeping things repaired even in a city's red light district. At least that was what she told herself as she swung out from the wall and dangled for a moment some twenty metres over the pavement.

The guttering groaned but it held. She snatched her heavy combat knife from her boot and took it into her teeth. Now she pulled her chin up to the edge of the guttering and held herself with one hand. Taking the knife she slashed it down through the tiled roof and anchored it into a solid piece of heavy plywood.

Four storeys below, she heard police sirens closing in from various points in the district. Using the knife, Kate pulled herself up across the guttering and then scrambled to her feet. She got her NVGs into place and pulled her .45, but Chernoff, as she had expected, had already retreated from the rooftop.

'T. K.?' Ethan asked.

'Josh is hit.'

'How bad?'

'He's conscious.'

Ethan dropped back and found T. K. holding Josh. 'It went right through my vest!' Josh gasped. He was scared.

'It happens,' Malloy said. 'The good news is maybe it's not real deep. Can you walk?'

'I don't know.'

Malloy was pulling Josh to his feet when the first police car pulled through the larger passage – across the courtyard from their position. Its sirens were screaming, its lights whirling.

'Inside!' Malloy whispered. 'They were at the back door to *Das Sternenlicht* when a second car entered the square, following in close behind the first. Ethan snapped on his headset, calling, 'Girl!'

Kate didn't answer, and they no longer had a visual on her.

Once inside Malloy pointed at the storage room, 'Through the bar!' he told them.

Josh was hanging on to Malloy's shoulder for support but he was at least moving his legs and carrying most of his own weight. Ethan kept his .45 down as they passed in front of a thin, homely dancer. Two men were in the audience. Another stood behind the bar. They all watched as Malloy and Josh struggled across the floor, but no one said a word or reached for a phone. When they got outside again, Ethan saw a police car slipping into the narrow passageway – sealing off the courtyard. 'Girl!' he said.

Still no answer.

He went ahead of Josh and Malloy and stepped into the street in front of a BMW that had pulled to a stop for the sake of the police car. 'HALT!' Ethan shouted, pointing the weapon through the glass and aiming at the man's head. The driver lifted his hands. Keeping the gun on him, Ethan moved to the side of the car and shouted in German, 'OUT!'

Malloy got into the back with Josh. Ethan let the driver back off and then slid into the driver's seat. There were shouts from the sidewalks, and then the police car came back out of the courtyard passageway in reverse.

Ethan floored it and caught the back fender of the police car as it backed into the street. He clipped a parked car on the rebound and then forced his way through an opening. From the back Malloy was talking almost conversationally. 'They've still got a visual, but no one is following yet.'

Ethan took a couple of fast turns.

'Looking good!' Malloy told him

Looking good, Ethan decided, meant they had about a ten second lead. He slammed on the brakes and skidded into the next side street – still free of cops. He saw what he wanted halfway down the block, a twenty year old Mercedes that looked well-tended. The older Mercedes models had less plastic and more steel – ramming power in other words.

Ethan shot the driver's window out and brought his combat knife under the dash as he rolled into the car. Malloy and Josh washed into the back seat slowly enough that by the time they were in and had the door closed behind them Ethan had brought the engine to life and was pulling away from the kerb.

'Still clear!' Malloy said, the tone of his voice edging up with excitement. They were almost out.

Ethan took the first right and met a police car coming down the road without sirens. He pulled politely to the kerb and watched the car go on. A moment later he hit it hard. Three, four, five seconds. . . 'Clear!' T. K. told him.

He turned again, slowing down to a legal speed.

'Are we still good?'

'We're good!'

Ethan tried to get his bearings. They were still in the district, but at the moment they were alone. *Alone* wasn't good. They needed to lose themselves in traffic. Otherwise a cop was going to make them.

'We need to get Josh to a hospital,' Malloy said.

'No!' Josh shouted. He didn't sound delirious, just frightened.

'I can't tell how bad it is,' Malloy answered.

'Doesn't matter. If I go to a hospital, I'll end up in prison.'

'At least you'll be alive,' Ethan told him. He decided he knew where he was and turned into a new street. Still at a legal speed he was starting to think – to hope, at least – that they had made it out.

'I'm begging you guys, no hospitals!'

'You could be bleeding to death,' Malloy told him, 'and I wouldn't know it!'

'I don't care! I don't want to go to prison – not here! I can't even speak the language!'

Kate found the roof access door locked and shot her way through it. She stepped into an enclosed stairwell carrying her .45 with both hands, her Kalashnikov still under her slicker. She kept her back braced against a brick wall and moved down the stairway carefully. Her thigh was aching from the sniper shot. She could feel blood running down her leg.

She stopped at the bottom of the stairs and pulled off her jacket, weapon, armour and blouse. She dropped her pants and took a look at the wound. The bullet had passed through. Her leg was trembling uncontrollably and blood ran steadily from the wound. Using her knife she cut thick ribbons of cloth from her blouse and began tying off the wound. The cloth turned red, and she wrapped another band around it. It too went red. She felt nausea creeping up in her throat again. She needed to quit moving or she was going to lose too much blood. She needed to get someplace safe and quiet. The trouble was if she stopped moving she was going to get caught. Move or die, she told herself, and thought back to the Eiger. Move or die. Kate put her armour back on, strapped her Kalashnikov back in place and then slipped on her jacket. She pocketed her NVGs and opened the door at the bottom of the stairs – again with her gun.

She stepped into the hallway of what looked like a hotbed hotel and saw a man running toward her – he had heard her silenced weapon. He was obviously freelance security and his gun was out, but it was not pointing at her, and when she levelled her weapon on him, he stopped. He looked like he wanted to bring his gun up, but a half second of hesitation took his chances away and he dropped the gun.

'Phone?' she asked.

He reached slowly into his shirt pocket and brought a phone

out. 'Back away,' she told him. He did as she said. Holding her weapon on him, Kate holstered his gun and crushed the cell phone under her boot. Then she went down the hall to yet another stairwell. She shot through this lock and exited into the back of an adult bookstore, finding as she did Chernoff's rifle and armour. Kate looked for Chernoff as she came toward the front of the shop, but she saw only men in the aisles.

Some of them watched her when they saw her gun, but it was the district, and not much seemed to surprise them. At the front door she stripped the security guard's weapon and tossed it. Then she limped across the sidewalk and into the street.

She looked both ways, but Helena Chernoff was gone.

'Move!' Chernoff whispered as she slipped into Carlisle's rental. Carlisle hit the gear selector and pulled forward but the traffic stopped him before he could make the turn. As he waited he risked a glance in the mirror and saw the figure of a woman limp into the street. He looked at Chernoff and saw her watching the woman with peculiar interest.

'Trouble?' he asked.

Chernoff watched her mirror until he was through the turn. 'Kate Brand got out.'

'How?'

'She climbed up the side of the building, David!'

Carlisle swore and then he laughed.

'What are you laughing at? She and her husband nearly killed me.'

'What about the others.'

'They were all down when I left – including my team. If they are not dead, they are going to be under arrest.'

'What about Malloy?'

'I hit him, but if he was wearing armour. . .'

'He needs to be eliminated. Don't you have someone on the police force who can get to him?'

'I have access to a detective in one of the intelligence units, but he's not going to want to commit murder.'

'Everyone has a price.'

Chernoff glanced at Carlisle and then turned her attention back to the street. 'I'll see what I can do. What about the Brands? How do you want to handle them?'

'I'll deal with them once I get back from New York.'

Ethan turned into yet another broad well-lit street, but the traffic he was seeking was slowing down. 'Roadblock!' Malloy called.

Ethan apparently saw the cops up ahead at the same moment and turned a one-eighty. Driving with only one hand on the wheel, he lost control and fish-tailed into a line of parked cars but got moving at once. Malloy watched the cops at the blockade running for their cars. Ethan got two blocks and most of another before they were moving.

'We can still lose them!' Malloy said.

Ethan took a hard right and then an immediate left. They were heading north along side streets again but it was getting late: traffic was too light to give them any cover. Ethan turned randomly and then again, and for a moment it seemed they had actually lost the two chase cars. 'Did you hurt your arm?' Malloy asked.

'I took a round just behind my wrist.'

How bad is it?'

'Broke the bone.'

Turning at the next block again, they could hear more sirens but still saw nothing. Ethan held the steering wheel with his knees, and reached inside his slicker. He tossed his phone over the seat. 'It's Girl!' he said.

'This is T. K.'

'Where's Boy?' Kate asked.

'Boy is a little busy driving at the moment.'

'You're in trouble?'

'Another minute or two, I'd say the cops are going to box us in.'

'Where are you?' Kate asked.

'Hard to know for sure, but probably due west of the Aussenalster somewhere.' He looked out the back window and saw a cop car pull into the street six blocks behind them. The cops had a visual again. He saw Ethan's eyes fix on the mirror. No need to tell him.

'If you're at the lake, you can't be far from the U.S. Consulate.'

'I can't get them involved in a hot pursuit.'

'You're going to have to!'

'We'd never get past the front gate.'

'What about the people coming in from Berlin?'

'They're still a good two-to-three hours away.'

'That will work. I want you to get to the Stadtpark and take cover. Can you do that?'

'They'll come right in behind us.'

'Not if you use your guns.'

'I'm not going to shoot police officers.'

'They don't know that,' Kate told him. 'Just hold them off a couple of hours.'

'Then what?'

'Then pray I can get the three of you out!'

'The Stadtpark,' Malloy said, as he handed the phone back to Ethan.

'We're going to have to cross a bridge to do that,' Ethan told him.

'They can't block them all.'

'Are you sure about that?'

A police car pulled into the road ahead of them and parked broadside before them. With two chasing them, they were trapped.

'Hang on!' Ethan called.

He hit the brakes and snapped the steering wheel to the left. This caused the Mercedes' passenger side to skid broadside into the police car. There was a heavy, hollow explosion of metal on metal. Malloy felt himself slammed against the door. He saw the cops almost next to him tossed about like crash dummies.

Josh screamed. There was breaking glass and then both cars were spinning. Ethan was still working the steering wheel. The Mercedes finished a ragged pirouette through the intersection and took off again. 'Everybody okay?' he called.

Malloy looked back. The chase cars were tangled up with the car Ethan had hit. He looked down at Josh, and saw him wide-eyed. 'I'm missing a show, aren't I?'

'We're fine back here!' Malloy answered. 'When we get to the park,' Malloy told Ethan, 'Girl says we need to take cover and hold the police off for a couple of hours. Is that going to be a problem?'

'Probably, but I guess we can try. Josh,' he added, 'I don't want to tell you what to do, buddy, but you might be better off just staying in the car when we bail. Let the cops pick you up and get you to a hospital.'

Tears came to the agent's eyes and he rocked his head. 'He's coming with us.' Malloy answered.

'I just meant—'

'No debate. He goes until he can't go any farther.'

'Okay. But when I stop the car, you've got to get to your feet on your own. If you can't stand up, we're gone.'

'I can stand up!'

Malloy looked at the city buildings flashing by. They had to be getting close to the park. He looked back. A car was three blocks back, but they were just following at this point. That meant they had called ahead to set up a roadblock they couldn't break through.

They crossed the Alster on one of a dozen or so of its bridges, going airborne in the process. Ethan had already turned off his headlights and was driving with NVGs. Malloy guessed by the noise some six-to-eight units were in direct pursuit, including two units coming up the eastern bank of the river and almost closing them off at the bridge. Ethan dodged an oncoming police van and then burst through a decorative metal fence that was placed at the Stadtpark entrance. He stayed on a wide dirt footpath, twisting through several ninety degree turns until he saw a large expanse of grass stretching out for a couple of hundred metres. The field ended with a stand of trees. 'The Alamo, guys!'

Saying this, Ethan cut off the footpath and raced directly across the meadow. When they were almost at the tree line, he made a hard right, skidding broadside and coming to a stop close to the trees. The Mercedes provided good cover as the three of them spilled out of the driver's side of the car. Ethan grabbed Josh and hoisted him over his shoulder. 'Lay down some cover!' he shouted.

Malloy did as he was told, taking refuge behind the front wheel of the Mercedes and firing a full clip. The effect of the automatic fire was immediate. The police cars turned broadside, forming a line some eighty metres out from the trees. As they did, Malloy slapped his reserve clip into the AKS-74 and dropped back. He heard some pistols, but the police were out of range for most handguns to have any effect.

After he had settled down beside Ethan and Josh, Malloy watched the next wave of cops driving along the borders of the park, presumably with the idea of closing down the perimeter. Once that was achieved, he thought that they would settle down in a defensive posture and wait for their SWAT teams to lay siege inside the park.

'You two stay here,' Ethan whispered. 'I need to take a look around. I should be back in about ten-to-fifteen minutes.'

As Ethan left at a full sprint across the next open meadow there was a moment when Malloy thought his friend wasn't coming back. Well, why should he? If he ran like that, he just might get out before the police had secured the area. Malloy looked down at Josh. Like it or not, Josh was going to jail. They both were. 'How are you doing?' he asked.

'I feel like someone hit me in the chest with a hammer and then threw me in a cement mixer.'

'First time taking a round?'

'Yeah. Have you ever been hit?'

'I took a few in the chest my rookie year in the field.'

'Sounds fun.'

'Mostly educational.'

'Yeah? What did you learn?'

'The only thing worse than pain is no pain at all. No pain means it's over.'

'In that case, I expect I'm going to live forever.'

'Hold that thought.'

After a minute or so of listening to the gathering sirens on all sides, Josh breathed hard, like he wanted to laugh. 'Boy took off, didn't he?'

Malloy looked across the meadow to their rear and felt the tightness in his chest letting go. No more secrets. 'If he's smart he did.'

'I should have stayed in the car. I mean, you had a chance without me. All I could think about was. . .'

'They don't have us yet, Josh.'

'They've got us, T. K. At this point. . . it's just a matter of time.' When Malloy didn't answer, he asked, 'You married?'

Thinking about Gwen, Malloy felt his eyes burn. 'Yeah.' How was Gwen going to handle this? Three, five years in prison. . .

'Kids?'

'I've got a grown daughter I don't get along with.'

'That's tough.'

'When I see her, it is.'

'I've got three girls and a wife who mean the world to me, T. K.'

'Listen, Josh, what Boy said about their charging us with murder probably isn't right. I mean they're going to throw that at you, but just for leverage to get you to talk. They're going to want to know about Dale and me. I want you to play dumb until you can get a lawyer – an American Embassy lawyer out of Berlin. Once you've got representation and can negotiate a plea you can handle, tell them everything you know. Don't hold anything back. Right now, we haven't hurt any cops and you weren't involved with kidnapping the man in the safe house. I'll tell them the same thing. That will get you maybe three-to-five.'

Josh Sutter seemed to calculate this new information. They were both coming to terms with surrender. 'Three years is a long time, T. K.'

'It's not as long as twenty.'

'Three years. . . a man can lose his family in that time. As far as my job is concerned, the bureau is going to cut me loose the minute they figure out I'm in the middle of this thing.'

'So you start over. Reconnect with the kids. Make peace with the ex-wife. Get a job and do what you want. Three years isn't the end of the world.'

'You think Jim made it?'

'I don't know, Josh.'

'Maybe they'd let Jim and me be cellmates. I mean so I'd have someone I could talk to. Kind of funny, if you think about it, giving a couple of FBI agents a cell together.'

Eighteen minutes after he left them Ethan returned. He was breathing hard – like a boxer in the last rounds. 'Come on!' he said, and took Josh Sutter up over his shoulder.

'Where are we going?' Malloy asked.

'I've found some decent cover for the two of you. Should keep you safe, at least until daylight.'

'So what's the plan?'

'I'll tell you when we get there.'

The spot Ethan had found required them to retreat from the tree line and cross a second meadow. After that, they followed a park road until they came to a sprawling rhododendron bush. He took a minute to cover their faces and hands with mud, exactly as he had done to his own face, and then helped them scoot under the heavy branches. At that point he swept leaves around them. Unless a patrol came wading into the bush they might stay safe for an hour or so – at least until sunrise.

'Kate wants your Berlin people to meet us east of the E22 –

on the road leading north out of Hoisburg. Can you get them to do that?'

'Sure. Where's Hoisburg?'

'As close as she could tell, the middle of nowhere. We should be there around sun-up – give or take an hour. If we're later than that, we're not going to make it.'

'How are we getting there?'

'Just get *them* there; Kate will take care of the rest.'

Malloy called Jane, checking his watch as he waited for her to answer. It was three-thirty in Hamburg, only nine-thirty in the evening in Langley.

'Yes?' she said.

'Where are the Berlin people?'

'They're on the road. Why?'

Malloy gave her the instructions Ethan had given him. 'We're going to be bringing some wounded with us.'

'What happened?'

'Ambush.'

'I'll get a medical chopper moving.'

'Put them a couple of hours south of the extraction point. If the Germans even think medics are coming for us, we're done.'

'The police are after you?'

'Only a few hundred.'

'Great.'

'I'm going black for a couple of hours, Jane. I'll call you when I can.'

'How bad are the wounded, T. K.?'

'A couple are ambulatory. The other has a chest wound. It's not deep, I don't think, but it could be serious if we don't get it treated.'

'I'm here when you need me.'

Malloy disconnected and looked at Ethan. 'They'll be there.'

Ethan took Josh Sutter's NVGs. 'Keep your headset turned off until five-thirty,' he told Malloy. 'You're going to need to save the batteries.'

Chapter Eight

Ussat-les-Bains, France
Fall 1932.

The affair lasted three weeks. In all that time it seemed to Rahn he was hardly ever away from Elise. That was not true, of course, but it seemed so because his thoughts never left her. Nothing but Elise mattered. They did not talk about the future. They lived either in the perfect present or the long-ago-past. As in their letters that previous winter, Bachman's name never came between them. They spent hours in melancholy adoration of one another. They drove into the mountains. They waded in cold streams. They explored the Sabarthès caves hand-in-hand. Everywhere they went, whether above or below the earth, they found some secret and quiet place to call their own. They kissed. They made love. He slept in her bed at night, coming late to it and then crawling out before dawn – lest the guests whisper. They would meet again a couple of hours later at breakfast. Over bread and jam and coffee they planned an excursion each day.

When they spoke it was always in praise of the moment. Had either of them ever been truly alive before this? Why did food taste so good? Was there any emotion equal to the feeling they got just by seeing one another? It was the stuff of newly-weds, the eternal language of lovers who never imagined something like this could happen and feel so perfectly wonderful. . .

Their only regret was not succumbing to their desires sooner. Sometimes in their moments of silence they would imagine the other was thinking about the coming storm, but neither admitted to such things. What were you thinking just now? How happy I am. Here. Now. Is it really true? Are you really, truly happy with me? Only kisses could answer such questions. Only lovers could be so blind to the inevitable.

When Bachman returned from Berchtesgaden he flew as far as Carcassonne and hired a driver to take him the rest of the way. It was a long day of travel, and he came into the village after dark. From the front lobby of the hotel, entering as stealthily as a thief, he saw them together at the bar quietly staring at one another. Bachman did not have to look at the bartender, whom he had paid to keep watch. He saw the truth in the flush of shame that washed over Rahn's face. He saw it too in his wife's fading smile.

Bachman's dark eyes shifted back to Rahn in accusation. *He* was to blame! Rahn sat frozen beside Elise, and Bachman knew it had been going on from the moment he had left. They had wanted only the opportunity and could not wait until he was down the road before they had turned him into a cuckold!

He thought he ought to kill them both. He might actually have done just that if he had been armed. As it was, he simply collected himself – his rage and humiliation – and he went up to his room. He got control of his passions. *He* could still manage such a feat! He felt a smile tearing out of him, cold, cruel and full of wise irony. This was what he had expected of them, of course! All the talk about purity, a perfect sham! How then could they disappoint him with their behaviour? He knew from the start this would happen! They wanted only opportunity! Where then was the betrayal if one never trusted?

Elise followed her husband to their room without a word to Rahn. In the morning, their bags packed, they left the hotel without explanation. Rahn watched them from his tiny, grim office to see how she behaved. Bachman did not seem to force her to go with him. Elise went willingly. She certainly gave no long, last look at *Des Marronniers*, not even a casual glance at the quaint village of Ussat-les-Bains, which she had told him only a week ago she loved because it was theirs. She waited for her husband to open her door. She watched the dirt at her feet. She climbed into the Mercedes and she studied her knees. As they drove away, the dust covered the road within a few seconds and seemed to erase the car from the landscape.

The days after Elise had gone were almost impossible to endure. He longed for the courage to kill himself. Later, trying to recall those first days of her absence, he remembered nothing at all. He might as well have died for a time. Almost a fortnight after they had gone and were surely back in Berlin, Rahn thought he must write some kind of letter, if only to explain. He got no further than dating the page. They had no future. Elise had made her choice. Besides, if he were foolish enough to write her what could he possibly say? What words had ever changed the past?

Michelstadt, Germany
January 1933.

At the end of the season, only a few weeks after Bachman and Elise had left, Rahn closed *Des Marronniers* and, with the last of the receipts in hand, headed back to Germany. He left a number of unpaid accounts in his wake but he did not care. He had no intention of ever returning.

He knew he could still pick up work at a commercial school teaching languages, but it was hardly a career and he was sick to death of the work. He wanted. . . he did not know what he wanted. So he went home. His parents could see the change in him almost at once. They worried but kept quiet for a time. Finally his father reached his limit after a few sullen weeks and announced to his son, 'You are almost thirty years old, Otto! What are you planning to do with your life?' So full of dreams and ambition only a year ago, he could only manage to say that he did not know. 'Tell me that you do not intend wasting your life chasing after buried treasure!'

'I'm finished with that.'

'I should hope so! In the real world, son, men *earn* their fortunes. They do not dig them up!'

'I know.' And it was true. If nothing else, this much he had learned.

One morning a few days later, he sat down and began writing. He could not have said what motivated him, certainly not his father's remarks, but later Rahn would understand that loss and emptiness had stirred within him the impulse to celebrate a doomed world in the last days before a war came that destroyed it forever. He started with a description of the sky one saw in the south of France – a blue that he had only ever seen above the Pyrenees. A page later he was simply writing.

He wrote for long hours at a time, fussing with his notes and research later. He wrote not like the trained scholar that he was but as a poet. There were sources and citations, of course. This was not a fantasy of a world that had never been, but it was not quite the dry stuff of history either. It was full of passion, his style a synthesis of history, poetry, and outraged narrative. He called his book *The Crusade Against the Grail* without ever saying what he thought the Grail was. He spent no time speculating about buried treasure or the fate of the Grail – these matters were for writers who had not spent the hard hours it took to learn the truth. He painted instead intimate portraits of the aristocracy, their love affairs, the political intrigue, the economic conditions of the regions, and the heroic enlightenment that had blessed the land of the Cathars above all the rest of Europe at that time. He talked about faith and love, and about knights who wrote poetry. He described a world in which Jews were not only allowed to live freely but in which they taught Christian children and no one thought it strange. He talked about women who were priests and love affairs that were never consummated.

He described the contours of the land, the infinite caves

beneath the Sabarthès range, and of course all the castles whose ruins still dotted the rugged landscape of southern France. He described the Blood Lance that he had seen painted in the *Grotto de Lombrives*, but he made no wild claims about it, not even a theory linking it to courtly love and the forever-potent desire of the spirit that it seemed to represent. He painted the world he loved in the last hours that it still breathed and, though it had all passed away centuries ago when the last fortress fell, it seemed to him that he wrote an autobiography.

Paris
1934-35.

It took less than a year between those first magic words pouring across the page and the printing of his book. As he had hoped, the book gathered some critical interest. His style was original. The depth of his knowledge was beyond anything ever written about the Cathars. Of course the proceeds hardly paid for the years on the ground Rahn had spent learning his subject, but that was to be expected. A book like this paid in other ways.

After finishing the manuscript and while he was still trying to sell the thing, Rahn went back to teaching in commercial language schools. He got some paying work as a translator and even flirted with the movies, writing the script for one of the new talkies in Berlin, working as a bit actor in another. With the publication of the book he began to aspire to greater things. He was only thirty. His life was still before him. He had always dreamed of becoming a literary critic at some point, but his years of tramping through the Pyrenees had not put him in the right circles. Good reviews and modest sales had not the force to pull him out of obscurity.

In the spring of 1935, caught up in preparing the French edition of the book whilst living in Paris for a few months, Rahn received an envelope with a Berlin postmark at his hotel one evening. Opening it he found a good deal of cash and a letter offering to promote his career if he would only come to 7 Prinz Albrechtstrasse in Berlin.

In their loneliest hours writers fall victim to every fantasy. They believe as a creed of faith the book they are working on will change everything. Personal grudges, moral failings, physical deficiencies: these will fade when the imagined book becomes a reality. When life goes forward in the same mindless crush as before, it comes as something of a shock. Quite incredibly the book is forgotten, copies go unsold, and no one speaks of what has taken years to achieve. The author then takes solace in some newspaper critic's random praise and nurses his bruised spirit with hopes that the book, though lost in its own time, might yet be recognised in a future age.

But cash in an envelope and an anonymous letter from a fan who promises to promote one's career? This was something even his boldest fantasy could not have conjured! Rahn laughed, pocketed the Reichsmarks, and tossed the letter aside. He had work to do! The French edition, which he had translated himself, was important – a second chance really. Had it not been for the money in the envelope, he would have written it off as a friend's idea of a joke. But the cash was very real. He told himself it was no doubt a madman or a homosexual. He picked the letter up again before he went to sleep that evening. He looked at it once more the following morning. It was written on fine stationery and the penmanship indicated good breeding. Though too brief to show very much, he thought the language was carefully chosen, even eloquent. So not mad. Probably a homosexual, or possibly. . . a patron. Did such beings really exist in modern times?

Berlin, Germany
Summer 1935.

Rahn had planned to visit Berlin again later that summer anyway. It would not hurt to go to the address and see what the anonymous letter writer had in mind. In the worst case, he could simply tell the fellow he was not interested!

He settled in an inexpensive pension and proceeded to 7 Prinz Albrechtstrasse, which turned out to be a government building. Rahn nearly turned away, quite certain now the letter was a hoax from a university chum with a great deal of money and a very lousy sense of humour, but then he thought no one sends enough money for one to travel from Paris to Berlin as a joke. On the off chance there might be some confusion about the address, some detail he was missing, he went inside and made enquiry.

The uniformed sergeant at the front desk greeted him without excitement, but his expression changed once Rahn had identified himself and presented the letter. He begged *Doctor* Rahn to be patient. Following a hurried, whispered phone call that left Rahn frankly uneasy, a military officer appeared.

'You will follow me, Doctor Rahn!' he announced.

It was almost the tone of a policeman preparing to make an arrest and, despite his pleasure at being addressed in the most flattering manner possible, Rahn endured a moment of regret. What had he got himself into?

'I wonder,' he said to the officer's back, 'if you might tell me—?'

'This way, please!' Apparently the young man had been instructed to explain nothing.

They walked through several hallways and came to an elevator where a corporal stood guard. Inside the elevator, still with his escort, Rahn examined the uniform. He thought it very handsome, very modern. The ancient runic script of SS on the collar was especially appealing. He knew of course the letters stood for *Schutzstaffel* – Security Division – and that what had once been a small faction within the military wing of the Nazi party had grown into a powerful organisation in its own right. Tasked originally with the Führer's security, the SS had now become very much like the Praetorian Guard that had served the emperors of ancient Rome – a force of elite soldiers who answered directly to the emperor. In the days of the

Roman Empire, the commander of the Praetorian Guard was the second most powerful man in the Empire, and it seemed that the commander of the SS, a young man named Heinrich Himmler, was on course to achieve pretty much the same status. On the young officer's finger Rahn saw a ring with a skull in the centre. He had seen the same distinct ring on the finger of a civilian on the train coming into Berlin. 'That is very interesting ring you have,' he offered congenially.

This got him an uninterested thank you, nothing more, and Rahn contented himself with staring at the elevator door until it opened. 'This way Doctor. . .'

The officer knocked at an office door and a voice called from inside. 'Enter!'

The young man opened the door, saluted a civilian who was sitting at a large desk, and announced that Doctor Rahn was waiting to see the Reichsführer. The man nearly jumped up, went around his desk hurriedly, and knocked on another door. Soon Heinrich Himmler appeared.

Rahn, recognising Himmler on sight, was flummoxed. He had thought. . . well, he had not thought one of the most powerful men in Germany wanted to promote his career! Himmler was in his mid-thirties, only three or four years older than Rahn. He had dark hair and though he was quite thin he seemed to be an energetic man. He had a peculiarly small chin and eyes set a bit close together, but he nevertheless made a good impression. He was educated and articulate, for one thing. For another, one could see from his manners he had been born to the aristocracy. What Rahn was not prepared for was Himmler's enthusiasm for *The Crusade Against the Grail*. Rahn's visit was unaccountably important to him, and he let Doctor Rahn know it in many ways. In fact, Rahn hardly knew what had hit him. One moment he was being led through a labyrinth of government hallways wondering if he might be under arrest. In the next he was listening to Heinrich Himmler tell him he had written the greatest book of the twentieth century! And Himmler *had* read the book. He was not eager to show off his knowledge before an expert, of course, but his questions showed a certain degree of understanding and background.

They spoke for nearly three quarters of an hour, Himmler seemingly having nothing better to do but pass his time chatting about the Cathars. Finally he broached the subject of Rahn's career. As he understood it, Dr Rahn had been forced to work at various part-time jobs in order to support his writing. Was that the case? Rahn admitted that his publisher's advance had been modest, as were the sales.

'But you are interested in pursuing a career as a writer and historian?' Himmler asked.

'I'm *interested*. Whether I am going to be able to do so is another question.'

Himmler smiled. 'What if I were to put you on my personal staff at, say, a captain's salary? I could give you an office and secretary as well. Would you be interested in such an arrangement?'

'I would be very interested. Of course I would want to know the nature of my duties. . .'

'That is the point, Dr Rahn! You would have no duties other than to pursue whatever research you wanted.' At Rahn's look of disbelief, he added, 'In addition to an office and secretary, I can provide research assistants as you need them, and, depending on the nature of the projects you decide to develop, ample funds for travel and research – even expeditions if you should care to lead any.

Rahn fought down his excitement but could not quite stop himself from asking, 'Are you serious?'

Himmler smiled. He was very serious.

Stadtpark, Hamburg
Sunday March 9, 2008.

The first armoured squads entered the park less than an hour after the police had established a perimeter. They wore night vision goggles and moved with military precision. Ethan, who had been running between various lookout points, opened light fire at the flanks of the squad and then sprinted to a position across the park where there was a marsh. Finding a second team staging at the perimeter some two hundred metres distant, he laid down a burst around them, hitting lights and steel mostly.

At a third staging area, he popped a couple more headlights and then pulled back toward the centre of the park, where the tallest trees stood.

'What is he doing?' Josh Sutter asked when he heard the gunshots.

Malloy didn't know, but as Ethan continued firing from different positions he said, 'Sounds like he's making them think the three of us are spread out and holding our ground.'

'What is that going to get him?'

'Time.'

'Is he one of your people, T. K.?'

'You mean is he an accountant?'

'Yeah. . . a *State Department accountant*.'

'No. He and Girl worked black ops for Dale – strictly contract work, as I understand it.'

'That Girl is a beauty, isn't she? I mean even in a flak jacket and combat gear. . . she was. . . I mean. . . if I wasn't married!'

'I take it you're feeling better?'

'Except for the cold, the pain in my chest, and the nausea, I'm doing just fine.'

A bit later Malloy said, 'I just remembered I turned fifty at midnight.'

Josh Sutter laughed quietly, but it took some effort. 'Man! And I thought *I* had it bad with a bullet in my chest!'

'You know Patton was fifty-six at the start of World War II? They say that old bastard couldn't wait to get over here for the fight.'

'They made the men tough back then, I guess.'

'They sure did.'

'You think Patton was ever scared, T. K.?'

'Everybody gets scared, Josh. Even old Blood and Guts.'

'When I'm fifty. . .'

'What?'

'I was going to say I don't want to be doing things like this, but the truth is I just might turn fifty in prison. That's like. . . twelve years from now.' He was quiet for a moment. 'Looked at that way,' he whispered, 'being out in the field at fifty and getting shot at. . . well, it looks pretty darn good.'

'Don't tell me you are actually looking forward to a desk job when you're fifty?'

'You can't tell me you *like* this?'

'Not *this* exactly, but. . . I don't know. Even this beats pushing paper while the kids are out in the streets having all the fun.'

'First time we met you, you know what Jim said? He said, "Accountants! I never met one yet that wasn't just balls-out-crazy."'

All three probe teams were deep inside the park by five. Within the next twenty minutes they had two helicopters hovering over the area and had doubled their number on the ground. Instead of running or burrowing as he gave ground Ethan went up. He heard two squads pass under him but could no longer watch them. The batteries on both NVGs were dead. A helicopter hovered for a few seconds over his position, casting its light about, even crossing over him once, but they were looking to the ground, not the treetops. A couple of seconds later, it moved on.

By six, the sun still thirty minutes or so away, the police had overrun the park. Ethan could hear the bark of the radio chatter and sensed a growing frustration, the gnawing fear that they had somehow let their prey escape.

*

A patrol walked along the narrow road next to Malloy's and Josh Sutter's position four different times in the last hour of the night. After the last of these passed, Malloy clicked on his headset, as per instruction, and heard Ethan's steady breathing. 'How are we doing?' he whispered.

Ethan didn't answer, but Malloy heard a single tap.'

'Can't talk?'

Two taps – no.

Twenty minutes later Ethan said, 'You're going to have to move in exactly two minutes. Head due north across the road and through the trees. Kate will pick us up in the meadow in three minutes.'

With another patrol approaching, Malloy thought better than to speak. He tapped once. Message received. He counted to sixty and then covered Josh Sutter's mouth, stirring him from his restive sleep. 'We're going to make a run for it.'

'I can't, T. K. I'm done.'

'Don't make me carry you, Josh. Remember, I'm an old man.'

'T. K., I can't do it.'

They heard the patrol leader say something. One of the squad ran toward them quickly. Malloy kept his hand on his Kalashnikov and prayed he would not have to use it. The squad leader called out, 'Check under those bushes!'

Malloy flipped off the safety and was about to roll free of the branches when a grenade exploded on the far side of the park. Seconds later a report came over the radio. 'All units to. . .'

Another grenade and then a third blew, each in a different sector. The entire squad took off at a sprint – following the sound of the closest grenade – and Malloy dragged Josh from under the heavy branches of the rhododendron bush. 'Come on!' he whispered, pulling the younger man to his feet. 'Don't quit on me now!'

Kate brought the Bonanza A36 in from the west at a speed of just under one hundred-fifty knots. When she had cleared the last stand of trees bordering the park and was sure she was heading precisely on the coordinates Ethan had given her, she lowered the flaps and wheels simultaneously. The effect was like putting on brakes. She watched the needle of the VSI plummet, and then for a moment she simply floated above the dark earth, getting her bearings with her NVGs. She hit the ground hard, bounced higher than she thought she would, adjusted the flaps, and came down solidly this time. She was running fast now, the ground relatively flat and even. She saw a squad of police moving toward her from the tree line on her right. They shone a light on her, but no one gave the command to open fire.

Whilst the plane was still moving, Kate brought the tail around, performing a bouncing half-pirouette and started back along the same track.

Ethan caught up with Josh and Malloy just as they crossed the road and broke into the meadow. Tossing his Kalashnikov aside, he scooped Josh over his shoulder and started toward the plane. A shot was fired from beyond the plane, but it was a handgun and wasn't quite in range. Kate pulled forward with a spurt of speed and then slowed the plane so as to give him cover.

A spotlight danced over him as a couple more handguns barked. Malloy, trailing a few steps behind, began squeezing off single rounds from his Kalashnikov. Once Ethan got Josh into the plane and then jumped in after him, Kate hit the throttle. Malloy tossed his weapon aside and started running. He heard shots in the distance from larger guns. The bullets zipped past him with a crack. Then a round hit his back. He stumbled and nearly went down. He heard more shots from other points. Kate was running out of space and was going to have to accelerate if she wanted to clear the trees at the end of the meadow. Before she did, Malloy gave one last desperate kick. Closing in on the moving plane, he dived through the open door and caught Ethan's outstretched hand. Ethan gave a scream of pain, but his grip never slackened. Three rounds tapped the fuselage and then Ethan shouted, 'He's in!'

Kate hit the throttle hard. At sixty knots the nose lifted and the gunshots suddenly stopped. No one wanted to shoot down a plane inside the city. A grove of trees loomed in the fore-ground. Malloy grabbed hold of one of the seats trying to get some kind of anchor and watched the dark branches waving before them as the plane tipped higher. The RPMs redlined as the engine screamed. They brushed the topmost branches and heard the clang of wood on metal, and then the plane banked to the north with the two police helicopters in pursuit.

Malloy, feeling the first bit of relief, looked at Ethan. 'How did you get those grenades to go off on the other side of the park?'

'I was up in a tree about sixty feet and just gave them a toss in different directions.'

'And you got down and caught up with us?'

'You two weren't exactly breaking any land speed records.'

'Just fast enough,' Malloy told him.

When they had lost the helicopters chasing them Kate turned on the lights and Malloy got his first look at Josh Sutter, who looked closer to death than he had imagined as they lay together in the dark.

'How are you feeling?' he asked.

'Like a free man.'

'You know what? You look like a free man.' He ripped the armour free and took a look at the wound. The bullet had broken bone and there was plenty of swelling. He prodded the wound tenderly and got a cry of pain for his trouble.

'I think I can feel the bullet.' That was the good news. The bad news was that the slug had probably fragmented – so there could be quite a bit of internal bleeding in the heart or lungs. He tried listening to Sutter's lungs, but the roar of the plane and his own thumping pulse made it impossible.

'How is the breathing?' he asked Josh.

'About like it was all night. Hard to get a good breath, but that's just the pain.' Maybe it was the pain and maybe his lungs had filled with blood.

'We have any medical supplies?' he shouted to Kate.

'How about some water! Do we have any water?' Ethan asked.

'There's a case of bottled water in the back!' Kate shouted. 'Medical supplies are up here.'

Malloy got water for Josh and Ethan, and then went to the co-pilot's seat, taking Kate a bottle. She thanked him for the water and then asked if it was a long night. 'Probably the longest of my life,' he said. 'Well, maybe getting shot in Beirut was longer, but I don't remember it. I was out for about forty-eight hours.'

'From what Ethan said I wasn't sure if I was going to be picking up two or three of you this morning.'

'Josh is not home yet.' He looked at the horizon.

'We lost them,' she said, as if reading his thoughts. She was running just over the treetops and city buildings, the sky still dark.

'So where is Hoisburg exactly?'

'About ten minutes east of here.'

Malloy checked the skyline again. Ten minutes was good. In twenty the police would be giving chase with planes.

'I'm going to see what I can do for Josh.'

Malloy took what passed for a first aid kit back to Josh, but all he could do was clean the wound and bandage it. He needed antibiotics and there weren't any in the kit. Finishing with Josh, he looked under the makeshift bandage above Ethan's wrist and whistled.

'At least the bullet went through,' Ethan told him.

He showed Malloy the exit wound, but it wasn't clean. 'I'm guessing you've still got fragments in there,' Malloy told him. After he had wiped down the area with alcohol and then bandaged it, he went back to the cockpit and settled in beside Kate. With the plane skimming just over the tree tops, the effect was disconcerting. It felt like they were going to crash.

'How's your leg?' he asked.

'How do you know about my leg?'

'I saw you limping right before you climbed up the side of that building.'

'I wrapped it.'

'Must be hurting pretty bad by now. . .'

'I've hurt worse.'

Malloy pulled out his phone and called Jane. It was just past midnight Jane's time. 'We should rendezvous in five to ten minutes,' he told her. 'We're in a plane, by the way – in case the Berlin people are wondering how we're coming in.'

'I'll let them know.'

'You have any luck getting a medical helicopter dispatched?'

'Your contact has the information.'

'We'll have three passengers for the chopper – one critical.'

'Why three?' Kate asked.

'Medical chopper for you, Ethan, and Josh. I'm going on to the Embassy in Berlin.'

'Just get us to a train, T. K. Ethan and I will take care of ourselves.'

'Maybe you ought to look at his wrist before you make that call.'

'If you can get us some antibiotics we should be fine.'

'Whatever you think is best,' he answered. He watched the tree tops slipping under them for a time, and then asked, 'When did you learn to fly?'

'Last year in France.'

'You have any trouble getting the plane?'

'I had a little trouble finding a private airfield, but I called a friend of mine I fly with and he told me where I could find one. After that, I stole a car, drove through a chain link fence and shot my way through a hangar door. By the time the night watchman woke up, I was already on the runway.'

Kate dipped one wing and buzzed two black SUVs parked on the shoulder of a country road. 'Are those your people?'

Malloy slipped on his NVGs and studied the figures. 'They look about right.'

'I hope so. I've had enough surprises for one night.'

Kate climbed to two hundred metres. Their horizon to the west was still clear, but Kate was apparently more interested in studying the road. Once she could see they had a clear runway she turned the plane in a long, descending arc and came back round, now heading toward the SUVs. The plane slowed when she lowered the wheels and then again as she extended the flaps. They dropped to within fifty metres of the road, which appeared to twist out from under them for a moment and then come back – now running straight out like a runway for nearly half-a-mile. There were some scrub trees at the side of the road, but the wingspan was only about ten metres and Kate settled the plane neatly between them. She touched down softly, braking gently at first, then more aggressively as they started closing in on the parked SUVs.

'Nice job,' Malloy told her as she pulled to a stop some ten metres short of the Americans.

The Road from Hoisburg to Uelzen, Germany
Sunday March 9, 2008.

'How can I help?' the American Embassy officer asked after shaking hands with Malloy and introducing himself as Brian Compton. He was a tall, well-built man with a military haircut and crystal blue eyes. Like the three men under his command he was packing a machine pistol and wearing armour.

Malloy gave him the address of his Neustadt hotel. 'You need to get someone to collect my computer and personal effects. If the Germans get hold of that computer, they'll know who was responsible for the trouble last night.'

'I think they already know.'

'Maybe, but they can't prove it.'

'We'll make it a priority.'

'Once the computer is secure I want one of your people to

check Sutter and me out of the Royal Meridien. The police will probably want to ask about a Mr Thomas with the State Department and Special Agent Sutter, but all your man knows is that Jim Randal got wind of something yesterday and went rogue. Thomas and Sutter reported him to their superiors and were then ordered to proceed to Ramstein at nine o'clock last night. You might want to make sure we have the flight records out of Germany to back it up, but there shouldn't be any rush on that. As far as your man knows, we are already on our way back to the States.'

'They're not going to believe a word of it,' Compton answered.

'What do you care? Your people all have diplomatic immunity, don't they?'

'Do you know the status of Dale Perry's safe house?'

'We got ambushed at the back door, plus there is a trail of blood leading right to it. I'm guessing the Germans have found it by now.'

'How about his computer?'

'I cleaned it.'

'You take anything out before you did?'

Malloy shook his head and lied out of habit. 'Didn't have time.'

'Okay,' Compton said after collecting himself. 'Not the best news, but not the worst either.' He went to the men in his command and gave them their orders. Two of them took off for Hamburg. The third got in the second SUV and waited as Compton helped Malloy get Josh Sutter out of the plane and into the van. Malloy took the front seat. Compton, who had the medical kit, climbed in the back with Ethan, Kate, and Josh Sutter.

'Agent Sutter will be getting on the helicopter. These other two have opted to find treatment elsewhere.'

Compton gave Malloy a surprised look.

'Don't ask.'

'Okay,' he said, 'let's see what we've got.'

'Agent Sutter may have some internal bleeding,' Malloy told him. 'Otherwise the wound is clean. How, I don't know, but it is. These two are the ones I'm worried about.'

Compton looked at Ethan's shoulder wound. 'Who's the surgeon?' he asked.

'She is,' Ethan said, nodding toward Kate, giving her a quick smile.

'Nice work, ma'am. You have any medical training?'

'I had a sewing class once.'

Compton's smile vanished when he unwound Ethan's bandaged wrist. 'This isn't good.' He pointed at Kate's thigh. I'm going to need to look at that too. Kate pulled her pants down and Compton cut the blood soaked blouse strips away. As he did, Compton sucked at his teeth disapprovingly. 'You two *need* to get on that chopper.'

'We *need* antibiotics,' Kate answered.

Compton searched through his bag. 'I'm equipped to treat a gunshot wound – not something like this.' He found some cephalosporin and held up the bottle. 'This,' he said, 'is good at *preventing* infection. I should give that to Agent Sutter. You two *have* infections. If you don't get help soon, you could be looking at septic shock. You do understand that is usually fatal?'

'Just clean the wounds and get us some drugs,' Kate told him.

The rendezvous with the army medics was southeast of Uelzen. Once the helicopter settled in a farmer's field Compton and his driver cradled Josh Sutter in their arms and carried him out. Malloy followed. Whilst Compton rummaged about with one of the medics for parenteral penicillin, Malloy told Josh Sutter, 'I'm going to find the people responsible, Josh.'

'Do me a favour. If you do, give me a call. I want to be there for the arrest.'

'You got it, buddy!'

When Malloy, Compton and the driver climbed back into

the SUV, Kate asked if he would mind driving them back to Uelzen. She and Ethan would take a train from there. 'We can drive you anywhere you want,' Compton told her as he passed them the penicillin and needles.

'Thanks, but we want to go to Uelzen.'

At Uelzen's gorgeous old train station Compton left his driver with them and went inside to shop for a change of clothes for Kate and Ethan. After a while the driver said he wanted to take a look around. Alone, Malloy pointed at the microphone in the overhead light, as if bragging about the technology. 'Amazing, huh? You wouldn't even see it if you didn't know it was there.'

Kate and Ethan, warned of the danger of talking, started in on technology and kept at it until the driver and Compton returned.

Compton stood outside the SUV, giving Kate and Ethan some extra room as they changed into their new clothes. When Ethan got out, he thanked Compton for the ride and shook his hand. As he walked away, Malloy climbed out of the SUV and pulled Kate away from the vehicle. Giving her the Swiss-style three kisses on her cheeks, he said, 'I'll be in Zürich tomorrow.'

'Right now I don't know where we'll be staying.'

'I'll call you.'

'No good. We're ditching the phones on the way out of town. I'll tell you what. Get in touch with Captain Marcus Steiner of the Zürich *Stadtpolizei*. I'll make sure he knows where we are.'

Malloy smiled. 'Is that your *guy*?'

'You know him?'

'He's an old friend of mine.'

'Well, *your* old friend is *my* old friend.'

'It's a small world,' he said.

'A small country at least.'

'One more thing,' he told her. 'You do understand Compton is going to try to follow you?'

Kate hadn't. Her eyes cut to Compton. 'In case some

administrator decides to turn you over to the Germans, they want to know where they can find you.'

'Would they do that?'

'Check your new clothes. He planted a tag somewhere on them or he's not really CIA.

Compton got in the backseat with Malloy and asked him where he wanted to go. 'Have you got medical facilities at the Berlin Embassy?'

'You, too?'

'I got some buckshot in my ass last night.'

'In the ass?'

'You know, it's not really as funny as it sounds.'

'We can probably take care of that.' He told the driver and then settled back tiredly. It had been a long night for him as well. After a mile or so, Compton asked, 'So what's the story on the Brit and her American boyfriend?'

'I don't really know. Dale got hold of them for the job. All I can tell you is they're good. Hadn't been for those two I'd be dead right now – or sitting in jail.'

'You seemed kind of friendly with the Brit.'

'Thought she might need a new handler. I wanted her to be sure she knew how to get in touch if she was looking for work.'

'Any idea why they would refuse treatment?'

'Maybe they don't have medical insurance.'

Compton smiled. It wasn't a friendly or reassuring expression. 'You don't think it was because they were afraid we'd turn them over to the Germans?'

'That's not going to happen, is it?'

'That's not for me to decide, but it's an option the D.O. is looking at.'

'Charlie Winger?'

'I take it from that look you know Director Winger?'

'We're old friends.'

'We're going to catch some fallout from the Germans on

this, T. K. Be kind of nice to give them the people responsible.'

The Road to Berlin
Sunday March 9, 2008.

With a two hour drive ahead of them Compton tried to establish some common ground before he started the debrief. Malloy played along, but it wasn't easy. They tried talking about their training instructors at the Farm, but having gone through in different generations that didn't get them much. After that they moved on to the leading personalities in the agency but once again they had virtually nothing in common. Malloy put in a good word about Jane Harrison when Compton called her the Iron Maiden. Compton defended Charlie Winger when Malloy said Charlie was a walking intelligence failure. Compton said in his opinion Mr Winger was one of the finest men he had ever known, which meant that the debriefing was probably going to end up on Charlie's desk without Jane Harrison being copied in.

After a couple of stories about the old days, one by Compton who was passing along a story he had heard from 'some old codgers', the other by Malloy, who could spin yarns all day without ever muddying the petticoats of truth, Compton ran through work at the U.S. Embassy in Berlin. Finally there was some common ground. Malloy said his father had worked at the U.S. Consulate in Zürich for seven years, back in the day when there was a Consulate in Zürich. 'That whole time,' he said, 'I never knew the old man was Company. You know when I found out? I was well into my third interview and my dad walked into the room. He said to me, "I want to know if you are as good as your old man when it comes to keeping a secret." '

Compton liked that even though the story was a bald lie. He asked more about Malloy's father, but Malloy told him the old man had kept all his secrets to himself. Eventually, Compton got around to the point of this show of camaraderie. He wanted to know what had gone wrong in Hamburg. To begin Malloy claimed he didn't know. That happened to be the truth, but ignorance is as good as a confession during an interrogation and Compton reacted by trying to blame Dale Perry. Had Dale made a bad call? Malloy went through the phone trace, mentioning that Dale's thoroughness had got them their lead in the first place.

'This was while you were kidnapping the attorney?'

'Dale told me the guy was dirty, and he was right. Ohlendorf was providing Chernoff with people and supplies.'

'I want to know how someone walked up and cut Perry's throat.'

'I wasn't with him. I didn't see it.'

'How does an assassin get that close to a trained operative, T. K.?'

'If I cut your throat open right now would that be bad judgement or a mistake on your part?'

Compton smiled but he didn't like the question. 'You're saying you think it was someone he knew?'

'I think it was Helena Chernoff.'

'Helena Chernoff just walked up to him and cut his throat?'

'We were all sure Chernoff was upstairs in bed with Jack Farrell.'

'So. . . bad intel?'

'The mistake was mine,' Malloy answered.

'How is that?'

'It was *my* mission. I'm the one who walked us into the trap.'

'All due respect, T. K., but it looks to me like you walked into a couple of them last night.'

Flying to Zürich
Sunday March 9, 2008.

Kate awakened with a start and realised she was on a plane. For a moment she could not imagine how that had happened. Then she remembered Ethan calling his friend in Bern, the long wait for him to arrive, the excruciating pain in her thigh throughout the day, the uncertainty of their even being able to get out of the country, and then settling into the fuselage and passing out. . .

'How do you feel?' Ethan asked.

She looked around and saw him sitting just behind her head. 'Thirsty,' she said.

He passed her some water, wincing as he used his arm. She laughed quietly. 'We're quite the couple, aren't we?'

'We'll be in Zürich in a couple hours. Marcus called. He'll have a doctor waiting at the hotel.'

'How are you doing?'

'A little sore, but I'll live.'

'I'm sorry I got you into this, Ethan.'

'What are you talking about? I had a great time.'

'Giancarlo told me I was going to get us both killed. . .'

'We're not dead yet, Kate.'

Kate smiled, and thought back to the Eiger and the terror she had felt clinging to a piece of rock as she hung over an abyss. *Not dead yet.* 'You know,' she said, 'when I lost Robert I didn't think I would ever fall in love again.'

'Everyone who has ever been in love feels that way.'

'It wasn't that I imagined I would never have feelings. I just didn't want them. I wanted to stay in love with him for as long as I lived. It was like I thought even with him gone I could still have something. . .'

'I know.'

'You *know*? You've been in a relationship like that? When was this?'

'I'm in a relationship like that right now.'

She laughed and looked away. 'You don't feel cheated sometimes – sharing me with Robert?'

'I guess I used to. I knew it was why you pushed me away; why you made jokes when I tried to get serious. After a while, I figured I had better leave or learn to live with it. I decided to live with it.'

Kate closed her eyes. 'If I had let Robert go, neither one of us would have been shot last night.'

'I'm not doing this for your first husband, Kate. I'm doing it because whoever sent those people to the Eiger meant to kill you. As far as I'm concerned, I'm not stopping until we know the truth.'

'Do you think we'll ever see T. K. again?'

'Doesn't matter. We'll do this on our own, if he decides he's had enough.'

'If I were in his position, I think I'd head back to New York.'

'No, you wouldn't. You might *want* to disappear, but you couldn't run away from a friend on a dare.'

'Is that why you love me?'

'It's one of the reasons.'

The American Embassy, Berlin
Sunday March 9, 2008.

Malloy's surgery was handled by one of the Embassy guards, who took out twenty-three pellets and then cleaned and bandaged the wounds. He finished with a shot of amino glycoside against infection. For the kidneys he gave Malloy a shot of glucocorticoids and a bottle of over-the-counter pain killers. Malloy caught a few hours of sleep afterwards and then got a hot meal.

He called Gwen from the secure line late that afternoon, early morning her time. She wished him a happy birthday and said she was hoping he would call. Was he going to do anything special for his birthday?

'Today is a travel day,' he said. 'I celebrated last night.'

'What did you do?'

'Drove around Hamburg with a couple of guys.'

'That's it?'

'We spent a few hours in one of the city parks – talking about the meaning of life. That kind of thing.'

'Oh, Thomas that sounds so boring! You're fifty, not dead! You're supposed to have fun!'

'I miss you, Gwen.'

'I miss you, too. When are you going to be home?'

'We turned up a bank account we didn't know about in Zürich, so I'll be there for a few days. When I see how long it's going to take, I'll give you a call.'

'Are you going to get him?'

'Gwen, forensic accountants can only do so much.'

They talked a few minutes more about things in New York. A gallery manager had talked to Gwen the night before about doing a retrospective of her work. It was nice, but a retrospective made her feel old. Was she old? 'I'm not old enough for a retrospective, am I?'

'You need another thirty years for a decent retrospective,' he said.

'They don't call *fifty* old for accounts, do they?'

'It's the prime of life.'

After Malloy got off the phone Brian Compton gave him an update on the damage in Hamburg. The police had found Jim Randal's body in a flat less than a mile from where he disappeared. They had not performed an autopsy, but death appeared to have been caused by a single shot to the temple. Quick and clean. At Ramstein there was better news. Josh Sutter was already out of surgery and doing fine. When Compton moved on to Company matters, the news was mixed. They had lost Dale Perry's safe house, as expected, but Malloy's computer and luggage had been recovered without incident.

Malloy asked about the cops. Anybody wounded? There had been a couple of injuries, Compton told him, whiplash mostly, but no gunshot wounds. Aside from Hugo Ohlendorf – and no one in Hamburg wanted to set his death aside – only a few Hamburg thugs had been killed. Compton ran through the rap sheets on the assassins at the scenes of both attacks, including a woman with a history of assault and weapons violations. They were all local except for a Berliner, everyone with a long history in the courts. They were all people Hugo Ohlendorf would have been able to contact through some kind of go-between like Xeno had been. None looked like the specialist Ohlendorf had mentioned.

'As expected,' Compton told him, 'the Germans are demanding the arrest and extradition of the State Department's Mr Thomas and Special Agent Joshua Sutter.'

'How are we dealing with that?'

'Charlie Winger ordered me to give them Dale's people.'

Malloy fought to keep his face a blank. 'Have you done it?'

'It turns out we lost them.'

'You didn't put anyone on them?' Malloy's tone evinced surprise – with just a touch of disappointment in the new breed.

Compton's face went sour. 'We tracked the GPS tag I put on the Brit girl to the Frankfurt Bahnhof before we realised a German businessman was carrying it.'

'Well, you screwed up,' Malloy told him with studied in-difference. 'I told you they were good. I figured you would know to put a physical tail on them.'

'We didn't have time to get someone!'

'Everyone's got an excuse after the horse is out of the barn.'

'We were ready to put a net on them in Frankfurt – in case we needed to pick them up. You don't have any idea where they were headed, do you?'

'If I did I'd tell you.'

Compton didn't look like he believed this. 'If one of them calls you, T. K. . .'

'You'll be the first to know.'

Chapter Nine

Dresden, Germany
Sunday March 9, 2008.

Malloy found some fresh clothes, courtesy of the Embassy, donned a new vest, and fitted an Uzi machine pistol deep inside a long winter coat. Into a new suitcase he slipped five hundred rounds of 9mm ammo, along with a toothbrush, razor, a change of clothes, a laptop, and an unopened bottle of Scotch that he had pilfered from someone's unattended desk.

An Embassy security officer drove him to Dresden.

Helena Chernoff learned Malloy and Brand had escaped capture late Sunday morning when she got a call from her source inside the Hamburg police. She immediately began tracking Malloy's cell phone number, which she had picked up from Dale Perry's phone. She located him on the move a couple of hours southeast of Hamburg.

With David Carlisle bound for New York and Ohlendorf eliminated, Chernoff was momentarily on her own, but she also understood that Malloy at some point soon would prudently discard his phone and pick up another. The opportunity to track him would not last. She had resources inside Berlin but the protocols that had protected her for nearly two decades prevented her from putting a team together quickly, so she drifted behind Malloy's signal until it ended at the American Embassy in Berlin.

She expected to lose him at this point, but several hours later Chernoff noticed his signal moving again. In Dresden Malloy's car entered the underground parking lot at the Bahnhof. A few minutes later the two men settled down in a restaurant inside the Bahnhof. Chernoff decided Malloy was probably going to take a train somewhere that evening. Of course he might have left Berlin by train, she thought, but Dresden was infinitely better for a man who felt his life might still be in danger. On a late Sunday evening there were not many people around the station, and the broad plazas to every side of the main building made any approach and exit by foot precarious. In Berlin an assassin could have used the crowds to get in close. Here her options were limited and dangerous.

She finally saw Malloy when he left the restaurant and walked across an open area with his bodyguard next to him. He stopped to pull a single piece of luggage from a locker and then ascended the stairs to an elevated platform. The man with him looked like government-issue, with a long wool coat, like the one Malloy wore. Both men, she decided, were concealing automatic weapons and were probably wearing body armour. Chernoff got a good look at the bodyguard's face, so there would be no surprises later, but as it turned out that wasn't necessary. After escorting Malloy to the upper platform, the bodyguard returned to the main floor and made his way out of the building. A few minutes later Chernoff saw Malloy briefly as he stepped into a first class sleeping wagon on the City Night Line.

Back inside her car, Chernoff pulled up the City Night Line schedule on her computer. There were two lines, one from Berlin, the other from Dresden. The trains joined at some point in the night and continued on to Zürich, arriving early the following morning.

'You said they couldn't get out,' Carlisle complained. He was talking about the ambush in Hamburg.

'David, you are missing the point,' Chernoff answered. She was in her car, heading west.

'No, I'm well aware of the *point*. You have a chance at

Malloy and you want to know how much more you can get from me before you decide if you want to do it.'

'I am not interested in more money.'

There was silence at the other end. 'What do you want?'

'Ohlendorf's network.'

Hugo Ohlendorf had managed a tremendously profitable and diverse organisation stretching from Oslo to Budapest with interests in drugs, prostitution, stolen goods, and any number of knock-off and pirated goods. In contrast, David Carlisle's and Luca Bartoli's organisations were something more like gangs – though they included decidedly more skilled personnel and demanded staggering sums for their services. With Ohlendorf gone, Carlisle had no doubt spent the last twenty-four hours considering how to take over the lion's share of the earnings without seeming to do so. Certainly it was not in his interest to upset either her or Luca Bartoli – the only two players still actively involved at this point. And now she had cornered him. If he wanted Malloy quickly, which she knew he did, he was going to have to pay for it.

Balanced against Carlisle's greed for Ohlendorf's profits was the certain realisation that his own network could end up being destroyed if Malloy survived another night. After a time of reflection, he said, as she expected, 'Helena, that isn't something for me to decide. We're going to need to vote on how we split up Ohlendorf's resources.'

'You control the vote, David. You always have.'

'Luca will want something if he agrees to give you Ohlendorf's responsibilities.'

'Then give him something. You have my price. Either pay it or find Malloy on your own – if it isn't too late.'

'The point was to kill Malloy whilst he was chasing Farrell!'

'His train has already left the station, David. Do you want me to let him go?'

Carlisle was quiet again, calculating the cost of pacifying Luca Bartoli. At last he said, 'Fine. The network is yours if you can eliminate Malloy tonight.'

Berlin, Germany
Summer 1935.

Otto Rahn had worked hard at meaningless jobs for over a
decade so that he might afford a month or two abroad to do
his research. Over the years he had literally stolen the hours he
needed in order to write. Suddenly, miraculously, he would live
well. He would have the funds he needed for research, funds to
buy any book he cared to own, access to every library in
Europe. He would have an office and a secretary – even
researchers if he needed them to bring him a book or a
summary or fetch him a cup of coffee! And best of all he would
take orders from no one. Himmler had promised him complete
autonomy. What writer, Rahn wondered, could resist such an
offer?

Within weeks of his meeting with Himmler, Rahn had settled
in Berlin. He went to his office each day for several hours,
leaving early if he felt like it, coming in late when he wanted.
He took time to meet others who were connected to the civil
branch of the SS and found himself amazed when various
individuals spoke to him about his book. They had all read it,
as it turned out. Asking about this, he learned that Himmler
had made a gift of his book to everyone on his staff.

One morning, as Rahn was busy outlining the necessary
research for a new project he was developing on the leading
aristocratic families of Europe, he heard a familiar voice in his
outer office. 'I wonder if it is possible to see Dr Rahn for a few
moments.'

Rahn's secretary said she was not sure. Dr Rahn did not
usually like to be disturbed. Rahn smiled at this. His secretary
was only twenty, but she had courage and took care to protect
him from the usual disturbances in a government office
building. Walking to the outer office, Rahn saw Dieter
Bachman. Bachman was wearing the military uniform of an SS
major. He was heavier by a few pounds, still hunched a bit at
the shoulders and still looking overly pale.

'Dieter?' he said. Rahn made no effort to disguise his astonishment and did not bother with the hypocrisy of a smile.

'Otto, my friend!' Bachman cried happily as his eyes lit up with affection. He acted as if nothing had happened between them. 'I hope you don't mind my dropping by like this. I simply could not wait until our paths crossed! I wanted to tell you how pleased I am you have joined the Reichsführer's staff!'

'I appreciate that,' Rahn answered. He was still uncertain. He hardly dared trust the friendly face Bachman offered him.

Bachman came forward and shook hands. 'It has been such a long time! It's good to see you, my friend. Did I catch you at a bad time? I thought we might talk for a moment.'

'Certainly,' he told Bachman. 'Come in.'

Behind closed doors, Bachman continued with the same enthusiasm, leaving Rahn off balance and curious. 'I told Elise you are here! She is as delighted as I am for your good fortune, Otto.'

'And how is Elise? I trust she is in good health?'

'Motherhood has made a new woman of her!'

'Do you mean to tell me you have a child?' A moment of dread and finality hit Rahn. Had he imagined some other fate for her? It had been three years! Of course she had moved on with her life!

'Only the most beautiful little girl in the world!'

'That is wonderful, Dieter!' Rahn struggled to smile, but it was a pale and feeble effort. He thought in fact he might be sick. 'I am really happy for you both!'

'Motherhood changes a woman, Otto. For Elise it has meant . . .well, it has meant everything! I dare say she is really, genuinely happy for the first time in our marriage.'

This cut Rahn with its unexpected bluntness, but it also had the effect of a *coup de grace*. Elise belonged fully to Bachman now. Rahn had nothing with which to hold her, no chance of changing her mind. This was why Bachman was here. This was why he was smiling! He wanted Rahn to know he had won! 'From the look of it,' Rahn told his old friend with a smile he could barely hold, 'fatherhood has changed you as well.'

'Well, one finds new priorities. What am I saying? Sarah is my buried treasure, my Holy Grail, the very light of my life!'

'Tell me something,' Rahn said with a tremor of discomfort. He needed to change the subject before he simply collapsed. 'Are you. . . that is, were you the one who recommended my book to Himmler?'

'I have it on good authority Himmler enjoyed your book enormously, Otto.'

'He has told me as much himself, but that is not what I asked you.'

Bachman's face seemed to tighten, though the smile never wavered. 'There are a great many people who give the Reichsführer books they think he might enjoy. You have won your appointment through talent, my friend, not because of anything I have done. Beyond giving him a copy of your book, I take no responsibility for your success.'

'What did you tell him about me, Dieter?'

Bachman seemed uncomfortable suddenly, but he answered promptly. 'After the Reichsführer had read your book he asked me about your background and character – if you might be the sort to stand with us.'

'And what did you tell him?'

'I said you are a True Cathar, Otto, the sort of man to walk into the flames of the Inquisition rather than renounce what he knows to be true!'

Rahn felt himself becoming emotional. If this was how Dieter Bachman repaid Rahn's betrayal, he was that rare soul in one's life – a true friend. 'I am in your debt,' Rahn answered.

'Nonsense!'

'I mean it! Ask anything of me, and I will do it.'

'In that case,' Bachman said with a sudden smile, 'I can insist you have dinner with Elise and me Saturday evening! How is that for repaying a debt of honour?'

'Dinner?' Rahn felt an odd surge of unreasonable panic.

Despite Bachman's assurances to the contrary he was quite certain Elise had no desire to see him. The thought of her face registering any sort of resentment at his intrusion was more than he could endure, and yet he had just promised *anything*.

If Bachman noticed his reaction, he did not show it. 'We are both eager to set things right between us again, Otto. Neither of us has any interest in stirring up unpleasantness. And of course we are both anxious for you to see what a beautiful child my wife has given me.'

Having no excuses ready and no reason not to go, Rahn accepted the invitation with as much enthusiasm as he could muster. Only later did he begin to worry. Bachman might say it, but did that really mean Elise would be happy to see him? Miserable was more likely. She would probably ignore him the whole evening or worse, treat him to cool, empty smiles. . .

Would she pretend, as Bachman had tried to do, that nothing had happened between them? Maybe tell him at some opportune moment how much she regretted their love affair? And how should he behave when she did? Agree that it had been a terrible mistake? What could he say, really, without sounding injured or foolish?

As he was dressing for dinner at the Bachman's townhouse that Saturday evening Rahn thought briefly about sending his regrets. It was not too late to come down with a headache, was it? A carefully worded note along with the flowers he had intended to take to them ought to be sufficient. He had no direct business with Bachman after all. Assuming he kept matters cordial between them there should be no problem from missing a dinner engagement!

But of course being cordial was all that was required of their evening together. He had simply to be polite and face the consequences. Why not take things head-on for an evening and be done with it? He was quite sure his first visit would be his last. Let them be the ones to end it. Besides, he could not keep from wondering if Elise had really changed. . .

Weimar, Germany
Sunday March 9, 2008

The distance between Dresden and Erfurt was easily handled in just over an hour by car. That allowed Helena Chernoff to park in a public lot close to the train station and then get a taxi back to Weimar, where she bought a ticket and waited for the City Night Line. Between Erfurt and Weimar she would have eighteen minutes – enough time to locate Malloy's compartment, make the kill, and then exit the train. By the time anyone noticed a problem she intended to be crossing the Czech border.

Wearing a hat to cover her face and carrying a hastily emptied suitcase for cover, Chernoff waited in the shadows until the train had stopped and then entered the train some six cars away from Malloy. She kept the hat but lost the luggage as soon as she was inside the train. Moving toward Malloy's carriage, she watched faces but saw nothing that alerted her to danger. Once in the first class carriage she found a narrow, empty aisle. The carriage offered a series of stairs leading to three separate compartments, two on the lower level, one at the top. The doors were numbered, but there were no names. Worse still, each door provided a peephole that would allow Malloy to look out and see who was at his door.

Chernoff walked to the end of the carriage and found a steward in a small cabin behind a glass wall. He said to her with some slight concern, 'May I help you?'

Chernoff pulled a Hamburg police badge and told him, 'Yes, I need to find someone travelling with you this evening – but very discreetly, if you will.'

His manner changed. 'Certainly, Officer!'

'A man travelling alone?'

'I have four this evening. Do you have a name?'

'Yes, but he is probably using an alias.'

The steward thought about this and then said, 'I have the identity cards of everyone in this wagon, if that will help. Would you care to have a look?'

Helena had a look and after a moment picked up the card of a Frenchman. 'This is the man.'

'Monsieur Dupin! But the American Embassy in Berlin made his arrangements! What has he done?'

'We think he might have instigated the trouble in Hamburg last night.'

The man was excited by this news, and bent over the table, reaching for a plan of the carriage. Consulting it, he pointed to compartment 106. Chernoff dropped back a step. The steward was a small individual, no larger than she, and she had no trouble lifting his chin with a quick, delicate move. Before he understood what was happening, she cut his neck open and pulled him to the floor. Whilst the man's feet still moved, Chernoff studied the strange designs of the blood splatter, and then touched the bloodied walls so there would be no doubt who had done this. Finally, she bent down to clean her knife blade and fingers on the man's coat.

Turning off the light she walked back into the aisle and found 106 at the top of a small set of stairs. She put her badge over the peephole, and tapped the door with the heel of her gun. Malloy called out sleepily in German with just a touch of a French accent. 'Who is it, please?'

She knocked again.

'Just a minute!'

At the click of the lock she began discharging her silenced weapon through the thin partition. She fired five evenly space shots. She heard a cry of pain on the third and then the heavy thump of a falling body. In the next instant, Chernoff pushed the door open, resolved to finish it.

The steward had come by at nine-fifteen, shortly after the train left the station. He had checked Malloy's ticket and taken his identity card – the Dupin alias Malloy carried but had not used in years. Promising to return the card with breakfast, he left a complimentary bottle of wine.

After that Malloy secured his room and settled down for the

night. He had tried to spend the time thinking about Hamburg but, after a few minutes, realised he was too tired and too close to the events to make much sense of it. Soon the gentle rocking of the train put him to sleep. He came awake briefly at one of the stations and checked his watch. It was still early. He was sitting on the floor. He thought he ought to try to stay awake, but the rocking of the train soon had its effect and he drifted back to sleep. At eleven-fifteen the train stopped at Weimar. He got up to have a look at the platform but saw only the shadowy outlines of the town against the night sky.

The moment the train started out of the station, he settled back on the floor, beginning to doubt his instincts. Then came the knock at his door and suddenly he was wide awake. He called out as he leaned down tightly against the floor. 'Who is it?'

A second knock.

He had balanced his suitcase on the table and kept a cord next to him so he could pull it and send the suitcase first into a chair and then down to the floor – a sound that he hoped might approximate a body falling in close quarters. His Taser gripped tightly in his right hand, Malloy called out, 'Just a minute!'

He reached up toward the lock and felt a moment of sudden panic. She was either coming through fast or she would simply start shooting at once. He turned the flimsy lock and saw his door splintered with bullet holes. He gave a cry that was supposed to approximate getting hit, but was in fact an eruption of fear and surprise. He remembered to jerk the suit-case from the table but did not even hear the thump and clatter of it falling. Five shots nearly crumbled the folding door.

Malloy watched the gun and silencer extend through the open door. He waited until he saw Chernoff's leg. The Taser's effect was immediate. Chernoff dropped her gun and fell down the steps. Whilst she was still trying to sit up, Malloy came after her, clipping her jaw with his knuckles. He saw the Hamburg detective's badge, her hat, and a couple of the shell casings next to her. He snatched the badge and began pulling her to her feet. Suddenly a door opened and a man in pyjamas looked out at him from the compartment directly below his. 'What is going on?' he shouted in German.

Malloy called to him in German, holding up the badge, 'Police business! Get back inside!' Another door opened, this in the suite adjoining his. A man wrapping himself in a robe came down the stairs, staring at Malloy and the unconscious woman in his arms.

'Back inside, please!' Malloy told him. He swung the badge toward the second man. 'Police business!'

Whilst both men retreated, Malloy twisted Chernoff's arm behind her back and half pushed, half carried her into his compartment. Once inside, he cuffed her and then began searching her for weapons. He found a switchblade, the handle tacky with the remnant of fresh blood. Tossing the woman into his bed, he bound her feet at her ankles with the rope he had tied to his suitcase. Before she was conscious enough to let out a scream he used her knife to cut his sheets apart and then gagged her.

He returned to the corridor and saw another interested onlooker. He held the badge up and commanded the woman back inside. Next he walked to the steward's cabin. The area was dark, but when he opened the door and switched on the light, he saw the steward stretched out on the floor. He snapped the light off and headed back toward his compartment. Outside, he saw lights in the distance. He hoped they were coming to a station within the next few minutes but could not remember the schedule in detail.

He saw spent shell casings and the hat she had worn on the floor in front of his compartment, but he left them as they lay. Another door opened, and he walked forward confidently with the badge held toward the man. 'Back inside, please! Back inside!'

He knew cell phones would be ringing police. He looked out the window again and saw lights in the distance. Inside his compartment, he saw Chernoff watching him with her dark, solemn eyes. Even in handcuffs she scared him, and he thought that maybe he should kill her. He checked his watch and then the schedule. There should be a stop in four minutes. He pulled out his cell phone.

'Yes?' He heard Jane's voice and the sound of people dining around her, even the odd sound of laughter in the background.

'I want you to call the Germans. Tell them Helena Chernoff is on the City Night Line bound from Dresden to Zürich. At the moment she is handcuffed and relatively secure in compartment 106 of the first class wagon, but if they don't move fast some Good Samaritan will probably help her escape.'

'Where are you?'

'We're coming into Erfurt.'

'There's no way you can get her to Frankfurt?' Jane asked.

'Frankfurt is four hours away. I'll be lucky to get out at Erfurt. Besides, we can use the goodwill with the Germans.'

'Are you at the station now?'

'Pulling into it in a couple of minutes.'

'Do you know what this lady can tell us, T. K.?'

'My guess is by the time we break her, what she knows won't get us very much.'

'Still, I'd like to try. . .'

'Make the call Jane. If we don't get the Germans moving on this, we'll lose her.'

New York City
Sunday March 9, 2008.

David Carlisle had chartered a private jet out of Hamburg at six o'clock in the morning. Having been up the entire night, he slept through most of the flight and arrived at JFK a few minutes past ten in the morning, U.S. Eastern Time.

On the limo ride from the airport he checked his phone and found Helena Chernoff had tried to call. He had quite a bit to do in a short amount of time and did not get back to her call until after he had finished lunch and was walking into Grand Central station. When she had told him the ambush at *Das Sternenlicht* had failed, his first reaction was quite naturally irritation. Then he had begun thinking about the consequences of that failure.

When Chernoff had told him about tracking Malloy as far as Dresden he had felt he had no choice but to agree to her terms. She was right about the vote. He could negotiate an agreement with Luca by giving him a cash payout. As long as his network remained unexposed, he would not be hurt too badly. What he did not like seeing was Helena Chernoff assuming the kind of power Ohlendorf's network would give her. Ohlendorf had always been easy to control. His respectability made him vulnerable to pressure. Once Chernoff got hold of it she was going to turn a ragged confederation of street level criminals into something he and Luca together might not be able to control. Still, he had no choice. The alternative was to give Malloy time to regroup.

After his call to Chernoff, he proceeded to rendezvous with a long-time informant who just happened to be a senior agent in the FBI. They passed one another like strangers, Carlisle taking a key from the man and proceeding to a locker. Inside it he found a marked route from JFK to the city, a set of motorcycle keys, a Port Authority patrol uniform, and a loaded service weapon. The address where he could pick up his ride was written at the top of the route map.

Erfurt, Germany
Monday March 10, 2008.

Malloy found a BMW close to the Erfurt station. He smashed the window and hotwired the starter. At the first main road he encountered, he headed southwest, in the direction of Frankfurt, calling Jane once he was on the highway. 'I'm going to need to change cars in Frankfurt – just to be on the safe side.'

They went back and forth about the details and then she told him she would get back to him. Twenty minutes later she called to tell him he could pick something up at the Frankfurt Bahnhof.

'Anything yet on Chernoff?' he asked.

'As I understand it they intend to board the train in force at Eisenach. That's. . . five minutes from now.'

'I've been thinking about how she handled this, Jane.'

'It's not really our problem any more, and I'm not inclined to pass our intel on her to the Germans.'

'That's the thing. I think Chernoff wanted to limit her exposure. That would put her on the train at Weimar and exiting at Erfurt – that's something like fifteen-to-eighteen minutes. If she had a partner, she had a ride waiting, and he's long gone, but if she was solo on this thing, then she left a car either at Weimar or Erfurt, and I'm guessing Erfurt.'

'The Germans will figure it out, T. K.'

'Right now, they don't know where this woman came from or what she was doing. And she's going to spend most of tonight trying to prove they have the wrong woman. That gives us maybe a twelve hour lead before they start looking for her car – checking a lot of different stations. She lost a lot of people Saturday night, Jane. And she had to have a computer with her if she was tracking my cell phone signal.'

'Why do you think her car is in Erfurt?'

'That's where she intended to step off the train. This late at night she might have had trouble finding a taxi. Better to have her car there than back at Weimar.'

'I'm on it.' Jane's voice purred with a touch of excitement. Cell phones and laptops were the treasure troves of her existence.

Malloy picked up a government issue SUV at the Frankfurt Bahnhof, leaving the stolen car sitting at the side of the road. He was pulling into Mannheim less than an hour later, when Jane called him. 'Any luck?' he asked.

'We're still trying to get someone to Erfurt to have a look.

That's not why I'm calling. Do you remember Irina Turner?'

Malloy frowned. 'You're talking about Jack Farrell's admin-istrative assistant?' The *sex-a-tary* Farrell had abandoned in Barcelona.

'That's the one. Seems she landed in New York three hours ago in the company of two investigators with the Spanish Federal police. They passed through Immigration and Customs and were met by two FBI Agents – according to plan. Our people were going to drive Turner and the Spanish Federales into Manhattan. That's the last contact anyone had with them.'

'You're telling me Irina Turner took out *four* federal officers and then disappeared?'

'Or she had help. Either way, I'm guessing she wasn't as dumb as we thought.'

'I need to think about this.'

'I thought you might. If you come up with anything, give me a call. I don't think I'll be getting much sleep tonight.'

Zürich, Switzerland
Monday March 10, 2008.

Malloy parked his borrowed SUV at the Offenburg Bahnhof and left the keys locked inside, as per instructions. A couple of hours later he dropped his cell phone in a trash container and caught an early morning train crossing the border into Basel, Switzerland. There he bought a tri-band cell phone from one of the local phone markets and caught a train to Zurich at just after ten o'clock. It was late in the U.S., but he took Jane at her word and called her home number. She answered, sounding wide awake. He told her to get a new cell phone, that the other had been compromised. Administrative details out of the way, Jane told him, 'We found Chernoff's car, T. K.'

'Anything in it?'

'Computer, cell phone, clothing, spare IDs, credit cards, guns, ammo, and cash.'

'I don't suppose you have told the Germans about our good

251

fortune yet?'

'I thought we might see how much they give us from their interrogations before I make nice with them.'

Malloy's next call was to Captain Marcus Steiner of the Zürich *Stadtpolizei*. 'Thomas!' Marcus announced. 'I was hoping I would hear from you today!'

'Just coming into town. I thought I might buy you lunch at your favourite bar, say around noon?'

'Sounds good. I'll see you then!'

From the Zürich Bahnhof Malloy took the Bahnhofstrasse exit and came to street level a short block away from the Gotthard Hotel. In good Swiss German he asked if he might have a room for the week. After a moment of thoughtful consideration the desk clerk checked his files and seemed suddenly quite satisfied with himself, like a man who has just solved a particularly difficult puzzle. 'I can give you the same room you had the last time you were here, Herr Stalder. Will that be okay?'

Malloy, who had not offered any of his names, smiled brightly. 'That would be fine!' He had been to Zürich on a couple of trips within the past year but the last time he had used the Stalder alias was at the Gotthard in the fall of 2006. He had always taken care not to shuffle his aliases too carelessly within a given city, and this was a perfect example of what could go wrong. A forgotten face, a passing acquaintance, a friend of a friend, a waiter, or a desk clerk with a long memory: one false name at the wrong moment and a cover could be blown. Sometimes that meant losing a passport, which cost money and time. Sometimes it exposed whole networks, which had the potential to cost lives.

The Swiss were especially troublesome in this respect. Most took one job and stayed there for years, if not a lifetime. Unlike the rest of the world, the *real* Swiss prided themselves on delivering service. That included remembering their regulars and apparently even the irregulars. This one was a real Swiss.

Malloy opened his wallet and found some Euro notes left

over from Hamburg. He passed a hundred Euros across the desk to the man – not quite a night's rent at the Gotthard. 'I appreciate the thoughtfulness.' When the clerk was not quite sure if he had been handled a gratuity or an advance on the room, Malloy added, 'That's just for you, but do me a favour.'

'Anything, Herr Stalder.'

'Make sure you spend it on something of absolutely no practical value.'

Virtue rewarded, the clerk folded the bill into his pocket and called someone to the desk. 'Watch the desk for a moment,' he said. 'I'm taking Herr Stalder to his room.'

The clerk had some trouble with the weight of Malloy's suitcase but made a brave face of it. Inside the elevator Malloy told him, 'Sorry about the luggage, but I'm packing extra ammunition this trip.'

Herr Hess, Malloy's new best friend, laughed politely.

Malloy's unspecified meeting place with Marcus Steiner was The James Joyce Pub, a couple of blocks off the Bahnhofstrasse, probably six from the Gotthard. Priced to keep out the riffraff, the pub was rarely crowded but always worth the visit. Malloy arrived first and took one of the comfortable booths at the back of the room. He had just ordered a beer when Marcus walked in.

Malloy had met Marcus Steiner forty-three years ago in the streets of Zürich. At the time Marcus had not spoken any English. Malloy, freshly imported from America, was a bit mystified by the fact that he couldn't understand anything anyone said. In a matter of months he was speaking Swiss German with his new friend and learning the basics of burglary. He may only have been seven years old, but Marcus had already discovered the Swiss fondness for keeping cash stashed away in various hiding places within their houses. He needed only an accomplice to distract his victims at the front door whilst he entered the house through an open window, and there were always plenty of those. By the age of ten the boys had graduated from the neighbourhood, where they had become suspicious characters, and had moved on to parts of town where they were not known. By twelve they were breaking into houses and taking everything they could carry. It was more dangerous but more profitable as well.

When Malloy's father and mother had finally returned to the States, young Thomas was fourteen. He knew Swiss German like a native and High German well enough to read and communicate. He also had the basics down on how to steal almost anything. All thanks to Marcus Steiner. The friendship, of course, did not survive the distance of an ocean. They weren't the pen pal sorts, and for the next decade the two boys went straight – at least young Thomas did – concentrating on getting an education and a decent job. When Malloy returned to Zürich on a three year assignment as an intelligence operative his first recruit was his old friend Marcus, who had perversely opted for a career in law enforcement. As Marcus had put it, the pay was good, the benefits were excellent, and it kept him close to the thing he loved.

After a few minutes of catching up – including an abbreviated telling of Malloy's troubles in Hamburg – Malloy got down to business. He needed a bodyguard for a few days. At his friend's raised eyebrow, he explained, 'Helena Chernoff may be out of play, but whoever hired her is still out there.'

They worked through the details, including a healthy advance that Malloy would deposit at a local bank under an alias Marcus used. That finished, Malloy asked his friend what he knew about the Italian mafia. This seemed to throw Marcus. He named a couple of the families operating in the north and finished, inevitably, with Giancarlo Bartoli, who was maybe connected and maybe just very lucky with his investments. Was Bartoli operating in Switzerland?

'He operates everywhere, Thomas. Giancarlo must sit on fifteen or twenty boards and probably owns that many more companies outright.'

'So what is his involvement with the families?'

'If you want rumours, I can give you everything you've already heard. If you want something more substantial, I'd say talk to Hasan.'

This of course was what he intended, but he had wanted what insights Marcus could give him before going to the Zürich branch of the Russian mafia. 'Can you set up a meeting?'

'I'll see what I can do.'

'Great. And one other thing. . .'

'Mr and Mrs Brand are staying at the Savoy for a few days under a doctor's care, but you won't get to them unless you ask for Peter Bartholomew.'

Malloy puzzled over this for a moment and then smiled. 'The guy who found the Lance of Antioch.'

'Ethan said you would understand.'

'How are they doing?'

'The doctor wants them both in hospital, which they won't do, and he wants Kate off her feet for a week or two. She's agreed to a couple of days. I saw them this morning. She asked me to get her a set of throwing knives and a target.'

'You're kidding me.'

'She tells me throwing knives can be very restorative.'

Marcus drove Malloy to one of his banks and Malloy arranged a wire transfer to cover the cost of his protection – all of them off duty Zürich police with arrest powers. Back at the Gotthard, a plainclothes policeman was already waiting at the front of the hotel when Marcus dropped him off.

Upstairs he pulled the shutters and took a long nap, but he slept in armour. His Uzi and a spare clip lay on the floor next to the bed. Meanwhile the cop who had met him at the front of the building stood outside his door. He woke up at nine that evening, but only because Marcus called him.

'Needle Park in an hour. Look for a friendly face.'

'A friendly face?' he asked, still trying to come up out of a deep sleep. There was no answer. Marcus had already hung up.

Malloy ordered a sandwich sent to his room, delivered by Herr Hess, and then called Jane at her office while he ate. Her secretary said she wasn't in, but a minute later Jane returned his call on a new cell phone. 'How's Josh Sutter?' Malloy asked.

'Agent Sutter is going to be flying home tomorrow.'

'Anything on Irina Turner?'

'About six hours ago Newark city police turned up a car in a parking garage registered to the FBI – four dead agents inside.'

'Did *she* do it?'

'A Port Authority motorcycle was found abandoned on I-278 not far from the I-495 exit. The operating theory at this point is that someone impersonated a Port Authority patrolman and stopped the car, but it gets worse.'

'I don't see how.'

'They think someone in the Manhattan office provided the route.'

'Someone *in* the FBI?'

'Something tells me this thing is a little bit bigger than Jack Farrell turning into a rabbit, T. K.'

'Any news on Helena Chernoff?'

'The Germans are telling us she's as silent as the tomb, but the computer is giving us quite a bit.'

'Any way I can get a copy of everything you receive?'

'I'll send the preliminary report to Bern on a secure line and have someone hand-deliver it to you tomorrow morning your time.'

They took a minute to set up the details. Then Malloy asked, 'What have you turned up on the H. Langer alias – from the cell phone Chernoff was using in Hamburg?' When Jane did not respond, he prompted. 'She had a bank account with Sardis and Thurgau in Zürich. . .'

'Right! They got back with us yesterday. Let's see. . . okay. They were holding eight hundred thousand Swiss francs up until the end of last year. At that point Chernoff or one of her agents transferred all but a thousand francs into another account – which of course we can't access.'

'End of last year?'

'You think it means something?'

'I think this is one alias she *wanted* to blow.'

Berlin, Germany
Fall, 1935.

At the front door of their townhouse Bachman shook Rahn's hand affectionately, like old times, and brought him into a palatial nineteenth century townhouse. Rahn carried a bouquet of wildflowers to give to Elise and an exquisite Bavarian doll for the child, both of which he handed to Elise when she walked into the parlour. The flowers were a courtesy, but the doll was something of a treasure. Elise told him it was wonderful. Sarah would love it.

She spoke with all the naturalness of a fond old friend and, contrary to Bachman's assessment, seemed not to have changed at all. She was still perfectly beautiful, as trim and serene as the first time they had met. She called him Otto, and actually looked pleased to see him. They kissed in the fashion of family and close friends, the touch of her cheeks stirring in him dark, intimate memories, but there was nothing in her expression to suggest similar sensations. In her eyes he saw the pleasure of seeing an old friend, nothing more. She showed him to a settee, and sat opposite him. Bachman left the room to fix highballs. Whilst he was gone Elise mentioned her surprise that he had agreed to join Himmler's staff. She had never imagined him mixed up in politics.

Rahn told her it was not really a political position. Himmler had simply assumed the role of his patron.

'He wants nothing in return?' she asked. Curious? Surprised? Or sceptical? He could not read her expression but had no time to ask what she meant.

'Don't be silly, Elise!' Bachman exclaimed as he returned

without their drinks. He had been listening. 'Himmler expects Otto to find the Holy Grail!'

Elise lifted her eyebrows. 'Is that all?' And then they all three laughed.

Bachman went back to the bar to finish their drinks. 'I loved your book,' she said. 'It was like reading one of your letters. When I had finished I turned back to the beginning and read it all again.'

Bachman popped back into the room nervously. 'One thing I did wonder about, Otto,' he said. 'You put *Grail* in the title, but you never say what it is! That's a bit unfair, don't you think?'

Rahn had heard the complaint before and gave his standard response. 'I thought I ought to leave something for a future book.'

'So you do have a theory about it – what it is, I mean?'

'Several, actually. I am just not sure which one is correct.'

The Bachmans' nanny brought Sarah into the parlour. The girl had already eaten her evening meal and was dressed for bed. She was obviously mystified by Rahn's presence but not especially disturbed. Elise introduced him to her as her Uncle Otto. From her age Rahn thought the child must have been conceived in the late summer months of 1932, exactly the season he and Elise had been lovers. She was now a few months past two years in age. She might have been Bachman's child, Rahn thought, but she certainly looked nothing like him. In fact, she looked like Elise – a perfect dark haired beauty. Casting a quick glance in the direction of Elise, Rahn imagined she might give him some sort of signal, *she is yours*, but he was disappointed. She was telling the nanny something. He looked at Bachman, and saw only a father's proud gaze fixed on his young daughter. If Bachman were at all uncertain about the child's paternity, it did not seem to matter to him. This was *his* child, no matter the biology.

At dinner they talked incessantly about the Languedoc as if they had all just returned from holiday. It seemed to them a different world, certainly one still shrouded in mystery and romance. Had Rahn plans to go back? Rahn had not been back since slipping out of the country with the hotel bankruptcy hanging over his head, but he did not care to bring up *Des Marronniers* and risk spoiling a perfect evening. 'I might go if Himmler wants me to find the Grail.'

'You have only to propose it and he will send you!' Bachman said cheerfully.

After dinner, Bachman finally turned to matters of politics. Germany had suffered from a lack of leadership, he said. One need only look at Berlin now – not even three years after Hitler had become Chancellor – to understand what a determined and talented man could accomplish. The city's transformation was nothing short of miraculous. Gone were the riots and squalor. Factories were running again and promised soon to be working at capacity. People had jobs, 'Even the likes of our Otto!' Bachman joked. 'And here is the greatest wonder of all,' he added more seriously, like a priest finishing a brief but pointed homily, 'it is the same in all the cities in Germany. We are a nation again!'

Before Rahn left, Bachman said he must clear the air. Elise and Rahn looked at their knees. Bachman was talking about their adultery. 'We were the victims of a weak and corrupt government,' he said. Rahn looked up in surprise. 'With our world having plunged into economic and moral collapse is it any wonder we lost our way? We discarded our sense of right and wrong because no one in authority could set a proper example! That's all that happened, and those days are behind us. I think it is time, and Elise agrees with me, it is time we forgive ourselves. Time we are friends again!'

Rahn found himself nodding in response to this. He suddenly felt a genuine admiration for Bachman. He had not tried to offer his forgiveness. That would have left Bachman the aggrieved party and sole occupant of the moral high ground. No, he counted himself as one who had lost his way, too. Best of all, their failings sat squarely upon the shoulders of others: the Communists, the Jews, and the bickering parliamentarians. Now, with a proper government, they could start fresh, their sense of right and wrong restored by the example of their Führer.

After that evening, the friendship resumed almost as if no time had passed. To Rahn's thinking, Bachman had saved him from teaching languages in a commercial school, which to him was comparable to saving a man's life. Not only that, he showed no jealousy. Rare was the week when the three of them did not sit down to a dinner together on Sundays. Often times they had drinks and supper on Thursday and Friday evenings as well. Bachman and Elise and Sarah became Rahn's family, Sarah even calling him Uncle Ot. Each time he appeared she was there to show him the details of her life: a toy acquired, a new piece of clothing, or a discovered knickknack from the park. She even began kissing him when he arrived and before she went to bed.

At work Bachman took the effort to introduce Rahn to people within the military branch of the SS who might prove valuable allies. What is more, they were all pleased to meet him and offered to have drinks or dinner with him as his schedule permitted. For her part Elise steered him into Berlin society, arranging for him to give lectures to prominent groups within the city. She found tickets to events that had been closed for weeks and even counselled him as to the kind of woman he should marry, because, she said, he must marry. Himmler was a great believer in family. He promoted married men, especially men with children, and left the bachelors to struggle. 'He is mad for aristocrats, Otto. Never mind if they have money, just make sure the woman you marry has blue blood in her veins and there is no limit to your future!'

'And if I am inclined not to marry for a while?' he asked her.

'You made a great many sacrifices for the sake of your art,' she answered, 'but those times are past. It is time to make a family whilst you are still young enough to enjoy it!'

To make her point Elise arranged dates for him with a number of prominent young women, but try as he might to make a go of it, the affairs were all miserable failures.

Wewelsburg, Germany
Winter 1936.

Early the following year Rahn joined the SS as an officer, though he was officially assigned to the civil branch. He too took the distinctive SS ring officers wore and was forever joined by a blood oath to the Order of the Skull.

A few days after the ceremony, Bachman came to Rahn's office. He said he must kidnap Rahn for the day. 'I hope you won't require me to take you at gunpoint?'

Rahn laughed at the hyperbole. All the same, there was something in Bachman's manner that suggested he was not really joking. 'What are you talking about?'

'Himmler has asked me to show you something. That's all I can say.'

Rahn shrugged. What Himmler wanted he got. 'So show me something.'

'It's quite a long drive. In fact we had better get going if we intend to make it back to Berlin this evening.'

They ended up a couple of hours south of Hamburg close to Paderborn at the village of Wewelsburg. In the distance they could see a plateau of land rising up over the village and the outlines of an old Renaissance fortress cutting into the grey skyline. 'Is that what we have come to see?' Rahn asked. Bachman had been talking about Sarah, a story about her crashing into their bedroom and insisting, with the innocence of the young, that the beds be drawn together so the three of them could sleep in a single bed.

'Magnificent, isn't it?' he said.

'I'm sure it was at one time. . .' Like so many of the old fortresses in Germany, Wewelsburg had long ago lost its strategic military value. It had in fact been abandoned without ever engaging in a battle and then languished in decay for more than two centuries.

Before they had crested the hill an SS sergeant came out of a small building close to the road and demanded their papers. Both men presented their credentials. In addition to these Bachman produced a letter signed by Himmler. The guard studied the letter and then went inside his hut. Rahn could see him on the telephone. When he came back out, he pointed at the gate in the wall. 'You may park inside, Major. If you need anything, just ask one of the guards. They are yours to command!'

Bachman folded the letter and started to put it away. 'Let me see that,' Rahn said. Bachman passed it to him, trying hard not to show his pride. The letter gave them permission to enter every part of the fortress without restriction. Himmler had signed the letter personally. With that name all doors opened.

Rahn looked up at the great walls, which were now towering over them. 'Without this letter we could not have got inside?'

'For the time being the Wewelsburg fortress is off limits to everyone but the SS squad assigned to guard it. Except for a handful of Himmler's generals and certain of his personal staff, no one else even knows it exists. One may enter it only if he carries a letter signed by Himmler himself. I suppose I should also tell you that if you mention to anyone where we have gone today, Himmler will have us both killed, as well as the individual you tell.'

Bachman announced this in such a relaxed manner that Rahn looked to see if he were joking. He was not. 'Why the secrecy?' he asked.

'The Reichsführer intends to see the SS continue to expand. I have heard him say he will not be happy until he can provide the Führer with a dozen divisions of elite armoured forces. Naturally, that kind of enormous growth can pose certain internal risks to the morale and confraternity of the Order. Certainly one man, even someone as energetic as Himmler, cannot oversee every aspect of such an extensive organisation, and yet for the SS to be effective that is what he needs to do. His idea is to create a secret order of knights within the Order of the Skull, like the paladins who served Charlemagne's court, a cadre of individuals fanatically devoted to the ideals of the SS. Once they are established he intends to give them Wewelsburg as a kind of retreat where he can meet with them and they can direct the affairs of the Order of the Skull.'

They passed through an enormous gate and entered a narrow courtyard. From inside the walls Wewelsburg did not seem that large. This had been a military outpost, hardly more than a citadel. It was sufficient to supply and defend a couple of regiments, no more. Triangular in shape with each of the three walls supported by a massive, perfectly round tower, it would have allowed for the rapid deployment of the soldiers defending it. No point along the wall was isolated or especially distant from any others, but the compact shape also reduced usable interior space. There were no plazas or roads here. In fact the ground inside the high walls stayed almost constantly in shadow and left the air ripe with the odour of damp rot.

Rahn could see at once that Himmler was intent on turning its dark intimate spaces into something quite inspiring, something worthy of the leadership of the Order of the Skull. Nowhere was this more evident than in the largest of the three towers, which had already been renovated. To get to it they descended a stone staircase and came to a small hallway. Beyond this, they stepped into a perfectly round room. At the centre was an open fireplace. Along each wall several stone benches extended from the smooth masonry, each bench sufficient for a single individual. The round walls had windows at various levels overhead encircling the room asymmetrically. These produced numerous beams of light splashing across the stone walls high above. At the top of the tower, past the chaotic sunbeams and deep inside the cupola, was a Swastika like none Rahn had ever seen. Attached to the end of each of the four branches was a long runic S that virtually doubled the size of the swastika. The change in such a familiar image was unsettling and vaguely traitorous, and Rahn could almost imagine that this inner core of SS officers, its paladins, would ultimately direct not only the Order of the Skull but Germany itself.

The real oddity of the room, and the effect was almost mystical, was the extraordinary echo when one spoke. In fact the crash of echoes made it impossible to understand anything that was said from the middle of the room. Curiously, if an individual sat against the walls on one of the benches even a whisper could be heard by someone seated anywhere in the circle. It was a round table of sorts – needing only knights and a Grail quest to complete it.

Before they left, they toured the officers' apartments, still unfinished but quite promising. In this area they found a crew of prison labourers hard at work. The men were rail thin and were watched closely by the squad guarding the castle. Rahn saw one of the men collapse as he hauled a heavy bucket of refuse out of the room. No one went to him. His fellow workers seemed not even to notice his exhaustion. Finally, a guard kicked him. Before the scene had played out, Bachman led Rahn back to his Mercedes.

'Where does he get these workers?' Rahn asked as he settled into his seat. They had been too thin to be healthy, sickly almost!

Bachman did not seem especially interested in the question but answered him easily enough. 'Himmler sweeps the streets for them.'

'Why show me this place?' Rahn asked on the long drive back to Berlin. 'I'm a historian, not one of his Generals.'

'Himmler is building his Montségur, Otto. What he wants from you is the Grail.'

'I am not at all sure the Grail ever existed, except in the realm of the spirit, of course.'

'You tell the legend in your book! Esclarmonde threw it into

Mt. Tabor!'

'But that is all it is – a local legend that an old man told me!'

'Himmler wants you to look for it, Otto. He will not ask you, of course. One who seeks the Grail must volunteer for such a quest – it is the Grail after all! But he will do everything in his power to assist you when you are ready to find it. You have only to ask his permission.'

'I have done with buried treasure. There are better ways to spend one's time.'

'You can have a look, can't you? I mean, all he has done for you, you can do that much for him, can't you?'

'I *have* looked, Dieter. I have been up and down the Ariege valley. I have plunged into snake pits and crevasses so deep and narrow no one has ever been there before. All I ever found were bones and cave paintings.'

'Let me tell you something about Heinrich Himmler, my friend. What he demands of his officers he gets. You cannot tell him it is impossible. In his mind nothing is impossible. If he wants you to find him the Grail of the Cathars that had better be something you want as well.'

'If he has brought me into the SS because he imagines I can find the Grail, he must be perfectly insane!'

'Take care, my friend. I will not allow you to slander one of the most important men in the Reich!'

'I only meant it's not there. He cannot *order* a miracle!'

'To refuse Himmler is the real insanity, Otto.'

'I am telling you it is a legend! Esclarmonde turned into a dove and flew off with the Grail. You laughed at the notion the first time I told you about it. Do you remember?'

'Himmler thinks there might be something to it.'

'It is a story, not a map to find buried treasure!'

Bachman was quiet for several minutes, Rahn sullen. Finally, Bachman told him, 'You must have another look, Otto. If I tell Himmler you have no interest in the Grail, I assure you this, you will find yourself quite suddenly shut out.'

'I don't understand.'

'Do you imagine Elise finds you tickets when none are to be had or that she knows so many beautiful aristocrats that she can set you up every weekend, one beauty after another? You are in favour! So long as you stand in the light Himmler provides you no man will dare resist you. The moment he sees no value in your efforts, you will find doors closing in your face.'

'He is paying me to write!'

'He was paying you to write. You are in the Order of the Skull now. Now he is paying you to do what he demands of you. And get serious about someone, whilst you are at it. You need a wife, Otto. You cannot love mine forever.'

Zürich
Monday March 10, 2008.

Malloy walked through the Bahnhof, shadowed discreetly by his guardian, and came out to the area once known as Needle Park. Inside a black Mercedes he saw a man he knew only as Max. Max was a forty-something Zürich detective with a perpetually sour expression, a haggard look, and the cool cynicism of a street-weary cop. Like Marcus, he carried a standard issue semiautomatic pistol in a shoulder holster, but his weapon of choice was a sawn-off, pump-action shotgun loaded with deer slugs. Whereas buckshot provided for an excellent margin of error, the deer slug, once pointed in the right direction, operated like a wrecking ball. Malloy had seen Max handle the gun once. After that he was always careful to treat the man politely.

'How's crime?' Malloy asked in English as he slumped into the front seat.

With a weary shrug Max told him, 'We had it on the run until you showed up.'

'I made my mess in Hamburg this trip.'

'You're not home yet, T. K.'

Malloy smiled bravely and looked out the window. No, he wasn't.

They drove to the back of The Gold Standard, one of Hasan Barzani's upscale clubs close to the banking district. 'Up the stairs before you get to the bar,' Max told him and then handed him a phone. 'Call me before you come outside again.'

Malloy found the back door unlocked but met an armed guard who seemed to be waiting for him. 'Have you got business here?' he asked.

'I'm here to see Alexa,' Malloy answered.

'Upstairs. Last door on your right.'

On the stairs Malloy had the odd sensation of being set up and kept his hand in his coat, the pocket cut way so he could keep his Uzi ready for a fight – just in case. He saw another guard at the top of the stairs but didn't speak to the man. At the last door on his right Malloy turned the handle and pushed into a tiny room fitted with a bed, a chair, a small chest of drawers, and a mirror. When he saw his old friend, Malloy said, 'They told me this was the place where I could find trouble.'

Hasan had stretched out on the bed and was reading a Russian newspaper. At the sight of Malloy, he dropped the paper and stood up, calling out cheerfully, 'Thomas! Marcus tells me every cop in Germany was chasing your ass yesterday!'

'They weren't quick enough,' Malloy told him and took the giant's bear-like embrace with a grimace of pain, his back aching. Malloy set his Uzi on the table next to Hasan's AK-47. Hasan was close to seven feet tall. He had had most of his height the first time the two had met some forty-three years ago. In those days Hasan was a rough piece of work whose sole pleasure was intimidation. Malloy had learnt a few self-defence tricks from his father, however, so when Hasan asked him for money to walk down *his* street Malloy had put the giant on his back. The move was so unexpected and so well practised that Hasan might have believed it was magic. It certainly had never happened to him before, not from a kid half his size! Rather than brood until he could get his revenge, which would have been easy enough to do, Hasan decided instead to make a new friend.

Having no more secret moves Malloy took the offer of friendship at once and proceeded to introduce Hasan to Marcus. Hasan, whose parents were refugees from the Soviet Union, had been dubious about the straight looking upper middle class Swiss kid until Marcus taught the giant how to pick a lock. After that their friendship was sealed for life.

By the time Malloy had returned to Zürich in his early twenties, Hasan was on the fast track for a long stretch in a Swiss prison. Malloy began managing things for him and within a year had him running the club where he had formerly worked as a bouncer. Within three years, and with two very public assassinations to clear the doubts away, Hasan had grabbed control of Zürich's small but lucrative market in sex, drugs, and stolen goods.

Hasan had not forgotten that Malloy had taken him from the street to the penthouse, but both men knew he had repaid his debt many times over with intelligence reports on a number of men it did not pay to anger. And there was another matter to consider as well. It had been a long time since Malloy's friendship had been of much use to Hasan. That made Hasan an asset Malloy was certainly not inclined to overuse or even trust beyond certain limits. The trouble was Hasan Barzani was the only person Malloy knew who could give him better intelligence than Langley.

'Marcus tells me you want to talk about the Italian mafia.'

'Actually I want to know what you can tell me about Giancarlo and Luca Bartoli.'

Hasan straightened to his full height, obviously not happy to hear the names. 'What is your business with those two, Thomas?'

'I think they might have tried to kill a friend of mine, but I can't prove it yet.'

'If those two want your friend dead, he has a serious problem!'

'Or they do.'

Hasan laughed with a bark of real enthusiasm. Yes, maybe it was the other way around!

'Giancarlo's fortune has tripled in the past decade, at least the accounts we know about. I want to know the secret of his success.'

'What can I say?' Hasan answered. 'Things are good right now in Italy.'

'Is he the new head of the families?'

'I hear that sometimes from people who don't know what they're talking about. The trouble is it's nothing more than a fantasy!'

'I've seen it written down in top secret reports.'

Hasan wasn't impressed. 'Here is the thing, Thomas. There are two families fighting for control of the north. In the south. . . things haven't changed since Caesar. From what I can tell, Bartoli pays protection to both families and stays out of the politics.'

'This lack of involvement. . . does that have anything to do with the assassination of his first son?'

Hasan lifted his shoulders. Maybe, maybe not.

'You're telling me he's not even connected?'

Another kick of the shoulder. He wasn't saying *that* exactly. 'The old dons are fighting over towns, Thomas, when they're not killing each other for the control of villages. They are fugitives hiding in farmhouses or prisoners sitting in high security jails and having their lawyers pass their orders on to their people. Giancarlo, meanwhile, is a major player in Europe. He pays his dues and stays clear of the old life.'

'Now see, this is why I wanted to talk to *you*. I'm reading reports that Giancarlo is really the new boss of bosses.'

Hasan shook his head, becoming more loquacious as Malloy laid on the flattery. 'Europe has changed, Thomas. Fifteen-twenty years ago, things were different. Every country had its own organisation and every organisation its own particular problems. The borders are open now. You've got Germans in Spain, Spaniards in France, English in Italy. . . and Russians everywhere!'

Malloy gave a shrug. The Russian mafia. They both knew about *that* mafia.

'The trouble with the Russians, they're not organised. They move in, take a piece of the street and hold on like pit bulls! But who are they fighting? Other immigrants! All of a sudden the people who ran things in the past are feeling the pressure. But what can they do? They can't start a fight on every street corner, and that's the only way to fight these immigrants. There is no organisation out there! It's just anarchy!'

Malloy nodded. 'The theory of *disorganised* crime.'

'Exactly! I mean if these people wanted to follow the rules, they wouldn't be criminals!'

Malloy smiled.

Hasan thought about things for a moment. 'But Old Money never goes away, Thomas. You know that. They start making alliances with the anarchists. They start specialising their services. People with contacts in South America or Africa bring drugs in, but now what? How do you take the drugs from one port into all of Europe? How do you get it to America? The pit bulls on the street corners don't know how to do this. They're running bags. The big picture. . . they don't even know the concept. It's a business like anything else. You've got a product, it doesn't matter what, women, cars, technology, counterfeit merchandise, gambling, bankruptcies scams, and-and-and! That's not even the end of it. After the product sells you have to think about the profits. You need to clean it up or you get caught with dirty money, and who wants that? And of course everyone always needs protection from the bloodthirsty politicians! So you've got two more industries coming into play.'

'So the Old Money lost control of the street corners, but they still get a piece of everything moving?'

Hasan lifted eyebrows and shoulders. What else? 'For a time,' he said, 'there was talk the Russian mafia was going to take over Europe. There's no talk like that anymore.'

'Why not?'

'Competition! New alliances. In-fighting. Politics. The

Russian mafia is like the old Soviet Union – it's there, but it's all in pieces.'

'So where do Luca and Giancarlo Bartoli fit into the scheme of things?'

'The old man runs a bankruptcy now and then to feed the dogs, but otherwise he's out of the game, Thomas. Who needs to go to prison at his age? Luca is another matter. He likes what he does. Like you, he's getting a little older but he can't stay home and live on the dividends. He's out making his deals, putting people together, making a reputation.'

'What does he do exactly?'

'Luca? Officially, he sits on a number of corporate boards, but the truth is he leaves his father's people to run the business side. He works with a couple of different crews out of Marseilles that move art and antiques through a couple companies in London. He has a top-notch counterfeit operation in Barcelona – good passports and EU cards. He is running some semi-legitimate businesses in Amsterdam to clean money and he has some people moving things out of North Africa into the islands and from there into the France and Spain.'

'Is he contracting assassinations?'

'Nothing like that. I mean when his brother was killed – this was years ago – that was different. He hunted down the family that ordered the assassination – every last mother's son. But that was personal.'

'He has to have some juice? People aren't going to give him their best markets without a fight.'

'The old man still has friends. You touch Luca's operations, you push him out of a market and bad things happen. Nobody bothers him that I've heard about, and he's fairly insulated from the police. . .'

'Would you call him a major player?'

'He runs a few crews. The money is good, but the old man taught him to keep a low profile.'

'I'm looking for someone capable of organising a political assassination.'

'That kind of thing I don't hear about. Me? I wouldn't touch a Swiss cop for the world. A politician? Forget it! When someone important is killed they never stop coming! They buy your enemies. They threaten your friends. If you want to kill politicians and get away with it there aren't many people willing to do it for you, and those who are cost a small fortune. If you want to spend like that, you might as well buy them.'

'I understand that. But someone is doing it.'

'Not Luca.'

'What do you know about a man named David Carlisle?'

Hasan shook his head, but there was a quick, nervous tick, a moment when the eyes lost focus.

'Are you sure? He's an Englishman. Maybe our age, a couple years younger. . . could be friends with Luca. . . ?'

Hasan lifted his hands, palms upwards, as if to say the name didn't mean anything. He was lying, but Malloy didn't push it. Knowing Hasan was lying to him was all he really needed to know. David Carlisle scared him, it seemed, and Malloy didn't know anyone who scared Hasan.

'Helena Chernoff?'

'Not a lady I want to meet.'

'You know the people she works for?'

He shook his head. 'As far as I know she's independent.'

'The past decade or so she's been involved with a cartel. . .'

'No. She has people working for her, Thomas, but she's free-lance – she goes to the highest bidder and always has.'

'Could she kill a politician?'

'If she had people who could arrange the contract and maybe organise the logistical support.'

'Do you know a man named Hugo Ohlendorf?'

Again, a shake of the head. This time probably legitimate.

Before he left Malloy asked about Hasan's family. The giant lost the tension in his face and talked easily about his daughters and sons. Then talk turned to old friends and the usual litany of misfortunes and illnesses that come with the passing of time. As they left Hasan said, 'You take care of yourself, Thomas!'

It was a kind remark and certainly genuine, but Malloy could not help remember that the last time he had been in trouble Hasan had offered to help. This time, it seemed, he was on his own.

After his phone call to Max, Malloy came out the back door of The Gold Standard and slipped into the Mercedes. 'Good meeting?' Max asked as his eyes scanned the shadows.

'Instructive.'

'So where to now?'

'I was thinking about having a drink at the Savoy.'

Chapter Ten

Zürich, Switzerland
Monday-Tuesday March 10-11, 2008.

A uniformed private security guard stood before the door to Kate and Ethan's suite. 'You have business here, sir?' he asked in Swiss German. Malloy said he wanted to see Mr Peter Bartholomew. 'And your name is?'

'T. K.'

The man knocked on the door without taking his eyes off Malloy. Ethan opened the door with an easy-going grin. 'He's okay.' To Malloy he said, 'Come on in. We were beginning to wonder if something had happened.'

Malloy walked into their suite and saw Kate sitting up in bed. She had a set of three throwing knives resting on her lap. A knife-scarred sheet of plywood with a human silhouette drawn on it leaned against the wall opposite the foot of her bed. She held one knife up and smiled. 'You care to try your luck?'

'Don't do it,' Ethan told him. 'She just wants your money.'

'The neighbours must love you,' Malloy said.

'The neighbours on either side are Securitas,' Ethan told him. 'They're getting paid to be miserable. You want a drink?'

'Thanks, but I had a beer at lunch and passed out for the rest of the day.'

'We're hopped up on meds and can't drink anything,' Kate answered. She sent three knives at the target in rapid succession, using her right, left, and right hands. Only the left handed throw was wide of the kill zone.

'Would you like some orange juice?' Ethan asked.

'Orange juice sounds good.'

'Any news?' Kate asked.

'Quite a bit, actually.' At their look of sudden interest, he added, 'The good news first. Josh came out of surgery without complications. He's flying home tomorrow.'

'Anything on Jim?' Ethan asked.

Malloy's face tightened. 'Jim was dead when Chernoff called us to make the trade.'

Kate and Ethan lost their smiles.

'As near as I can tell Chernoff or one of her operatives drove him to an apartment about a mile away and then recorded him telling me to help him. Chernoff set her trap at the back of *Das Sternenlicht* and called Josh. She was already on the roof with the recording when I talked to her.'

'You think Jim told her where we were hiding? Ethan asked.

'I don't think Jim had any idea where we were. He was lost without GPS. I think Chernoff got our location from my cell phone.'

'How would she have got that?' Kate asked.

'From Dale's cell phone. There were only two numbers in the address book, and one of them was in America. She was hooked into the provider and found the phone – the same way Dale found the phone we thought belonged to her.'

'I hope you've changed phones,' Kate said, trying to make it sound like a joke.

'Not until I used the old one to bait Chernoff into coming after me.'

This got the expected reaction: disbelief, surprise, and ultimately, with the news of Chernoff's capture, a profound sense of relief. At their insistence, still not believing it, Malloy went through everything from Chernoff's take down and arrest by the Germans to the capture of her cell phone and computer. At the mention of Chernoff's computer files Ethan wanted to know if Malloy thought it might lead them to Jack Farrell. That had been the point of going to Hamburg after all.

'I think it's safe to assume Jack Farrell was dead when Irina Turner left New York,' Malloy told them.

'What are you talking about?' Kate asked.

'We've been chasing a ghost.'

Ethan stirred. 'I thought they had proof Farrell was at the Barcelona airport and then inside the Royal Meridien. Photographs, fingerprints, DNA. . .' He looked at Kate for confirmation. They had seen it all on TV.

'Irina Turner needed a stand-in for the surveillance photos and bank transactions, but the DNA and fingerprints were easy enough to leave behind.'

'How did she. . .?' Ethan stopped himself. Between test tubes with bodily fluids and severed digits, it wasn't that difficult to leave trace evidence for crime scene teams to find. With Irina Turner's story to support the evidence, everyone had just assumed. . .

'So why make it look like Farrell was running?' Kate asked. 'I don't understand. What was the point?'

'Chernoff's employer got wind of what I was doing with the SEC investigation and decided to silence Farrell before he could do any damage. While he was at it, he had Irina embezzle roughly four-hundred-sixty million dollars. To cover his tracks, he made it look like Jack Farrell had done it and was on the run with the money. The police raid on the Royal Meridien put the pressure on, and the person I had used to start the investigation against Farrell sent me over to do what I could to make Farrell go away.'

'You're saying Chernoff's employer knew you were involved in this before Farrell even disappeared?' Ethan asked.

'They knew all three of us were involved. From what I can tell, we were the targets in the multiple assassinations Ohlendorf mentioned.'

'But that was. . . a couple of months ago!'

'Phase one was to get Irina Turner in place. She was the specialist Chernoff needed. She moved the money off shore and then apparently killed Farrell. Next came the pretence of flight, and finally the publicity. The near-miss at the Royal Meridien was the bait that was designed to draw the three of us to Hamburg.'

'Why not just find you in New York and us in Zürich?'

'If the three of us had been killed in Hamburg, my people would have denied any knowledge of what I was doing, but they would have known I was on assignment and that would have answered any questions they might have had. If someone shot me down in New York – or if I just had a heart attack – there would have been some interest in what I had been doing, and that would have led to Farrell and Robert Kenyon and the Council of Paladins. So instead of shutting down the enquiry, killing me in New York would have generated a lot more interest.'

'How could anyone know you instigated the investigation against Farrell?' Kate asked.

'I made a number of enquiries about Robert Kenyon. In some cases, I hired people to check out certain addresses or acquire certain records. Apparently Robert Kenyon's killer found out what I was doing and decided Farrell was a liability he could not afford.'

'Giancarlo told me I had to let this thing go. He said if I didn't he couldn't protect Ethan or me.'

'When was this?'

'A few weeks ago – at the party.'

'About the time Farrell disappeared. . .' Malloy thought about it. 'So he was telling you not to go to Hamburg. . .'

'He couldn't have known that was going to happen.'

'Maybe he contacted you to find out if my investigation was connected to Robert Kenyon's murder.'

Kate thought about this without answering.

'How do they know about the three of us?' Ethan asked.

'Helena Chernoff worked for Julian Corbeau – back when the three of us took him down. She had our names and at least some basic information about all of us. I have been assuming she was hired by the paladins to kill us, but I think it's possible she provided some of the intel on me before she arranged the trap for us in Hamburg. That could mean she is in partnership with some or all of the people we've been looking at – not just a contract assassin.'

'I don't understand something,' Ethan said. 'If Jack Farrell had to be killed because he knew too much, why bother coming after us?'

'Because Farrell isn't the only one with the information we're looking for. I think Ohlendorf could have taken us to Kenyon's killer, and I think Giancarlo and Luca know the truth. In fact, at this point, I think we have to admit that Ethan has been right about this thing from the start. The paladins or some faction of them were involved in Kenyon's death.'

'There are nine paladins,' Ethan told him.

'Ohlendorf represented four of them: Johannes Diekmann and the other three founding members. Once you remove the emeritus members from the equation you have Jack Farrell, Farrell's father, Robert Kenyon, Hugo Ohlendorf, Giancarlo and Luca Bartoli – all active at the time of Robert Kenyon's death. At this point they are all dead except for Luca and Giancarlo.'

'We don't *know* Jack Farrell is dead,' Ethan said.

'Farrell was a businessman. As far as I can see he wasn't involved in much except for laundering money and working some bankruptcy scams with Giancarlo. I don't think he was capable of arranging what happened to us in Hamburg.'

'That's why he hired Chernoff.'

Malloy shrugged. 'Okay. It's a possibility, at least until we find the body.'

'What about the other two paladins?' Kate asked.

'David Carlisle replaced Kenyon. Christine Foulkes joined the council a couple of years later, after Jack Farrell's father passed away. I suppose Carlisle could be involved. He seems to have gained by Lord Kenyon's death, but Foulkes doesn't make sense. I put her with Diekmann and the socialites – not really involved in the criminal activities.'

'So what do we know about Carlisle?' Kate asked.

Malloy lifted his hands in a gesture of frustration. 'The guy is a ghost. He has a permanent address in Paris, an apartment in the city actually, but he's never there. Never. Different people occasionally use the apartment, there's a regular maid service, and someone goes by once in a while to pick up mail and restock the place, but no one, including the landlord, has ever met Mr Carlisle.'

'There is quite a bit about him in the annual reports the paladins put out,' Ethan said. 'I've seen pictures of him and summaries of his activities. Outside of that, I can't find anything about him.'

'I've seen some credit reports, some activity on his UK passport, but nothing conclusive,' Malloy told them.

'How much do we know about his history?' Kate asked.

'Just the bare bones. He was born and raised in Liverpool. As a young man he kicked around the docks before he finally drifted into the armed forces. No immediate family is left and his cousins haven't seen him since he was a kid. Old friends from school don't even remember him – so he is either a very frightening individual or he didn't have much personality. From those who do recall him, it could be a bit of both.'

'He served in the SAS for six years,' Ethan added.

'The people he served with told my investigators he was a loner. They also said he was very good at what he did, but of course the SAS doesn't take any other kind. After he left the service, under some kind of suspicious circumstances as I understand it, he went off radar for about three years – no jobs, no travel, no contacts with his old friends. That usually means some kind of criminal activity. . . or living on the streets. The next time his passport surfaces he's travelling in Africa and South America and working for a security firm that's contracted with some of the big oil companies.'

'A mercenary?' Ethan asked.

'They call it security, but in some of those places a person with the right credentials can earn six hundred to a thousand dollars a day. That went on for a couple of years and then he began travelling in the Balkans – back when it was the last place on earth a reasonable person would want to go. At about the same time Robert Kenyon was there. Since Carlisle had served under Robert Kenyon's command during the Falklands War, my guess is they were operating together, but just what they were doing is anybody's guess.'

'Robert was buying paintings and antique furniture,' Kate told him.

Malloy smiled. 'Robert was more than likely with British intelligence. We know his maternal grandfather was an MI6 operative after the War and was actually the one responsible for organising the Knights of the Holy Lance as a cover for a number of activities that he launched behind the Iron Curtain. Lord Kenyon might have been buying and selling antiques in the Balkan countries, but I promise you this, that wasn't all he was doing.'

Kate looked at him without responding.

'For years no one in Europe wanted to get involved in the Balkans,' Malloy told her. 'Not officially at least, so people were sent in undercover. The paladins sent humanitarian aid into the region – which can be an excellent cover for people involved in covert activities.'

'You think Carlisle is in hiding because of something that happened in the Balkans?' Ethan asked.

'That could be the case, but the really dangerous people are all dead or locked away. I'm more inclined to think he's in league with Chernoff as some sort of partner in assassination. He may also be supplying mercenaries and weapons to different places. At least, that is how he profiles.'

'Maybe Carlisle wasn't working for Kenyon,' Ethan said. 'Maybe he was working for the other side.'

'That would explain the low profile, but not his association with the paladins.'

'Carlisle sounds like a man we ought to talk to,' Kate said.

'I had three viable choices other than Giancarlo or Luca

Bartoli when we started looking at this thing last year: Jack Farrell, Hugo Ohlendorf, and David Carlisle. There were a lot of reasons to go to Farrell, but obviously Carlisle is the only choice left. So if we can find him, by all means we'll talk to him!'

Ethan looked at Kate. 'Giancarlo might know where he is. It wouldn't hurt to ask him, would it?'

'He might be willing to tell Carlisle how to find us. . .'

Malloy smiled and shook his head. 'After what happened in Hamburg, I'm not sure that's such a good idea.'

'So what do we do?' Ethan asked.

'Mend,' Malloy told him. 'Wait. Look at some fresh information from Chernoff's computer that's coming in tomorrow. If she was partnering with Carlisle the information ought to be there. If it comes fast enough, we might even find the guy before he goes to ground. But for now, unless you want to talk to Giancarlo or Luca about their involvement in Robert's death, that is where it stands.'

'They're out of the question,' Kate answered.

'You want to know what happened,' Malloy answered, 'and they have the information. . .'

'They're family, T. K.'

'That's where most violence occurs.'

'It's not an option.'

Malloy looked at Ethan for support, but in this he had no ally. 'Then we'll find David Carlisle,' he said.

Zürich, Switzerland
Tuesday March 11, 2008.

Malloy called Gwen on the hotel phone when he got back to his room. It was late in the evening in New York, but Gwen answered like she had been waiting for his call. Nothing was certain yet, he said, but he thought he might be coming home in a few days. He was running out of leads. Gwen told him she missed him terribly. He said he missed her as well and realised just how lonely he was as he said it. *Home* had a nice sound to it.

He started getting ready for bed after his call but decided he wasn't really ready to go to sleep. His nights and days had got turned upside down. Cracking open his purloined Hart Brothers Scotch, he sat down and began going through the files on Hugo Ohlendorf that he had taken from Dale's computer.

Dale Perry of course had found Ohlendorf through his contact with a Hamburg hoodlum on the rise. From those meetings Dale knew Ohlendorf was involved in *something*, but he didn't know what it was or the extent of Ohlendorf's involvement. Accordingly, Dale had made a comprehensive study of the man over a period of several months. He had listed every organisation to which Ohlendorf belonged, including the Knights of the Holy Lance, and his involvement as the representative of Johannes Diekmann and the three Berlin socialites who had helped to found the Order in the summer of 1961. Despite nearly a thousand hours spent on the investigation Dale had unearthed very little Malloy did not already have.

The Order of the Knights of the Holy Lance had taken shape under the direction of Sir William Savage, an Englishman living in West Berlin in the early years of the Cold War. Sir William had been a VP in a major construction company, but as records now indicated he was in reality part of British Intelligence. As soon as West Berlin came under siege Sir William persuaded one of his key operatives, a German aristocrat and a former SS officer named Johannes Diekmann, to help establish a resistance organisation. . . if the unthinkable occurred. Diekmann had suggested they recruit a number of socially prominent individuals in the city who would dedicate themselves to raising consciousness in the West about the importance of keeping West Berlin free. Using these individuals to conduct a public relations campaign, Diekmann and Savage had then gone quietly about recruiting individuals capable of crossing into East Germany and establishing covert operations amongst the disaffected and quasi criminal classes.

As tensions had eased over the years, Sir William's operations reached farther into the Communist-run countries of the East Bloc. Whilst the operations were undoubtedly funded by British Intelligence at the beginning, Sir William and his fellow paladins had taken pains to create a financial base through corporate contributions that were in fact only partially legitimate. By the 1980s the paladins had established a complex and a rather cosy relationship with a number of the major criminal factions in Europe.

With nine paladins sitting on the council, each with one vote, the Order had been seemingly independent of Sir William from the very beginning. In fact, Savage had appointed friends and family to the council, starting with his daughters' husbands, the fathers of Jack Farrell and Robert Kenyon, and two Italian businessmen with whom he had a long and intimate relationship, Giancarlo Bartoli and Giancarlo's father.

By the time of German reunification Lord Robert Kenyon was representing Sir William's interests on the board. Following Sir William's death, Robert Kenyon had assumed his grandfather's seat with the full authority of a paladin. By the time Luca and Jack Farrell became paladins, the world had changed. The threat of Communism had faded, and the paladins responded by changing the mission of the Order of the Knights of the Holy Lance. What had not changed, at least until the death of Robert Kenyon, was the control of the paladins. Sir William's faction of five had trumped Johannes Diekmann's four votes – effectively guiding the Order in all things great and small. This meant that until 1997 the paladins sanctioned no activity that was not at least marginally in the interests of the Crown.

The dynamic had changed when the next two paladins joined the Council. David Carlisle and Christine Foulkes had no allegiance to either faction. That gave them the power to forge temporary alliances with either Ohlendorf or Bartoli. It was tempting to imagine that Kenyon's death was connected to some kind of internal discord within the paladins, but Malloy had found no evidence of it. The paladins seemed to have a direct interest in large sections of the black market economy throughout Europe. That was indisputable. Whether or not there was discord amongst the leadership, he could not say.

This much he had worked through. First, Hugo Ohlendorf had access to, if not control of, a great deal of criminal talent. These were individuals willing to commit murder in league with one of the most notorious assassins in Europe. David Carlisle, with his mercenary and perhaps political contacts in various countries, was undoubtedly capable of dealing in weapons, drugs, and mercenary soldiers. Jack Farrell, like his father before him, had worked with Giancarlo Bartoli in a number of ventures on both sides of the Atlantic – sometimes legitimately and sometimes otherwise.

Finally, there was Christine Foulkes. She was an oddity. A one-time celebrity party girl, Foulkes had joined the Council of Paladins and virtually withdrawn from public scrutiny. Like Carlisle, one found file photos in the annual reports, one read about her activities on behalf of the Order, but no one else encountered her. That meant the paladins were lying about her activities, or she was travelling under assumed identities. David Carlisle might use multiple identities to travel, but Malloy could not see why Foulkes would take that kind of risk.

After skimming Dale Perry's summaries, Malloy ran file searches on Christine Foulkes, David Carlisle, Giancarlo and Luca Bartoli, as well as the inactive paladins whom Ohlendorf had represented: Johannes Diekmann, Sarah von Wittsberg, Lady Margarite Schoals, and Dame Ann Marie Wolff. The result was a gold mine of information, but like any gold mine, most of it was rock and mud. At five, almost ready to close down, he came across a series of surveillance photos of David Carlisle. When the photographs were taken, Carlisle had been meeting Hugo Ohlendorf in Paris in 2005.

As these were relatively current and showed a somewhat different face from the file photographs of David Carlisle that the paladins published each year, Malloy copied them to a memory stick, along with a number of general files about the paladins. He thought Ethan would have most of this, but it did not hurt to be thorough. He hoped to have something more substantial after picking up the summaries Jane was sending him the following morning.

In the meantime, he closed down his computer and tried to get a few hours of sleep.

Berlin, Germany
Spring 1936.

After his trip to Wewelsburg Rahn promised himself he would not see the Bachmans, at least for a while. He was certainly too angry with Bachman to spend an evening as if nothing were wrong! But when Saturday came round, he showed up at their door. He had a picture book for Sarah, wildflowers again for Elise, and a bottle of good Riesling wine for Bachman. He took the kisses of the girl and her mother – all that he really had in the world – and settled down to drink and talk. Nothing at all was different between them.

As he was leaving, Elise said to him whilst they kissed good-night, 'Dieter tells me you might be having problems with Himmler. . .' She looked worried. He had not seen worry in her eyes before and understood suddenly that his dismissal of Himmler's absurd idea might create serious problems for Bachman, and by extension for Elise.

He shook his head and tried not to show the tension he suddenly felt. 'Not at all,' he said. 'I was simply confused about something Dieter told me.'

'You must be careful, Otto. Himmler is fickle with his affection. Keep him happy and the world is yours.'

'So perhaps I should find him his Holy Grail!'

'Keep him hopeful, as Dieter suggests, and he will feed you honours and acclaim. Ignore him and—'

Bachman walked toward them. 'What are these whispers?'

'We are plotting to kill Hitler!' Rahn answered, but he forgot to smile as he said it.

Bachman blanched at the joke, but then he laughed. 'And I thought it was something I should be worried about!'

Rahn found Bachman at his office late the following week. 'I have been thinking about what you said. I want you to arrange a meeting for us with Himmler – whatever time is good for the two of you.'

'You are not going to do something foolish, I hope?'

'On the contrary, I have a proposal for the both of you.'

Bachman looked relieved. 'That is wonderful news, Otto!'

'Will he fund an expedition, do you think?'

'If you think there is some chance of success he will!'

'Are you interested in joining me?'

'Only say the word, and I am there!'

The meeting came the following evening in Himmler's office. Himmler had put in another long day and seemed only to want to get home to his family. 'What can I do for you?' he asked. His smile flickered politely and died.

Feeling a moment of panic take hold of him, Rahn's voice came out with trembling uncertainty. 'Major Bachman tells me. . . that is, I understand. . . from him. . .' Rahn took a deep breath and tried to steady himself. He was like a school boy facing examinations before the master! 'I understand you have some hope of my finding the Grail.'

Himmler did not look at Bachman, nor did he appear surprised. His curious gaze remained settled on Rahn. 'You said in your book that it was at Montségur before the surrender. As I recall, you tell a story in your book about how it was taken and hidden somewhere *in* Mount Tabor.'

'I said it was a legend the locals told amongst themselves – something no outsider had ever heard.'

Himmler's face remained expressionless. 'That was what appealed to me. I am curious, have the caves all been thoroughly explored?'

'There is of course a great deal of interest at the moment, but no, I think there are many that have been overlooked. The thing is I am not convinced the Grail is even an object.'

Himmler's eyes cut to Bachman, and Rahn understood everything. Bachman had given Himmler more than his book. He had convinced Himmler that Rahn needed only the funding in order to find the Grail. He had probably told Himmler that Dr Rahn had secretly been in search of the Grail for over a decade but had not had the funds to make a proper go of it. Once upon a time Rahn *had* thrown himself into the search, but that had given way to the actual beauties of history he had discovered along the way and ultimately to the story that he had realised he wanted to tell. But Himmler had no interest in history unless it served him. He wanted to believe the Cathars were Aryans and keepers of the Grail and of course persecuted by an evil and corrupt Church.

'That is not to say,' Rahn added, 'that there was no sacred object at Montségur.' He had the sensation suddenly of listening to himself as if from some perspective beyond his own body. 'In fact, I have always believed they worshipped the Blood Lance that Percival witnessed in the Grail Castle.'

Himmler moved in his chair. 'The Blood Lance?'

'The Blood Lance, of course, was never identified as the spear that had pierced Christ at the Crucifixion. It was simply a lance of pure ivory that dripped blood into a gold chalice.'

'You think that is what they possessed?' Himmler asked excitedly. The exhaustion Rahn had seen in his eyes only moments ago had simply vanished.

'From what I can see, the Cathars accorded the Blood Lance a higher honour by far than the Cross. If you recall Eschenbach's narrative, Percival saw it carried through the banquet hall at the Grail Castle and no one gave a word of explanation about its origins. For many years, I have to admit, I imagined the Lance *guarded* the Grail, which was either the cup or something inside the cup that Percival could not see. I think now, however, that the Grail refers to the blood – that which dripped from the tip. You have only to look at the word *Sangraal* to see the possibility. We normally break the word down into *San Graal*, the Sacred or Holy Grail, but if we break it down as *Sang Raal* you see that *Sacred* becomes instead *blood* and *raal* is a pun on *real* – meaning Royal. In other words *Sangraal* means Royal Blood – the blood which flows continuously from the Lance!'

'You are telling me the Grail *is* the Blood Lance?'

'More precisely the *blood* of the Lance is the Grail.' Rahn held up his hands. 'This is only theory, you understand, and I do not mean to suggest that there is actually an ivory lance that bleeds. This is what you have to understand: the Blood Lance and gold chalice are divine visions. The Cathars, after all, were a spiritual people. They rejected the world and its treasures. They took no succour from its pleasures because they sought something much finer in the world of the spirit. And that spirituality was embodied in their vision of the bleeding Lance.'

Himmler's eyes lost their lustre. He did not care to be disillusioned.

'That is not to say they did not possess *something*. The problem for me has always been to determine just what the relic was exactly. It is difficult, as you can imagine, to be certain without actually finding it, of course, but I am now convinced that the relic they possessed is the Holy Lance Peter Bartholomew discovered at Antioch during the first Crusade. If you recall your history, Reichsführer, the Crusaders had laid siege to Antioch for seven months, all the while hoping for reinforcements and supplies that never came. Just when they were convinced they were going to have to retreat, one of the barons arranged for someone inside the city to open one of the gates. That was all it took. By the end of the day, Antioch belonged to the Crusaders. The following morning, however, an army of two hundred thousand Turks arrived on the plain before Antioch. A day sooner and they would have annihilated the Christians. As it was, the Turks were forced to lay siege to the city, whilst the Crusaders enjoyed the protection of Antioch's impressive defensive works, including some four hundred towers. The problem for the Christians was this: they had no supplies and no way of getting any.

'They consumed what rations they had within the first few days of the siege. After that it was every man for himself and all that comes of an army in the grip of famine. Soon the army could barely climb the walls to defend the city. When a fire broke out one evening – a common enough occurrence in medieval times – the men did not even roll out of their beds to try to put it out. Against Christians they would have sued for peace. Against the Turks surrender meant massacre. So they starved instead and prayed for a miracle. Then even the prayers ceased. They were dead men, every last one of them, and every last one of them knew it.

'Now it was just at this point that a cleric named Peter Bartholomew went to his priest and told the man about a vision he had had on a number of occasions. In it St. Andrew would tell him the Holy Lance – the spear that had pierced the side of Christ – was buried under the floor of a church some-where inside the city. In those times, something like this was more than a curiosity. It was a sign from God to be taken very seriously, and the priest went at once to Bartholomew's feudal lord, Raymond, Count of St. Gilles. Raymond went to his fellow barons with the news. After some obvious scepticism the barons agreed to lead Peter from church to church through the city and see if he could recognise the place he had seen in his vision. When they came to the church of St. Peter, Bartholomew cried out, "This is the place I saw!" Within a few hours they had dug a deep trench under the floor in front of the altar. Exhausted and discouraged the last of the enthusiasts were ready to leave when Peter threw himself into the trench and began clawing into the mud. A moment later he screamed to them it was here, he had found something. Then as they waited he brought a piece of mud-caked iron out of the earth.

'He had not even got out of the trench when Raymond fell

to his knees at the edge of the trench and, according to the chronicles, bathed the mud-smeared object with his tears and kisses. Naturally word of the discovery spread through the army, and a faith that had gone dead suddenly stirred again inside every man's heart. God himself might as well have appeared in the skies to promise them victory. This was a sign and every man knew it: the Lord had willed them to take Jerusalem from the infidel and the Jews. They had only to stand up and fight. Victory was theirs for the asking!

'Instead of manning the walls to defend the city, the army *insisted* they be given the chance to face the enemy in the open. The Lance held high on a stake so that every man might see it, the Crusaders marched out in formation and broke the enemy's force in the course of a single afternoon.

'Now,' Rahn said, 'here is the interesting part of the story.'

Himmler tipped his head forward – enamoured of the tale.

'For a time, everyone turned to Peter Bartholomew before the army made any decision. He would hold the Lance against his chest and declare whatever vision or thought came into his mind. Eventually, of course, the priests, all of them slaves of the papacy, became jealous and they stirred resentment against Peter Bartholomew's divine oracles.'

'Yes!' Himmler whispered, for he hated the Church, even as he had once loved it.

'To put an end to Peter Bartholomew's authority, the priests baited the poor man into a trial by fire to prove his relic was genuine. In those days, Reichsführer, a trial by fire was not a metaphor. They set a large area afire and waited until it had burned down and only white coals remained. Then they sent a man walking across the coals to see if God protected him. Peter, clutching the Lance to his chest, crossed the coals in his bare feet, and he would have made it, but certain of the priests came pushing their way to the edge of the trench and told him he had got turned around. He must go the other way to cross the coals. Naturally, the poor man turned and started back the way he had come – every step melting his flesh. His friends tried to help him out of the pit, but poor Peter wanted to prove his Lance and so he stayed in the pit until he had returned the way he had come – so confused he nearly collapsed and died where he stood. And he would have. . . if not for the Lance.

'It was of course too much for any man, and Peter lay close to death, but he would not let go of the Holy Lance. He held on to it for thirteen days before he died – some even say he was murdered. Whatever the truth, it ended for him on 20 April, 1098.'

'The twentieth of April! That is the Führer's birthday!' Himmler cried.

Rahn nodded, afraid to show too much enthusiasm. 'I thought too it was a propitious omen.'

'But what happened to the Lance!'

'At Peter's death the Lance passed into the care of his feudal lord, Raymond of St. Gilles. According to eyewitnesses Raymond had a reliquary made for it. By later standards it could not have been very impressive, and it was certainly not very large, but he had it gilded and then covered the lid with the pearls and rubies he had in his personal treasury. Then he arranged to have armed priests guard his relic night and day and carry it behind him everywhere he went. You have to understand, a relic of the Passion, as he believed this was, could buy a kingdom in those days. Naturally, something of that value could turn an otherwise quite religious man into a thief. This object, after all, had been covered in their Saviour's blood and had proved its miraculous power at Antioch and then again when Peter Bartholomew survived what would have killed any other man!

'For five years Raymond's priests carried the Lance of Antioch in a procession behind him – even into war – and for five years the army that marched behind Raymond was never defeated.'

'The True Lance!' Himmler whispered.

'It seemed so,' Rahn admitted, 'but then, on the occasion of Raymond's visit to Constantinople, it simply disappeared.'

Rahn hesitated, watching Himmler, then Bachman. Both men waited for more – the point of his narrative. 'That was the story Raymond gave, at least. As far as I'm concerned he had good reason to lie and absolutely no motivation to admit to having the relic still in his possession. You see, as Raymond was leaving Constantinople, an old rival of his, the Prince of Antioch, kidnapped him. According to the custom of the day, he demanded a ransom for Raymond's release. Obviously the prince, a fellow Crusader, expected to be given the Lance in exchange for Raymond's freedom. He wanted it returned to Antioch, which is understandable, but Raymond told him it had been taken from him in Constantinople. Despite continual torture and interrogation for over a year, Raymond held to his story. He had lost it! He could not return what he did not have. A year later, apparently convinced, the prince accepted gold instead of the relic he desired, and nobody has ever heard of the Lance of Antioch since.'

'But he had it all along!' Himmler cried.

Rahn smiled. 'If Peter Bartholomew could walk over burning coals Raymond was man enough to hold out against torture. After his release his health was broken, of course. He was an old man at the start of the Crusade. He knew he had only a few weeks to live before his body gave out, and he arranged his affairs as best he could. To his eldest, an illegitimate son, he gave command of his forces in the Levant. To his infant son, and rightful heir, he gave his possessions in the Languedoc and sent the boy home in a ship. And with the boy, I believe he sent the Lance of Antioch as well.'

Himmler sat back in his chair, his eyes lit with passion.

'Now you must understand,' Rahn told him, 'the Lance was nothing more than a piece of twisted, corroded iron. It did not even look like the head of a lance. That much we know from eyewitness descriptions, but what it had inspired was undeniably miraculous. As the story was told from one to another over the years the relic became something more than a piece of iron. Its rust became in the imagination of those who venerated it the *Sang Raal* – the Sacred Blood. Its twisted, corroded form became the ivory lance that bled continuously into a gold chalice that could never be filled.

'To follow this vision was to follow the way of the Cathars, to yearn continually after the world of the spirit. When all else was lost at Montségur, the knights surrendered their lives but not the relic that had inspired the divine vision. *That* they would not surrender to the hated priests of Rome.

'Can you imagine over two hundred men, women, and children walking into the Inquisitor's fire on the morning of 16 March in 1244? Can you see them leaving the fortress and walking into the flames without a single voice crying out in terror until the flames actually consumed them?'

Himmler's eyes glittered at the image.

'They did not trust in the mud-stained relic Peter Bartholomew had found. They believed in and followed the divine image of the Blood Lance. They walked into fire, even as Peter Bartholomew had done.'

'But the Lance itself? You think they buried it *in the mountain*, as the legend tells it?'

Rahn shook his head, giving the man a taste of doubt. 'No one knows. I saw the image of the Blood Lance and Chalice in one of the chambers inside the *Grotto de Lombrives*.'

'You mentioned that in your book!'

'I showed the painting to Major Bachman soon after we met. You remember seeing it, don't you, Dieter?'

Both men looked at Bachman, who nodded confirmation.

'They might have hidden it there, in the Lombrives, I suppose, or any of the other caves in the region. Mount Tabor is literally honeycombed with caves. Of course it is also possible that the legend is nothing more than pure nonsense – like most of the rest of the stories one encounters. It is entirely possible that nothing at all is waiting to be found – that the vision of the Blood Lance is purely a gift of the spirit that only a True Cathar can attain.'

Himmler considered the matter with a sudden look of

caution. 'You are saying then, that all you really have is the legend an old man told you when you climbed the mountain – and a painting on a cave wall?'

Rahn let one shoulder kick up. 'I told Major Bachman that a couple of weeks ago. It is hardly promising, as I told him, but since our talk I have been thinking about it. . .'

Himmler's head tipped; he was listening.

'Esclarmonde, according to the legend, threw the Grail into *Mount Tabor*.' Himmler waited with a look of uncertainty. 'Mount Tabor is the name of a mountain north of Galilee – where the Transfiguration is thought by some to have occurred – when Christ appeared to three of his disciples as something other than a mortal being. It is exactly the same with the Lance. One looked upon a lump of iron that had been *transfigured* into something divine – the Blood Lance of Eschenbach's Grail legend.

'There is also the rather curious fact that Mount Tabor's peak in the Languedoc is called St. Bartholomew.'

'After Peter Bartholomew, do you think?'

'It could be just another coincidence, except that the caves themselves into which the Grail was thrown, if we can believe the legend, are known as the *Sabarthès* – a simple corruption of Saint Bartholomew.'

Himmler's caution faded. This was the clue that would take them to the Lance! Rahn maintained the thoughtful countenance of a scholar still probing for a working hypothesis.

'Peter Bartholomew's example of courage must have inspired all those who were about to face the flames of the Inquisition – and of course he too was a victim of the clergy and fire. From a simple, humble cleric, his faith had turned him into the first knight of the Blood Lance.'

'But this is incredible!' Himmler cried excitedly. '*The Sabarthès!* The caves hold Peter Bartholomew's relic!'

Rahn smiled sheepishly. 'I had every piece of evidence in front of me for the past five years, but until Major Bachman pushed me to consider an expedition I just could not see it! Now. . . of course I cannot promise success, but I think there is perhaps. . . *some* small hope. . .'

'What do you need to find it?' Himmler asked. 'Tell me, and it is yours!'

Rahn managed to look surprised, as if hardly expecting Himmler to respond at once, but in truth he was ready. 'I am thinking. . . a dozen to twenty men. They ought to be miners or men used to hard labour underground. If it is anywhere, it is deep inside the mountain, somewhere beyond the reach of smooth-fingered priests.' He turned toward Bachman. 'I will also need a squad to support the expedition: transportation, equipment, and a base of operations. I don't think it would be wise to let on we are going in search of anything. The French might be very reluctant to cooperate. In fact, we might make a show of sending me somewhere else so no one suspects our real intentions. . .'

'That can be arranged easily enough,' Bachman said. He looked at Himmler. 'He might sail to Iceland, looking for evidence of the Hyperboreans.'

'A ship would be good,' Himmler nodded. 'We can make a show of having a double of Dr Rahn entering a ship and then be done with the charade.' He turned to Rahn, 'But tell me, Dr Rahn, how soon can you start such an expedition?'

'I want to see some people in Switzerland who have explored a number of the caves. Then I would like to arrive in advance of the expedition by a few days so that I might establish a protocol for a systematic search. I can start at once. If Major Bachman could be ready in say. . . a month that would be ideal.'

Himmler turned to Bachman. 'That won't be a problem, will it, Major?'

'No problem at all, Reichsführer,' Bachman answered.

'One thing,' Rahn answered, almost hesitating to interrupt.

Himmler looked curious. 'Certainly, what is it?'

'I should like to see the Order of the Cathars established

within the SS – if we are lucky enough to find the Lance – with the Lance of Antioch as their own.'

Himmler smiled with the indulgence of an older and wiser man. 'Let us find your Lance of Antioch first, shall we, Dr Rahn? Then we can worry about its fate!'

Bachman was pleased. He could not understand why Rahn was not. 'You have your expedition! What more do you want?' he asked when they met to work out the details.

'What do we tell Himmler when we have searched the last cave and it does not exist?' Rahn asked him.

Bachman looked stricken. 'But we know where to look!'

'They *buried* it, Dieter, because they did not want anyone to find it! That is, *if* it even existed!'

'But you made it sound like it would be no great problem!'

Rahn looked away angrily. 'Where do we stand when we come home with nothing?'

'But Otto, you said—'

'Where do we stand?'

Bachman reflected. 'It won't be good, of course. . .'

'I am going to need money, Dieter. A great deal of it.'

Bachman raised his eyebrows. 'Certainly, whatever you need.'

Chapter Eleven

Mount Tabor in the Languedoc,
Summer 1936.

After several days with an old friend in Geneva, Rahn travelled
to Provence and then on to the Languedoc. He settled for a
night close to the ruins of Foix, where Esclarmonde had been
able to look to the south toward Mt Tabor and the Ariege river
valley. On the following morning he hiked one of the most
beautiful trails in the south of France, the Way of the Cathars.
It was an ancient path that started in the Valley of the Elms
under Mount Tabor's eastern skirt, traced the borders of the
peak where Montségur defended the holy mountain and
ultimately climbed up over St. Bartholomew's summit before
tracing its way down to the mountain's western foothills and
the Sabarthès caves.

He camped overnight not far from the fortified caves of
Bouan and Ornolac: the latter located beyond the baths
of Ussat and filled with serpents; the former a virtual castle,
complete with keep, stairways, towers and a water tank. He
moved on, combing the region's forgotten potholes and establishing a method of search for the expedition. Two weeks later,
his programme set, he telephoned Bachman to tell him he was
ready.

The miners came into the country as members of the Thule
Society. Bachman, the spokesman for the group, represented to
French officials that the purpose of their visit was to spend a
few weeks exploring the cave system along the Ariege valley.
Bachman's support detail of over a dozen SS junior officers

entered the country separately. When they were not stationed at the campsite to work as guards, these men stayed at various hotels in the region like tourists, usually changing their locations every week or so. Ostensibly having nothing to do with the members of the Thule Society, they were in fact responsible for bringing supplies and equipment into the campsite, supervising the work inside the caves, and guarding the camp at night.

There were a few encounters during the expedition with fortune hunters who were working in the same caves, but the mix of cash and intimidation that Bachman offered them inevitably persuaded them to look elsewhere for treasure. In the first weeks of the expedition Rahn and Bachman often left the campsite to have a drink in one or another of the local villages, but one evening a local roughneck who had had too much to drink began complaining about the Germans who were overrunning the area. Hadn't they their own country to pollute? The man's fury was aimed at tourists in general, Bachman and Rahn included, but afterwards Bachman declared that the members of the expedition must take greater care to remain inconspicuous.

The miners, of course, were not a problem in this respect. From the moment they entered the country, they virtually disappeared into the landscape. Even in camp, they kept to themselves and spoke only when asked a direct question. Rahn soon learned that they were all prisoners who had been promised parole at the completion of their journey. As a further incentive for their cooperation, Bachman told him, each man had been assured a substantial financial reward should the expedition be successful. Despite these generous motivations, Bachman trusted none of them. They were escorted into the caves at sunrise, and when they had finished their workday, invariably long after sunset, they were brought back to the campsite under the watchful eyes of Bachman's officers. At night two men stood guard over them. Even deep in the caves, Bachman took no chances. Someone was always assigned to monitor their activity.

The work was hard and sometimes dangerous. As a matter of routine the men were ordered to descend into narrow defiles and deep crevasses. At times they were asked to force open channels that might once have been accessible but had partially filled up. They sought out collapsed veins and possible false walls. They were seeking, as Rahn had told Bachman on more than one occasion, a small gilded box. He was convinced, he said, that the artefact had been preserved in the reliquary Raymond had constructed for it. It could be anywhere, of course, but he was fairly sure it would be hidden away in a place that would have turned back 'a smooth-fingered medieval priest.'

They did not hurry their search but pushed through the caves systematically. In many they found prehistoric tools and bones, in some they discovered medieval artefacts. In one cave the miners followed a crack in the earth down to a surging underground stream, where they encountered the bones of a nineteenth century explorer. He had apparently fallen to his death. On Bachman's orders they left the skeleton as they had found it.

After a month, Bachman's faith began to waver. Rahn was quick to remind him that he had said this is how it could possibly end. Then he added that there were still caves to explore, and they must not get discouraged. One evening Bachman wondered aloud if the Cathars might not have dropped their treasure in the tarn close to St. Bartholomew's peak. Wasn't there some legend about the waters? Rahn knew the legend, of course. The deep waters were said to hold the accursed treasury of ancient Thebes, but he dismissed Bachman's theory. The Cathars, he said, would not have thrown a sacred relic into unholy waters.

'But it could be anywhere!' Bachman answered. At his whining tone, Rahn lashed out at him in fury.

'*You* wanted this expedition, Dieter, and promised Himmler God-knows-what to get it! Well, now you have it. So stop your complaining!'

'But you were so confident, Otto!'

Rahn turned away, his eyes scanning the valley. 'Not until you had pushed us both into a corner with your wild promises to a madman.'

In his dejection, Bachman forgot to defend Himmler's sanity.

There were enough caves to house a city of cave dwellers. Some went on for miles. Others were simple hermitages, offering only a few rooms or simply a bit of shelter from bad weather. Many were nothing more than a deep crack in the earth and a great pit waiting below. Deep inside the caves Rahn sometimes got away from the others and worked an area on his own. He liked the perfect solitude of the work and, as the weeks passed, he went out on his own more frequently. There were days when he lost time. In these moments, he was not sure if he had gone mad or attained perfect sanity.

Sometimes he turned off his torch and thought about Elise. He wondered what she would be like with him if Bachman were not constantly hovering close by. She had her child, yes, and she was a different woman in some ways, more comfortable with her fate at least, but she was not happy. She was never going to be happy married to Bachman! In the darkness he would recall her face and think back to the time before she had again become the good wife.

She had been right to stay with Bachman of course. What life could he have offered her back then? Of course now things were different. Rahn was a celebrity by declaration, one of the new intellectuals! When he returned with the Lance of Antioch, Himmler's Blood Lance, it was anyone's guess how the Reichsführer would reward him. Certainly he would have enough income to support her if she wanted to file for divorce.

He liked to imagine Elise and Sarah living with him. He spent a great deal of his time each day trying to decide the kind of house they should purchase. Maybe something in Potsdam, where the air was fresh. He would not need to go into Berlin more than once or twice a week, unless he simply wanted to be in the city. In Potsdam they would have beautiful countryside for Sarah to enjoy, and he could work in solitude on the novel he had always dreamed he could write.

But then he would pull himself up short and recognise the sheer madness of his fantasy. Elise was never going to leave Bachman. It was not the money, not even the affection. It was her oath! In the face of it, she would not undo her destiny no matter her desire for Rahn. She would stand with Bachman until death because she had said she would. Rahn could love her, and he was sure she loved him, but it was never going to change their fate – the troubadour knight and his titled lady!

Six weeks into their search Rahn staggered out of the bowels of the mountain at dusk one evening and was met by Bachman. 'It was hidden in the Bouan, Otto!' he cried excitedly, 'so deep in a fissure that we nearly missed it. Covered with snakes!'

'What was hidden? What are you talking about?'

'We have it, Otto! We have found the Lance of Antioch!'

The fortified cave of Bouan was part of a complex of caves bordering the Toulouse-Barcelona highway not far from the Puymorens Pass. Halfway up an embankment that was reinforced with walls topped with parapets was an impressive, manmade entry that led into a number of chambers. Rahn knew it well and was careful of the snakes as he walked back to where the treasure waited. The men had cleared the box of snakes without anyone suffering snakebite – a miracle in its own right – but they had waited for him to open the treasure. The box was small, as he had said it would be, gilded and decorated with tiny rubies and small, ill-shaped pearls.

Opening the lid, Rahn saw that one of the hinges had rusted through. He was careful to avoid cracking the other. Inside he saw a piece of iron no larger than his fist. It lay upon a faded linen cloth. Rahn showed it to Bachman and his men. He then carried it to each of the six miners who had been on the detail when they had found it. The miners stared uncertainly at the thing, unsure of what they were looking at. Not one of them spoke.

Outside the cave, standing in the dark with Bachman, Rahn heard his friend tell him, 'Himmler will crown you with laurels for this, Otto!'

'This was your doing as much as mine, Dieter.'

'I thought you would be happier, my friend.'

'I am delighted, only a bit tired, I suppose.'

'I have the cure for that! Let's break the rules on our last night here and go have a drink in the village. What do you say?'

Late the next morning, their celebration finished, Bachman's support squad arranged to drive the twelve miners back to Germany in three vehicles. Rahn rode back with Bachman.

It took three long days of driving to get to Berlin. They got in late and Rahn stayed at the Bachmans' townhouse in their guest room. The following morning, they took the relic to Himmler. Himmler was pleased, of course, but at the sight of the thing his face registered a moment of inevitable disappointment. The Lance of Antioch may have convinced an army of medieval Crusaders, but it hardly seemed worthy of its legend in a less credulous age.

'I am not sure it is even the head of a lance!' Himmler complained.

'It may not have been,' Rahn admitted. 'There is a school of thought which holds that the head of a Roman standard was actually used to pierce the side of Christ.'

'I did not know that.'

'That is not really the issue, Reichsführer. The issue is what this object inspired. What you touch today is the object that by force of the imagination the Cathars transformed into a divine vision of blood and ivory and gold.'

Himmler nodded, and tried to imagine it. After a moment,

he looked up at Bachman with an air of one attending to the details. 'I assume you have taken care of the miners?'

'As soon as they were back on German soil.'

Himmler reached in his desk and brought out four passes to the upcoming Olympic Games. Handing them to the two men he told them they had done an extraordinary job. He meant to see that both were amply rewarded for their efforts. For the time being, however, until he could arrange the proper honours for such an accomplishment, he wanted them to be his guests at the Games. Himmler spent a few minutes talking to them about the festivities and the importance of the Games to Germany's new standing in the world. As he finished he seemed distracted, certainly disappointed that his Grail quest had not ended with a beautiful cup and spear. He seemed nearly to push the two men out of his office.

Bachman seemed not to have noticed. He was no doubt savouring his likely promotion to the exalted rank of Colonel. 'That went well, I think.'

Rahn nodded.

'What is it now, Otto?'

'What did he mean by his remark about taking care of the miners?' Rahn asked.

'The ones who saw the relic in the cave may have said something to the others, so we arranged for them all to be executed once they had crossed back into Germany,' Bachman told him. 'For security reasons.'

'You did *what*?' Rahn stared at the man in horror.

'We needed to make sure our discovery remained a secret, Otto! How would you have dealt with it?'

'You *killed* those men? My God, Dieter! You killed *twelve* men for the sake of that. . . that piece of *rubbish*!'

'Of course I didn't kill them! I ordered it done! Come on. Let's have a drink and a decent lunch. It's time we made a proper celebration!'

'They are *all* dead?' Rahn was trembling, close to vomiting.

He collapsed into his office chair because he was no longer able to stand.

When tears filled his eyes, Bachman said to him, 'For God's sake, Otto! Get hold of yourself! Didn't you happen to notice or are you perfectly blind? They were only Jews!'

Zürich, Switzerland
Tuesday March 11, 2008.

Kate rarely thought about the Eiger. She recalled virtually nothing of her various interviews with the police after coming off the mountain or even the memorial service for Robert at the family chapel in Devon, shortly before the property was sold at auction. She had a vivid memory of sitting in London with the Kenyon family solicitor and her father, however. The solicitor had told her that Lord Kenyon's investments shortly before his death had been *unfortunate*. He had, in fact, been so careful not to mention the word bankruptcy that Kate had not really understood the situation until her father had explained it to her rather bluntly afterwards.

The financial loss so soon after Robert's death had seemed only a very sick joke to complete the utter ruin that inhabited her soul. She had not even the ability to care. For weeks, then months, nothing stirred inside her. She forgot even her promise to find Robert's killer. That oath had faded from her memory like much of what had happened in the immediate aftermath of events on the Eiger. Giancarlo came to Zürich after the bankruptcy, their second meeting since the Eiger. He had found a great deal of information about the Austrians but admitted it led nowhere. Kate listened numbly to everything he told her, certain now she would never learn the identity of Robert's killer.

As they had parted, Giancarlo offered to let Kate stay at his house in Santa Margherita, a resort town south of Genoa. 'Sometimes,' he told her, 'only the sea can answer.'

She did not want to go. She had met Robert at Santa

Margherita! How could she stand to see the place again? Roland told her that was perhaps the best reason to go. She could not really face life in Zürich. She had no plans to go back to university, no plans really to do anything at all, and so she called Giancarlo to accept the invitation. For the first week at the house she had the glorious Ligurian Coast and Bartoli's great villa entirely to herself. Eleven years later, she could not remember how she had passed her days, but she knew she had stayed close to the house – like an invalid. She had a vivid memory of staring at the place where she had first seen Robert. She could not remember anything they had said to each other that evening. She remembered instead the feeling that she was falling helplessly in love with this man. Eleven years later that feeling was still as bright as on the night she first experienced it. What were words compared to that? For that matter, what was touch or taste? It was a moment one carried into eternity, she thought, the last memory she would have before death itself took her. Next to that evening everything else in her life faded. She knew it then, and she knew it still. Robert Kenyon was the only man she had ever really loved with all of her heart and soul.

Santa Margherita, Italy
September 1997.

Luca arrived a week or so into Kate's stay at the Bartoli villa. He claimed not to have known Kate was staying there, but he came alone and settled into the house without the usual plans to throw parties or have friends drop by. He did not invite her to swim or take a walk with him. He seemed to want to give Kate space. They pitched in together to make their dinner, drinking wine as they worked, but their days were their own.

Luca had been Robert's age, a good deal older than Kate. Growing up, Kate had worshipped him without really knowing much about him. In the last stages of her adolescence she had finally managed to seduce him – without any great trouble. Luca was married with a family, of course, but Kate was young enough not to consider the consequences of her choices. Besides, it was hardly Luca's first affair. A few torrid weeks under the hot Italian sun had made life seem perfect, but the romance began to fade once Kate had finally understood they hadn't very much in common. It was not exactly heartbreak she endured; more like waking up to reality. But Luca was charming and full of energy, so she had stayed in his circle and played the wild girl for a summer or two. All that had ended the night she saw Robert Kenyon. Not even a year had passed since that first meeting, but to Kate it seemed a lifetime ago.

Luca was well past the shock of Robert's death – life had gone on for him – but his attention and kindness to Kate was remarkable. When they finally had a long talk about Robert and how she was dealing with it, he seemed to understand what she was feeling. Maybe everyone understood, one had only to lose the world to know the feeling, but for Kate Luca's empathy let her open up and say the things she could not speak to others. Luca had never been one for soul searching conversations, but he knew Kate's most extravagant follies, so there were no secrets between them.

'I don't think I can ever climb again,' she told him when he had asked her if she had even thought about climbing since the Eiger. 'Leaving the house, coming down to Italy, that was almost more than I could manage.'

He pressed to know why, and she told him bluntly that she was afraid. Luca was curious at this. Kate Wheeler afraid of something? He could not imagine it. Afraid of what? That was the thing. She was afraid of everything. She could only feel safe in very familiar places. Even then she had terrible fantasies of gunmen breaking through doors or crashing through windows. Sometimes they were waiting silently round the next corner. On bad days, as she walked, the floor would seem to fall away. The effect was to leave her on the brink of a hallucinatory abyss.

And the worst of it was this. Having lost her nerve to climb, she realised she had nothing at all in life. For years climbing was all she knew, all she really wanted to do, and now she found she had lost it along with everything else. 'Not a day passes,' she whispered, 'when I don't consider killing myself.'

Hearing this grave confession Luca asked, 'How would you do it?'

'What do you mean?' she asked.

'I mean you *think* about it. How exactly do you see it happening?'

'I don't know. . .'

'Knife, gun, gas, pills. . . you have to have thought about how you intend to do it!'

'Luca, you're not supposed to help me think about something like that!'

'Why not? I am curious!'

'You're supposed to tell me that with thoughts like these I had best get to hospital! Seek professional help!'

'Why should I tell you what you already know?'

'You don't take me seriously!'

'You are not serious. You are only morose.'

She went to her room in exasperation, but minutes later Kate stormed back out. 'I want to die by falling! That's how I want to do it!'

'Won't work,' he said.

'I don't see why not.'

'Fear of heights. You probably can't even get up a stepladder.' And with that she had exploded with curses. It was *her* suicide, and she could imagine it how she wanted! Then they were suddenly both laughing. She could not remember ever laughing so hard. They had ended up spending the evening proposing the perfect suicide and then finding fault with the method until they had both agreed there was no good way out. Besides one did want to see what came next – bad as it was.

The following morning Kate awakened, quite hung over, but with a feeling that something had broken in her – or the ice in her soul had finally thawed out. 'I want you to teach me how to shoot a gun,' she said as they nursed their hangovers.

'You've shot a gun before, haven't you?'

'Actually, I haven't.'

'There is nothing to it, Katerina. You aim the gun and pull the trigger – like in the movies.'

'I want you to teach me everything you know, Luca. Velocity, calibration—'

'Calibre.'

'You see? I'm desperate for training.'

'Any reason in particular?'

'I promised myself I was going to find Robert's killer. I think it is time I get ready to deal with him, when I do find him.'

'If you want to be *ready*,' he told her, 'you had better do a good deal more than learn how to shoot a gun. What if he is standing on a hill? How are you going to get to him with your fear of heights?'

'I'm serious, Luca!'

'So am I. If you want to fantasise revenge, leave me out of it. There is no point in learning to shoot a gun because it is never going to happen and it is a waste of time for me to teach you. If you want revenge, if you *really* want it, then you must learn everything.'

'I'll do whatever I have to.'

'You are going to have to learn to climb again. You cannot nurse fears and delusions if you are chasing a killer! If something frightens you then you must face it. Do you imagine the person – or persons – who sent those assassins to the Eiger has never seen someone with a gun? There are people in this world, Kate, who see a gun and know what to do! If you go after someone like that you had better know you are stronger, faster, and smarter! And you better know how you intend to do it. People who murder people and get away with it know something about taking care of themselves. In a fight nothing is ever what we think it is going to be. You cannot think that because you are hurt by this person you will win. Victims stay victims. You must be prepared to win at any cost and by any means. Is that what you want – to win at any cost? Or do you want to feel a gun in your hand and *pretend* you have taken your revenge each time you pull the trigger?'

'I want this man in his grave, Luca.'

Luca studied her expression for a moment, and then retreated to his garage. He returned a few minutes later with a set of throwing knives and a sheet of heavy plywood that he leaned against a wall. He took chalk and drew the rough outline of a man. Then he took two of the knives and stood with his back to the plywood. Taking three long steps away from the target he turned and threw the first knife. The knife buried itself deep in the wood as he stepped forward and threw the second knife with his opposite hand – inches from the first.

Kate stared at the knives for a moment and then looked at Luca. 'Think of the man you want to kill,' he said, 'as being *that* good,' he told her. 'You have to be better – or you must let go of the fantasy.'

Kate returned her gaze to the two knives. Finally, she walked up to the target and took the knives in each hand. 'Show me how to do that,' she said.

Zürich, Switzerland
Tuesday March 11, 2008.

Eleven years later she could still remember the sensation of prying those two knives out of the wood.

'Are you okay?' Ethan asked.

Kate smiled. 'Fine. Just bored.' She snapped two knives toward her target, left, then right handed. The throws were good – dead centre.

'You didn't look bored,' Ethan told her. 'You looked like you were thinking about something.'

'Luca didn't kill Robert. Neither did Giancarlo.'

309

'Maybe, but they know who did.'

She looked out of the window, wrestling with the incongruities. 'How could they know and not tell me?'

'They're a part of a secret society,' Ethan told her. 'Whatever they're involved in, you can be sure of two things. When they joined the Council of Paladins, they swore a blood oath to keep the secrets of the Order and to come to the aid of each other no matter the risk or cost. When you make that kind of promise, you don't talk about exceptions. Family and friends come second – even favourite god-daughters.'

'But Robert was one of them. Why would the paladins kill one of their own?'

'If it wasn't infighting. . . maybe he betrayed the Order.'

'Why was I part of it? If they wanted him dead for something like that, why include innocent people as well? Luca taught me. . . everything. And it wasn't so I could make a living as a thief. That came later, after he taught me how to take revenge. He was teaching me to how to kill someone, Ethan! When his brother was killed, he hunted down the people who were responsible. He told me about each man that he found and killed, how they reacted, how they had got ready for him and what he did to get around their defences. He wasn't bragging. He was showing me by example what I needed to know for the time when I found Robert's killer.'

'Or killers.'

'He was making sure I understood everything he knew so I would be ready for the fight. I might be exhausted; I might end up being the one who was hunted down. I might not have a gun when I needed it. I needed to know a great many things. He taught me all the skills he had. Why would he do that if I was going to come for him someday?'

'I don't know, but he knows what happened. He and Giancarlo are keeping the truth from you. You need to face that if you're ever going to find out what really happened.'

'I know, but I won't touch them. I won't! Not unless they killed Robert, and I don't think they did. It just doesn't make sense.'

*

Kate was moving about the hotel room on crutches when Malloy arrived late that evening. Ethan offered him a drink and this time he accepted. 'Scotch and soda, if you've got it.'

Whilst the ice crackled, Malloy settled in a comfortable chair. 'I had a long look at what they've taken from Chernoff's computer. There's quite a bit of material that is going to produce good intelligence. We're going to be able to figure out her key contacts, and at least some of her finances. The trouble is at this point we're racing against time. I mean if we find a telephone number that takes us into a network of phones, we have to get to it before the owners ditch them. Otherwise, we just end up chasing shadows and picking apart aliases.'

Ethan handed him his drink. 'So we're two steps from locating the guy – and still three or four days from knowing anything?'

Malloy took a sip of his drink. 'We could get lucky, but that's all it would be. Carlisle hasn't shown up, at least not as Carlisle, but if he wired money to Chernoff late last year, or contacted Ohlendorf in the past couple of months we might turn up one of his aliases.'

'If this guy is smart he has to know he's in trouble,' Ethan answered.

'I think he's known he was in trouble for several months. That's why he came after us.'

'But the whole world wasn't looking for him,' Ethan said. 'If your people link him to Chernoff, he's going to have to crawl into a hole. Once that happens nothing you get from Chernoff is going to take you anywhere close to the guy.'

'I know.'

'So what's the plan?' Kate asked.

'I found some files in Dale's computer before I cleaned it. If nothing else I turned up a set of decent surveillance photos of the guy. What they're publishing in the annual report doesn't give us very much. With these we can at least make an ID on him. He pulled a memory stick from his pocket and

311

handed it to Ethan. 'They were taken in Paris three years ago.'

'So our ghost gets out now and then?' Kate asked as she swung over on her crutches and stood behind Ethan.

'He was having a meeting with Hugo Ohlendorf,' Malloy told them as Ethan slipped the key into his computer. 'Dale's people were tracking Ohlendorf, but they did the follow up on Carlisle for the ID.' He pointed at the screen as the files came up. 'Those other folders are for you as well. Once Dale had a name, he put together a dossier on Carlisle. I'm not sure there's anything there we don't already know, but sometimes all it takes is the right eyes looking at something.'

'I'll take anything you've got,' Ethan said as he opened the picture file and hit the Slide Show prompt. The first photograph showed Carlisle and Ohlendorf sitting at an outdoor café. Carlisle it seemed had banished his working class roots, looking every bit the social equal of Hugo Ohlendorf.

'A good looking guy,' Malloy remarked.

The third photo came on screen and Malloy glanced at Kate, who stood frozen behind Ethan, staring at the screen as if stricken. 'What's the matter?' he said.

Ethan turned from the computer screen as well. Kate's eyes were fixed oddly on the screen as the sequence ran but she said nothing. 'What is it?' Ethan asked. His voice betrayed his concern. As well it should. Kate looked like she was having a stroke.

'It's. . . Robert,' she whispered.

'What? What are you talking about?' Ethan asked.

'That's not David Carlisle we're looking at. It's. . . Robert Kenyon.

Kate's face grew oddly serene as she seemed to come to terms with the fact that she was looking at her first husband some eight years after his presumed death on the Eiger.

'*Cut the rope,*' she whispered at last and only then did Malloy see the first tear forming. 'One of them said something. I didn't really understand. What about *her*? *What do we do with her?* Something like that. And Robert said: *Cut the rope.* I was groggy from hitting my head, but I knew Robert couldn't have said something like *that*. I mean. . . I just didn't believe it.'

'It answers a lot of questions,' Malloy said as he began reviewing the odd pieces of evidence that had never made sense.

Finally Ethan stirred. 'It raises a lot more.'

'Not really,' Malloy told him. 'Think about it. Robert Kenyon makes a foolish investment and loses everything – including Kate's money. Who are the beneficiaries of the bankruptcy? His life-long friends. They didn't take the money, they funnelled it – at least most of it – into new accounts in David Carlisle's name. The guy managed the impossible: he died *and* he took it with him.'

'So what happened to Carlisle?' Ethan asked.

Malloy shook his head. 'David Carlisle was a mercenary in the Balkans in 1994. That's the last official record of him anywhere until 1997 when he became Kenyon's successor on the Council of the Paladins. My guess is he got killed and is buried somewhere in Serbia or Bosnia. Kenyon just took his identity because they looked something like each other.'

'Robert climbed out that night,' Kate said, her eyes still fixed on the man she had married almost eleven years ago. 'By the time the moon was up he had got to the Traverse of the Gods. He probably made the summit by three or four that morning and was off the mountain before dawn.'

'I don't get it,' Ethan said. 'Why would Kenyon give up his identity?'

Malloy waited for Kate, but she had no theory. 'There's only one good reason,' he said. 'He was in trouble. Whatever it was, he had time to make financial arrangements, so it sounds to me like some kind of investigation into his activities.'

'Six months,' Kate said. 'That's how long it took for the two of us to fall in love and get married. That's how much time he had.'

'The acquisition of the company was in that same time frame,' Malloy remarked.

'I understand the bankruptcy scam,' Ethan said. 'He needed money and he didn't want to leave a paper trail, but why involve Kate? Why get married?'

Malloy looked at Kate. Her tears were gone. 'Every magician knows the key to a successful illusion involves distracting the audience at the critical moment,' Malloy told them. 'In this case the distraction was the Eiger, more exactly Kate's bad luck with it. A well-publicised honeymoon climb to beat the mountain? What could be better? And when it failed, when the two Austrian climbers described watching Kate, her husband, and their guide going over, that was supposed to be all anyone would talk about. Kate's bad luck with the mountain.'

'So the climbers were just supposed to be witnesses?' Ethan asked.

'They weren't *just* witnesses,' Kate answered.

'But they were hired because they had no criminal record – no known association with you or Kenyon or for that matter your guide. The idea was they would report the thing and show people the spot where they could reasonably expect to find two bodies. When no one found Kenyon's body – well that kind of thing happens on the Eiger.'

'Robert probably only learned what had happened to me a couple of days later,' Kate said.

'And when he heard the story you were telling it was actually better than what he had planned, so there was no need to eliminate you.'

'By then I had told Giancarlo everything. Giancarlo listened to my story without batting an eye, and then he promised me, *promised*, he would find Robert's killer if it was the last thing he ever did.'

'He was in on it,' Malloy told her. 'He and Luca and Jack Farrell, Hugo Ohlendorf and Jack Farrell's father – all the active paladins.'

'So what do we do about it?' Ethan asked. 'I mean we still don't know how to find the guy.' He looked at Kate. 'We *are* going after him, aren't we?'

'Definitely,' Kate told him, her jaw grinding. 'We are definitely going after this man.'

'Well, we still don't know how to find him,' Ethan muttered.

'Giancarlo will tell me where he is.'

Berlin, Germany
1936-38.

There had always been plenty of drinking. It came with the literary life, the need to socialise after hours of poring over texts. With money and a social schedule to keep, it got worse instead of better.

Himmler noticed Dr Rahn's behaviour early in 1937, not long after his first promotion, and he made sure Rahn was notified that he had been seen acting in an unseemly manner. In the summer of that year Rahn published his second book, *Satan's Minions*. There were problems with the proof, improvements and 'clarifications' that Rahn flatly rejected. When the changes went through anyway, in accordance with the official view about racial purity, Rahn said nothing more publicly about the changes but, in private amongst friends, he seethed with anger. That made his being watched essential. And there was that title to his book, as well. Explain as Rahn might that Satan was the light bringer to the world, a Promethean figure, there was, inevitably, the concern that Rahn had intended an oblique barb at Hitler's Reich . . . or worse, Himmler's SS.

It was time for a reality check for Dr Rahn and, when September came, Himmler had him sent to Dachau to work as a guard until December. He came back chastened and obedient, but then Himmler had reviewed a number of disturbing reports about his behaviour at the camp – remarks made in confidence to another guard that bordered on treason

– and it became necessary to tap his phones and open his mail.

In January of 1938 one of Himmler's aids remarked that Dr Rahn had not submitted a Certificate of Racial Origin. Everyone joining the SS from 1935 on had been obliged to submit the form. Dr Rahn, of course, had been recruited. There had been none of the usual requirements to fulfil and no one had thought to ask about the racial purity of the Reich's new golden boy. Was there a problem? Himmler's subordinate would not back down. There was no problem so long as he provided a certificate! Himmler said he would make sure Dr Rahn was informed of the situation. Papers were pushed through. The request was made politely but firmly. Rahn, the prima donna, said he would take care of it. He then proceeded to ignore the request, as he had all the others.

Berlin, Germany
Fall 1938.

In the spring of 1938 Hitler effected the annexation of Austria. That it was accomplished without a shot being fired had the effect inside the Reich of confirming Hitler's policies and silencing forever the feeble voices of protest and moderation. The move into the east was not aggression but reunification. Austria and Germany were not two nations, but one. As if to confirm this, fate cast two teams of climbers onto the impregnable north face of the Eiger in July of that year, one Austrian and one German. After racing up the better portion of the rock, the teams tied their ropes together just under the summit and finished their climb as a single team. To commemorate the triumph, the Führer shook the hand of each man and took the occasion once more to speak of Germany's destiny and of course Aryan supremacy.

In an act that was hardly noticed by the outside world but was celebrated with great pomp within the Reich, Hitler moved the Lance of St. Maurice from the Schatzkammer Museum in Vienna to the cathedral of Nuremberg, where it had once lain as part of the insignia of the Holy Roman Empire. Thought by some to be the spear that had pierced the side of Christ, the Lance of St. Maurice was believed to have been discovered in Jerusalem by the mother of Constantine. Its storied history placed it in the hands of such warrior kings as Attila the Hun, Charlemagne, Otto the Great, and even Napoleon. The legend went that whoever possessed this lance held the fate of the world in his hand. By taking the Lance back to Nuremberg, Hitler was in effect reclaiming the authority of the long defunct Holy Roman Empire and placing himself in the glorious tradition of the warrior kings who had carried the spear of destiny from triumph to triumph.

Once the relic had been installed at Nuremberg, Hitler ordered Himmler's leading historians and scholars to prepare a detailed history of the Lance, confirming with scholarly scrutiny the wild legends associated with his exquisitely preserved relic. Himmler naturally turned to his best man. In a tediously documented treatise Dr Rahn concluded that Hitler's newly acquired artefact, though undoubtedly possessing a long history within the European houses of royalty, was produced in the Carolingian period – from the time of Charlemagne, some eight centuries after Christ. The Lance of Longinus, kept in the Vatican, he wrote, was of far greater antiquity and possessed as well a more credible provenance. That lance, he explained, was very likely the relic pilgrims to Jerusalem in the seventh century had reported seeing. It had gone to Constantinople after Jerusalem fell to the forces of Mohammed. Inexplicably broken, its tip had come to Paris with the Crown of Thorns via Venice when Baldwin II of Constantinople had sold a number of sacred objects to Louis IX in the thirteenth century to finance the crumbling defences of his empire. Though venerated for centuries it vanished following the outbreak of the French Revolution at the end of the eighteenth century. The body of that same spear head had been captured by the Turks in 1452 and was sent to Rome in 1492 when Sultan Bajazet presented it to Pope Innocent VIII.

Also a contender for authenticity, Rahn noted – and perhaps mostly likely to be genuine – was the so-called Lance of Antioch, found and then lost again during the first Crusade. That spear, he wrote, may well have left Jerusalem only a few decades after the Crucifixion.

A thorough man, Himmler read Rahn's report before he passed it on to Hitler. Once he realised, with a dawning sense of horror, that Rahn had dismissed Hitler's precious relic as a medieval forgery, he had no choice but to have the report rewritten by certain of Dr Rahn's subordinates. As a matter of prestige he kept Rahn's name attached to the document, but ordered the historian to be sent to the SS-run work camp in Buchenwald.

Only an impassioned plea by Colonel Bachman had convinced Himmler to let Dr Rahn serve as prison guard rather than enter the camp as an inmate.

Elise had first seen the change in Rahn at the 1936 Olympics. Everyone had been in such a famous mood that summer – except Rahn. At first she credited it to his tendency for moodiness. She had seen the same deadness in his eyes when he ran his hotel. After the thrill of his sudden fame, a bit of depression was understandable. Only it did not pass away. She saw him laughing sometimes, but there was no happiness in it, and even when he looked at Sarah, whom he adored, he seemed wistful and melancholy. His wit got sharper. The cynicism that comes of middle age grew more fixed and cruel. He had an encyclopaedic knowledge of all things esoteric. But gone was the man's passion.

There were more women after that summer, too. Some very horrid stories, to be honest. Elise listened to Bachman's edited narration of the gossip he had heard and even seen, and she tried not to be shocked. She said it was all the consequence of too much to drink, and Bachman must encourage him to cut back, but secretly she knew the alcohol was only the trigger. Rahn's problems ran deeper than that.

After his tour of duty at Dachau in the late fall of 1937, he had tried hard to be the old Otto, but *trying* was all he accomplished. His cheerfulness was excessive and oddly timed. He talked about writing not one book but four or five of them at once. He had even dipped back into a novel that he had begun years earlier. Nothing came of his plans of course, and his desperately bright smiles turned leaden again after a season. He seemed to age, his hair to thin, his skin to go ashen. He gained weight. He was still a handsome man, but at thirty-four he was quite suddenly middle-aged. He and Bachman no longer seemed so very different from one another. They began to fit together like the odd old men who sat together sometimes in the dreariest cafes, even down to the detail of their sagging shoulders.

In her own youthful fit of passion Elise had said once she wanted to think of Rahn forever sitting in the grass beneath the ruins at Montségur, she at his side, as they listened to the wind and imagined it to be the voices of those martyred for their faith. That was no longer what she thought about when she thought of Otto Rahn. Life had got close and messy. She remembered him getting sick from too much to drink. She sometimes thought of him in France as the hotel keeper. In her nightmares she could imagine him standing guard at a detention centre. On the better days he was the stodgy scholar addressing the Berlin ladies about Satan, who, as it turned out, had suffered bad press in Rome but was actually a quite fascinating fellow. . .

When she looked for the causes of his ruin she always thought about Bachman. That probably was not fair. Rahn had made his own choices, but he had been such a free spirit, so excited about. . . everything. How had he lost it? The answer was clear – if not exactly fair and accurate. Bachman had attached himself to Rahn's vitality and then sucked the life out of him, turning him in the process as grey and old as himself. Elise had fallen in love with him, but in the end Bachman had won Rahn's soul. The evenings they spent with him, the Sunday meal Rahn almost always attended so he could see Sarah, this was Bachman showing off his latest conquest: the tamed and broken adulterer.

Bachman would have been shocked to know her thoughts. He was really very fond of his friend. He never spoke a bad word about him, and he was genuinely worried when Rahn's actions got him in hot water with Himmler. Once, in a fury of concern, he had said of Rahn, 'All that intelligence! Why can't he see he's destroying himself?' He had been talking about a report Rahn had filed with Himmler that had got him exiled to the Buchenwald detention centre, but he might have said it about a dozen other incidents as well.

January 1939.

When Rahn came back from his tour at Buchenwald in January of 1939, he made no effort to be diligent in his work or pleasant in society. He began saying things, things not wise to say. Bachman ignored some of it, but grew angry at other times. Did he intend to get himself *and* his friends killed?

'Do we kill men for their thoughts now, Dieter?'

'They are killed for much less than that, Otto, as you well know! I tell you, you must take care. You walk a very fine line at the moment.'

'Because I would not tell Hitler his spear is genuine?'

'Your troubles are more than a single report, but you are a fool to put truth ahead of common sense.'

'He wanted the history of his spear, and I gave it to him.'

'He wanted confirmation of his own opinion!' Bachman's smile was cold: 'And who are you to say he is wrong?'

'An expert!'

'It is your attitude, Otto! You sit at the right hand of the second most powerful man in Germany and you act as if this is all a great inconvenience for you!'

'Have you considered the problem might not be *my* attitude – but that of everyone else?'

'Have a drink, Otto. You scare me when you are sober.'

It was not always like that, of course. They could not have endured him if he was always so morose. Sometimes he talked about a girl he had met. He claimed to be thinking of asking her to marry him. Neither Elise nor Bachman had met her, he was very secretive about her, but he assured them both they would like her. Then he smiled and said he was thinking of inviting *the Heini* to his wedding. *The Heini* was Heinrich Himmler. Only his intimates and perfect fools referred to him by his nickname. Rahn was not an intimate.

Bachman told him the Reichsführer would be pleased to be included. 'At the very least it will bring his attention to the fact that you are getting serious. Who knows? He may even attend! He has told me more than once your problem is singular. You need to get married and have children. Otherwise you will have nothing to anchor your feelings.'

'Astrid will anchor me deep in the ground,' Rahn told them. 'I will be a changed man, that I promise! You will see!'

'When are you going to ask her to marry you?' Elise asked.

'I'm working up my courage. . . but soon, I think.'

'I would not delay,' Bachman told him. There was a warning look as he said this, and Elise could see that Rahn saw it as well. Something terrible was about to happen.

That evening as they prepared for bed Bachman said that he was worried about Rahn. Elise tried to console him. Things were improving. He had stayed mostly sober, hadn't he? And the girl, Astrid, he seemed serious about her. As she said this, it occurred to Elise that Rahn had been grimly serious about Astrid. She even wondered if Astrid was some kind of morbid joke – a dark reference to suicide. Something very awful seemed to lurk in his eyes when he spoke about her, and she worried, because despite everything she loved him.

'I am not at all sure he can save himself at this point, Elise. Himmler has ordered an investigation. I am under orders to say nothing about it to him, but the situation is very delicate, and our friend could very well lose everything.'

'Why? What has he done that is so terrible?'

'It's not what he has done. It is what he is.' At her look of confusion, Bachman added, 'There is some concern he has been concealing things.'

'What sort of *things*?'

'That he is a Jew for one. He has been very coy about the matter when pressed to submit his documents confirming his racial purity, and so Himmler has decided he must have something to hide. He has put a request through channels for someone to take a serious look at the family's history.'

As her own ancestry included East European Jews who had become financially successful after their move to Germany, Elise felt a tremor of fear pulsing through her. Had it come to that? That they were digging up family histories?

'I think this evening ought to be our last dinner together with Otto for a while,' Bachman remarked. 'We should get some distance from him, just in case the report confirms the worst.'

'And what do we tell Sarah? She is very fond of her uncle!'

'Tell her what you have said before. He has business and can't come by as frequently as he used to do.'

'But you are talking about stopping his visits entirely!'

'If it turns out he is a Jew, Elise, none of us must have anything to do with him. Especially Sarah!'

Soglio, Switzerland
Thursday March 13, 2008.

The village of Soglio lay on the side of a mountain overlooking the Bergell Valley and the year-round glaciers atop a range of mountains that included the Piz Cengalo and Piz Badile. The village had come into being some three or four hundred years ago and was made almost entirely of grey fieldstones and old timbers. At its centre lay the Hotel Salis – formerly the Palazzo Salis. The hotel had been in operation for over a century, but the name Salis was one of the oldest in the region. The family had originally made its fortune selling Swiss mercenary soldiers to the monarchs of Europe.

A single road wound up the mountainside through lush groves of enormous chestnut trees and came finally to a large parking area at the outskirts of the village. Driving into the village required a permit. At this time of year, on a cold, sunny March day, the parking lot was mostly empty – cluttered only with the cars of the some thirty or forty year-round residents.

The Hotel Salis was open for business, of course. A seventeenth century palace, it had rooms for guests and advertised fine cuisine. At the front of the building there was a plaza where three cobblestone alleys converged. At the back was a garden featuring the two tallest trees in Europe – sequoias brought back to the Old Country in the late nineteenth century. Beyond the garden lay a high grey wall. Beyond the wall was a vast wooded mountainside.

In March of 1997 Roland Wheeler had brought his daughter here to meet with her godfather, Giancarlo Bartoli. Father and daughter had spent the night in the hotel. Giancarlo had come over the Italian border by car the next morning and had met with them in Kate's room.

Kate got the same room this trip and spent a surprisingly comfortable night – the result no doubt of the fresh mountain air and the kind of silence modern people rarely experience. She had a light breakfast early the next morning, and then limped back upstairs on her crutches. Once in her room she sat down to wait for the man she had once trusted like a father.

Giancarlo arrived with a driver and one additional body-guard. His dark green Mercedes had no permit, but no one asked his driver to move it when he parked in the middle of the plaza. Giancarlo seemed uneasy as he crossed the plaza. He sent one of the bodyguards to Kate's room. Kate thought the man might just shoot her, but that was simple paranoia. Giancarlo would not want to be so close to his crimes.

The bodyguard said he needed to check her room before

Signor Bartoli came upstairs. Kate allowed him his freedom. After he had looked for recording devices and weapons on her person and throughout the room, he ran an electronic scan across the walls looking for any kind of transmitting devices. That finished, he took Kate's cell phone and went downstairs. A few minutes later Giancarlo climbed the stairs and stepped through Kate's open doorway. The old man gave the room a curious look, checking his memory, it seemed, and then nodded, as if pleased by Kate's sense of irony. It was in *this* room he had made his promise to find Robert Kenyon's killer.

They did not kiss as they always had done. Giancarlo stood self-consciously by the door and set Kate's cell phone on a table close by. Kate remained seated in her chair. No smiles and no greetings.

'Did *I* kill Robert?' he asked her, his lips offering the pale imitation of a smile.

Kate's message had told him she knew the identity of Robert's killer. She had said she wanted to meet in Soglio at the Hotel Salis at ten o'clock Thursday morning.

'Nobody killed Robert,' Kate said. 'You know it, and now I know it.'

The old man smiled almost genuinely now. 'Is this the point where I tell you I don't know what you're talking about?'

'Don't do this,' she said, feeling her passion at his betrayal choking her. 'Don't lie anymore. Kill me if you want, but just stop lying!'

'All right then. Robert is alive and well. Are you happy?'

'Getting there,' she said. 'But I want to know why.'

Giancarlo shook his head. 'It's old business. No longer very important.'

'It's important to me.'

'There were people in the House of Lords who had started an investigation against him. There was talk about bringing him up on charges of treason.'

'You let me go up that mountain to die – for the sake of a traitor.'

'No! I helped Robert arrange his financial affairs. He did not tell me you were a part of his disappearance.'

'It was murder, not a disappearance.'

'Luca and I knew about the money, but Robert handled the rest on his own. If I had known. . .'

'You knew. I saw it in your eyes at the wedding. I thought. . . I thought you were sentimental! But that wasn't it. *You knew*.'

'I knew he meant to break your heart! I knew that he meant to leave you a widow!'

'A very poor widow.'

'You never suffered financially, Katerina.' The old man's eyes cut away from her.

'It was for the money, wasn't it?' she asked. 'His marriage to me? He saw a ten million pound trust fund that had just passed to my control, and he took it because he could!'

'Robert cared for you deeply.'

'Robert only cares for himself. What I find so impossible to understand is that *you* don't see that.'

'I have seen the affection in his eyes! His regret at losing you!'

'Let me tell you about that regret. He sent assassins to kill me in Hamburg.'

'Because you would not stop looking for his killer! I told you—!'

'Tell me where I can find him.'

Giancarlo shook his head. 'I can't do that.'

'You owe this to me!'

'I cannot betray an oath.'

'An oath?'

'I swore a sacred oath – as he did. We are bound by it, Katerina. I am not sure you can understand such a thing, but I cannot betray it.'

'It seems to me no matter what you do now you betray a sacred oath. You *do* remember when you stood in a house of God and swore to protect me if anything should ever happen

325

to my parents? Do you remember *that* oath?' Bartoli did not respond. 'My father and mother are dead, Giancarlo. Where is my protection?'

'Katerina. . .'

'I am not your *little Katherine*! Not anymore. Honour your oath. Stand beside me as a father stands with his daughter. Tell me where he is!'

'I didn't know he meant to hurt you!'

'Are we talking about the first or the second time he tried to kill me? Was he there? Was he in Zürich watching us as we talked? Watching me?'

'Let me talk to him. If you agree to let this thing go—'

Kate shook her head. 'No. I agree to nothing. His word – *his oath* – means less than nothing at all! Just tell me where I can find him, and your obligation to me is finished. Believe me, I will never ask anything of you again.'

Giancarlo stood before her without answering. He looked, she thought, like a man lost at a crossroads.

'What do you want?' she asked when it seemed he would not break his silence. 'Do you want money? Do you want. . . I don't know. . . ten million Euros? Twenty? I know how important it is for you to have *enough*. God forbid you lose all your money and end up in the gutter!'

The old eyes went dark and cold at the insult. 'Are we finished?'

'No. You and I are not finished until you tell me where he is!'

'Are you threatening me?'

'Do you really want to go to war for the sake of a man who murders his friends? Do you want to know why I am still alive? It is because Robert is greedy. He could have murdered me and put an end to his problems, but he saw a chance at Jack Farrell's money and he could not resist taking it. Did he tell you about that part – that he murdered his own cousin so he could steal half-a-billion dollars?'

'That's not true! Jack is—'

'Jack Farrell is dead. You didn't know? You thought he got away? Let me tell you the truth about your friend, the good Lord Kenyon. If he thought he could get away with it, he would come after your money too.'

When Giancarlo did not answer her, she pushed on. 'Do you know what I think? I think you *want* to tell me where he is. I think Robert has become a disappointment to you – with his treason and his larceny and his attempts at murdering me. I think the fact that he failed to kill me in Hamburg amuses you. I think you are loyal to him for the sake of some oath that once meant a great deal to you but doesn't mean anything to you now. I think secretly you must hate him *and* the oath you swore!'

Without answering her, Giancarlo turned and left her.

Kate stood at the window so he might see her when he came out of the hotel. She saw his driver and bodyguard come to attention the moment Giancarlo appeared. She watched his tall, gaunt frame as he walked into the plaza.

The bodyguard opened the back door of the Mercedes and stood at attention, but before he got in, Giancarlo took off his coat and folded it neatly. He looked round the plaza as he did this. Did he expect a bullet from a rooftop, or was this a signal for his men to move in? She could not read him and realised with a sudden emptiness she never could. Like Robert, his affection was counterfeit.

Giancarlo sat down in the backseat and the bodyguard went to the front passenger seat. For a long beat the village was silent. Finally, inevitably, he looked up at the window where Kate stood. Their eyes met briefly, and then the car drove off.

Kate looked at the rooftops and alleys. The village was still quiet. She waited until he was surely gone and finally decided she had misjudged the old man's sense of decency, along with everything else. She was getting ready to call Ethan and Malloy, who were waiting at the bottom of the mountain, when her room phone rang. 'Yes?' she said.

'I have been thinking,' Giancarlo said to her. 'You haven't

been to my farm in Majorca for years. Maybe you should go there for a day or two to let your leg mend. Just make sure you get there before next Monday. I understand bad weather may be coming by then.'

'Thank you,' Kate whispered.

'Be careful.'

Majorca, Spain
Saturday March 15, 2008.

The island of Majorca, famous for its beaches, celebrities, and all night parties, was still mostly agrarian throughout its interior. A few good highways connected the coasts and a few more serviceable roads linked the villages, but throughout much of the island the roads were rough and narrow.

The pace was Old World. Farmers typically stopped their trucks to speak with their neighbours. It was a slow, peaceful existence that carried on much as it had when Giancarlo Bartoli's father built his great house atop a high plateau over-looking successive terraces of olive trees.

Robert Kenyon had never appreciated the farm. It was too quiet, too isolated. He and Luca had brought parties to the house to make life bearable when they had come to the island as young men. The first time he had gone to the farm with his new identity – the old life cut off and left behind – David Carlisle understood what Giancarlo loved about the farm. Not long afterwards he had arranged to lease the property from one of Bartoli's companies. For the past several years he had spent as much time as he could here. The farm was safe. He did not have to consider the chances of an accidental meeting with a face from his past or shuffle passports at border crossings. Here something was wrong if the neighbour did not pass by his front gate at ten in the morning and come back at eleven. The wine was good. The rocks were challenging and the heat, even in springtime, baked out the fears that gnaw at every fugitive.

At this point the isolation of the farm was more than a

luxury. Helena Chernoff was missing. As they had last spoken before she went after Malloy he could only imagine that she was undergoing interrogation. It was perfect nonsense to think anyone could resist interrogation. In the end everyone talked. Everyone! One measured courage by the hour in a situation like that.

Chernoff's Christine Foulkes alias would be exposed. When that happened people would want to talk to all the paladins. They would all confess to knowing nothing about Chernoff's involvement, but they would *meet* with investigators. Since the death of Robert Kenyon, they had all been careful to avoid any sort of public contact with David Carlisle and Christine Foulkes, having sent their representatives to the annual meetings of the paladins. They could claim – and no one could prove otherwise – that they had no idea that Foulkes was Helena Chernoff or that David Carlisle was in fact Robert Kenyon back from the dead. Carlisle, on the other hand, could not survive even a cursory investigation. He was going to have to slough off his identity and start over. Most of his cash was safe, he had already moved his money into banks that would not give him up without a fight, but his less liquid investments, some fifty million pounds tied up in real estate, were going to be lost. The cost of doing business.

Luca was coming to Majorca on Monday with three pristine passports – less than forty eight hours to wait. Even if Chernoff broke quickly, which wasn't likely, he thought he had that much time. Of course he wasn't sure. She might have worked out a deal. For the sake of a private cell with a window she could have told them where they could find him. Still, waiting here was better than risking a border crossing. His current aliases might already have been flagged. Even with new passports his troubles were not completely behind him. Phone numbers and safe houses he had once trusted could now turn into traps. His friends and contacts might be under surveillance or ready to give him up for the sake of their own freedom. Virtually anyone he had ever known had become a potential threat. So it was not just a change of name. He was going to have to start over.

Majorca, Spain
Sunday March 16, 2008.

Wearing night vision goggles and body armour, Ethan and Malloy worked their way up the terraced hills of the Bartoli farm under a pale half-moon. They finally stopped on a ridge just over a hundred metres out from the perimeter wall. 'This is the area,' Ethan said, checking his navigator. Besides an Army Colt at his belt, he carried a DoubleStar Patrol rifle with a silencer. The attached night scope was a Morovision-740 G3. The gun was configured like the popular M-4 that U.S. tank squads used. It had a short barrel and an abbreviated banana clip similar to the Kalashnikov. He carried several extra ammo clips, though neither of them expected him to need them. Loading the first clip, he chambered a round and took his first look through the scope. 'Nice,' he whispered. He was looking, Malloy knew, at a night landscape that had suddenly turned green. A red pinpoint of light functioned as the gun sight.

'You can check the sighting out here.' Malloy pointed across the terraces to a place about equidistant to the house. He double-checked the area for life forms to be sure. It looked good. Ethan settled the gun on a tripod mount and set the selector to fire a single round. He took a moment to steady himself and then squeezed off one shot toward a stand of gnarled olive trees. The silencer was state of the art. Only the mechanism ejecting the shell made any significant noise. Ethan tampered with the scope and then tried again. After a third shot he said, 'It's good,' and turned back to the house.

Malloy carried a MilCam LE thermal scanner. It was capable of finding heat images – even through some walls. On his first scan of the house he found no one on the ground floor. In what Kate had called the master bedroom on the second floor he discovered the heat signatures of a man and woman, both in the same bed. At the gatehouse, some eighty metres south of the front of the house, he found two males in separate bedrooms. According to Kate the gatehouse was used for security personnel, usually Bartoli's people when he came to the farm. Otherwise the gatehouse was unoccupied. These people were undoubtedly Kenyon's bodyguards.

Malloy handed Ethan the thermal scanner and pointed toward the house, letting him get a fix on the man and woman. 'What do you think? Irina Turner?'

'In the best of all worlds it is,' Ethan whispered.

Malloy used his cell phone and heard Kate's voice, 'Yes.'

'A man and woman in the master bedroom. Two men on the second storey of the gatehouse, separate bedrooms.

'Three minutes,' she said.

He told Ethan, and began scanning the yard. There was a broad well-lit expanse of lawn at the front of the house, then the gatehouse and perimeter wall. Beyond the wall to the east was a rocky patch of pastureland leading to a natural rock wall and a mountain wilderness beyond it. To the west the plateau continued for nearly half-a-mile before rising abruptly into a mountainous terrain. In this area Malloy found some buildings, including a caretaker's cabin. The caretaker was in bed with his wife, who was also the housekeeper and cook. According to Kate, this was a working farm, but other than the caretaker and his wife all the workers came from the village three miles down the mountain.

He continued scanning for the heat signature of a lookout, but the hilltop was quiet. About a minute or so after the call to Kate, Malloy heard the distant whine of a small plane. He swept the scanner above the house and saw the dark, cold forms of the boulders that fortified the back of the Bartoli farm. The rocks rose up almost vertically for a couple of hundred feet. Beyond the boulders he could see only a wilderness of more rocks and steep ascents – safe haven for a climber. The boulders were probably three hundred metres away – still in the outer range of Ethan's gun.

He brought the scanner down across the perimeter walls and stopped at the gatehouse for another look. The two males were still quiet. At the house, Kenyon was tossing in his sleep.

Malloy heard Kate on his headset. 'I'm at five hundred metres.'

A moment later the security lights around the house blinked off – the whole mountain crashing to black.

David Carlisle had not slept well since leaving New York. He wanted to blame the flights from Hamburg to New York to Majorca with the six time zones each way, but he knew better. The truth was he was suddenly vulnerable. Worse still, there was nothing he could do but wait it out. Two sleepless nights had just become three.

He got up and trudged through the dark to the master bathroom. As he washed his hands in the well-lit room he studied his face in the mirror. For eleven years he had been David Carlisle, even to his closest friends. Lord Robert Kenyon was dead. He had wanted no slip-ups and above all no rumours to the contrary. Not once had anyone called him Robert. He even thought of himself as David Carlisle. But that was easy, really. A name was not a part of the essence of a man. Change the name and the man was exactly the same creature. The inner voice had no name, as he had only realised once he killed Robert Kenyon. A name was a convenience for the world to use, not a way into one's self. Curiously, however, he now understood that a name fixed one in the world. Without it, his essence continued unaffected, but there was no connection to anything. That meant at this particular moment he was quite suddenly without identity and therefore without anchor. Was he David Carlisle the fugitive? Or should he think of himself in terms of his next alias – whatever name and nation and family Luca decided to give him? Or had he become the resurrected Lord Kenyon – despite the name on his new passport? On the Most Wanted lists he would surely be Robert Kenyon with all his titles included. One could only imagine how the tabloids would play the whole thing up with the inevitable sobriquet of the English Assassin. And yet, as none of this had happened, was he still David Carlisle?

He snapped the light off. The *me*, the *I*, and the *you* of his inner thoughts, the holy trinity inside one's head, had never been blurred before. Aliases had never been more than tools, but now he was not sure: he was a man on an island living on top of a mountain. . . nothing more.

He made his way back to his bed, checking the digital clock. Twelve-fifty. The dead of the night and here he was thinking about rubbish. It was actually a fairly decent time to go to bed if he had not been so tired from the last two sleepless nights. His shoulders hit the mattress and his eyes opened. This was insomnia. He smiled. There had been a taunt in the old days when one did something especially despicable to a woman, *I hope you can sleep at night!* Talk about tripe! Guilt had never kept anyone awake. No, fear and worry were the culprits. He looked toward Irina without seeing her. She had done her best to exhaust him earlier and now slept the sleep of the just – murderous bitch that she was. He could still remember watching her face as she executed the Spanish and U.S. federal officers in that Newark parking garage. She *liked* it. For him killing had never been pleasant. One killed for a reason and when one had finished with it that was it. Other than the adrenalin that came of one's natural fear of getting caught or killed he felt nothing at all when he took a life.

Instead of turning on his light and reading, as he probably would have done had he been alone, he lay quietly in his bed trying in vain to empty his mind. Nothing to worry about. The world was going to go on no matter what happened. He was going to make it as he always did – or perish as everyone must. No reason to lose sleep over it.

For Irina starting over had always been part of the overall plan. She had taken a third of Jack Farrell's fortune for her troubles and gave up a life of confidence games in the service of one of Hugo Ohlendorf's captains. In return for her troubles she got a new identity and a seat on the council. He had taken her new passport to her in New York and they had got her out of the country with only a little hair dye to modify her looks. She said she found it liberating to be someone new. Of course when she had said it she was still revelling in the blood and stink of murder. *Was* it liberating? He thought back to his first days as David Carlisle. There had been some pleasure, he had to admit. Coming back to murder those who had come after him was an especially liberating experience, but on the whole it was a mixed bag, certainly not something he had ever wanted to do twice in a lifetime.

He looked at Irina's shadow next to him. She could have moved on after a day or two at the farm. That had been the plan originally – a bit of celebration and then they were to separate so she could get on with establishing herself in her new life. Once they knew his situation had become precarious, she had decided to stay. He might have thought of her as loyal if he had not known human nature so well. Irina was positioning herself. Helena was suddenly gone. Someone was needed to replace her. Who better than her protégé? She had even mentioned taking over Hugo Ohlendorf's network. At least there was no shortage of ambition.

He could not say how long he lay in that twilight between dreams and consciousness as he tried to work through things that ought to have been settled. There were some moments when he might actually have crossed into sleep, but he kept coming back to consciousness. Call it a crisis of identity. Then something happened. A sound. He came awake suddenly and listened. No. Not a sound. That wasn't quite right. He had been listening to a sound – and it had suddenly ceased. The house was too quiet. Then it came to him. A pump had been running. Mid-cycle it had stopped. He turned and saw his digital alarm clock had gone black. He looked out the window and saw the grey sky. The security lights that always shone at night had been extinguished.

Someone had cut off the electricity.

Chapter Twelve

Majorca, Spain
March 16, 2008.

Kate dropped from the Cessna at two thousand metres. The wind screamed in her ears like mad furies and her heart pounded with adrenalin as it always did when she left a plane and began a freefall. She loved the raw terror of the acceleration, the seconds dragging out as she rushed toward the earth.

Until her jump Kate had thought only about taking down her target. *Target*. A nice way of thinking about the man she had married. She had worried about the details as she always did when she planned a job. That part was finished now. Things went as she had anticipated or they didn't. There were no more adjustments, no modifications, and no contingencies that were not already in place. It was no longer the *target*. It was Robert: the traitor, the mercenary, the assassin, the liar, the thief. The *ex* in every bitter sense of the word.

When they were still talking about the man who had killed Robert, T. K. had profiled him at one point and suggested that he was something of a coward who lacked the courage to take care of his own problems. It had been a reassuring insult against a hated and still unknown antagonist. Now that she knew the man she came for, Kate was not ready to admit anything of the sort. She was convinced Robert had courage. He would put up a fight – kill her if he could. But there was something in his character she could not define. Sociopath that he was, there was *some* feeling in the man. *Cut the rope.* He had bumped her on purpose and sent her off the ledge. She

335

knew that, but he had also known she was tied into an anchor. Pushing her over the ledge was not an attempt to kill her. And he had not cut the rope as he ought to have done if killing her was the point. He had told one of the Austrians to do it, almost as an afterthought.

Why? The face she saw before her as she went over the ledge still troubled her. She had never understood the expression, but she thought maybe he had fallen in love. In which case it was regret. He had certainly put on the act as an affectionate lover. And in those last days she had seen him grow thoughtful, as if wrestling with some decision. That night on the Eiger he had seemed melancholy. Had he been reconsidering his options, wondering if he had to lose her along with everything else? Thinking about. . . *not* killing her? Telling her he was in trouble and hoping she would run off with him? He should have known he had only to ask. She would have gone with him into hiding. She had harboured no doubts about the man she loved; she had held to no morality except love. So why hadn't he said something? Why had he taken her up the mountain to die?

She could tell herself it did not matter. He had made his choice that night and they had both lived with it, but his refusal to cut the rope still nagged at her. Easy enough to do. She was hanging out of sight. All he was looking at was a piece of rope. He could have cut it rather than tell one of the Austrians to do it. The only logical conclusion was that he had felt something for her and could not bring himself to kill her with his own hand.

What she hated most about him was that flicker of humanity in his soul – if that is what it was. It made her doubt herself and what she was doing. It made him something more than a despicable coward who needed to be destroyed. After the years of mourning she had devoted to him she wanted to end things cleanly. She wanted him to feel the hurt he had caused. Instead, she spent her last moments of her freefall thinking about why he had not cut the rope himself!

Robert had become larger than anyone in her life, greater in her mind than her own father. She had let Ethan stand in Robert's shadow. And Ethan, who was the smartest and bravest man she had ever known, had endured her silent comparisons without a murmur of complaint. He had accepted second place to a dead man because it was the only place she would allow him. And for all of that there was no danger he would not risk for her. He had even let her come alone because it was *her* fight. T. K. had resisted, but Ethan had understood. This was what she needed. Even if it killed her, it was *her* revenge, the thing she had waited over a decade to accomplish.

Robert had been playing at love. If it had taken him at the end, if he had actually developed feelings, he had not let it sweep him away. He had overcome his affection for the sake of the money. That was the point. He was at the bottom of it all a confidence man. He used the emotions of others for his own gain. He was a pretty *face*. His smiles were rare and beautiful, his wit quick without being cruel, but there were hollow places where there ought to have been heart and soul.

Even Luca knew it. That was why he had taught her how to fight. He would not betray Robert. He had sworn an oath, the same as Giancarlo, but if it happened that she could find Robert on her own, Luca wanted her to be ready.

That was the kind of friendship Robert Kenyon inspired in those who *really* knew him.

Carlisle rolled toward Irina as soon as he understood what had happened. Touching her he whispered. 'Someone is here!' But he was thinking, *Kate*.

He heard Irina moving without seeing her until she crossed in front of a window, her naked silhouette black against the grey moonlit sky. Turning away from her, Carlisle found a pair of pants and a sweatshirt on a chair close to the bed. He rummaged in the closet for his climbing shoes and a jacket. He found his handgun and holster in his bedside table.

Then he heard glass breaking at the gatehouse.

*

Kate's canopy unfurled with a reassuring snap, slowing her hundred-mile-an-hour plunge over the next several hundred feet. With her NVGs strapped into place she spent the next few seconds sighting the house and working the toggle lines. She was on course to land on the rooftop but was anxious to find the direction of the wind before she got too low. There were always currents this close to a mountain, but they were quiet and sometimes as uncertain as a spring rain.

She risked a glance toward the gatehouse and then looked at the mountain looming up behind the Bartoli farm. When Kate had come here with Luca to learn to fight she had spent hours on those rocks, not once using a rope – at his insistence. For weeks she had practised using weapons and cracking alarm systems. The rocks had been a terror at first, but then they began to clear her head and take her back for an hour or so to the innocence that had died on the Eiger.

At five hundred metres, Kate called out her position. At three hundred she drifted in a lazy circle, finally catching some wind. Before she got too low, she took both toggles in her left hand and pulled the grenade launcher free from one of her two thigh holsters. The weapon appeared to be nothing more than an oversized revolver. She fired three grenades into the windows on the upper storey of the gatehouse. When she heard the glass break she tossed the weapon away.

Carlisle went to his bedroom window. The lawn was dark, the trees and gatehouse completely blacked out. Kate was out there. He just could not see her yet. This was how he always knew she would come – whenever he had let the thought take hold of him. *Hell hath no fury.*

Three explosions rocked the gatehouse in succession – then a gas line blew – sending fire and smoke soaring high, the blast illuminating the front lawn briefly.

'What happened?' Irina asked.

'The gatehouse,' he answered. That was not how the police would have handled a raid. This was Kate.

'How many are coming, David?'

He searched the shadows. He thought about Kate, Ethan Brand and Malloy. They had got out of Hamburg in one piece and were coming to kill him. Exactly as Giancarlo had told him it would turn out.

'I don't know. I can't see anyone. . .'

Kate drifted toward the gently sloping roof, turning out with the wind and then back into it so her canopy caught the breeze at the last moment and let her step into her landing softly with her weight on her good leg.

As soon as she was down she gathered the canopy and wrapped it around one of the chimneys to keep it from giving away her position. She pulled a long rope from her belt and tied it off to the master bedroom's fireplace chimney. Then she walked down the slope keeping the rope taut. She leaned out beyond the guttering to have a look at the bedroom window. Next she let the rope dangle beside it to get a fix on the length she needed.

She brought the rope back up, taking hold of it just beneath the point where it had dropped below the window frame. Walking back up the slope a couple of steps, she whispered, 'Where are they, T. K.?'

'They're directly under you,' Malloy answered into her headset.

Kate pulled her Uzi free from her second thigh holster, fingered the safety off, took a deep breath, pointed the weapon toward the roof and then squeezed the trigger.

Something like forty rounds came through the ceiling in the first seconds of the assault. The bullets tore out plaster chunks and thumped into the plank floor. Carlisle and Irina dived toward the doorway and spilled out into the hall before either of them responded with a volley of pistol fire into the ceiling.

They were still firing into the ceiling when the second volley came – this time breaking the bedroom windows. The bullets came snapping through the walls and crashing crazily around them.

As she went down the roof Kate picked up speed and jumped off her good leg. She went out, turned toward the building and squeezed down on the Uzi for a second burst. The clip emptied into the glass and wood and broke the window frame apart before she got to it.

She swung into the window, letting go of the rope as she did. Kate dropped only a couple of feet, but she tried to favour her good leg. In doing so she came down on a chunk of plaster and lost her footing, slamming hard into the floor.

Her night vision goggles flew off. Her Uzi skittered across the plank floor. She felt woozy and could tell her wound had started to bleed again, but she came up fast with her Army Colt extended and ready.

She knew the shape of the room. Using the pale light of the windows to get her orientation she made her way toward the stone wall of the fireplace. That was the only spot in the room where their bullets would not penetrate through the walls.

Just as she touched rock, she heard a volley of pistol shots from the hallway. Some thirty bullets broke through the wall. When it had finished she heard two clips bouncing to the floor, fresh ones snapping into place.

'They're pulling back,' Malloy said as Kenyon and the female finished emptying their guns. 'Kenyon is moving toward a window! Girl? Girl! Are you there?'

'Is she okay?' Ethan asked.

'We've lost contact.' Malloy saw the male climbing through a window. 'Kenyon is going out a window!'

'What about the female?' Ethan asked.

'I can't find her.'

'What do you mean?'

340

'There's no heat signature! Girl? Give me a signal if you can hear me.'

The moment the clips dropped Kate swung out from the fireplace and cut the wall with her Colt – seven rounds waist high – then rolling into the open doorway she dropped her empty clip and slapped in a second.

But suddenly the house was quiet. She could feel plaster dust still falling, see the frame of a window in the room opposite her own – a grey square of pale light. Everything else was black.

She waited, heard something – the creak of a shutter, she thought, and fired through the walls again. This time whilst she reloaded, a pistol answered – ten rounds in controlled bursts, one of them smashing into her armour, missing her skull by inches. Kate jerked in fear and surprise, then rolled out of the line of fire. She heard the wood cracking behind her. She emptied her third clip through the wall and reloaded with a quick snap.

In the other room there were no more shots fired. Running? Dead? Or saving ammo? Kate needed the NVGs, but she did not dare give up the ground she had fought to take. If she retreated back to the centre of the room she would be exposed and vulnerable to a counterattack. She had them hiding from her at the moment, and just maybe running out of ammo.

She needed to take the fight forward, not fall back.

'I still can't find the female.'

'Maybe she went out the window,' Ethan told him.

'I can see all the windows,' Malloy said. 'Girl, can you hear me?' he said. When Kate still did not answer, he told Ethan, 'This is not good.'

Irina Turner had settled against the heavy fieldstones of the fireplace in the guest bedroom. She had fired out most of two clips and had maybe five-to-seven rounds left. No more clips and no armour. And not a word from David. None from the gatehouse either, not that she expected anyone to have survived that explosion. That meant she was alone. The good news was her assailant appeared to be alone as well. More must be coming, she knew, but for the moment Irina had a chance. She felt about the fireplace until her fingers closed on a metal handle. She lifted the thing carefully. She had the shovel. She set it back into its holder and felt for the companion piece. This time she got some weight. The poker.

'I give up!' she shouted in Spanish, then in English. 'I surrender!'

'Throw your gun down!' a woman called to her. British. And not a tremor of fear in her voice either. This had to be Kate.

'I'm throwing it down!' Irina answered. She sent her gun sliding across the plank floor nearly to the doorway. 'I'm in the bedroom across the hall from you! I just threw my gun out.'

'I want you to come out with your hands over your head and stand in the doorway!'

'I can't put both hands up. I've been hit!'

'Step out and keep one hand on your head!'

'You're not going to shoot me?' Irina was frightened, and she let it show in her voice.

'I'm not going to shoot you, but you are going to have to step out now!'

Kate crawled from the master bedroom out to the open hallway, her weapon extended. She could see the shadow of the gun just inside the doorway to the next room.

The female came out of the shadows with one hand behind her head. When her body was suddenly inside the frame of the window in a perfect silhouette Kate said to her, 'Stop right there!'

'Don't shoot me!'

Russian, she thought. *Irina.* 'If you move I *will* shoot you! Do not move!'

'I'm not moving!'

'Where's Robert?'

'Who?'

'The man you were sleeping with!'

'I don't know! I think you must have killed him.'

Robert could be hiding behind the door or back against the wall under the window, just waiting for her to come forward.

Kate fired twice into the wall on either side of the door then into the baseboard to either side of the woman's silhouette. She dropped the clip and reloaded.

The woman shrieked and flinched at the sound of the .45. 'Please, don't shoot me!' she whimpered.

'Girl has the female!' Malloy announced.

Ethan brought the red dot down across Kenyon's back and tightened his grip on the trigger. 'I've got Kenyon,' he said.

'Then take him out,' Malloy answered.

'Get on your knees,' Kate told the shadow.

'Please, don't hurt me.'

'I'm going to handcuff you,' Kate told her. 'I'm not going to hurt you.'

The shadow went to her knees, still whimpering. 'Please be careful, I'm hurt!'

Kate stepped to the side of the woman and took her wrist. She needed to holster her Colt in order to reach for her cuffs. As she started to do this, Irina moved with surprising agility. Kate's back and elbow lit up in pain.

'Girl is down!' Malloy shouted. 'Girl is down! Open fire!'

Ethan pulled his sights from Kenyon. He swept the gun barrel down toward the house and flipped the selector to auto.

'Give her cover NOW!'

Kate hit the floor. The armour she wore had protected her spine, but her right elbow was broken, the pain worse than anything she had ever felt. She tried to focus, tried to understand what was happening, but the pain was numbing her thoughts. . .

CRAIG SMITH

She heard plaster popping, the crackling of bullets as they snapped through the air overhead. She could not hear the gunshots. So it was Ethan. Giving her cover. . . but why?

Then it came to her! She rolled away just as the steel rod that had shattered her elbow cut into the wood next to her head. She kept rolling, going for distance, and then saw the shadowy figure of the female snag the gun in the doorway and roll across the floor toward the fireplace and darkness. The bullets kept coming until the clip had emptied. Then suddenly the room was silent. Kate was breathing plaster dust, her eyes burning from the stuff. She had her combat knife out. Pure instinct, she could not remember losing her gun or grabbing the knife.

She looked behind her, then swept her gaze round the room. Three windows. The room was large, nearly the size of the master bedroom. With the patches of grey light on the floor and in the window frames there was enough ambient light for Irina to notice any movement, even in the shadows. A creaking board, the rustling of clothing, a piece of plaster crumbling underfoot. Anything. . . and Kate was dead.

'Cease fire!'
   'Is Girl okay?'
   'She's hurt. She's hurt!'
   'I'm going in!' Ethan told him.

The gunfire had lasted only seconds, but it came like a swarm of bees. The plaster was still in the air from the first shots, so now it was like snow flurries.

In the silence Irina had time to think. The bullets had come from somewhere beyond the house. From the olive groves, she thought. No sound of an entry team downstairs. Nothing moving in the front yard. No lights. No helicopters.

She still had time. Irina swept the big gun in front of her. Seven rounds left – give or take. One move, one sound and she would have Kate.

Listening, waiting, watching the shadows, Irina got nothing. Dead? Or playing dead?

Leaving his rifle behind, Ethan scrambled down an incline of dry earth laced with the roots of olive trees. Slipping continually, even falling once, he ran toward the wall. Fearing the worst, all he could think about was Malloy's panicked, *She's hurt!*

What did it mean exactly? In trouble, wounded. . . dying? How much time did she have before the woman finished it? What were her chances? Irina Turner, if that was the woman in the house, was almost certainly fighting in the dark. Kate had a pair of NVGs. If she still had them, and if she still had her gun. . .

He swore softly as he slipped again and tumbled across an especially steep pitch. Coming to his feet, Ethan tried to hurry, only to slam face-first into a low-hanging branch.

Kate had wanted this, he told himself as he staggered out from under the gnarled branches. She had waited eleven years for it. She deserved it. That was the argument, and Ethan had gone along with it over Malloy's protests. Why hadn't he thought it through? With something like this nothing ever happened quite the way you planned it. So you went in with a partner. Together you covered each other. You handled the unexpected. But he had wanted to believe what Kate was telling him – that this was her fight. All Ethan had really wanted was to make her whole again, to let her take her revenge and put Robert Kenyon behind her once and for all. He realised now that he had wanted too much. His mistake was going to cost Kate her life.

It would have meant nothing but some lost pride for Kate if Ethan had insisted on coming along. They had always worked together. Why did she think she had to do this alone? He ought to have said to her. . .

He ought to have said Kenyon wasn't worth it. Let the police take him as Malloy had suggested! But of course she would never have agreed to that. No. She had found him, and she was going to make him answer – even if it killed her. But Ethan could have gone in with her, if he had only insisted. He should have gone with her!

Kate kept the knife at waist level, holding it with her thumb close to the blade. She could sweep with it if Irina came in close suddenly or throw it if it came to that.

Better on her terms, she thought, and slowly, so the rustling of fabric would not draw gunfire, Kate put the blade of her knife in her teeth and pulled her last clip free of her vest. She began thumbing the bullets out into the palm of her numbed right hand. When she had emptied the clip, she turned her hand over and took the loose bullets and the clip in her left hand. She tossed the bullets and clip across the room – sending them high to give her time.

She caught the knife handle in her left hand as the bullets rained down like marbles on the wooden floor. Kate used the distraction to step in closer. She saw a muzzle blast some fifteen feet in front of her – firing toward the sound. On her next step Kate cocked the combat knife behind her ear and snapped it toward a point just behind the sparks.

When she heard a cry of pain, Kate dived toward the sound. She heard two more shots – seemingly wild and random – and then heard the gun hitting the plank floor. Kate collided with Irina's legs and brought the woman down to the floor. She swept her good hand over the naked body as she listened to the woman's ragged cries of agony and found the knife buried in her shoulder.

'Please!' Irina groaned. 'I'm hurt!'

Kate ripped the blade out of her flesh and went for the throat.

Kate heard bullets tearing into the front door and then Ethan's shout, 'GIRL!'

'I'm up here!' Kate answered and rolled off Irina Turner as

the woman bled out, her limbs twitching slowly as she died. Suddenly all that Kate could feel was the paralyzing pain of a broken bone. Even standing up was too much.

Ethan called again from the hallway at the top of the stairs. 'I'm in here,' she said, her voice filled with the exhaustion that suddenly swept over her.

When Ethan knelt beside her, Kate realised that she had lost consciousness for a moment. 'Are you hurt?' he asked, his hand cradling her head.

'She broke my elbow.' Still holding her head, Ethan slipped his hand across her shoulder and touched the bone. The pain came like an electric shock. 'That's the one!'

Easing her head back to the floor, he asked, 'Where's your headset?'

'In the master bedroom,' she answered. 'Somewhere by the window. . .'

Ethan snagged the headset and opened the channel. 'Are you there, T. K.?'

'How bad is it, Boy?'

'Girl's elbow is broken, but she's conscious. The woman is dead. Have you taken down Kenyon yet?'

'I saw him close to the top of the rocks, but I couldn't get a shot off. I'm going to make the call, Boy. I don't think we have any choice at this point.'

'Give me a five minute head start before you do.'

'Let the police take him, Boy.'

'That's still not an option, T. K.'

'I'm going after Kenyon,' Ethan told Kate as he handed her the headset. 'Just stay here and keep talking with T. K.'

'Let him go,' she said with a sigh. 'He's not worth it. He's. . . nothing.'

'He doesn't get to do this to you and then walk away.'

'*She* did this.'

'No. This is Kenyon's doing, and he's going to pay for it.'

Before Kate could stop him, Ethan took off at a sprint down the stairs and out the back of the house. The rocks lay some fifty metres behind the house and soared up over three hundred feet – huge boulders and monolithic slabs of dark porous stone. Though there were open faces here and there that offered technically challenging climbs, there were also slots and gentle slopes that allowed Ethan to scramble up most of the way quickly. He made one traverse across an open face that was difficult but only because he was wearing hiking boots instead of climbing shoes. Near the top, he was forced to leap across a small chasm so that he could finish his ascent on a gently sloping pillar that took him all the way to the top.

Before he left the rocks, Ethan peered out across the terrain. In front of him he saw a moonlit field that was covered with rocks, trees, brush, weeds, and shallow gullies. A quarter of a mile on, the mountain's summit took the form of a series of jagged points, a climber's paradise of exotic forms. This was Robert Kenyon's backyard – his refuge if the farm ever came under attack – and for a moment Ethan hesitated.

Without quite being conscious of his sudden fear at facing the man, Ethan looked back. He saw the outline of the Bartoli farmhouse almost directly under him. The dark terraces of olive trees where Malloy still waited were approximately three hundred metres distant. Malloy would still be able to see him at this point, but once he left the rocks, he crossed into a no-man's land. Out there he would have no cover and no backup. Not even a plan.

'Tell me something,' a voice close to him said. 'Is Kate still alive?'

Ethan drew his weapon and turned in the direction of Kenyon's voice, but even with his night vision goggles, he could not find the man's location. Kenyon was below him some-where, usually the inferior position, but at the moment he apparently had excellent cover. Ethan, on the other hand, was utterly exposed – his silhouette cutting into the skyline with the clarity of a target. Worse still, Ethan had no fallback. His only chance of eluding a bullet was to attempt a thirty foot slide down the pillar, finishing with a ten foot drop into a chasm of boulders.

And so he stood up straight and faced his adversary. He could at least do that much. 'She's alive,' he said, 'and no matter how far or how fast you run she'll be coming for you if it takes the rest of her life.'

'But she'll be on her own, won't she?' Ethan felt a chill at the words. He realised that Kenyon was taking a moment to enjoy himself before he finished things between them. 'It must burn you knowing that when Kate was sleeping with you all these years that she was really in love with me. How did you live with something like that, Ethan?'

'Kate would have gone to the end of the world for you, if you had asked her. I'm curious. Are you sorry now that you didn't?'

'It might not be too late. Once you're in the ground. . . and she has some time to reconcile herself to the idea. . . she might see that getting back together again only makes sense.'

'You're not really that stupid, are you?'

'You don't think I could tempt her?'

Ethan had found Kenyon's position, but he had no shot at the man. He could see nothing but rocks. 'If you think Kate is still in love with you, why did you run away?'

'Actually, Ethan, I came up here hoping you would be the one to come after me.'

'You know, *Bob*, I never met a coward yet who wasn't ready with an excuse the minute he turned rabbit.'

The shot that hit Ethan sent him stumbling back along the pillar. The second bullet knocked him down. As Ethan slid and then tumbled down the pitch, he kept his eyes on the rocks below him – gauging his fall without quite controlling it.

He managed to stay on the pillar all the way to the base, but that was it. When he dropped over the edge he slammed into a boulder four feet under the rim. His armour saved his ribs, but his face slapped stone and he lost consciousness as he dropped the last six feet.

When he came to, Ethan moved his legs slowly, almost curiously. Not paralyzed, he thought, but his body ached, and he could not be sure if anything was broken. His pain was too general to know anything with certainty. He struggled to sit up and wondered if Kenyon was close by. He looked overhead, realising Kenyon might already be taking aim. He saw only the grey, moonlit sky.

'Are you still there, Bob?' he called.

There was no answer.

'It's okay, buddy. I dropped my gun when I fell. I won't put up a fight if that's what you're afraid of. You're going to have to look me in the eye though when you do it. I know that might be hard for a man who hires other people to do his dirty work, but it's got to be done. . .'

Kenyon's shadow cut across the skyline. He was standing at the base of the pillar ten feet overhead. Ethan saw him swing his arm: taking aim. 'Tell me something, Ethan,' he said. 'Was she worth it?'

Malloy knew Ethan was in trouble when he drew his weapon and then didn't move, but there was nothing he could do except watch and wait for a shot if Kenyon showed himself. He could hear nothing of their conversation, of course, but he could almost imagine the bile between the two men. That alone explained Kenyon's willingness to double back and risk everything for the chance at Ethan.

Ethan staggered before Malloy heard the gunshot. A second gunshot stepped on the echo of the first. By then Ethan was already sliding across the rock. From his vantage point, Malloy had no idea if Ethan's armour had protected him or if Kenyon had shot him in the head. He could not even tell how far Ethan fell after he dropped out of sight.

He felt his gut go hollow as he watched, the ache of possibly losing a man who had become a close friend, but he hadn't the luxury of indulging in his grief. Kenyon was going to have to move or risk getting caught by the police, and he wanted to be ready.

His first chance at Kenyon was a fleeting one. Kenyon's body was in profile only a moment before he went behind yet another boulder. Not wanting to give himself away with a bad shot, Malloy waited for a better opportunity.

Then Kenyon emerged from the rocks and stood stock still for the space of a second or two on the pillar from which Ethan had fallen. His body faced Malloy. His weapon was aiming down at Ethan's position.

Putting the red dot over Kenyon's heart, Malloy squeezed off one round without hesitation. He heard the soft spit of the bullet, watched Kenyon drop at almost the same instant, and then heard the well-oiled slide of the mechanism as his weapon ejected the hot shell.

Malloy and Kate and Josh Sutter were waiting for Ethan at the front gate when the police helicopter ferried him from the rocks to the brightly lit front lawn. As soon as he touched down, Ethan stepped out of the saddle and walked toward Kate, who came toward him as if every step hurt. 'The police tell me Kenyon asked if he could talk to you. They're willing to give you a couple of minutes, if you want to see him.'

'He can go to hell,' Kate said.

'You're not going to have another chance for a long time, Kate. Maybe years.'

'The man is dead to me, Ethan. I never want to see him again. I don't even want to hear his name.'

Ethan reached out to hook his arm around her.

'Careful,' she told him, wincing at the gesture. 'Everything hurts.'

'I know the feeling,' he answered, letting his lips brush against her forehead and hair, thinking to himself, 'Most definitely worth it.'

*

Malloy walked Josh Sutter back toward the helicopter that contained Robert Kenyon, two Spanish police officers and a medic who was busying working on his patient. 'You're kidding me,' Josh announced incredulously. His voice was as bright as the day they had first met. 'You were aiming at his *heart*?'

'You didn't really think I wanted to hit him in the foot, did you?'

'The *Federales* were telling me you shot him there because you wanted to be sure we could take him alive.'

Malloy laughed. 'Makes a good story, I guess, but it's just not true. I was going for the kill and screwed up.'

They stopped well beyond the whirling blades of the police helicopter. Josh needed to go, but he seemed to want to say something more. 'I appreciate your insisting that I fly over for the arrest, T. K. That was. . . it meant a lot to me.'

'I told you I would.'

'I know you did but, you know, people say things, and then they forget. You have no idea how good it felt to put the cuffs on that guy and read him his rights.'

'I thought you'd want to see him in the ground. I sure did.'

'Jim always said it was better to take a scumbag alive. That way the lawyers got to peck at his liver for a few years before we finally strapped him down on the gurney and took him out of his misery.'

'Jim was a hard man – but a good soul.'

'He was the salt of the earth, T. K.'

'Are you going to be all right with the Bureau – after what happened in Hamburg?'

'My supervisor told me he wanted to send me back to Germany to face charges when they were screaming for me to be extradited, but then the Germans decided they didn't need to talk to me after all. I mean, they actually said they didn't think I had done anything inappropriate, so he cooled down some. You wouldn't happen to know anything about why the Germans changed their minds about me, would you?'

'Someone gave them a list of names from Chernoff's laptop.'

'*Someone?*'

'One of the senior accountants I work for. Anyway, the Germans were so happy about getting the information they decided to accept our explanation of what happened.'

'That Jim and Dale went rogue, and you and I went home?'

'That's the story I like.'

Josh thought about this for a minute. 'What about the siege at that park where we spent half the night?' he asked. 'Jim and Dale can't get the blame for that too, can they?'

'Those guys were probably Chernoff's people, don't you think?'

Berlin,
February 1939.

The letter had no return address, but like all his mail for the past year or so it showed signs of having been opened. Inside Rahn found a note that read:

You are being investigated.

Elise had not signed it, but he knew her handwriting. He knew as well that she had put herself at risk by mailing such a warning. Of course he had suspected for some time that they were reading his mail and tapping his phone. If Himmler had ordered an investigation, that was another matter. It meant they were not going to be content until they had everything. A stray remark, a fool-hardy tryst, an intercepted letter such as this one, and of course a detailed racial profile. . .

The world had changed in the past two years. Not so much in direction as speed. He had seen terrible things at Dachau in 1937, but those things had paled against the open hostility in the worker camp – the slave camp – at Buchenwald. They were no longer interested in containment. Buchenwald had become a death camp in all but name. They were not marching people to the walls and shooting them, of course. They simply worked them to death. In the end it all came to the same. They drove the people to exhaustion, and those who did not go quickly, the young and strong ones, they starved. Then there were the ones who got special treatment from the mad wife of the camp director who, even among the guards, was called the Witch of Buchenwald.

What he was still trying to understand was how he had got into the middle of it. He was not that sort of man! But of course there were a great many men who were not at all *that sort*. Truth was they had moulded him into their image by giving him what he wanted most. He had enjoyed the comforts Himmler had extended to him. He liked his salary. He liked notoriety. He enjoyed the company of intellectuals. He liked the women who came to him for the asking and performed. . . anything. He liked fine restaurants and the best seats at the opera. He even liked giving speeches to adoring ladies and respectful old gentlemen.

He could chide himself for the deal he had made with Himmler, but he had enjoyed every second of it until he had understood that in the process he had become a murderer like the rest of them! It had been a Faustian bargain – his soul for the freedom to write! And the joke of it was this: he could no longer write. The better part of his second book he had written long before Heinrich Himmler had made him a knight of the Order of the Skull. The rest was taken from him and rewritten so that it seemed he had ranted against the Jews. Why hadn't he quit when they rewrote his book? Of course he knew the answer – he just didn't like it. No question really. He hated what they did to his book, but still enjoyed the splendour of knighthood, the runic SS, the handsome men with their eyes watching him, the beautiful women for the asking. . . the whole great show of the Reich rising up to the terror of its enemies! Until the blood of the twelve miners splashed across his soul, it had been a fine run! Now, seeing what he had done, he hated the runic double SS more than Hell's Gates. It physically revolted him when he looked down at his hand and saw the ring that bound him by a blood oath to the Devil's own.

He had not long to wait for the investigation to be completed. He knew that. They would find him out soon enough, learn his darkest secret – that amongst the pagans and heretics of his ancestry there were Jews as well. In 1935, though it had been policy to do so, no one had bothered to require him to fill out a certificate of racial purity. Certainly no one had asked about his grandparents. Why should they? He was not trying to join the SS, *they* were recruiting *him*! Of course in the first days after he had joined the Order no one had dared approach him about paperwork that he needed to complete. He had received the form some months after joining and, seeing the problem at once, he had ignored it. No one said a word, nor had he expected them to. He was Himmler's darling. His time was his own, and he might not be pleased about being ordered to fill out routine paperwork. But times had changed. *Krystalnacht*, the Night of Broken Crystal in the fall of 1938, had been a declaration of war on the Jews in Germany and Rahn's exalted position had eroded. He could no longer ignore a request for information about his ancestry. What he did not provide, they would find on their own. It was only a matter of time.

It was strange to realise he was an enemy of the Reich. Absurd, really. He remembered the miners Bachman had murdered. He had not really thought about the deadness in their eyes as they ate their meals in dull silence. He had written it off as exhaustion, but he had seen that look again at Buchenwald. It was the look of doom. Sometimes, in the mirror, he saw it in his own eyes, too. No one survived the camps, not in the end. So he went about his business each day, still nominally a member of Himmler's civilian staff, wondering at the day and hour when they would arrest him and pack him off to join the rest!

Sometimes, at the absurdity of it, he would laugh. It was beyond believing! Sometimes, his guts churning in fear, he was sure they were coming and that he would be better off killing himself. A bureaucratic investigation was inevitably slow but it was also careful. At some point, they would realise they had recruited a Jew! He saw men looking at him and realised word of the investigation had leaked out. They were very good about that kind of thing. He saw them get quiet as he approached. Bachman dropped by to tell him Elise was not feeling well. 'No dinners this week, I'm afraid!' A moment later he was gone. The next week it was Sarah's turn to be under the weather.

He went once, uninvited, to their townhouse, knowing Bachman was away. The maid told him Frau Bachman was engaged and could not receive him. Was there a message to give her? He had thought she would agree to see him. When she refused, he knew he was lost.

He did not decide to act because of that. The idea simply presented itself one day as he was scanning the usual reports that crossed his desk – a note about work at Berchtesgaden. The Eagle's Nest – a splendid Bavarian-style cabin cradled high among the rocks – would be completed that spring, deep inside the compound. It would be presented to the Führer on 20 April, the culmination of a national celebration of his fiftieth birthday.

Berchtesgaden was guarded by SS troops.

For the first week after the idea had simply boiled up from the chaos of his fears, Rahn managed to push it away completely. He went to his office each morning. He worked long days, his head bowed into his books. He ate and drank alone at night, watching his door with the curiosity of a fugitive as he wondered if they would come on this night or if he might be free a few nights more. Old friends happened not to notice him when he walked in the streets. When he rang up the worst sort, even they had business that kept them from seeing him socially. Secretaries kept their eyes averted when he appeared or they had errands that chased them from their stations. 'I am a ghost,' he whispered into the mirror one afternoon, and saying it, he realised that he must do something. He must at least try to get out. Then the idea came back to him – this time something more than a fantasy. Running was not the answer. Not for a knight of the Blood Lance.

February 28, 1939.

On the last day of the month, Rahn passed an envelope to one of Himmler's assistants. 'Make sure the Reichsführer sees this first thing tomorrow,' he said.

'What is this?' the man asked with a degree of suspicion that made Rahn uneasy.

'My letter of resignation.'

The man's face washed pale. 'You took an oath!'

'If the Reichsführer is interested I will be glad to explain my reasons in person. For now, if you will, simply give him my letter.'

Rahn was not sure he would make it out of the building, but he had decided he must resign. If all else failed, if the Gestapo arrested him before he could act, he had at least declared he was no longer a sworn knight of the Order of the Skull. Whilst his letter still lay unopened on Himmler's desk, he proceeded to the car pool and took a staff car for an early morning trip. With a near-perfect forgery of Himmler's signature, the paperwork was impeccable, and Rahn proceeded out of Berlin holding his breath the entire way.

On the following afternoon, Rahn presented another letter written over Himmler's signature to the SS guard at the entry to Wewelsburg. The corporal made a phone call, and seemed to take longer than before. Every nod of his head, every answer he gave, spelled doom in Rahn's overworked imagination, but he finally signalled Rahn through. 'You may park inside the gate, Dr Rahn!' As he had anticipated, his resignation would take several days to filter through the bureaucracy. On this day, at least outside of Berlin, Dr Rahn was still an important man.

Himmler kept the relic Rahn had given him in a locked room close to the officers' apartments on the upper floor of the fortress. A sergeant had directed Rahn to it and even unlocked the door for him. Then he waited whilst Rahn retrieved the thing.

Himmler had not responded well to the Lance of Antioch because he was, in the end, a profoundly unimaginative man. That was not to say Himmler had no interest in the object. He was mad for occult ceremonies, secret societies, and anything at all that hinted of being a magical talisman. He believed in ghosts and the power of objects that had been touched by destiny. And though Himmler might tell the Führer the Lance of St. Maurice had pierced the side of Christ, in his heart he believed Rahn, believed as well that *he* owned the True Lance – and with it the destiny of the world. But for the time, still a young man, Himmler had kept his secret talisman locked away in his secret castle.

Nothing, Rahn knew, would cut as deep as losing this – especially as a Jew had stolen it from him.

Elise told the maid not to admit Dr Rahn. When he appeared, her maid following him helplessly, Elise told the woman to go upstairs. 'Shall I telephone the police, Ma'am?'

'No,' Elise said with a calmness she did not feel. 'I will handle it.'

Alone, the two of them seated on the settee in the parlour, she told him, 'Otto, we cannot see you anymore. I am sorry, but Dieter insists we keep our distance – at least until you are cleared.'

'That's not why I am here,' he told her. 'I came to ask you if Sarah is ours.'

Elise seemed startled by this, but answered him honestly. 'I was certain you already knew the answer to that.'

'Does Dieter know as well?'

'There has been nothing between us for years. He can hardly imagine Sarah is his own.'

'Will he protect Sarah – if she is threatened?'

'*Protect?* You think she is in trouble?'

'If anyone finds out she is my daughter she will be.'

'No one will ever know that. Dieter has been very good about keeping our secret. It is in his interest as well – as you have probably guessed.'

'I don't understand.'

'Haven't you ever noticed his affinity for young men?'

Rahn was surprised. He had always. . . well, he had seen things, but he had not been willing to believe that Bachman might actually. . .

'I suppose maybe I knew. . .'

'Sarah and I protect him from scandal, but he is also genuinely in love with both of us. Sarah means the world to him, and he is very good with her. He is a very kind man, Otto.'

Rahn lifted the rucksack he had set at his feet and placed it between them. 'If you show this to Dieter, he will take it from you and you will have nothing that can help you and Sarah if they come to take you away.'

'I don't understand. Why would anyone—?'

'If you keep it hidden from him until it is needed I think he can use it to save you.'

'Otto, no one is going to take us away! Our secret is safe!'

'No secrets are safe anymore. It takes only a maid looking at your letters or a bureaucrat checking *your* family. . .'

'You think *I'm* Jewish?'

'I can do basic genealogical research, Elise.'

'You know then?'

'Go on,' he said. 'Have a look. It just might save your life.' She observed the rucksack with interest now.

'What is it?'

'Open it.'

She brought the gilded, battered box out of the bag and set

it on her lap. 'Have a look inside,' he said. Opening the lid, Elise saw the lump of iron and the rotted linen cloth beneath it. She looked at Rahn without understanding. Bachman had obviously kept everything from her. 'You are being very mysterious, Otto.'

'Promise me you will hide this someplace where no one can find it.'

'I don't understand!'

'It is something Himmler wants, and with it Dieter can save you if he has not already given it back.'

'Otto, what have you done?'

'Elise, promise me you will only tell Dieter about this if you and Sarah are in trouble – for Sarah's sake if not your own!'

'You don't think he can be trusted – even if he knows it will save Sarah's life?'

'He will convince himself nothing is going to happen to Sarah. He is very good at lying to himself. I think we all are, actually.'

'If Himmler wants this he will find it! You aren't saving me with this, Otto! You are getting me into the middle of something horrible!'

'We are all in the middle of something horrible, Elise. Besides, he isn't going to know to look at you. He is going to be following *me*.'

Her eyes fixed on him with an expression of utter tragedy. He had never before seen her face like this. 'You aren't coming back, are you?'

'I want to see Sarah before I go.'

Kufstein, Austria
March 15, 1939.

It took two days for Himmler to learn that Otto Rahn had stolen a car from the motor pool, three to discover he had taken the Lance of Antioch from Wewelsburg. The moment he realised what Rahn had done to him, he called off the Gestapo and put Colonel Bachman in charge. 'No matter the cost, no matter the time involved,' he said, 'You *will* find out where he has hidden it!'

'Of course, Reichsführer!'

'As for Dr Rahn, once you have recovered what he has taken, I want him brought back to Berlin so that I may have a word with him before he is shot.'

Operating directly under Himmler's authority, Bachman directed a nationwide manhunt. Additionally, he sent men to the south of France and to Geneva, Switzerland, where he knew Rahn had a number of old friends. Bachman set up his headquarters for the search in Berlin, coordinating a number of teams. He kept a plane on standby night and day. He gave orders to call him the moment Rahn had been detained. On the fifth night after Rahn had run, Bachman was spending another sleepless night when he suddenly sat up in bed, wide awake. They had not found Rahn in France or Switzerland or at any of the border crossings, he realised, because Rahn was *not* running. He was still in Germany.

'*We are plotting to kill Hitler!*' That was what he had said as a joke one evening when Bachman had caught him whispering to Elise, but there had been something in his eyes when he had said it. . .

The following morning Bachman ordered everything in Otto's office and apartment reviewed a second time. It took three days and ten agents before they found he had taken a look at the plans of the Eagle's Nest. Hitler was going there for his birthday in just over a month, and Rahn – the doomed romantic with his deluded notions of right and wrong – intended to be there!

Bachman flew to Berchtesgaden on Monday, 13 March, and began directing a discreet search of the villages and towns. They were looking for a soldier on leave who was passing his time quietly. Late on Wednesday, one of his agents reported a tall, fairly young captain in the SS who was renting a room from a widow in the village of Kufstein – not more than forty kilometres from Berchtesgaden.

Bachman moved in just after dark.

Rahn travelled by car to central Germany, then by train as far as Munich. He got ahead of the first investigators and hitch-hiked southeast to the village of Kufstein on the Austrian side of the border. His papers were checked at the border, but his forged papers had stirred no interest. He got a room with a widow by telling the woman he was on medical leave from the army and wanted to do some hiking in the area for a few weeks before he reported to Berchtesgaden for active duty. She did not ask for proof, but to assuage her curiosity he left his orders to transfer to Berchtesgaden on 19 April out on the bureau for her to find. His uniform, he kept hanging in his closet.

He sometimes spoke with the woman about his parents and a fiancée who had broken off the engagement with him without explaining herself. He told a good story, and won the old woman's sympathy with it. She told him he ought to make up with his parents before it was too late. There would be a time when he would be sorry for the quarrel. As for the young woman, it was her loss. He just needed a little time getting past a broken heart! He told her she was probably right, but for the time being he just needed some time to himself. She seemed to understand, and certainly showed no concern when he stayed locked in his room or went alone into the woods as the weeks passed.

On the night they came for him, Rahn heard her answer the door and then her cry of surprise as they pushed into the house. Rahn got his military uniform and his papers together before they hit the bedroom door. In the mad scramble to get away, he had nothing else. He went out through a window, threw his boots and uniform to the ground and risked descending by the drainpipe. Neither man giving chase was willing to risk a fall. They watched as he ran. They might have shot him easily enough. When they didn't, Rahn knew Elise had done as he had asked her. If Himmler had any hope of retrieving his Lance he needed Rahn alive.

He changed into the uniform when he got to the base of the Wilder Kaiser. He hid close to a fine ledge, where in ancient times prisoners of war had been tossed. It was a good place for a soldier to die.

The Wilder Kaiser, Austria
March 15-16, 1939.

Bachman brought several squads in from the roads to converge on the mountain. Once the search was started, he did what he could to reinforce the area quietly. He did not intend for Rahn to slip free, but neither did he want the villagers to notice any sort of military action.

They found his civilian clothes an hour past midnight. Twenty minutes later they found Rahn. He was wearing a captain's uniform but hiding like a runaway slave inside a hollow log. By the time Bachman arrived, the soldiers had been standing around with their captive for nearly an hour. As per instructions Rahn had not been hurt, but they had stripped him of his officer's hat and of course his *Totenkopf* ring. A sergeant presented Bachman with the forged transfer papers.

Bachman considered the transfer with his torch and then walked toward his old friend with a smile that evinced no affection. 'It never would have worked, Otto. They would have arrested you the moment you showed these papers. I was on to you! I know how you think!' He let this fact settle, before adding, 'You understand I am going to have to kill you?'

Rahn smiled. 'You, or someone you order to do it, Dieter?'

'I don't suppose it is going to matter much to you who does it, but you may want to consider how much pain you want to endure. Reichsführer Himmler has given me complete autonomy in that respect. I can still be your friend, Otto. I can make it very quick. You will feel nothing. But for that, my friend, I am going to need what you took from the Reichsführer.'

Rahn looked at the men holding him and then at Bachman. 'Swear it – on the eyes of your daughter! Swear to me you will make it as painless as possible!'

'I swear it on the eyes of my daughter!'

Rahn nodded. 'Then I will tell you the truth – but only you, Dieter.'

Bachman considered his old friend quietly for a moment. 'If you are lying. . .'

'I am not lying. I owe you the truth, Dieter.'

'Leave us alone!' The soldiers backed off some fifteen metres, establishing a circle around the two men. On three sides the ground was reasonably level and covered with trees. On the fourth side the cliff waited. There were twelve men in all, each aiming his torch at Bachman and Rahn. The two men stood close to one another, their faces illuminated by the artificial light.

Rahn rubbed his wrists and stamped his feet, trying to restore his circulation. 'Where have you hidden the Lance?' Bachman asked him.

'You must understand something, Dieter. Once I tell you the truth you will end up lying to Himmler about it. It is really better for you not to know.'

'It is touching that you are so concerned for my well-being, Otto, but I will take my chances with the truth. Where have you hidden it?'

'Are you talking about the Lance of Antioch?'

'What else do you think?'

'I haven't hid it anywhere. How could I? I've never seen the thing!'

'You and I both know better!'

'Oh, that! You are talking about what we brought out of France! That isn't the Lance of Antioch, Dieter. What you thought was a reliquary I paid a Swiss metal worker to gild and then paste with jewels that I had bought in a shop. Why do you think I asked you for money? Credible forgeries cost a good deal! As for the piece of iron inside, what you are calling the

Lance of Antioch, I had more luck. I dug it up by chance from your garden.'

Bachman stared at him without comprehending. 'What are you saying?'

'I am saying you killed those men – we killed them – for nothing! I planted Himmler's precious relic in that cave, Dieter. It's why I insisted I go ahead of the expedition, why I directed the search the way I did. All of it was a show so that we could deliver a piece of nonsense to a mad man and keep our precious status as his darlings!'

'I don't believe you!'

'You don't want to believe me, but I swear it is the truth. On the eyes of *my* child, I swear it.'

'No.' Bachman shook his head. He tried to smile. 'This is a tactic – a ruse! You will say anything to avoid being tortured! You *know* where it is!'

'I know the Lance of Antioch disappeared in Constantinople over eight hundred years ago, Dieter. No one knows where it is. As for the Blood Lance of the Cathars – that rests in the heart of every true knight!'

'But you said Raymond sent it back to the Languedoc with his infant son!'

'If he had possession of it and chose torture instead of surrendering it, then he was a greater fool than Peter Bartholomew, and this much I know: Raymond was no fool.' Rahn laughed suddenly at Bachman's utter consternation. 'I keep trying to imagine how Himmler is going to take it when you tell him this. You know he is going to blame *you* for it, don't you? No one likes being tricked – mad men least of all. My advice? Tell him I took the secret to my grave. Tell him you won't stop looking, but that I got away and there was nothing you could do. But on your life, my friend, do not tell him the truth or he will have you murdered!'

'True or not, what you stole is what I will take back to him!'

'I can't let you do that, Dieter.'

'You have no choice!'

'A man always has a choice. . . even if it isn't pretty.' In the next moment Rahn was running toward the ledge. Three of the men guarding it were close enough to move in to intercept him, but he had the size and the will to get through them. He drove hard toward the strongest of the three and stumbled when they collided. The other two tried to grab his coat as he kicked out two more steps.

In the next he was gone.

The Wilder Kaiser, Austria
March 16, 1939.

He heard the wind as he plunged. He saw the black face of the mountain blurring. He thought of Elise. She was sitting beside him on Montségur. Kissing his cheek lightly, she told him that she wanted to think of him always just as he was that day, the two of them high over the world and resting for a moment amongst the beautiful ghosts.

Berlin
April 11, 2008.

A couple of weeks after their return to Zürich, Ethan received a letter from Frau Sarah von Wittsberg, one of the paladins of the Order of the Knights of the Holy Lance. She invited him to visit her at her Berlin apartment on the afternoon of 11 April. She had, she said, a favour to ask.

Frau von Wittsberg lived in a nineteenth century flat that had been renovated without quite losing all of its original charm. Set in the former East Berlin, the neighbourhood had a friendly, Bohemian flavour to it, and Ethan was surprised to find that the former dame of Berlin society fit so easily into such unpretentious surroundings.

She was in her mid-seventies and still quite the beauty. She had silver hair, and round, intense black eyes. She possessed the posture and confidence of aristocracy, the manner of one who had hosted diplomats, the unflinching character of one who had survived the camps.

In her front hall and living room there were no photographs on her walls to commemorate her three-decade-long struggle to keep West Berlin free. Instead she had filled her walls with several canvases by different German artists who had been driven out of Berlin in the 1930s. Their art had been deemed by the Nazi authorities to be decadent. Ethan recognised the artists, but not these particular pieces, so he took a moment to study them whilst the lady prepared a pot of tea.

'Giancarlo tells me you used to steal paintings like these and got rich doing it,' she said as she set a silver service on a small table in front of a settee.

Ethan smiled affably. 'If you're worried I might come back and get these, don't be. I'm retired from that life.'

'He told me. He said you had got religion or something.' She studied the paintings as if looking at them for the first time in years. 'You know, I don't particularly *like* any of these. I don't understand them really, but I absolutely love what they stand for. These artists stayed true to their own vision even though it ruined them. These days artists sell out for money they don't even need.' After a moment of thoughtfulness, she added, 'I was in the camps, you know.'

'Yes, ma'am. I read about that in one of the early articles the Knights published about you.'

'My mother and I spent most of our first year at Buchenwald.'

'And today is the anniversary of its liberation?'

'Very good. *Very* good, Mr Brand.' She reflected for a moment. 'Giancarlo told me I would be impressed with you. I'm beginning to see why. My mother was still quite lovely at the start so they used her as a prostitute for the guards. After a year, when they had ruined her beauty, we got shuffled off to one of the sub-camps where they tried to kill us by hard work and starvation. They would have done so too if they had had a little more time. But Buchenwald was where it started. Buchenwald is where I go when I dream of Hell.

'Do you want to know a very cruel irony?' she asked after a moment of contemplative silence. When Ethan said nothing to this, she continued, 'Several years after the war my mother confessed to me that my father had served as a camp guard at Buchenwald. We were there at the end of 1943 and through most of 1944. My father had served only a few months in the fall of 1938.

'He was one of the people Himmler personally recruited – one of his historians, actually – sent to the camps to work as a guard for unspecified disciplinary reasons. For years after I found out, I imagined that *my* father must have been different from the guards my mother and I had encountered. I knew him as a decent, sweet tempered man. My mother told me he was the most honourable man she had ever known.

'As I have got older, Mr Brand, I have to admit to myself he probably behaved *exactly* as the rest of them did. It breaks my heart to believe it, but you see there were a great many decent, honourable men working in the camps. . . and every last one made God weep.

'But I will tell you one thing about my father that was different from the rest of them. Fact, Mr Brand, not a daughter's wistful speculation. When he had finished his three month tour at Buchenwald he resigned from the Order of the Skull. Himmler wouldn't have it, of course. They made it sound like it was a climbing accident – but it was murder. They gave out a press release about his death and covered him in praise even whilst they were disposing of his corpse somewhere without so much as a marker to commemorate his existence. *Exactly* as Himmler treated the victims of the camps.'

Frau von Wittsberg smiled, but there was no happiness in her expression. 'Are you familiar with the story of Percival?'

Ethan looked at her, wondering what could have inspired such a change in topic. 'Percival was the knight who encountered the Blood Lance and Chalice in the hall of the Fisher King,' he said when it was clear she wanted him to speak.

Frau von Wittsberg nodded and said, 'It is a lovely pagan legend the Christians appropriated, but good for all, I think. When he saw the Lance and Chalice carried by a procession of knights and ladies, Percival was obliged to ask, "Whom does one serve who follows this?" Had he asked that question, the Fisher King would have been healed of his lameness and the dying land would have bloomed into life again. Because he failed to say anything at all, Percival fell into a deep slumber and when he awakened he found himself alone in a wasteland.

'My father knew that legend better than any man of his generation. He was a scholar of the Grail, and yet he committed Percival's error. He saw the great show the Nazi's put on, the brilliant uniforms, the colourful banners, the great triumphal processions and he forgot to ask, "Whom does one serve who follows this?" Like a lot of Germans of that generation, I suppose. . .'

She walked over to the tea service and poured two cups, then signalled for Ethan to join her on the settee. 'I do not mean to speak to you in riddles, Mr Brand, but I find to my utter embarrassment I have committed my father's and Percival's error. The sin of omission, if you will. What is worse, I haven't even the comfort of blaming my youth and inexperience as they might have done if they had been the sort of men to make excuses. I was old enough to know better and had even the memory of my father's failing to remind me. More than that, I am a child of the camps. I know human nature's ugliest face. . . and still I failed to ask the essential question!'

'You're talking about the Council of the Paladins?'

'I fought for West Berlin's safety from the moment it stood in peril until the Wall came down. In all it was a twenty-eight-year-long siege that absolutely no one expected to end with victory. I spent lavishly on the cause. I spent the better part of my fortune, actually. Courting politicians and diplomats is not a game for the poor. I fought a war, Mr Brand, as surely as if I had carried a weapon, and I did not blanch at the alliances we made along the way. There is no other way to put it. We were not choosey about our friends – not so long as they served our cause.

'When it was finished, when the Wall came down, I expected the Order of the Knights of the Holy Lance would quietly dissolve. We had no further reason to exist. I spoke my mind about so many things over the years, but not about that. Of course we had money and networks in place, and the Communists were on the verge of collapsing in the Soviet Union. So we could not stop with Germany reunified. We had to keep at it!

'And when the Soviets fell and war broke out in the Balkans it did not seem right to turn our backs on the genocide. . .'

She shook her head slowly. 'It never occurred to me that my war had ended and I ought to resign my seat. I was proud of what we had accomplished, because I knew that we had resisted a great tyranny and we had won. My seat among the paladins meant I had made a difference. It was the brightness in my adult life that brought balance to the darkness of my childhood. It was proof I had done more with my life than just survive.

'Instead of offering my resignation, I stepped aside and let Johannes Diekmann represent me. I trusted Hans. I knew he would do the right thing. When he was no longer able to participate I let him give my vote to his nephew. We all did. Herr Ohlendorf was a tremendously persuasive man, Mr Brand. Very charismatic and bright. . . and as corrupt an individual as I have ever encountered. And I knew the Devil himself.

'We had become a humanitarian organisation – committing our good deeds in the sunshine and God knows what atrocities by the pale light of the moon. For nineteen years I did not ask to see the accounts, accounts I had a right and responsibility to examine. I did not even *consider* Percival's question, and now I find I have awakened in a wasteland. We sold weapons and mercenaries to the worst men on earth. We sent assassins against democratically elected leaders. We stole a great deal of money in a dozen different ways. We ran drugs, people, and goods for no other reason than to make money, and finally we began murdering our friends.

'I speak as one who did it, because I had the power to ask for explanations and I was happy instead to look elsewhere whilst the monsters danced.

'That ends today, Mr Brand. I cannot undo my silence, but I mean to take responsibility for it.' She nodded toward an old steamer trunk in the corner of her room that functioned as a plant stand. 'Have a look inside that chest, if you will. There is something in it I think you might appreciate.'

Ethan walked to the trunk, removed the potted plants from it, and then opened the lid. He found a tray filled with miscellaneous objects: coins, rings, tiny glass vials, and porcelain knick-knacks. 'Remove the tray,' she told him. When he did, Ethan saw a small gilded container that was not much larger than an ordinary music box. It was bedecked with tiny, misshaped pearls and rubies. The workmanship was dis-appointing – until one realised it was a nine-hundred-year-old medieval reliquary.

'Open it carefully,' she told him. 'The hinges have rusted away.'

Ethan lifted the lid to have a look and saw a lump of iron the size of his fist. That explained the weight of the box. Tucked into the corner was a card with a typed inscription and the horrible mark of a Swastika stamped beneath. The note read:

The Lance of Antioch: discovered by Doctor Otto Rahn in the Sabarthès caves of the Languedoc, 1936.

At the bottom of the card Ethan recognised the signature of Heinrich Himmler. He looked up at the woman in disbelief.

'When my mother died in 1960 I found out she had kept a lockbox in a Zürich bank from 1939 on – renewed every ten years. Naturally I went to have a look. If you want to know the truth I was hoping for stock certificates in some old Blue Chip that might have gone up in value a hundred-fold, but this and the love letters my father wrote her in the winter before I was conceived are all that I found. The card was buried under the silk. I am not sure she ever saw it.'

'Do you have any idea why Otto Rahn would have given this to your mother?'

'Of course I do. Otto Rahn was my father, Mr Brand. On my birth certificate it states that I am the child of Sarah and Dieter Bachman, but my mother told me otherwise, and the letters she kept confirm it.

'On the day he sent his letter of resignation to Himmler, I am fairly sure he came to our townhouse and gave this to my mother. I remember his visit, because it was the last time I ever saw him. It was a cold winter day and he was wearing the uniform of an SS officer. I had never seen him dressed as a soldier and did not recognise him at first.

'He was my Uncle Ot, a part of the family for as long as I could remember. Unless I am deluding myself with fantasies, I am quite sure he had a package with him that was not much larger than that reliquary you are holding. I thought it was a gift for me. I always got something when he came to visit, but on this occasion he had forgotten to bring me something. He spoke to my mother in whispers. I wish I could tell you what they said. I only know that they were both very earnest and I think frightened. And later she cried.

'A few weeks later my legal father told me Uncle Ot had died – an accident whilst he was climbing a mountain in Austria. Dieter Bachman was killed in Poland a few months later. My mother remarried and, when he was killed in Sicily, his relatives denounced her as a Jew so they could have her fortune. After the war, we were like everyone else – standing in a wasteland and starting over. By the time we had built Berlin back into a city I was married and my mother had passed away. She saw so much in her life, but she never had to look at the Wall.

'I found out about the lockbox a few days after her funeral.

Less than a year later the Russians built a wall around West Berlin, and Hans Diekmann came to me to ask if I would help organise a defence of the city. I had already brought this back from Zürich by then and had been reading about the siege of Antioch at the time of the first Crusade. As Hans was explaining what he and Sir William were planning, he said we were under siege and though it might look hopeless we must keep faith. That got me thinking about what had happened at Antioch, and it seemed to me like a sign from God.

'I told Hans I would do anything he asked of me – seduce politicians if I must. My husband was wealthy and we both had a great many social contacts, so we were well placed to help. On a whim, I suggested to Hans that we call ourselves the Order of the Knights of the Holy Lance, as our situation seemed nearly as desperate as that of the Crusaders at Antioch.

'We were all very modern back then, Mr Brand, and Hans was not inclined to establish an order of knights – not so soon after Himmler's Order of the Skull – but then I showed him my father's treasure. Hans had become a very devout Christian after the war. At the sight of that relic, he told me that he *knew* we were going to make it through.

'We used this amongst the leadership – the paladins – to take our oath. I cannot tell you the fire that built amongst us as we passed it from one to another, swearing by its holy power. When we had finished with our oaths, we made war exactly as the Crusaders at Antioch had done – never for the moment doubting that it was God's will that we should tear apart that Wall one day.

'Now here is the thing, Mr Brand. The paladins have authorised me to dissolve the Order. It is long overdue, and, as you can imagine, there is a great deal of work to be done – including extensive meetings with various law enforcement agencies. All of that, I can handle. My mistake was a moral one. I committed no crimes in a legal sense. I will not, however, try to keep as my own what I have repudiated with my silence.

I don't deserve to keep this, and I will not tempt Providence by pretending otherwise.

'That is where you come in. Giancarlo assures me you will know where it belongs.'

Ethan stirred from his shocked silence. 'I have to be honest, ma'am,' he said. 'I have no idea what to do with something like this.'

'Then I suggest you pray for guidance. Take all the time you need. . . and then do what you must. I do not care to approve or even to know what you finally determine. But do remember this, Mr Brand. There are those who believe that whosoever possesses the Holy Lance can determine the destiny of the world.'

Epilogue

Kufstein, Austria
June 15, 2008.

'You're absolutely sure it's not genuine?' Kate asked. She and Ethan were sitting at an outdoor cafe in the village of Kufstein, Austria. Otto Rahn's Lance of Antioch lay on the table between them like an ugly paperweight. Ethan had already sent the reliquary to the curator of a private institution in Texas. Despite Ethan's detailed reservations about the reliquary's provenance, Dr North had been excited to receive it and had asked Ethan to write a monograph, which North's organisation proposed to publish. He had said he would be happy to do it and had already begun the work. The fate of the relic itself, however, still needed to be settled. So he and Kate had come here. 'You don't think it is even *remotely* possible you could be wrong?'

'The Crusaders needed a miracle at Antioch,' Ethan told her, 'and Raymond of St. Gilles came up with one.'

'But *this* was the miracle. He saved the army by calling this the Holy Lance. That makes it a piece of history – something people would like to see.'

Ethan could not decide if Kate really believed her argument or if she only wanted to play the devil's advocate so he would have no second thoughts afterwards. 'Faith in God saved the army. This was just a prop for a stage play.'

'How do you know it was a counterfeit? I thought you said they found it buried under the floor of one of the churches?'

Ethan shook his head and smiled. 'The priests had workers

tear away the floor. Then they spent the better part of the day digging through the sub-flooring and dirt. Once it was clear that there was nothing to find, they ordered the men out. That was when Peter claimed he saw something and jumped in to have a look. A few seconds later he brought a piece of iron up out of the mud. Raymond was right there to take it from him and kiss it and praise God for the miraculous sign from heaven.'

'Peter had it in his pocket?'

Ethan shrugged. 'Even by medieval standards the scam was transparent. Of course anyone smart enough to understand what had just happened was also smart enough to realise that a miracle was the army's best chance at getting out of Antioch alive.'

Kate picked up the corroded knot of iron from the table and turned it in the sunlight to have a closer look. 'What doesn't make sense to me is why Peter Bartholomew would submit to a trial by fire – knowing this was just a piece of iron.'

'The trial by fire occurred almost a year after the siege of Antioch. By then Peter was directing all of the military decisions of the army. The barons flattered him when they weren't actually offering him gifts and bribes. The priests deferred to his judgment – much as they hated doing it – and the rank and file exalted him as the expedition's holy man. It was heady stuff for a commoner, but he knew that if he refused the challenge he was going to lose everything.'

'And if he accepted it he was going to burn to death.'

'He believed the Holy Lance would protect him.'

Kate let the object drop on the table with a dull thud. 'He didn't have the Holy Lance. He had this thing.'

'In Peter's mind it had become what he said it was.'

Kate shook her head. 'I think his willingness to walk through fire proves he actually found something in the mud. That's the only way his action makes sense.'

'Then you have to accept that he was visited by a vision of St. Andrew, who told him where this was buried. Of course that would mean this is the lance head that pierced the side of Christ.'

Kate was quiet. She wasn't ready to go that far.

'Magical thinking was a way of life in the Dark Ages. Rational thought was still about three or four hundred years away. Given the general level of naiveté and superstition in the culture it wouldn't have taken much effort for Raymond to persuade Peter that the Lance – not their scheme – had made Peter a great man in the army. Once Peter believed that, it was easy enough for him to imagine that it would protect him from fire.'

Kate offered a wry smile. 'The first step into the pit ought to have shown him otherwise.'

'He put himself into an ecstatic trance before he ever touched the coals. It's likely he didn't feel much of anything until he was almost through, but as he was leaving the pit, the priests apparently turned him around and sent him back the way he had come. That's what killed him.'

'They *wanted* him dead?'

'The Lance wasn't the problem. Peter's visions were getting in the way of good military tactics, and no one had the authority to shut him up. So they baited him into a trial by fire to get rid of him.'

'You think he actually believed this was going to protect him?'

'All I can tell you is he was still holding it when they pulled him out of the pit, and he kept holding it all through the thirteen days it took for him to die.'

Kate shook her head at the pathos of it. 'Why would Raymond talk Peter into killing himself? Or was *he* deluded as well?'

'Owning a relic of the Passion made Raymond first among equals. No other leader of the Crusade could boast anything like it. And it wasn't just prestige. As long as people believed it was genuine, it had tremendous material value. Debunked, it was worthless.'

'You're telling me Raymond sacrificed Peter's life for money?'

'Some things never change.'

'But after Peter died this ought to have been discredited.'

'Once Peter was eliminated the priests were more than happy to declare the lance head genuine. They had their authority back. More importantly, Jerusalem still needed to be taken, and the legend had already set root among the rabble that an army carrying the Holy Lance in its vanguard could never be defeated.'

Kate looked around the village thoughtfully. 'What brought Otto Rahn here? If he had friends in France and Switzerland, why not go there?'

Ethan shook his head. 'All anyone really knows is that an early morning hiker found his body at the base of the Wilder Kaiser on 16 March 1939. As soon as the Austrian SS found out what they were dealing with, they called in the German SS troops stationed at the Berchtesgaden. They drove in that morning and took the body away.'

'At which point it disappeared?'

'The public heard about the climbing accident of the Reich's pre-eminent Grail scholar, but those inside the SS got an object lesson about the fate of anyone daring to betray Himmler.'

'Do you think Rahn was a decent man – as his daughter imagines?'

'I don't know, Kate. I expect a great many *decent* people got mixed up in the SS. I don't think any of them purposefully set out to be monsters. From their perspective, they belonged to something that was noble and pure. In the end those who were still alive were probably not much different from Peter Bartholomew – holding on desperately to the lie, even as they burned.'

The Wilder Kaiser, Austria
June 15, 2008.

At the base of the Wilder Kaiser, Kate and Ethan found the grove of trees where Otto Rahn's body had been discovered in the late winter of 1939. They studied the dark face of the mountain rising up vertically over them with the practised eyes of rock climbers. Ethan pointed to the ledge from which prisoners of war had been thrown in earlier times. It would have been a three or four second plunge. He decided that was just enough time for the man's prayers and regrets to strangle in his throat – unless he was at peace with God.

Ethan wanted to believe that a person could win his way to grace no matter the sins of his past, but his own experience left him less than confident that it was so. Good intentions seemed only to take one so far. In the end, he thought, the things we do define what we are, despite our regrets and sorrows. Otto Rahn had served in two different SS concentration camps. That was one time too many for him to plead ignorance about what was happening. He might have suffered doubt in the cause he served, might even have been spiritually crippled by what he had seen, but so long as he stood with Himmler he was a part of the most hated regime in history, and all the worst for him that he was a Jew.

Was he really something of a Percival awakening in a wasteland, as his daughter wanted to believe? Or had they found out what he was and chased him down when he ran? Knowing that life is rarely pure, Ethan thought there must have been many reasons for Otto Rahn to break his oath and resign from the Order of the Skull – some noble, some self-serving. That was not what mattered. What mattered came afterwards.

Two weeks might not seem like much in a lifetime, but it was all Rahn had left and he must have known it. In that desperate and lonely time the forgotten romantic in him must have imagined that he joined the sublime company of those doomed and heroic troubadour knights he had celebrated when he was still a free man with a beautiful soul. And if it were so, if he really became a knight of the Blood Lance, if only for an hour or two, then surely he had died with them as well.

'It belongs to him now,' Ethan whispered. He gave the relic a gentle toss, and together he and Kate watched the thing tumble across the black earth and settle at last in a patch of wildflowers.

Historical Notes

The Cathars have always provided fertile ground for the imagination, but they did indeed perish by the hundreds of thousands during the early decades of the thirteenth century. Their notion of courtly love was revolutionary and far reaching. As to the nature of their heresy, opinion is divided, but their image of the Blood Lance seems at some point during the conflict to have replaced the Vatican's Roman Cross as the unifying symbol of their sublime faith.

The Lance of Antioch, which is much discussed in this novel, is universally credited with saving the army of the first crusade. That event almost certainly inspired the legend that an army carrying it into battle could never be defeated.

The life of Otto Rahn has not yet been thoroughly researched. Nevertheless, I have tried to follow the precise outlines of the last decade of his life. He held numerous jobs before and after the publication of *The Crusade Against the Grail*, the oddest being a failed business venture in France as a hotel owner, though no one can say where he got the money for it. Rahn was labouring in obscurity in Paris when Heinrich Himmler contacted him anonymously with a note offering lavish praise of his book and cash to travel to Berlin for a meeting. Himmler subsequently spoke with Rahn and ultimately recruited him into the SS, where he became a trusted member of Himmler's inner circle. For a season Rahn was golden – the toast of Berlin – his book becoming an overnight bestseller in Germany some three years after its first appearance.

The accounts of Otto Rahn's final years reflect a personality sinking rapidly into conflict and disillusionment. They include carefully veiled references to drunkenness, profligacy, and numerous ill-advised remarks against those in authority. His death at the Wilder Kaiser was noted in the newspapers at the time, but there is no subsequent mention of his funeral, and as far as anyone can tell Rahn's body, recovered by SS officers, was never returned to his family. It was only discovered after the war that Rahn had resigned his commission a fortnight before his death. It is left for us to imagine why Himmler chose to wait until after the report of Rahn's death before he personally signed and stamped the letter, signifying his acceptance of the resignation.

Dieter and Elise Bachman, and of course all the characters in the contemporary story, are products of the author's imagination. For more on *The Blood Lance* visit my website at: *www.craigsmithnovels.ch*

Acknowledgements

I am grateful to Harriet McNeal, Burdette Palmberg, my wife Martha Ineichen Smith, and my mother Shirley Underwood for reading an early draft of this novel. Their unique perspectives and unfailing encouragement helped me enormously during the rewriting process. I also want to recognise my old friends Matthew Jockers and Britta Luehr, Matt for helping over the rocky parts of the story, Britta for showing me Hamburg. Many thanks also to those who over the years have so generously shared their resources when I needed them most: Herbert Ineichen, Doug and Maria Smith, Don Jennermann, and Rick Williams.

I want finally to give special thanks to my editor Ed Handyside and to my agent Jeffrey Simmons. Without their hard work and unflinching faith this book could not have been made.

CRAIG SMITH lives with his wife, Martha, in Lucerne, Switzerland. A former university professor, he holds a doctorate in philosophy from the university of Southern Illinois. His first novel, published in the UK as *Silent She Sleeps* and in the US as *The Whisper of Leaves*, won bronze medal in the mystery category of ForeWord magazine's Book of the Year Awards.

The Painted Messiah, the first of his novels to chronicle the exploits of T.K. Malloy, was first published by Myrmidon in 2007 and is available in both hardback and paperback editions.